LOVE ME

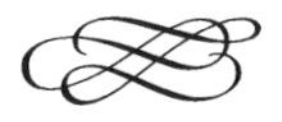

TIFFANY PATTERSON

NOTE TO THE READER

Dear Reader,

Thank you for choosing to read Love Me. Before you begin, please know that topics such as sexual assault, inter-partner violence, and chronic illness are discussed. There are no graphic scenes of sexual assault, but they are mentioned, and many of the characters' actions occur as a result of these issues. With that said, if you choose to continue, I hope you enjoy Diego and Monique's story.

PROLOGUE

Diego

"I'm moving to New York."

Those four words hang between us for an indeterminate amount of time.

I stare into my best friend's honey-brown eyes—the same pair of orbs where I've witnessed laughter, happiness, fear, and pain.

The eyes and face I know so well stare at me with apprehension.

"Did you hear me?" she asks.

Somehow, I hear the words over the pounding of my heart. I avert my gaze and concentrate on a point above her head. The fractured, beaten-up wooden boards that manage to hold up the abandoned barn we're standing in start to mirror my internal condition.

Moving?

To New York?

That wasn't the plan. After our respective graduations from college, we always intended to move back home to Williamsport.

Monique graduated last week. While I have one semester left, I was biding my time until we were finally back in the same city permanently.

Aside from that, my probation doesn't end for another two years. I'm not allowed to move out of the state until then.

"Why?" The word comes out of my mouth, sounding hoarse.

"I got a job," she answers quickly before plastering a smile on her face.

I've memorized every expression of hers. This one is fake. Forced.

She continues to watch me as if waiting for my reaction.

All I can think of is how perfect she looks with the afternoon sun streaming in through the broken windows. Its rays make her tawny skin glow.

She bites her lower lip.

Is she afraid?

Could my reactions frighten her?

Taking a step away, I run my palm over the back of my neck.

"You applied for jobs in New York?" I finally ask.

She peers out of the window, glancing down at the stream that runs behind the field where this abandoned barn sits.

Our barn.

Our spot.

We've come to this place since we first discovered it at eleven years old. It's where we've shared every important milestone of our life with one another.

Where we shared our first kiss—to get it out of the way.

Where we came when each of us had our first actual break-up.

That terrible day, when Monique found out the truth about her biological father and how she was conceived. The memory of her crying in my arms after learning her mother was assaulted still burns in my brain seven years later.

The day we opened our college acceptance letters together.

All of those memories and more happened right here in this old, abandoned barn.

"The opportunity for a job at The Museum of Modern Art came up. One of my professors put in a good word for me."

That doesn't surprise me. As an art history major, who always performed at the top of her class, what professor wouldn't want to vouch for her?

"This is my chance to not only work amongst some of the best curators in the country but to build the connections I need to open my art gallery one day."

Dual emotions war inside of me. I hate and love the excitement in her voice. I want nothing more than her happiness. But why does it have to be so far away?

"Because I can't stay here."

I blink in surprise, not realizing I asked that question out loud.

"Why not?"

"I can't move back home," she says, almost above a whisper. She shakes her head. "I won't become a burden to anyone any longer."

"Don't say that."

Ever since she discovered the ugly truth about how she was conceived, she says shit like this.

"You're not a burden—"

"Aren't I, though? My entire life started with one horrible night for my mom. Then she got kicked out of her house. I got sick, and she had to abandon her dream of attending college because she needed to pay so much to take care of me."

She gestures to her arm, showing the glucose monitor. She's lived with type one diabetes since the age of five. Though she's learned to manage it well over the years, it's obviously still a big part of her life.

"None of what happened to your mother is your fault," I say sternly. "She's doing well now. Both of our moms are."

"Thanks to my dad's help," she mumbles, avoiding eye contact with me. "If he hadn't come along, she'd still be working a job she hated."

We won the lottery when our mothers, who were single parents, met and married our fathers.

My birth father is a piece of shit who manipulated my mother into a lie of a relationship.

Carter Townsend isn't my stepfather. He's my dad. The only man who's loved me wholly from day one.

Damon Richmond is the same for Monique.

"It's been seven years. You should talk to your mom about this—"

The shaking of her head stops the rest of my sentence. "She can't know. It would only hurt her more.

"Besides, it's fine. I've just graduated from college. This is what I'm supposed to do. Go off and flee the nest."

She starts to pace.

The walls close in on me.

"They got me through college. I won't be a burden to them anymore."

"You're not a fucking burden to anyone," I say louder than intended.

Doesn't she know how much she means to everyone who loves her? To me?

"Yeah, and what about you?" she asks suddenly.

I jut my head back in surprise. "What about me?"

"It's my fault you don't have that job offer waiting for you after you graduate next semester."

"Fuck that job," I say through gritted teeth. "You think I would still want to work for that family after what that son of a bitch did to you?"

Her ex.

Slater Cullen.

The bastard who dared to put his hands on her.

His family is well known in the field of architecture. I was supposed to go to work for their company once I completed my degree. Since I put their son in the hospital, that deal is off the table.

Due to my family's influence, I got away with only a few years of probation and some anger management classes.

"But you've been blacklisted," she replies. "And for some reason, you won't take the job your uncles keep offering you at Townsend Real Estate."

I tighten my fists at my sides. "It's complicated," I tell her.

She shakes her head. "It's not. I have to move to New York to start my career and make connections so that I can open my art gallery within the next five years. That's how I'll pay back the sacrifices my mom made for me. And my dad.

"I owe them this. To stand on my own. And I won't be the weight on anyone I love anymore."

She looks me directly in the eyes as she says this.

I know what she's not saying. I step away from her. That dark cloud of anger that comes over me when it feels like life is spiraling out of my control takes over.

This is the real reason she's leaving.

My inability to control my anger, the rage that sometimes takes over. Like when I put her ex in the hospital.

I inhale deeply, trying to get enough oxygen into my lungs. It's useless.

She's leaving.

And I know it's not solely because of this new job opportunity.

It's because of me.

She's blaming herself, but the truth is, this is my fault.

She feels like a burden because of me. My uncontrollable temper got us here.

The words of my biological father come rushing back to my mind. *"You'll never amount to anything."*

He was never one to mince words when it came to how he felt about me.

A mistake.

An affair baby.

An accident he never wanted.

All things he would tell me when my mother wasn't around. Though I've only seen him a handful of times since I was young, his words stick.

"Diego?" Monique calls, pulling me out of my thoughts.

I look over at her.

"We'll still be close." She smiles, but again it's forced.

My heart feels like it just cracked in half. This isn't how today was supposed to go. I was going to tell her about the money I've been saving ever since she first told me about her dream to open her own gallery.

We were back in high school.

I put every other paycheck I received from my internships into savings for her gallery. This was going to be my graduation gift to her.

I clamp my mouth shut, keeping that truth to myself.

"It's only a plane ride away. But I have to do this. New York has such a great art scene. My new job will put me in contact with a lot of people in the field and I'll be able to create my plan to start my gallery."

It's as if she's trying to inject happiness into her voice.

The lump in my throat is so large that I can't speak.

I look around the hollowed-out room, sunken in ceiling boards, and decrepit wood surrounding us. Brokenness I never noticed before stands out now.

She's leaving.

And she has no plans to return. To get away from me.

"Please be happy for me. This is my dream," she finally says.

How come her dream just turned into my nightmare?

CHAPTER 1

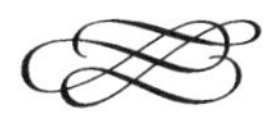

Monique

I twist my key in the lock, anxious to get inside to open the letter burning the palm of my hand. It's from the National Institute of the Arts. I recently applied for their creative small business grant.

I toss my bag and other belongings that I carry with me to work at my day job as an art curator onto the table by my front door, then heel-toe my shoes off.

After shutting and locking my door, I just stare at the envelope in my hands for a beat. The contents of this grant could determine my life's next steps.

It would mean finally having enough money to start the art gallery that I've longed to open for years. A place to showcase women artists who otherwise wouldn't have the opportunity to get into a gallery.

As a curator in New York City, I know how hard it is to break into this very exclusive world. At the upper echelons, it's a space reserved for people with at least a seven-figure net worth. More like eight figures, though.

I want to provide women artists who aren't wealthy enough, come from rough backgrounds, or aren't worthy of being seen in the eyes of the larger society, with a space to call their own.

I take a deep breath and rip open the letter like peeling off a band-aid. My fingers tremble slightly as I unfold the letter.

My eyes scan the first few sentences.

"Ms. Richmond, though your application caught our attention," I mumble-read. "we regret to– Ahh!" I yell in frustration.

Without reading the rest, I crumple up the rejection letter and toss it across the room.

It hits the wooden door of my apartment and bounces a little, landing a few feet away.

Yet another disappointment in a string of disappointments.

Disgusted, I spin away from the door and head straight to my kitchen. I uncork my favorite bottle of red wine and pour myself a glass. Before I take a sip, though, I check my blood sugar numbers on my wristwatch.

I'm in a safe enough range that a few sips of wine won't do any harm.

With a sigh, I down half of the glass. I desperately want to chug the entire thing and then go back to the bottle for seconds.

Even after more than twenty years of living with type one diabetes, I have moments where I wish it wasn't such a damn factor in my life. The desire to drown my sorrows in a bottle of alcohol is one of those moments.

Especially when I recall that my illness is why I'm currently single. My stomach twists in a knot thinking about my ex.

But I shake my head and pull my emotions together enough to set the half-filled glass aside.

I have a phone call to make.

Ms. McClure is the mother of the leading artist I want to feature in my gallery. I promised to call her when I heard the news about the grant.

"Hello?" she answers on the third ring.

"Ms. McClure, it's Monique Richmond."

"Oh," she blows out a breath, "perfect timing. I just put Mikey down for the night."

A pit forms in my belly. Mikey is her grandson. Her daughter, Sharia, is his mother. Sharia McClure, the artist with so much talent, who'll never paint another picture again.

"I won't keep you long. I know how busy you are." I brace myself before saying the words out loud. "My grant proposal was rejected. We won't be getting the money."

"Ah," she says, sounding contemplative. "And the other grants were turned down, too, right?"

I nod, though she can't see me. "Yes, ma'am." I'd applied for a total of five grants to start this gallery and they all got shot down. While I have some savings, no bank is willing to grant me the sizable business loan I would need to start my gallery in the city.

And while this is my dream, I refuse to turn to my parents for help ... although I know my father would jump at the chance to write me a blank check.

I've asked too much of them over the years. I refuse to be another burden to them, even as an adult.

"But this doesn't mean there isn't hope," I quickly say. "We can try something else." What that something is, I'm not sure of at the moment.

"Well, I didn't want to tell you this until we found out about this grant application, but ..." she trails off.

I know I'm not going to like what comes next.

"I've gotten an offer from another, established gallery."

My chest burns at the word *established.*

"Which gallery?"

"The Richards Gallery."

"I see." It's a decent-sized gallery in Brooklyn. But I can't give up. "Ms. McClure, I'm sure their offer was great, but from experience, I know how a lot of these galleries take on more stock than they can feature in a timely manner.

"At my gallery, I can guarantee Sharia's work will be front and center. Her work deserves to be seen and valued by the masses. I promise this is just a bump in the road."

There's silence on the other end of the line.

I bite my bottom lip to keep from pushing her. She's a woman who's already experienced the murder of her daughter, and is now raising her two-year-old grandson.

"I'm sorry, Monique. I know how passionate you are about Sharia's art. But with the mounting costs of just living, I've already had to dip into my retirement savings to pay for home repairs to keep it safe for Mikey."

The sigh that she emits steals my own breath.

A part of me, which I prefer to keep buried, thinks about my mom. I wonder if she sounded this exhausted when I was Mikey's age. Though she was much younger—only eighteen when I was born—she was all alone.

Burden, burden, burden.

The chant echoes in my mind.

I shake my head to refocus.

"I'm sorry. I can't even imagine how difficult the past six months have been for you," I tell her. It's been half a year since Sharia was murdered by Mikey's father.

"I won't ask you to wait until I can get it together, but please know that I'll always support you and Mikey in anything you need. Sharia was a rare talent, and her beauty will live on in the works she created."

"Thank you, Monique."

A few minutes later, I hang up more dejected than when I called her. I glance over at the counter at the glass of wine. A few more sips won't hurt anything.

Right as I start toward the counter, a pounding on my door scares the hell out of me.

"What the?" I murmur at the same time I look toward my bedroom, wondering if I need to retrieve the weapon I keep in my bedroom for intruders.

"Monique!"

A relieved sigh whooshes from my lungs when I hear Diego's voice on the other side of the door.

"Coming," I shout when he continues to knock like something's on fire. "Diego, what's wrong?"

The sight of my best friend standing in front of me wild-eyed like he's ready to attack someone or something has my heart racing.

"What happened? Why're you here?"

"Are you hurt?" he asks, his cinnamon eyes searching my face.

"No. Why?"

He brushes past me, leaving me to close the door behind him. He's stalking around my half-furnished living room like a caged animal.

"You're freaking me out," I tell him. "Did something happen at home?"

He stops in the middle of my living room and looks at me again. "That fucker didn't do anything to you, did he? I'll beat his ass again if he did."

The words come out through gritted teeth.

I move closer to him and take his hands in mine. Meeting his gaze, I ask, "What the hell are you talking about?"

He towers over my five-foot-six body from his six-foot-one height, searching my gaze.

"Don't lie for him, Monique. I caught his ass on the beach in Miami dancing and kissing another woman. Did he cheat on you?" He pulls his hands from mine. "I knew I should've knocked his ass out cold. He cheated on you, didn't he?"

"Who ... Are you talking about Lawrence?"

My ex-fiancé.

Yet another disappointment in the last few months.

"He was dancing with some woman on the beach while engaged to you. He said you broke up with him though."

My stomach muscles tighten. I shouldn't be surprised he found someone else to keep him company at his big showcase.

I'd be lying if I said it didn't hurt a little.

Especially considering the reason he dumped me.

I push out a breath. "He must be down there for Art Basel. Is that what you were there for?"

"Answer the damn question," he insists.

Frowning, I cross my arms. "He didn't cheat on me … that I know of." I shrug and do my best to ignore the slight pain in my chest. "You would've known he broke off our engagement if you'd answered my phone calls. Where have you been?" I ask suddenly because I don't want to think about my ex.

Or his reason for dumping me.

For the first time since I opened the door for him, he has the sense to look contrite. He scratches the top of his head, ruffling the dark curls that rest there.

"Work keeps me busy."

"Mhmm," I reply.

Diego's eyes narrow as he looks me over in that unnerving way of his. Sometimes it feels like he can see right down into my soul.

Most of the time, I almost crave that attention from him. But not tonight. I don't want him to see the truth in my eyes tonight. I feel too vulnerable, and the last thing I want is to unload all of my problems onto him.

He doesn't give me that option, though.

"Wait, did you say he broke up with you? That son of a bi– What aren't you telling me?"

"Noth—" The lie dies on my lips as his eyes narrow even more.

"We don't keep secrets from each other." His voice is so deep, a tinge of darkness in it that sends a chill through my body.

We used to not keep secrets from each other.

When I don't say anything, Diego moves closer and cups my face with his hands. Warmth fills me.

"He didn't want to deal with me being sick," I admit.

Diego raises one of his thick, dark eyebrows. I can see a muscle in his perfectly square jaw bulge, even through his neatly trimmed beard.

"He dumped you because of your diabetes."

I swallow and step out of his embrace. "Not exactly."

"Then what exactly, Monique? Because I'm about to get on another flight back to Miami to whoop his ass a second time."

"No." I grab his wrist firmly. "Don't do that."

"What happened?"

My mind scrambles as panic starts to take over. I can't let Diego fly off the handle again for me. Not like he did last time.

"It's not that big of a deal." I try to bring some levity into the conversation. "Anyway, did you really get on a plane and fly here from Miami for that?"

* * *

Diego

She asks the question like a three-hour flight is even that big of a deal for us. I don't answer.

"What happened?" I ask again. I try to keep the demand out of my voice, but it remains evident.

"I got sick a few months back. My blood sugar wasn't adjusting to the insulin from my pump. Ended up in the ER for a few hours. I still don't know what went wrong, but that was when I decided to go off of the pump for a while and go back to self-injections."

My stomach muscles tighten because I didn't know she'd gone off of the pump. Over the years, she's gone between a pump and injections.

She shrugs. "Anyway, that happened to be the night of a really important showing of his."

I'm shaking my head before she finishes. "Tell me he didn't choose to go to a show over staying with you at the hospital."

Her eyes lower, and I want to put my fist through a wall.

"His career is important to him," she says by way of an answer.

"And you aren't?" Taking a step away, I run my palm over the back of my neck. "Why didn't you call me when you were in the hospital? I would've been here."

"I know." She holds out her arms. "It wasn't that big of a deal.

Honestly. Everything stabilized within a few hours. I was back home before the next morning."

"But?" I prompt.

She looks at something over my shoulder. "But, a few days later, he came to me and said that he couldn't go on like this. With his career taking off, he needed someone who could keep up with him. Not hold him back."

"I'm going to crush his fucking skull." I start for the door.

"No!" Monique runs to get in between me and the door. "You will not do that! Please. I've already had a bad enough day."

I'm suddenly thrown back to eight years ago. Our junior year in college. The scene is almost the exact same. Monique standing in between me and a door, begging me not to go and beat the shit out of the guy who hurt her.

I didn't listen last time.

Guilt courses throughout my body. That decision rocked our friendship to its core. I won't make that mistake again.

Besides, I already clocked him once on the beach before I hopped on a plane. There are other ways to make someone suffer aside from putting my hands on them.

I take another step back with my hands up. The back of my heel hits something.

I turn and see a wadded-up paper on the floor.

"What's this?" I ask, picking it up and starting to open it.

"Nothing." She runs over to snatch the paper out of my hand.

I raise my arm out of her reach before she can get it. "You don't leave random scraps of paper on the floor." My best friend is meticulously neat and organized.

A by-product of having to keep vigilance over her health for most of her life.

She blows out a frustrated breath and goes to plop down on her sofa. "A rejection letter."

I unfold the paper and read it. "Baby ..." The word slips out of my mouth without my thinking. I know how much starting a gallery means to her. "You know, I—"

"It's not a big deal." She takes the paper from my hand as I sit next to her and tosses it behind the TV. "There are other grants, and eventually, I can get a loan."

I adjust my position so I can look her in the face. For a moment, I simply take her in. The tawny complexion of her skin, eyes that are so big like pools of honey.

Her perfect nose that has a small mark on the right nostril from the nose ring she used to have. I held her hand when she got it pierced during our senior year of high school.

She's styled her natural curls into crochet locs, which are piled in a high bun at the crown of her head. The hairstyle accentuates the catlike shape of her eyes.

And her smile, marked by full, pink lips.

Her smile isn't right, though.

Monique reaches her hand to one of my curls. Her fingers begin to twine in my hair, betraying her words.

She plays in my hair when she's lost in thought or something is wrong.

"Tell me the truth," I implore.

Her lips press together. "You always know. This is the third rejection I've received. At this rate, it'll be years before I can open my gallery here."

I sit up, causing her hand to stop moving.

"Why does it have to be here?"

She gives me a curious look. "What do you mean?"

"That asshole said you told him you were planning to move back to Williamsport. Why wasn't I the first person you told about moving back home?"

I hope like hell she doesn't hear the hurt in my voice.

Her face wrinkles before realization dawns in her expression. "I told him that the last time we talked." She shrugs. "I just said it without thinking."

My heart sinks a little, but I don't believe her words for too long.

"You said it because home is where you belong."

Monique's eyes widen. My eyes fall to her lips. The same lips she's pressing together. The movement she does when she's at a loss for words.

Finally, she pushes at my shoulder and says, "I just said it to make him think he wasn't the only one who was moving on."

She tries to infuse her voice with levity.

I flex my fingers to keep from balling them into fists. Everything inside of me wants to make another trip back to Miami for the pleasure of beating her ex-fiancé's ass again.

Once wasn't enough.

"I should've called you sooner," I say, regret lacing my tone. I won't tell her how difficult it became to hear her voice after she got engaged.

Knowing that she would be spending her life with another man ripped a mile-wide hole in my chest. It was as bad as the moment she told me she wasn't returning to Williamsport. Only worse.

"You should have," she retorts. "I'm tired of talking about me. What about you? Are you still with that lame ass architecture firm instead of at your family's business where you belong?"

"That architecture firm is one of the best in Williamsport."

"It's not Townsend Real Estate."

"Nothing is Townsend Real Estate," I reply. "And we're not done talking about you. Why does your art gallery have to open here?"

Her head cocks to the side. "Because this is where I live."

"You don't have to live here."

Her eyes bulge.

"My job is here," she insists.

"There are art museums in Williamsport the last time I checked."

"I have an apartment and a lease I can't just walk out on." She waves her arm, gesturing to the space we're in.

For the first time I notice how bare her apartment is. "Where's all your furniture?"

Frowning, she glances around also. "Lawrence took half of it since we both went in on the furniture."

I crack my knuckles.

"Don't start that," she says, knowing me too well.

"You can break a lease." I turn my attention back on her. "I'll pay the fee."

"No." She points her finger at me. "You absolutely will not do that."

"Why not?"

"Because."

I smirk at the exasperation in her voice.

"You're worse than my dad sometimes." She sighs. "You know he wanted to buy a freaking building when I first moved here."

I chuckle because I know very well that her father tried to buy some prime real estate in this city to allow her to live in one of the apartments rent-free. Unfortunately, that real estate deal fell through.

"When are you coming home?"

She rolls her eyes skyward and drops her head to the back of the couch. It lands on my forearm.

"I have friends here," she says, less adamant than a minute ago.

"You have family and me back home." My voice comes out surprisingly low.

Her eyelids flutter and a smile creeps across her face, revealing a dimple. My stomach contracts at the sight of it.

"A move takes time."

"I could have movers here this weekend." I glance around her space.

She gets quiet, and as her hand goes back to my hair, she lays her head on my shoulder. "You're so damn insistent."

"So, it's decided then?"

Her head pops up. "No, it's not decided. I never agreed to moving."

"You never really disagreed either." I know her. If she didn't want to do something she would flat out say it.

"You could open your gallery back home. The one you've always wanted to start," I tell her. "Real estate isn't as prohibitive back home. Besides, there you have more resources to work with."

"No." She shakes her head. "I will not have my father or anyone else do something crazy like buy a building and convince your bank friends or whoever to give me a loan to start my business."

Always wanting to be Ms. Fucking Independent.

"Why struggle if you don't have to?"

She sits all the way up and crisscrosses her legs, facing me. "Because this is *my* project. I've gotten so much from my parents and family over the years." Her head drops, but not before I see the sadness that invades her eyes at the mention of her family.

"I can't ask any more of them." She shakes her head. "I want this for me and for the women whose work will be featured in my gallery. I want ... *need* them to have a voice. I can't do that if the means by which I started the gallery is solely through family connections and nepotism."

I push out a breath on a long sigh. "I get it," I admit reluctantly.

It's the same reason why I haven't gone to work for my family's company yet. The need to feel like you aren't living off of your parents, but that you're fulfilling the promises they put into you by raising and loving you all of these years.

"But we can still support you." I raise my hand to stop whatever is about to come out of her parting lips. "It's a reminder that you're not alone. You've been away from home for too long."

Six years ago I wasn't in a position to convince her to stay. Then I thought I permanently lost her heart when she became engaged.

It's different now. She's not engaged, and from where I'm sitting, there's no reason for her to fight so hard to open a gallery here over Williamsport.

I've learned to control my temper over the years. I won't betray her trust by falling into the darkness that once threatened our friendship.

Her mouth closes and the corner kicks up into a half grin. The expression is fleeting when she quickly stuns me with a right jab to my chest.

"The hell?" Grimacing, I rub the spot she just punched.

"That didn't even hurt." She rolls her eyes.

"It did. You sucker punched me," I protest.

"*That* is for not calling me back in weeks. All I got from you was some short text responses."

"I'm sorry." I hate that my selfishness prevented me from being there for her when that asshole broke up with her. I should've known better.

"Don't let it happen again."

It's my turn to return the half smile. "We'll see more of each other once you bring your ass back home."

Her hands go to her hips. "Is that an order?"

"Depends," I quickly reply. "Are you going to follow it?"

Her lips morph into the cutest frown. "I'm not in the military."

"Would you like me to beg?" I wiggle my eyebrows.

"Yes, get down on your knees and beg," she replies, laughing.

I start to move to the floor, but she grabs my arm.

"What are you doing?"

"What? You've never had a man beg you before?" My question charges the air.

A weighted silence falls around us. We stare into one another's eyes. I find comfort in the honey coloring of her irises that I know so well from memory. My heartbeat speeds up just a notch when I notice the twitch of her lips that reveals she's biting the inside of her cheek.

It's one of her tells.

"I've missed the hell out of you, Mo." My words come out slightly strained. "Move back home."

CHAPTER 2

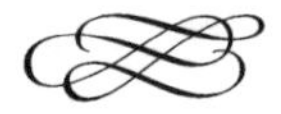

*M**onique*

"Hey, Monique, where does this box go?" my seventeen-year-old brother, Damian, asks, walking into my new condo carrying one of my large cardboard boxes.

"Um, it says 'bedroom' on the box," my fifteen-year-old sister, Avery, says with a roll of her eyes. She's so sassy sometimes.

"You can stick it in the main bedroom," I tell Damian. "Thanks, bro. You don't have to carry any more boxes. The movers will do it."

"Like hell they will," my dad's voice booms through the door behind my brother. "He can be helpful. Especially, since he decided it was a good idea to get a 'C' in his physics class last semester."

My dad eyes Damian, who's named after him.

"Leave my baby alone," my mother interjects, emerging from the hallway.

My entire family has come to help with my move, despite my father hiring the most expensive moving company in the city of Williamsport to bring my minimal amount of belongings from New York to my new place.

"You're too easy on the boy," my dad says.

"Like you aren't the same way with Monique and Avery."

"Hey," my sister and I say at the same time. We both look at one another across the room and crack up laughing, because, yeah, it's true.

"I treat my princesses special because they are."

I watch as my dad sidles up to my mom, towering over her, but looking down into her eyes with such affection. Their chemistry practically ignites the entire room. For a second, I swear it's as if the three of us, plus the movers coming in and out, disappear from their consciousness.

"But I treat my queen the way she deserves," I hear him murmur.

My mother's entire face lights up. She lifts on her tiptoes and leans in for a kiss.

I look away. Also, because something ripples through my chest. A yearning I can't ignore but don't quite understand.

One would think that since I recently broke up with my fiancé, he would be the one who my heart yearns for.

But it's not him.

A knock at the door startles me out of my musings before I have time to put a face to the name my heart is calling.

My dad pulls it open. His six-foot-plus height obscures my view of who's on the other side. However, his following comment alerts me to who it is.

"I figured you'd show up eventually," he says with a familiar scoff in his tone. "This boy is always lurking around somewhere."

When he steps away, my lips curl as my eyes lock with golden brown irises that I've known since I was nine years old.

"Diego!" Avery yells and runs to throw her arms around him. "Monique said you might not come over to help because you probably had to work. I told her it's Saturday, but she said you've been working a lot lately."

He looks at me and cocks his head to the side. My gaze is drawn to the grin on his pink lips.

"Are you lying on me, Mo?"

"Are you calling my Short Stuff a liar?" my dad interjects before I can answer.

"Damon, leave Diego alone," my mother orders before she steps around my father and gives Diego a hug.

"Daddy, how long are you going to call me that nickname?" I ask.

He lifts an eyebrow. "Until I'm good and gone. Which won't be for years and years and years to come," he replies. He kisses my forehead.

Familiar warmth passes through me from my father's loving words.

I've missed this.

I've visited my family over the years, and they came to visit me as well. This is different, though. I'm actually home. To stay, not just for a few days or a week.

That realization settles over me when I look over at Diego again. *"I've missed the hell out of you, Mo. Come back home, please."*

After he asked with such sincerity and longing in his voice, it was no longer a choice. While I had a job, volunteer work, and friends in New York, it didn't feel like enough. The pull of moving back to Williamsport was more significant than everything else combined.

"I didn't lie," I finally say to Diego. "I thought you would've had to work overtime since work keeps you so busy."

There might be a slight bitterness in my voice. I may still be slightly miffed that he hadn't answered my calls in the last few months of my relationship with Lawrence even though he's been present since I agreed to move back home.

A shadow passes over his face but he quickly covers it. I tilt my head to the side and give him a look. Our gazes lock, and he squints ever so slightly. His way of letting me know he doesn't want to talk about it right now.

"They're doing it again," my dad says with that slightly irritated edge in his voice.

I peer over at him, frowning.

My mother approaches his side and wraps her arm around his waist. "Doing what?" she inquires.

"That silent talking shit they always do." My dad looks between me and Diego. "Been doing it since they were kids. I told you they had a secret language between them. They could be plotting the downfall of society and none of us would know."

Diego and I look at one another and crack up. It's true. We've always had our own language, a way of speaking without words. It's not even a conscious thing anymore.

It's just us.

"Leave them alone," my mother protests, defending Diego to my dad the way she always has. Though, he doesn't need any defense. I suspect my dad loves Diego as much as the rest of us do.

"I'm glad you came, but you don't have to help us move. I don't have much stuff anyway," I tell him, waving him inside. "Most of my furniture is being delivered next weekend."

"Cool." Diego removes his suit jacket. "I ordered lunch. Figured you would all be hungry after moving."

"That's sweet, Diego," my mother says. "But Damon made a reservation for us at that new Thai place across town. It's my favorite."

His face drops. "Oh."

"I have to unpack my stuff anyway," I say. "You all should go."

"If your family made plans—"

"That's right," my father cuts in. "I made plans on my baby girl's first full day back home."

"Damon," my mother says, giving him a look.

Frowning, he looks between me and Diego. I have no idea what he's thinking or what that look my mother just gave him is all about. The truth is, I'm a little drained from my move.

I arrived back in Williamsport yesterday, and though the movers have done most of the work, I still had to arrange things.

I spent much of the morning picking out furniture with my mom. Which she and my dad insisted on buying.

"You look tired anyway, honey," my mother says.

"Let me check your watch."

"What are your numbers?"

Diego and my dad speak at the same time. Diego reaches me first, taking my wrist into his hand. He immediately checks my watch's display, reading my blood sugar levels.

"You're a little low." He frowns.

I don't even bother to scold him or my dad about their overprotectiveness. I've missed them. I check the number. Diego's right, but I'm still in the safe range.

"I put the orange juice in the fridge already."

Diego's at the refrigerator before I can even finish my sentence. He hands me a carton of the juice and watches as I open it.

"Drink," he insists.

I mean mug him at the same time I take my first sip.

"Happy?" I mutter after swallowing.

"We'll see in a few minutes."

I glance at my parents, ready to ask them if they can believe him. But I notice a half smile on my father's face. The smirk disintegrates when he sees me eyeing him, and he clears his throat.

"The first thing he should've done when he came over here," my father gripes.

"Stop it," my mother insists, swatting at my father before approaching me. "We'll have lunch some other time, right?" She looks me in the eyes, searching.

I nod at my mom before excusing myself to go to the bathroom and do an injection of insulin once I know Diego's brought my favorite quinoa bowl over for lunch.

My mother's hands wrap around me as soon as I re-enter the kitchen. She hugs me tight for some reason. It's a reminder of the distance between me and my mother. The one I've unconsciously placed there for years.

Ever since—

I don't finish the thought before Diego slides the meal that he brought for us to eat in front of me. He knows my body's needs as well as I do.

A small smile touches my lips as I take my first bite of the quinoa bowl.

I've missed being home.

"We'll have lunch soon," I tell my mom as she prepares to leave with my dad and siblings.

She smiles, but her eyes continue to search mine. Then, her smile turns genuine. "I'm glad you're back home."

"Me too."

Minutes later, my entire family leaves. About fifteen minutes after them, the movers finish up, and I finish my lunch.

It's just Diego and me left.

I go to ask him if he's going to eat, but he scoops me up in a massive hug before I can say anything.

"What's this?" I ask with a laugh when he stays like that, just holding me.

"I'm glad you're back home," he mumbles into the crook of my neck.

I force myself to ignore the shudder that rattles through my body. But I can't ignore the goosebumps that sprout up along my arms.

Diego pulls back. "Are you cold?" A genuine expression of concern is plastered on his handsome face.

I look over his bronze skin and thick, dark brown eyebrows that match the color of the curls on top of his head. While my hands are no stranger to the feel of his silky curls, when my eyes land on the neatly trimmed beard that covers his sharp jawline, they itch to feel the hair there.

I clasp both of my hands to stop myself.

"Not anymore," I say, barely audible.

The way Diego's eyebrow lift makes me wonder if he knows what I was thinking.

* * *

Diego

"I can't believe Kyle, of all people, is getting married," Mo says.

"Is already married," I correct while pulling my own meal out of the bag and placing it on the counter.

"Forks are in that drawer." She gestures toward the counter by the brand-new, sub-zero fridge.

"Your dad didn't spare any expense, did he?"

She frowns. "The man is unyielding. You should've seen him almost flip his shit when I even suggested that I pay rent for this place."

"He owns the building."

"No," she insists, "his company owns the building. Everyone else has to pay their mortgage or rent here. Why shouldn't I?"

"You're his daughter." Before sitting to eat my lunch, I grab her wrist to check her numbers. They look good.

"You're just as bad as he is." She snorts.

With a shrug, I tell her, "You could've moved into my building."

She glares at me. "Then I would've had to fight with you over paying rent."

I chuckle at the same time I kick my leg over the stool across from her at the kitchen island. It's true. Townsend Industries owns the building I live in. My cousins, Kyle and Kennedy, both also live in units in the building.

Correction: Kyle used to live in the building. While he still owns his place, he's moved in with his new wife, Riley. They'll probably end up buying a larger home somewhere else soon. Kyle's already mentioned wanting more space for Riley's eleven-year-old niece, and he's brought up having more kids.

I can hardly believe his change over the past few months.

That brings me back to my original plan for coming over. Kyle asked me something a few months ago that led me to make a decision about my relationship with Monique.

"It was either move into this place for free, or he would've insisted on giving me the seed money to start my gallery somewhere in town," Monique continues. "And I am not letting that happen."

"So you've said," I say.

"You sound like you think I'm being stubborn." She holds her hand up, stopping my reply. "I'm not. This is how it has to be. I know it's taken longer than the original five years I planned, but the women featured in my gallery deserve me to go as hard for them as they go for their work."

I nod in agreement.

"Doing this on my own is a promise to them. I can't explain it, it just is," she continues. "I've already applied for a couple of grants and a business loan. I have some savings I can use for a deposit on a place. I have three appointments next week to look at spaces."

"Where?" I ask.

"One's not too far from here. Walkable. The other one is a few blocks from Williamsport U."

"Your mom would love it if you opened a gallery there." Monique's mom has worked as a sociology professor at Williamsport University for the past seven years. She made the career change from paralegal after completing her Ph.D. program.

"Yeah," Mo replies, staring at something over my shoulder.

I place my fork down. I've seen that same withdrawn expression overcome her more than once when talking about her mother.

"Where's the other place?" I ask, moving the conversation along.

"A few blocks from the Williamsport Museum of Natural History."

"That's an awesome location for an art gallery." I nod. "Right in the art district. All of those locations are," I add.

"Which is great, but I don't know about start-up costs. Hell, I don't even have artists yet."

"What happened to that one artist you were telling me about?" I snap my fingers as I try to remember. "Sharia? You said her mom was looking for a gallery to feature her work, right?"

A new sadness invades her eyes.

"You never told me about why her work is so special to you."

A small, sad smile touches her lips. "She was one of the women from the shelter where I volunteered. I met her when she was living there with her baby. She didn't want her mom to know where she lived because her mom had never liked her boyfriend.

"He turned violent after she got pregnant. It only worsened after she had the baby," Monique shakes her head. "One night, while I was volunteering, we started talking. She mentioned how she missed painting. She had some paintings in storage that she never told her ex about because she feared he would do something to them.

"He stalked her for months and eventually found and killed her." Her voice becomes shaky.

I reach across the table and clutch her free hand in mine.

"Her mom came to the shelter, and I told her about Sharia's storage unit. We found her paintings, and I was in awe of her talent. I knew right then that I wanted to feature her work. Her art deserves to be seen and adored. She poured so much passion into every stroke. I —" Her voice cracks.

I squeeze her hand. When she turns her hand over, giving me her palm, I intertwine our fingers. We sit like that for the remainder of our meal while she recounts how Sharia's mother took in her grandson but wanted to keep her daughter's memory alive through her art.

"The last time I spoke with her, she told me she had an offer from another gallery in the city. I hope it goes through for her. Sharia deserves that much."

She's sincere, but there's regret in her voice.

"It's selfish, I know, but I wanted to be the one to have Sharia's work on the walls of my gallery. To explain to buyers how awesome she was in life as a mother. And how, even though her voice is gone, her art remains timeless. She had this special technique she did with watercolors ..."

I listen as my best friend lights up as she talks about the artwork of a woman whose life was cut off so young.

"I'll leave work early to meet you next week," I tell her an hour later as we sit on the couch.

She gives me a curious look. Instantly, my gaze drops to her lips, twisted to the side.

The urge to run my thumb along the seam of her lip is almost overwhelming. The feelings pushing through me solidify the decision I made about the course of our relationship. Things need to change between us.

Now isn't the right time for that discussion, though.

"You're going to leave work early? Won't that big, fancy architect firm you work for have a problem with that?" She teases.

I give her a one shoulder shrug. "I don't give a shit what they do or don't think. Besides, I don't work for them anymore."

Gasping, she pulls back. "Did you get fired?"

I frown, and she laughs.

"Of course you didn't. So you quit. What are you going to do now?"

"What? You think I'm going to go broke?"

She rolls her eyes. "That'll never happen."

"I got a new job."

"So, you were at this new job this morning. Please, tell me ..."

"Yes," I finally say. "You're looking at the newest director of architect design at Townsend Real Estate."

"Yes!" She moves around the island and leaps into my arms, wrapping her body around mine.

The deep laugh that pushes through me is more about having her this close to me—right where she belongs—than my joy over my job.

Before I can get my fill, she pulls back and then pushes my shoulders.

"What the hell took you so long? Why wasn't that the first thing you told me when you walked through the door? Wait, when did you make the move? Is Uncle Joshua excited to have you there finally?"

"I needed to make the move in my own time. Your family was here, and then you started to talk about your gallery. I just completed my first week. And yeah, he's stoked to have me as a part of the family business."

I answer her questions all in one shot.

"You look happy about it," she says, her smile growing wide.

"I am."

"I knew this move was coming," she says cheerfully. "I could feel it. You're going to do amazing things at Townsend. I fucking know it."

Pride swells in my chest at her words. My best friend has always been my biggest and loudest cheerleader.

"You're going to paint the Williamsport Skyline with your innovative building designs," she continues. "You've already been doing that at the other firm, but now, you'll have your name on the designs you create instead of the firm whose name you're not attached to."

"Design is a team effort," I tell her.

She waves a dismissive hand. "Yeah, yeah. But *you* are the star. Your art is the buildings you create. Me?" She points to herself. "I can't draw a straight line to save my life, but I know real art when I see it, and I've always known you would make an impact in this field because you're so damn talented."

She cups my face with her hands. Her eyes start to water.

Just as I grasp her wrists with my hands, she says, "I'm just sorry this didn't happen sooner. It's my fault you—"

"Stop." My one word command cuts her off.

A long, lingering silence falls between us. Sentiments I hate to see pass in those honey eyes of hers.

Sadness, regret, shame.

I want to kill every memory of hers and mine that put that look there.

Taking one of her hands from my cheek, I kiss the inside of her palm. A soft sigh escapes her lips.

"Not a damn thing that has or hasn't happened in my life is your fault," I say sternly. "I make my own decisions and am responsible for my actions."

I kiss her palm again because the urge to do so becomes overwhelming. Her hands are so soft in mine. They are so delicate, I never want to let them go.

A demanding wave of emotion overcomes me. I'm barely able to hold it back. The way I want to take my best friend into my arms. This is what I've been holding back for too long.

Calm down.

I have to remind myself to hold back. Not to come on too strong. To be the nice guy she needs. Not the dominant man my base urges are telling me to give into.

When I kiss the inside of her palm again, a hiss of air escapes her lips. I can't ignore the way my cock responds in my pants.

"Be my date to Kyle's wedding."

Her perfectly arched eyebrows raise. "What?"

It might just be my overwhelming desire, but her voice sounds breathless.

"My cousin's wedding."

"Where you're the best man?" she asks as if she doesn't already know.

I nod. "I need a date, and you're it." I give her a smile I know she can't turn down.

Her eyes drop to my lips. I almost groan when her tongue slips out and runs along her bottom lip.

"I'll take that as a yes."

CHAPTER 3

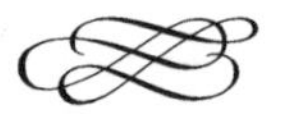

Diego

"I don't like it," I tell the group of architects before me. We're in the conference room on the twentieth floor of Townsend Industries.

This is our second meeting with me as the lead architect on an upcoming project. It's my first significant role at Townsend Industries, a somewhat controversial move for my uncle to have made, given I'm a new employee.

"Diego," Dan, one of the other design architects on the team, says, looking around as if he's ensuring he has the agreement of the rest of the group. "With all due respect—"

I lift an eyebrow. "When someone starts a sentence with all due respect, in my experience, they're about to be disrespectful as hell."

Dan's mouth remains ajar, but no words come out.

"Is that what you're about to do?" I ask.

He quickly shakes his head. "N-No. Of course not." Another look around the room. Everyone else stares down at the table in front of them.

"I only wanted to mention that this project has been on the table for months. And you're rather new to the company."

"And?"

"Uh, well, it might be a good idea to take some time and look over the designs properly before you make a rash decision."

I run my hand through the neatly trimmed hairs of my beard to calm my temper.

"Don't be such a hothead," my mother used to tell me all of the time when I was a teenager. Only things that mean something to me can get me riled up.

My family.

My career.

Monique.

Not in that order. Two out of those three I will go to war for. But now, my career is inextricably tied to my family. Hence, the added irritation at Dan's comment.

"Let me make sure I understand what you're saying," I tell him.

He sits up higher in his chair.

"You believe I didn't take the time to look over the submitted designs and that I'm somehow being hasty in my decision when I say these plans don't work?"

His eyes balloon. "I didn't say that—"

"I'm pretty sure you did," I start without giving him time to finish. "The close to twelve hours I spent pouring over the designs over the past three days isn't enough time to figure out that they do not coincide with what the client is asking for."

"I ... we just submitted the designs yesterday."

"And I had an inside look at them before they were submitted and took them home last night to study the designs. Is that not enough time for you?"

He glances around the room. All heads are lowered.

"This client is very picky. I'm surprised he even let someone with such—"

"Such what?" I ask through gritted teeth.

"So new to the company, is all I wanted to say." He holds up his hands. "I think I speak for all of us when I say that all we want our client's satisfaction."

"You don't speak for me." I glare at him.

"What?" He genuinely looks confused.

"The client's satisfaction is not my main concern. It's for the well-being of the Townsend Real Estate name. This is not our first client, and it damn sure won't be our last. My primary concern is that Townsend Real Estate delivers an end design that looks good and is functional in all areas.

"The client wants an eco-friendly design, but his measurements, as well as yours, are off. They're outdated."

I glance around the room, looking at the architects before me. "We can do better. And if we can't, maybe we need a new team."

The room falls silent.

Dan is the only one who meets my gaze head-on. A slow, unfriendly smile crosses my lips. The bastard is testing me.

"We'll take the next couple of weeks to develop a better design," is the last thing I say before ending the meeting.

Even as everyone piles out of the room, I can feel the back of my neck burning from irritation.

I don't mind having my ideas questioned. Questions can make for a better result. The problem is who the questions are coming from.

I'm well aware Dan doesn't like that I'm in this position. He believes it should be his. What he doesn't realize is he has more ambition than actual talent. He's lucky I didn't say as much during the meeting.

As I exit the conference room, I come face to face with my uncle, Joshua. There's a half-smile on his face.

"You overheard that, huh?"

"You sounded dangerously close to the CEO or the COO of this place," he jokes, referring to my uncles, Aaron and Kyle, his son, my cousin, and closest friend besides Monique.

I snort. "I wasn't that bad."

He lifts a dark eyebrow.

"The designs weren't right. We can do better."

His smirk grows to a full-on smile as he grips my shoulder. "It took me years to finally get you to come over to work for us. Are you going to tell me what finally changed your mind?"

His sharp, emerald green eyes stare me down, and it's on the tip of my tongue to tell him the truth. I might crack if I wasn't used to the intensity that my uncles and father share.

But my reasoning isn't relevant. Not anymore. The past is the past.

"It was time," I say.

His shoulders slump, and his hand falls away from me. "Keep your secrets for now. I'll eventually get to the truth. Let me know if Dan or anyone else is an issue on this project. He's cocky as hell and a sound designer and he knows it."

"But not great," I finish for him.

He nods and continues, "He might be jealous that you're leading this project right out of the gate."

I cock my head to the side. "Did it sound like he was a problem?"

He chuckles. "And they say *we're* cocky."

"I don't know anything about this fictional *they* you speak of."

He pats me on the back. "Because they're fucking irrelevant. Speaking of family, don't even think about working next weekend."

"I'm the best man. I don't have time to work even if I wanted to," I say. Next weekend is Kyle's wedding. Second wedding, actually. He and his wife, Riley, are already married, but no family was present for that wedding. He swore it was only about revenge.

Yeah, right.

I could see him falling for that woman from the moment he met her.

"Are you bringing a date?" my uncle suddenly asks.

"Monique," I reply without thinking.

His eyes light up. "Damon's happy as hell she moved back. I know you are, too."

I can't help the smile that parts my lips. She's back home where she belongs. Correction: she's almost where she belongs. Getting her to agree to be my date to Kyle's wedding was another step in the right direction.

"I have to go—"

"Hey, Dad," my uncle's words are cut off by his seventeen-year-old son, Cole. "Hey, Diego." Cole nods in my direction. "My dad told me you were working here now. That's cool," he says as I pull him in for a hug.

"I was here a lot when I was your age, too. Maybe you're the next architect." I lift an eyebrow.

He shakes his head before ducking it. "I'm just here to see my dad."

"No, this kid's got legal matters on his mind," Uncle Joshua says, wrapping his arm around his adopted son. The two look nothing alike with my uncle's dark brown hair, green eyes, and freckles. Cole has light blond hair, blue eyes, and no freckles in sight. Yet, they're family.

Even with Cole's, at times, reticent behavior, one can see his admiration for his father.

"We're heading out," Uncle Josh tells me.

We exchange goodbyes as I check my watch. I've got about twenty minutes before I need to leave for the day to meet Monique at the first spot she's looking at to open her gallery.

She was also supposed to hear about another grant she applied for. I'm eager to find out whether or not she got it.

"Mr. Townsend, you have a visitor to see you," my assistant, Rebecca, says once I reach my outer office.

I pause because I don't have a meeting on the calendar.

"Who is it?" I question.

She nods her head toward the lobby. I can only make out a man with dark hair from this distance. His back is to me.

"He says his name is Gabriel Garcia."

Ice floods through my veins at hearing that name. "That's impossible."

"No, I'm pretty sure that's the name he gave me," she says, double checking the notebook where she read his name.

I don't reply because I'm too busy staring at the guy. He takes that moment to stand and turns to face me. My heart rate kicks up, but I swallow the lump in my throat.

It's not him.

Gabriel Garcia is my biological father.

Was.

He finally died weeks ago. The bastard.

This is his son, who was named after him.

"Diego," Gabriel Jr. calls across the room, smiling like we're fucking buddies.

"Wait five minutes and then send him in," I tell Rebecca without answering or looking at Gabriel.

I head for my office to pack up my belongings for the day. I have another ten minutes before I need to leave the office to meet Monique on time. I don't know what Garcia is doing here, but I plan to get rid of him as quickly as possible.

As soon as I close my briefcase, there's a knock on my door. "Come in."

In walks my assistant, with Gabriel Jr. following closely behind her.

"You can close it on your way out," I tell her.

"What the hell are you doing here?" I ask him as soon as the door closes.

The fake ass smile on his face drops. "Is that any way to greet your brother?"

"I have one brother, and you sure as fuck aren't him. I'll ask for the last time. Why the hell are you in my office?"

He doesn't immediately reply.

I look over Gabriel, who is close to fifteen years older than me. He's three inches shorter than my six-foot-one height, and his skin is olive while mine is more bronze, but I can't deny the similarities in hair, eye coloring, and similar facial features.

I fucking hate it.

Gabriel and his brother, Victor, are the products of Gabriel Garcia's marriage to their mother. I'm a product of an affair. The one Gabriel Garcia Sr. manipulated my nineteen-year-old mother into and then used me as a pawn to control her for years.

Needless to say, there's no love lost between me and that family.

"That's cold. Did that family of yours teach you to be like that?"

"Strike one, you've shown up to my family's business out of the blue. Strike two, you just insulted them. One more strike, and I will break your fucking jaw in this middle of my office."

His gaze lowers to the tightened fists at my sides. I dare this motherfucker to give me another reason to lay him on his ass.

"Hey." He holds up his hands in surrender. "I thought maybe we could talk. Seeing as how our father recently passed away."

"Your father," I correct.

His lips tighten. "He didn't see it that way."

"He should've. He was never a father to me."

"Then why did he leave something for you in his will?"

My head juts back because I wasn't expecting that question. "What are you talking about?"

"That's why I came to see you. We're having the reading of his will soon, but it requires all of us to be there."

"Who the fuck is *us*?" I'm damn sure not a part of that family.

"Like it or not, Gabriel Garcia is your father. Your *real* father."

I take a threatening step in his direction.

He steps back for the first time, fear invading his eyes.

"I just mean, you share his blood. And he took that seriously."

I scoff. "Seriously enough to lord it over my mother's head for years." I know all about the way my father manipulated my mother. He used his money and influence to put me in school and used that as a way to keep her from dating anyone else.

That is until she met Carter Townsend.

The man who adopted me and raised me as his own.

His nostrils flare, and his eyebrows dip to a V. The angered expression passes quickly, though.

"He wanted you to have something of his to remember him by, I guess."

"What?" I ask.

"I don't know. We'll find out at the reading of the will, but you have to me there."

"Do it without me. Now get the hell out, and don't show your fucking face around here again."

I yank my door open, gripping the handle so tight that my knuckles turn red.

"We need you there. The attorney said—"

"Figure something else out because I want nothing from him, you, or anyone else in your goddamn family. And if you show your face around here again, I'll break it."

The unmistakable urge to follow through on that threat rushes through me. My sight begins to cloud, and the back of my neck starts to heat up.

I run my hand across my neck, but the move is useless.

Seeing the face of Gabriel Garcia Jr. is like looking into his father's face. I despite them both.

I was relieved when I heard he'd died. I thought I could finally bury that old demon of mine. But now, standing face-to-face with his spitting image, brings that familiar anger back.

Garcia's eyes balloon.

"Get the fuck out," I order between clenched teeth.

"Father said you had a temper," I hear him murmur as he tosses me a glare over his shoulder.

As I step in his direction, he picks up his pace toward the exit.

I slam my office door and run my hands through my hair. I had plans to visit Monique, but I can't go to her like this. Not with how disturbed I am over seeing that bastard.

When I send her a quick text to let her know I'm going to be a little late to her viewing, she replies that the meeting just got pushed back anyway.

A sigh of relief releases from me.

I know exactly where I need to go to get rid of this extra energy burning through me right now.

CHAPTER 4

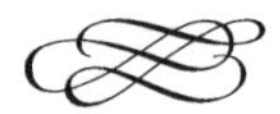

Diego

I look around the dark, dank basement of the brick building I entered. Over the years, I've learned to control my anger. I've managed to filter the rage that's gotten me into trouble more than once in my life.

One main way was in this room.

The smell of sweat, blood, and adrenaline meets me as soon as the heavy metal door opens.

"Diego," the beefy guard greets with a sharp nod.

"Mike." I give him the same courtesy.

As I step over the threshold, the door slams behind me. A chorus of grunts and cheers greets me. A crowd gathers around the thirty-foot octagonal cage on the other side of the sparsely lit room.

"Are you here to fight or to watch?" Mike asks behind me.

I look at him over my shoulder but don't say anything.

He gives a slight nod. "Fight."

This is one of the ways I've learned to manage my anger. After the last time my rage boiled over and caused massive amounts of upheaval in my life, my father introduced me to Uncle Josh's underground fighting ring. One of our family's worst kept secrets.

Or best. Depending on who you ask.

"It's been a while since I seen you down here, kid," Buddy, an old friend of my grandfather's, greets me.

I don't know how old Buddy is, but he's been running this fighting group for years. He still looks like he can take on just about anyone who passes through those doors, though.

"Something must've really got your goat if you're down here in the middle of the week." He's always saying weird shit like that.

I nod but don't go into details. We don't talk about our feelings down here. Our fists are the language we use. Right now, my hands are itching to hit something or someone.

An image of Gabriel Garcia Jr. standing in my fucking office flashes across my mind.

"I need a fight," I say.

Garcia Jr. looks so much like my biological father that I can't help but see his face also. I hate that man. I'm glad he's dead but somehow his ghost decides to haunt me from his grave.

"You know where the changing room is," Buddy says.

In a matter of minutes, I change into a pair of boxing shorts, a T-shirt, and wrap my hands. I don't bother using gloves. Wraps are all I need.

"Townsend, you're next," Buddy says over the yell of the crowd as soon as I exit from the changing room.

I crack my neck on each side before rolling my shoulders back and forth. I can feel the tightness throughout my body as I attempt to loosen up my muscles. Everything inside of me burns to hit something.

"You'll never amount to anything."

The words Gabriel Garcia used to say to me when my mother wasn't around come back to memory.

I never told my mother about the shit he would say to me. Once she married my dad, I thought Garcia was out of my life for good. But words have a lasting impact on a child's psyche.

"Alright, you both know the rules," Buddy says as my opponent and I step into the center of the octagon. "Keep it clean. No shots to the balls. And steer clear of the face." He pauses and looks between us.

"Or don't. It's your face not mine." He shrugs and then lifts his hand. "One, two, three. Fight!" he yells at the same time he jumps out of the ring.

My opponent isn't new to me. We've gone toe-to-toe before.

I watch his midsection as we circle one another. He tests me with his left jab a couple of times.

I dodge each one. When he goes in for a fast takedown, I see it before he makes his move.

I'm able to leap out of the way right before his fist makes contact with my ribs. I give him a shove to the back, which sends him flying.

My heartbeat quickens. This is exactly what I needed. A fight to work out all of the bullshit swimming in my head.

Between the stress of a new team at work that questions my position and the memories of Gabriel Garcia, my irritation rises to a level that I don't ever want Monique to see again.

So, I bring my rage to this cage. I'll let it out on my opponent because he signed up for this.

He moves faster than I predicted. A side swipe of his right leg sends me to the ground. In the blink of an eye, I'm on my back. I tuck and tighten up enough to prevent any real damage when he lands an elbow against my ribs.

I let him climb on top of me, seemingly giving him the upper hand. Then I raise my legs to lock him into a triangle chokehold. I can feel the fight leaving his body. Each second that passes his face grows a little more red. But I don't want this fight to end too quickly.

Releasing him from the triangle, I let him regain his composure. We both rise to our feet. He's not giving up, yet. Which is just what I wanted. He's the only person I'll be fighting tonight since I plan to visit Monique and her gallery as soon as I leave here.

I can't spend too much time on this.

"Let's go," my opponent grunts while slapping his head with his hands.

His added aggression causes the corners of my lips to lift into a smile. He swings, and I duck the right hook that comes close to connecting with my jaw. I let him swing a few more times, though I easily duck and bob out of the way.

I land a few blows to his ribs. Each time I make contact with his body, I can feel the stress and tension ebbing out of my muscles. The words from Gabriel Garcia about not being good enough start to slow until they're no longer echoing through my mind. His words are replaced by my real father's words.

"I love you, son."

"I'm so proud of you."

I can't even begin to count the number of times Carter Townsend, the man who raised me, told me those words. Remembering them, reminds me of who the hell I am. A man who can control his temper.

Once that realization comes to mind, I'm done with the need to fight.

It's my turn to send my opponent to the mat with a leg sweep. He goes down hard. I don't give him time to recover before I'm on him. Less than ten seconds pass before he taps out.

I immediately stand and start for the cage's exit. Buddy stops directly in front of me.

His wise hazel eyes meet mine, searching for something. He often does this right when I'm about to leave.

"You got what you needed," he says. It's not a question even though he nods. Then he steps out of my way.

I don't think to ask what that's all about. All of us that end up down here get something we need. For most of us, it's a way to work out whatever bullshit the day has thrown our way.

Though the area where the cage is set up is dank and dark, the bathrooms and changing rooms are a complete contrast. The sparkling black tile is broken up by a white tile path that leads to the showers.

I shower in the steaming hot water and let it wash away the remaining tension. Twenty minutes later, I emerge from the changing rooms in an entirely different mood than when I first stepped into this room.

I can now go to Monique tempered, being the nice guy she needs. Not the animal with an uncontrollable anger.

CHAPTER 5

Monique

"As you can see, the developer took their time with the new design. The sconces were carefully painted to give the historical look that this neighborhood is known for," the real estate agent tells me.

Scanning the sconces, I frown. Though they look appealing, I instantly recognize that they will not give off enough lighting to illuminate the artwork I plan to hang on the walls.

"How much will it cost to replace them?" I ask.

Steve, the realtor for this building, raises an eyebrow. "Ms. Richmond, I assure you the sconces, along with all of the other additions to this space, are top quality." He sounds too close to being dismissive for my liking.

"We know what looks best in this space."

That comment causes me to cock my head to the side.

"Your clients will have no trouble with this office. In a building such as this one, the price you'd be paying is almost a steal." He shrugs and holds out his hands if he's just dropped his ace of spades.

"Is that right?" I ask slowly, looking around at the brick walls.

"It is."

"Then why has this particular space remained unoccupied for the past six months?"

His eyes balloon briefly. He pushes out a deep breath. "My client is looking for the right renter for this space. Your office would fit beautifully here."

"Gallery," I correct.

"Right. Art gallery."

With a slow nod, I add, "To be quite honest, for this neighborhood, the price isn't all that great. Especially considering it looks like there's some early mold over in the corner there."

I point toward the ceiling in the far corner. "I suspect there's some sort of water leak coming from the second floor bathroom. That would take at least a month, and who knows how many thousands of dollars to fix."

I look back at the realtor. "I hope your client doesn't expect that cost to come out of my pocket."

His face turns red either from embarrassment or anger. Either way, I don't care. I know this guy and his client are full of shit. I recognized the lackluster and shoddy renovation work as soon as I entered this place.

"I-I must have m-missed that," he stutters out. "I will let him know. That, of course, will be taken into consideration when we talk about pricing."

"Don't bother," a deep voice I know by heart states from behind him.

Steve startles and turns to come face to face with a pissed off looking Diego.

"Hey, you," I call, drawing his attention to me. When his golden orbs land on me, a serene calmness washes over me. A peace I didn't even realize I was lacking invades my bones. Despite nothing going the way I want it to today, I feel calmer because he's here.

"C-Can I help you?" Steve inquires.

"Yes," Diego answers abruptly, cutting him down with his glare.

Steve visibly shrinks back from the expression on my best friend's face.

"Once you leave here, you can give your client a call and tell him this place is a dump and if he ever wants to rent it out, he needs to cut the price by at least twenty percent." He takes a step to the side, then looks between Steve and the door. "You can go now. Make that call."

"Diego," I say. He's right about Steve and this place, but he doesn't have to be so rude about it.

"Now," he reiterates without looking my way.

"Ms. Richmond is the potential renter I'm working with, not—"

"Was," Diego corrects. "She was. She's no longer considering this space. Are you, Mo?" He glances over Steve's shoulder to me.

"No," I answer with a shake of my head. "I'm sure my father would drop dead if he came in here and found out I'd rented this place."

"Father?" Steve inquires.

"Damon Richmond."

A look of pure surprise comes over his expression. "As in—"

"Yes, Richmond & Associates Development. As my friend just said, you can go now. I won't be in contact."

My father's development and realty company is well known around the city. The curious expression on Steve's face right before he makes his exit tells me he's wondering why I'm seeking a space on my own if my father is Damon Richmond.

I don't feel the need to give him an explanation.

"Can't believe that motherfucker," Diego gripes once Steve leaves.

"You were mean to him."

"He was trying to swindle you," he quickly replies. He moves closer and peers down into my eyes, as if searching for something.

I tell myself I should look away—the eye contact feels entirely too intimate—but at the same time wholly and completely us.

Without me realizing what he's doing, Diego's hand moves to my cheek. Butterflies fill my belly as he strokes the side of my face.

"What are you doing?" It comes out as a whisper.

"Are you okay? You look disappointed."

I pivot my head slightly, turning into the palm of his hand to nuzzle it. I can't remember a time when I didn't feel comforted by his touch.

"I am," I admit. "Although I honestly didn't have high hopes for this place, it's the third location I've looked at this week and nothing is clicking." Frowning, I turn away, taking in the space again. "Hell, even if I did find a better space, I doubt I could afford it."

My shoulders slump underneath the weight of failure yet again.

"This place was never going to suit you," Diego says as he glances around. "Not enough light. And those sconces are fucking ugly." He frowns, a look of horror overcoming his handsome features.

Despite my dour mood, laughter spills out of my lips.

"Come with me." He takes my hand, not even waiting for me to agree.

He gives me just enough time to grab my handbag from the chair at the corner of the room before we're out of the door.

"Where're we going?"

"To find your dream," he responds.

* * *

Diego

"Whoa," Monique says a minute after we enter the first floor office space.

"It used to be a dental office, but the owner retired a month ago," I tell her of the office. "The total area is ten thousand square feet. Once the furniture is moved out of here, it'll be the perfect location."

"Diego ..." Her voice trails off.

I hear the doubt in her tone, but I also see the wonder in her eyes. She turns to face me.

"Is this place even on the market? There's no sign out front, and I didn't see it available on any of the listings I researched."

I jut my head toward the door. "Aunt Mia's coffee shop is a few blocks from here," I say, referring to the wife of my family's long-standing head of security.

"I stopped by a couple of days ago and overheard the owner of the building talking about putting this place on the market soon. I asked him to hold off until I got a chance to look at it with you."

She blinks, a small smile creeping over her mouth. I shove my hands in my pockets to keep from reaching for her.

"You did that for me?"

She has to know I'd do this and so much more for her.

"Of fucking course I did." I hold out my arms. "Look at this place. It's perfect. The art district isn't too far from here, and with that new place that just opened across the street, we can see the district is growing in this area.

"It's the perfect location to be on First Fridays," I tell her, mentioning the monthly event that galleries and museums in Williamsport host for lovers of art and culture.

"You're right." She sounds breathless, and I know the idea is growing on her. "How many square feet did you say it is?"

"Ten thousand. If you decide to knock that wall out, I bet you can make it to fifteen."

Her lips push out in a pout. "That's a lot of space."

"Exactly what you need when this place is filled with art from all of the artists you'll be featuring." I snort. "Hell, in a year or two you'll probably need a second space."

She rolls her eyes playfully. "You say it with such confidence."

Before I realize what I'm doing, I'm standing in front of her, my hand tipping her chin up so she can't look anywhere but at me. "I say it because it's the truth. Your gallery is going to be a huge success. I can feel it."

She doesn't say anything for almost a full minute.

We remain standing like that. Me holding her chin, her looking directly into my eyes, mine searching hers. As if it has a mind of its own, my thumb lightly runs along the seam of her bottom lip.

Monique inhales sharply but she doesn't pull away. When her mouth falls open slightly, the muscles in my stomach tighten. The urge that has been more and more difficult to fend off comes close to erupting inside of me.

Lowering my head, I bring our faces within inches of one another's. She doesn't pull back, and I take that as a win. However, when I start to go all in, the bell over the door chimes as someone enters.

Monique startles and pulls back, forcing me to release her. I hadn't even realized my hand was wrapped around her waist.

"Mr. Townsend," Donald Rucker, owner of the building, greets. Though he's a stand up guy, at this moment, I want to knock his damn head off.

"This must be the young lady and future owner of a world famous art gallery that you told me about?" he says, smiling at Monique.

"I don't know about that," she replies with a laugh. "I'm Monique."

"Richmond," he finishes. "Your friend has told me a lot about you. He's very proud of everything you've accomplished so far."

She looks at me. "I haven't done anything yet."

"As I told you, Mr. Rucker, she's too modest for her own good." On instinct, I wrap my arm around her shoulders, pulling her into me.

He looks between the two of us, and his smile grows.

"I'm sure he's told you about this place, but how about we have a look around, and I can answer any questions you may have?"

We spend the next thirty minutes with Donald Rucker. Monique asks insightful questions on the space, the cost, timeline for renovations, and a host of other logistical inquiries. She's thorough, yet another sign that I know her business will be the success she's aiming for it to be.

"Thank you, Mr. Rucker. I'll be in touch," she says as we exit the building.

"I'm hungry." She glances down at her wristwatch. "I'll need to do an injection first."

"Aunt Mia's coffee shop is less than a ten-minute walk from here," I suggest, referring to my Uncle Brutus'—our family's long-time head of security's— wife. I always keep a few granola bars and orange juice on me just in case she needs them. It's a habit I've had since high school.

Even when she lived out of state, it was something I continued to do.

"Yeah, that'll work," she says, checking her watch.

I call ahead of time to order the lentil brown rice bowl she likes, to make sure it's ready when we arrive.

Minutes later, we arrive at the *Cup of Joy* café.

"I'm going to head to the bathroom."

I nod, and then make my way to the counter to pick up our order which is ready for us.

Minutes later, we're eating at one of the tables by the window.

"What do you think of the place?" I ask.

When her shoulders immediately slump, my heart sinks. I thought this would be the perfect spot for her gallery.

"It's perfect," she says, her words contradicting her expression.

"But," I prompt.

"But I can't afford it." She sighs. "It's out of my range. The places I marked down to look at were all in my budget."

"They just weren't the right fit."

She shakes her head in response to my comment.

"Then let me write the check for the difference." The words flow without hesitation.

Her eyes balloon, and a smile makes its way to my lips. The way I could stare into her eyes for hours at a time is pure insanity. Yet, it makes total sense to me. I reach across the table to take her hand in mine when I see her eyebrows draw downward.

"Here me out," I hedge. "I know you don't want to ask more of your parents or anyone else—"

"I've already gotten so much from everyone … And I won't ask you to do me any favors either."

"You're not asking. I'm offering," I remind her.

She shakes her head adamantly. "It's still the same. Taking something from someone else instead of figuring it out myself."

"Why the hell do you have to figure it out on your own?" I can't help the bite of frustration that laces my tone.

She blinks. "Because." She sounds just as frustrated.

"That's not an answer."

Monique lets out a groan. "You wouldn't understand."

"Me? I wouldn't understand. The man who knows everything about you." Just saying that out loud causes a thunderous jolt to course through me. It's the truth. I know her inside and out. Our souls have been intertwined since the moment we met.

Our gazes clash.

"Did you really think I made you move back home just so I could stand on the sidelines and watch you struggle to open this gallery all by yourself?"

"You didn't *make* me do anything. I decided for myself," she chides.

A chuckle falls from my lips. "Of course you did."

Her eyes narrow to slits, which makes the grin playing at my lips grow even wider. For some time, no words are exchanged between us. I glance down to notice my thumb making tiny circles along the vein of her wrist.

"Why are your knuckles bruised?" she asks suddenly.

Shit.

I didn't want her to see the bruises from my fight. She thinks underground fighting is something I did once or twice years ago.

"I forgot to wear boxing gloves in my gym class this morning," I lie, hating the twist of guilt in my stomach.

Her eyes narrow on me. But the café employee bringing us our meals interrupts her thoughts.

Neither one of us pulls away even as the employee has to reach over our entwined hands to pick up the dishes.

"The space," I say, getting us back to the more important topic.

"No," she finally says. "It would cost too much."

"I've got it to spend," I quickly retort.

"You're not pulling money out of your inheritance to help me."

"It wouldn't come from my inheritance." As a Townsend, inheritances are a part of all of our lives. I first received access to it three years ago at the age of twenty-five. But every five years, I receive a larger sum.

"Or from your income."

"It's not from my income either."

She pauses and looks at me with a question in her eyes.

"It's been close to six years since you first mentioned opening your own gallery one day. Do you remember what you said when you told me?

"You said," I start without giving her a chance to answer, "all artists deserve to have a space to feature their work. All of them."

"You remembered," she says, smiling.

Her eyes dip, and I fight the urge to tip her chin to make her meet my gaze head-on again. Even though she's sitting right across from me, her hand still firmly in mine, I miss her when she's not looking at me.

For a brief moment, I wonder how the hell I survived all of these years with her living so far away for so long. I don't even want to remember the hell I went through when she told me she was getting married.

"Since that day, I started saving money to invest in your dream."

"What?" she screeches.

I tighten my hold on her hand when she attempts to pull it away.

"No, you haven't."

"Would I lie?"

Stilling, she meets my eyes with hers. I can tell the exact moment she recognizes the sincerity in mine because my name falls from her lips in a whisper.

"Diego. Wh-Why would you do that?"

"How can you even ask me something like that?"

"But how?"

"I knew you would never let your parents help you. Even if you did, I wanted to help make your dream a reality, too. It's the least I can do. Because I know your gallery is going to be amazing. I can't wait to see how the lives of the artists you feature will be transformed because of your hard work."

"Their hard work," she corrects.

With a shake of my head, I counter, "Yours too."

A long exhale makes its way out before she says, "I'll think about it."

"While you think, let's go look at the space again." I stand and hold out my hand, which she takes with ease.

I want to demand to know what the hell there is to think about, but I know I'll have time for that.

We've been just friends for long enough.

I kick myself multiple times a day for not taking this step before. But maybe the timing was never right. Either way, friendship isn't enough for me anymore.

Not when I know I'm in love with my best friend.

CHAPTER 6

Monique

"Oh my gosh!" I squeak as I plop down on my couch right next to Diego. I lay my head against his shoulder and let out a sigh that's eerily close to a groan. "It's been so long since we've gone museum hopping."

After we left the café, we went back to the space so I could look it over again. It truly is perfect and, of course, Diego would be the one to find it. The location is great, and my mind couldn't stop racing with all of the ideas of artists I could feature in the space.

I almost gave in right then and there, but I held firm. I need to make this decision on my own.

After that, Diego suggested we head over to the Williamsport Museum of Natural Art, which turned into us visiting the African-American and Latino-American Art Museums which were nearby.

"I hadn't seen the new exhibit at LAM," Diego says, his arm curling around my shoulders.

I move in tighter to his body to rest my head more easily against him.

"I forgot that a new artist was even featured this month."

"Good thing we went. His exhibit ends next week."

He nods in agreement.

"Today was great." Our time at the museums and art stores really lifted my mood. "I have to admit, as much as I missed Williamsport's museums, I do miss The Met," I say of New York's premiere art museum.

"Nothing beats The Met," he concedes. "Do you remember the first time we went together?"

My head pops up and I give him a look.

"What?"

"How could I forget? We almost got kicked out because you kept wanting to touch the paintings."

He chuckles. "I was sixteen and hadn't seen anything like it before. That was when I became a fan of artwork."

I nod in agreement and start to play with one of his tendrils of curls in his hair.

"Does that mean you're missing New York?" he asks, and something in his voice sounds almost … fearful?

The shake of my head is instant.

"I love New York. It's an amazing place that'll always have a piece of my heart."

His lips tighten, and I wonder what that's about.

Sighing, I lay my head back on his shoulder, still with my hand in his hair. My position is awkward, but I love playing in his hair and resting my head against his shoulder so much that it beats out any possible discomfort.

"I have to admit something."

He stills, but I keep going.

"I enjoyed my time in New York. I met some wonderful people. Made great friends. But there was a part of me that was so lonely there." Pausing, I run my teeth across my bottom lip before admitting the last part.

"Though I had a full life there, there were some days I would go to The Met to feel a little closer to you."

Diego pulls back enough to look down at me. I don't say anything else. I want to allow my admission to hang in the air alone, but something else feels almost compulsory to admit.

I snort. "Ironically, the day before Lawrence dumped me, I had one of those days. He had just found out he would be featured at one of the shows at Art Basel in Miami," I say, speaking of my ex-fiancé. "While I was happy for him, all I wondered about was if you were going to be there."

I look up at Diego.

"We hadn't talked in a while, and you didn't pick up when I called. Then I remembered our first time traveling to New York after freshman year of college. After work that day, I ended up at The Met."

"Alone?"

I nod.

"What did you do there?"

With a shrug of one shoulder, I tell him, "I laughed by myself because I imagined all of the jokes you would make about the people around us or how you would growl, furious with someone, if they dared to step in front of me at an exhibit."

"People need to watch where they're going," he gripes.

"See? That's exactly what I pictured you saying." I lay my head back down on his shoulder. "Anyway, I remember going to bed that night with a pit in my stomach. Maybe I had a sense things were ending between me and Lawrence.

"The next morning is when he broke up with me."

It's not exactly pain that I feel as I relay that part of the story. Well, not pain about the breakup. It's more so the reminder that, yet again, my mere existence is more of a hardship for someone than a joy.

An image of my mother pops into my mind.

"Hey," Diego's uttering calls my attention. "What's going on up there?" He taps my temple with his finger.

I start to shake my head, but he stops me by cupping my chin. "SK. Remember?"

I swallow. Our childhood codenames for one another. Secret keeper.

A smile spreads my lips as I lay my head back against his shoulder. "I really want this gallery, Diego," I tell him. "Not for me. There are so many artists who are overlooked because others choose to believe there's something wrong with them. I want to shine my light on their talents."

He remains silent for a beat, then sits up to turn to face me. "You'll have your gallery. And it's going to be fucking amazing. I can't wait to see you shine when it opens."

For a brief moment, his words drown out all of my doubts. I can't hear any of my previous insecurities over the surety of his comments.

"I've missed you," I say just above a whisper. The words come without me thinking.

Before I know it's happening, his hand palms my cheek. It's so warm and comforting that I barely notice the way he leans in closer.

His lips brush across my forehead. An involuntary groan pushes out of me.

Another kiss to my forehead brings out a sigh. Affection between us has always been a natural part of our friendship. It's never been awkward or weird.

But something about this feels different.

Warmth spreads through my body suddenly, and it takes me a second to realize that it's because Diego has placed his hand on the back of my neck. The move prompts me to turn my head up to meet his gaze.

His eyes burn in a way that I've never seen before.

I swallow and look away because I can't quite form words.

But he does the last thing I expect him to do.

He places his hand underneath my chin, returning my face to his. I don't have time to ask what he's doing or thinking before he dips his head. His lips brush against mine in a similar way he kissed my forehead.

Tiny sparks of electricity flow throughout my body. A shiver courses through me when he brushes against my lips again. In the back of my head, my subconscious screams that this shouldn't be happening for some reason.

However, I can't deny that this feels like the most natural thing in the world.

I part my lips slightly. A small smile breaks out on Diego's handsome face. He moves in closer, lowering his head once again to meet mine.

Right before our lips touch, for real, my ringing phone startles the shit out of me.

"What was that?"

"Your phone is ringing." His voice is so calm and steady, just like he's always been in my life.

I dive for my phone, which is sitting on my coffee table.

"Avery?" I answer, seeing my sister's name on the screen.

"Nique, hey. It's me," she replies like I didn't just answer her by name. "I have a show coming up in a couple of weeks, and I wanted to make sure you're still coming."

Avery has a fantastic singing voice. She's in a local chorus group and performs in school musicals.

"I-I remember." Closing my eyes, I turn away from the couch, knowing I sound flustered. "I have it in my calendar."

"Okay, good. Because we haven't seen you often and I was hoping you didn't forget about me."

"I would never forget about you." My heart sinks because the truth is I haven't been over to visit my family as much as I know they would want me to. I keep telling myself it's because I'm busy setting up my art gallery, finding artists to feature, applying for grants and loans, and looking for a location.

While all of that is true, I could visit more than I do.

Sometimes, a piece of me feels like an outsider in my family. It's not their fault, and no one has ever treated me this way. However, it's a result of knowing how my life began. My siblings will never have to contend with that reality, and I'm grateful for that.

"Good," Avery replies. "It'd be cool if you came to one of my practices, or maybe we could get lunch together?" The hope in her voice tugs at my heartstrings. "Mommy says she'd love to grab lunch with you, too, but you're always busy."

I swallow the lump in my throat.

"I know. I'm sorry. Starting a business is a lot of work." It feels like a lie as I say it, but I hope she buys it.

My sister isn't a fool, though. "Daddy runs his own company, and he has time to have lunch with Mom at least once a week. Uncle Joshua and Daddy also make time to have lunch with each other, and they both run their own companies."

Diego's hand lands on my arm. "I'm going to give you time to talk with your sister."

I whip around and almost trip over my feet at the sound of Diego's deep baritone behind me.

"Shit," he whispers at the same time his hands wrap around my waist to keep me from falling. "Be careful, babe."

I almost lose the hold I have on my phone.

"Is that Diego?" My sister's voice breaks me out of my thoughts.

"Yes." That one syllable comes out slowly because I essentially told my sister I don't have time to visit or have lunch with my family, who live less than twenty minutes away. Yet, I have time for Diego.

"Can I talk to him? I want to invite him to my show, too."

Without thinking, I pass the phone to my best friend. He immediately lights up at hearing my sister's voice on the other end. I make myself look away because the butterflies in my belly start to become too distracting.

What is happening to me?

In my periphery, I watch as Diego promises my sister that he'll attend her concert. He makes mention of Kyle's wedding and even consoles her by telling her something is for the best.

I can only guess what that is, but I knew my sister had a crush on Kyle Townsend for a long time. The ten-year age difference didn't matter to her, but Kyle never saw her as anything more than one of his younger cousins. Even though there's no blood relation.

That brings a smile to my face.

After a few minutes, Diego disconnects the call. "She had to go but said she'll see you this weekend at the wedding."

I nod as I turn back to face him. "I think she might be experiencing her first heartbreak."

"I told her she'll find someone ten times better than my cousin who'll cherish her."

I shake my head. "Remember, at that age, so many things seemed like life or death?" I reminisce. "Like when Darryl Brunson broke up with me, and I thought I'd never get over it."

A laugh spills from my lips from the memories of my first boyfriend in high school.

"He never deserved you."

"You say that about all of my exes."

He moves closer and takes my chin between his thumb and forefinger. "Because it's the truth." His voice is low and tender but somehow dominating.

I can't look away from his eyes as his thumb begins to stroke my bottom lip. The air around us quickly charges with the electricity it held right before my sister's call. Breathing becomes slightly more difficult. The magnitude of what's building between us feels unconscionable.

"Diego." His name is a whisper.

"I'm going to get going," he says, making my heart sink slightly, which is ridiculous. He definitely should go. "I'll pick you up as soon as I get off work on Friday."

I blink and blink again. "This weekend?"

"For Kyle's wedding."

"Oh." I snap my fingers as reality begins to sink in again. I'm Diego's date for the wedding.

The word date takes on a whole different meaning now.

"Right."

A half smile crosses his lips. The muscles in my stomach tighten.

He leans in and kisses my forehead. "Are you feeling okay?"

"Yeah, why wouldn't I be?" It's a stupid question, but I ask anyway.

He doesn't say anything but takes my wrist, the one with my smartwatch on it, and scans it intently. I know he's searching for my numbers.

"You can connect this to your phone, right?" he asks.

I nod. "Yeah. I can track my numbers on any phone."

"Good." He removes his cell from his pocket and pulls something up on the screen. "Connect it to mine, too."

"What?"

"I should have your numbers in my phone. Just in case."

"In case what?"

"You never know." He doesn't even wait for me to explain how to do it before he downloads my monitor's app to his phone. My blood glucose levels display on his phone screen in a matter of minutes.

"I should've done that a long time ago," he says regretfully.

"I was in a different city."

He shrugs as if that makes no difference.

"You're a little low. It's been a couple of hours since we've eaten."

Without a word, I head to my kitchen and grab a granola bar. I make a show of unwrapping it and taking a huge bite.

A satisfied look crosses his face. "You have enough insulin, right?"

"Diego," I growl. I'm the one who's lived with this disease for more than two decades.

"This weekend," he reminds me, backing off the diabetes stuff. Before I know it, he's standing in front of me, planting another kiss on my forehead.

"Lock up behind me," he orders.

Even as I close the door, I can feel his presence on the other side, waiting until he hears the telltale *click* of the lock sliding into place.

"Happy?" I yell out.

"Not yet," he replies, and I wonder what that response is all about. "But I will be."

I tap the screen on the side of my door, and the camera turns on. I watch as his long legs carry him away from my door.

All I can think of as I watch him go is, *Did I kiss my best friend?*

CHAPTER 7

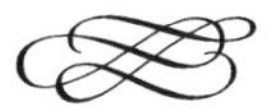

Diego

"Dearly beloved, we are gathered here today ..." The officiant for my cousin's wedding starts.

I glance at my cousin, and even though he isn't facing me, his profile reveals the mile-wide smile on his face.

As Kyle and Riley recite their vows, it's as if they're the only two people in the world. That thought has me looking at our friends and family watching this union take place.

When my eyes lock with Monique in the second row, I also catch her watching me. Neither one of us look away. The words of the preacher fall into the background as I watch her.

My lips spread without consciously thinking about it. I know I'm giving her the smile I unconsciously reserve only for her. In return, the expression on her face reveals her dimples. A warm sensation rushes through me.

"The ring?"

I startle and turn to see my cousin glaring at me.

Shit.

A part of me wants to burst into laughter, but I won't ruin my cousin's big day. I pull out the ring box from the pocket of my tuxedo pants and hand it to him. Though he already has a ring, the crazy bastard went and had both of their rings engraved with the words 'truth or dare'.

Apparently, it's an inside thing between them.

I look back to Monique, who is sadly now watching the couple whose wedding it is, instead of me. Selfishly, I want her eyes back on me.

Until now, I've suppressed it, but this growing need I have to have her is becoming overwhelming.

I'm sure it has to do with seeing my cousin so fucking in love. I'm happy for him, without a doubt. He loves Riley, and despite their rocky start, she's good for him. But it makes me regret how long it's taken for me to claim the woman I love.

"Whoop!" our friends and family shout when Kyle dips Riley by the waist and grants her a kiss that neither one of them will forget.

Claps and laughter erupt around the room. I, again, search for Monique. She's joining in on the excitement, clapping. All I want to do is scoop her up and do the same as my cousin.

In time.

In fact, tonight. I've already decided. That half kiss we shared at her place earlier this week wasn't enough. I'm done wasting time.

She's mine, and I intend to make that clear by the end of the night.

* * *

Monique

"I can't believe how beautiful everything is," I gush as Diego and I stand on the dock of the manmade lake behind Townsend Manor. The lake sparkles with floating lanterns, lighting up the evening sky. Each lantern is a different color because Kyle said his wife likes color.

Overhead, the night sky shines brilliantly with stars. It's as if every star has come out tonight to shine specifically for Kyle and Riley's reception.

"It's amazing, isn't it?" Diego says from beside me.

It's just the two of us out here on the dock. Diego wraps his hand around mine, and I lean against his shoulder. Warmth and safety that I haven't felt in a long time envelope me, and I close my eyes to soak it all in.

"You look handsome, by the way," I say after a few beats of silence

"You think so?"

I laugh. "You look good in anything," I tell him without thinking.

His arms tighten around my waist even as I turn to face him.

He peers down at me, holding me in a way that leaves no space between our bodies. I reach up and entwine my fingers with one of his locks. I've always loved the silky feel of his hair. And he never minds when I touch it.

"I'm surprised you still keep your hair this long." It's not ponytail length or anything but long enough to comfortably run my fingers through his mane. However, the sides and the back are kept closely shaved.

"Have you considered my offer again?"

The question confuses me. "What off ..." I peter off as I remember what he's referring to. "I can't take your money, Diego." I've come to my conclusion.

If I'm going to start this gallery, it'll be on my own.

"You're not taking it. I'm offering it," he counters. "Besides, it's already been earmarked for your gallery for years. There's no other purpose for that money besides investing in your dream."

My heart rate quickens. To know he's been saving for years for my dream makes feelings I can't put into words rush through me.

How the hell do you say no to something like that?

"You want to say yes but you're being stubborn," he says firmly.

"I'm not stubborn."

"You are," he retorts. "You somehow think you're justified in believing that you've taken too much from the people in your life."

He holds up a hand when I open my mouth to say that's not the truth.

"You know it and so do I. Do us both a favor and don't lie to me."

I clamp my mouth shut, hating and loving how well he knows me.

"Do you know why I keep my hair this length?"

I squint at the sudden change in subject but shake my head. "You like it," I reply, not understanding what this has to do with anything.

"Because *you* like my hair long. During our junior year, the first time I ever let my hair get longer than an inch, you commented that you like it long. That was around the time you developed the habit of playing in it. Since then ..." He trails off.

I'm speechless because I never put two and two together.

"That was years ago."

He nods. "And I've kept my hair the way that you like ever since. Just like I put away money to fund your dream. And just like the other night in your apartment felt like I took my first deep breath in fucking years," he confesses.

I inhale sharply because he's talking about those kisses we shared. I knew we couldn't avoid talking about them, but I didn't know how to approach it. He, obviously, doesn't have that same problem.

"You've always been more than my best friend, Monique."

"What have I been?" I ask, needing to hear his answer.

"Mine. You've always been mine."

He punctuates his declaration with a soul binding kiss.

This kiss is nothing like the soft brushes of his lips we shared in my apartment.

What Diego and I are sharing right now is his claim of me. It can't be called anything less than that. And I don't attempt to resist. His lips on mine feel too right.

I can't think straight. All I can do is surrender to the embrace.

Unsurprisingly, what I discover is that I could kiss my best friend for a long, long time and never get tired of it.

A tiny moan escapes my lips, and Diego pulls me flush against his body, deepening the kiss.

All space and time evaporate.

Too soon, Diego pulls back.

"Dangerous," I murmur while staring at his lips.

"Never to you," he declares while running hand down my cheek.

Our eyes lock, and his burrow into mine as if he's asking me to believe him. I don't have the faintest idea why. I know he would never do anything to harm me.

I didn't mean that type of dangerous.

Instead of saying that out loud, however, I say, "I don't remember our first kiss being anything like that."

It's meant as a joke. Our first kiss was with one another in our spot when we were eleven. We did out of curiosity after watching that 90's movie *My Girl.*

It felt weird and awkward at eleven, and we barely spoke about it afterward.

This kiss was nothing like that.

"We aren't kids anymore," he says just above a whisper. His gaze is glued to my lips.

My heart races, and it takes a full minute before I can say, "You shouldn't have done that."

"Why not?"

The answer should be obvious. Because we're friends. *Best* friends. And obviously, I'm a bit of a mess when it comes to relationships.

"Diego," is all I can sigh out, though.

"Mo—"

"Diego!" a deep voice calls from behind us.

I pull away from Diego to find his father, Carter Townsend, standing at the far end. He wears a tuxedo similar to the one Diego has on.

"They're going to head out soon." Mr. Townsend waves us in.

I start to head up the dock, but Diego takes me by the hand. He leads us in the direction of the backyard of the main house. We enter the doors of the reception area, hand-in-hand. For the briefest of moments, I look up into Diego's eyes and he meets mine.

I've never wondered what it means for the entire world to fall away when you're looking at someone. I've known that feeling since I was very young. Diego could take up my entire world for hours at a time and I wouldn't notice.

The look he gives me tells me that I'm not alone in this feeling.

Fear seizes me.

What am I supposed to do with the magnitude of these emotions?

"Come on, baby girl. Give your pops a spin on the dance floor," my father says, breaking the stare off between Diego and me. "Can you give my Short Stuff some space, please?" He glares at Diego.

"Uncle Damon," Diego says to my father, using the name he started calling him when we were kids. He refers to my parents as aunt and uncle the same way I refer to his, since our families are so close—practically family.

"For the remainder of this song I will," Diego continues. "But I'm not going far."

My eyes bulge at the same time my father says, "What the hell does that mean?"

"Let's dance, Daddy," I say, knowing that my calling him that will take his attention off of Diego. My dad is always picking on Diego for some reason.

"I told you that boy was trouble," my dad says when we start dancing.

I laugh because he's being ridiculously overprotective. "You know I'm twenty-eight, right?"

"Is that supposed to mean something?"

"And I've lived in another state for years."

"Don't remind me." He rolls his eyes before taking my hand and spinning me around. "Those years were torturous for me and your mother. I'm glad you're back home, Short Stuff."

As irritated as I want to get at the pet name my father has called me since even before he became my father, I can't. It's the tone of voice he uses whenever he says it. It makes me feel utterly safe and loved.

"I love you." I lay my head on his chest. I close my eyes, and not for the first time I wish that he was my biological father. That it was him who my mother met all of those years ago, when she was just eighteen and they made me.

Him, my father instead of the monster who actually conceived me.

"It does no good to think about the past and wish things would've turned out differently."

My head pops up from his chest because it feels as if he heard my thoughts.

"I don't have any regrets about my life because they all led me right here. With my family." He glances around the room. His eyes stop, and the most beautiful smile breaks out on his face.

I don't even have to look to know that he's found my mother somewhere in the crowd. I track his gaze, and sure enough, there she is. Dressed in a long, green dress that looks stunning on her petite figure.

I take after her in so many ways.

Her natural hair is styled in stunning updo, and when she looks over to see my dad looking her way she smiles as well.

It's not the first time I've seen such an exchange between them. My childhood was littered with those moments. As I look around the room, it's hard not to see similar interactions happening with many of the married couples that are present. It reminds me that both Diego and I were brought up surrounded by love.

We're the lucky ones.

Yet, that type of burning, compassionate love that exists between the couples that raised us, has felt elusive for so long in my adult life. Maybe because I'm not entirely sure that I'm deserving of it.

"No regrets at all," my dad says again before looking down at me.

"Thank you for loving my mom," I tell him. "And me."

He shakes his head. "Loving the both of you wasn't even an option, baby girl. It just came naturally."

My heart feels like it's about to explode from all of the love in this room. This space is not big enough to contain it all, it feels like.

"You know your Mama wants to see more of you, don't you? We all do," my dad tells me.

"I know. As soon as my gallery—"

"Your gallery will come together. Even though you won't let us help you with it. But nothing is more important than family."

"I know," I say, hating that I haven't been acting like I know this.

"Your gallery—"

"It's going to be amazing," Diego cuts in.

When I look up, he's grinning down at me. Slowly, he pulls his gaze away to look over at my father.

"Song ended." He says it as if he had a timer to reclaim me.

My father looks between me and Diego. He surprises me by not commenting. In fact, a slight smirk crosses his lips. He quickly replaces the look with a stern glare at Diego.

"Take care of her," he says like Diego is taking me away somewhere.

"Always," Diego replies before I can say anything.

"Did you enjoy the dance with your father?" he asks, taking me into his arms.

"Yes."

"Good. Because I don't plan to let you out of my arms for the rest of the night."

My heart almost comes to a complete stop.

CHAPTER 8

Diego

"How many rooms do you have available?" I ask the clerk behind the front desk of the boutique hotel where I've rented a room for the night. The hotel is close to Townsend Manor, and I convinced Monique when I asked her to be my date that it would be better to stay out here for the night instead of driving back into the city.

The only problem is she insisted on having her own room.

Like that was going to happen.

"You're in luck, Mr. Townsend. We have five rooms available. Two of them are singles, while one is a—"

"I'll book them all," I cut him off to say.

He stutters and looks completely confused before saying, "Excuse me?"

"All of them. Book all of them under my name."

"Sir, the price on that is—" He breaks off when I flash my black card in his face.

"Book 'em. Make sure you have absolutely no more rooms available in this hotel. Understood?"

He continues to look dumbfounded even as he makes the reservations, but I don't let up. I'm not giving Monique a chance to back out. A more reasonable man would probably go about it a little differently, but hell, I am who I am.

"What took so long?" Monique asks as I make my way back to the lobby area where she's been waiting.

"Bad news." I fake a frown. "They somehow don't have your room reserved."

"What? Why?"

I shrug. "They lost it."

She sighs in frustration. "I can just make another one. I'll see if they have any other rooms available—"

"I tried that," I say, taking her arm before she can walk off to the front desk. "It's a no-go. Nothing's available."

"Are you sure?" She glances over at the front desk in desperation.

"Positive."

"I guess I could catch a car back ho—"

"Don't even finish that sentence. You're staying with me."

Her head begins to shake vigorously. "I can't."

"Why not?"

Her lips part but nothing comes out.

"Is it because you're afraid we'll pick up where we left off earlier tonight?" We hadn't had much alone time at the wedding or the reception. That one stolen moment at the pier and our one dance on the dance floor was it.

I love my family to death but dammit if I didn't want to get rid of most of them just to be alone with her.

"We shouldn't."

"You said that earlier, and for some reason, I'm not believing you. Let's go." Without letting her get a chance to respond, I take her bag and put it over my shoulder and then wrap my hand around hers.

The entire walk to the elevator she protests, giving bullshit reasons as to why we shouldn't spend the night together.

"This is hardly the first time we're sleeping in the same bed," I remind her as we get off of the elevator.

"Yes, but those times ..." She trails off.

I don't need her to finish the sentence. Those times weren't after we kissed like we were the air one another breathes.

"It's late. We've both had a long day and you don't have a room. It'll take at least thirty minutes to get back to your place, and I have a huge bed waiting for us. Not to mention there are obviously some things we need to talk about, and I still need to convince you to take this damn money to start your gallery."

I push the door open to the suite I've reserved and pull her inside.

Silence fills the room as the door swings closed behind us.

"This is not how the night was supposed to go," she murmurs, looking around the suite.

"Yeah?" I ask. "How was it supposed to go?"

"With me politely and lovingly turning down your offer to help fund my gallery."

"Not going to happen," I retort.

"How're you going to tell me what I'm going to do with my business?"

I grin.

"And what about the other thing?" I say instead of responding to her sass.

"What other thing?"

"This." I cup my hand around the back of her neck and yank her body to mine. My lips cover hers before the gasp entirely escapes her mouth. This time, my kiss is urgent, demanding, and unyielding.

I feel the power of our connection coursing throughout my entire body. It makes me feel like I can do anything, even conquer her fears and mine.

We're both panting by the time the kiss ends. I can feel my cock stirring in my pants. I run my fingers up and down the length of her waist. I want nothing more than to strip her down and claim all of her, the way I should have done a long time ago.

"I can't think straight when you kiss me," she says.

"What's there to think about?"

She looks at me like I have two heads. "Everything." She steps out of my hold, making me frown from the loss of skin-to-skin contact.

"This has the potential to ruin everything. We can't keep—"

"We can and will," I promise.

Pushing out a breath, she runs her hand across her forehead. I take her hand and bring it to my lips, kissing her knuckles.

The way she rubs her lips together tells me she enjoys the feel of my lips on her body.

"This could ruin our entire friendship," she finally says.

"Or make it even better than it's ever been."

Her eyes float closed, and I take that as an opportunity to cup the side of her face. I run my thumb along her cheek, noting how soft it feels.

"What if it all falls apart? I don't think I'm all that good at relationships, Diego."

"That's because all of the losers in your past weren't worth your time." I put a finger to her lips. "Don't defend them to me. Not tonight."

No, not all of the guys in her past were exactly losers. But there were some bastards.

I force myself to put the past out of my head.

She shakes her head. "I'm not defending *them.* You know my past as well as I do. Besides, not all relationships work out."

"Ours will."

"How do you know that?"

"Because it's you and me," I say it with all the confidence I have in my body because there isn't a doubt in my mind about this. "I won't screw this up," I declare.

She presses her lips together and wrinkles her forehead. "It's not you I'm worried about messing anything up."

My mind flashes back to all of the mistakes I've made. How I've let my anger get the best of me at times. I've learned to control it, in a variety of ways. I won't let any of my darkness impede our relationship.

Not again.

"I have a proposition," I say.

She gives me a wary look. "Your propositions often end up with me doing something strange."

"You'll be doing something strange tonight," I mumble.

"What?"

"Nothing. Back to the money, first."

"Diego—" She stops when I raise my hand.

"It's yours. For your gallery. There's no one in the world I trust more to put it to good use, and it will be wasted because I promise you I won't touch it for anything else. So ..." I draw out the word as I move closer to her, placing my finger under her chin to make her look up at me. "It's yours. And in return you'll give me three months."

She blinks and then blinks again. "Three months for what?"

"To let me show you how good it can be between us. Three months to make you love me." I bend low and kiss her forehead, then the tip of her nose, each cheek, and finally her lips.

A miniature earthquake of a shiver runs through her. I run my thumb along the seam of her bottom lip, noticing the slight tremble.

"Three months. And if things don't work out, we'll go back to being just friends." It's a complete lie. I know it but I say it because I know it will give her some sense of security.

"Three months?"

I nod, again, knowing it's a fucking lie. I'm not going anywhere in three months and I'm sure as hell not letting her go anywhere.

Pushing out a breath, she glances around the hotel suite. "You planned this, didn't you?"

"I have no idea what you're talking about." Each word is punctuated by me taking a step forward.

She takes steps backward until her back hits the wall.

I bracket her in with my arms. "Is that a yes?"

"You know you're the only person I can't say no to." Her eyes fall to my lips.

By now my cock is straining against the zipper of my pants to be free.

"I know," I tell her, a cocky smile on my face.

"But if once the three months are up and it's not working out, we can go back to being just friends. And I'll pay you back the money."

"Abso-fucking-lutely not. The money is yours either way."

"You're such a pain in my ass," she gripes.

Letting out a laugh, I bend low, meeting her eyes. "I should be a gentleman and say that I'm okay with taking things slow."

I press my face into the crook of her neck, inhaling the floral scent. She's worn the same perfume for years. I get her a bottle of it every year on her birthday.

Her natural sweet smell mixes with the perfume to create a scent I can't get enough of. I would say I want to bottle it up to carry it around with me always but there's the chance I'd lose it. And some other fucker could find it and know exactly what her scent is.

That ridiculous thought pisses me off.

"But we've both waited long enough for this to happen, Mo," I growl in her ear before biting her earlobe.

Her entire body shudders.

"Tonight, I'm going to make all of you mine."

* * *

Monique

With that declaration, Diego lifts me up into his arms and carries me to the bedroom. The room is massive, and that's when I become one hundred percent certain that he set this whole thing up.

Diego is a planner and a perfectionist. He doesn't miss when it comes to even the smallest of details. It's what makes him a great architect and an even better friend.

Tonight, I have a feeling I'm going to find out it's also what makes him a superior lover.

Tingles move throughout my body when he runs his fingers up and down my legs.

"Have I told you how much I love seeing you in these heels?" He moves to the end of the bed, lifting my right leg. He kisses the inside of my knee.

"They'll look perfect over my shoulders tonight," he growls.

My nipples harden to the point of pain, and I've already soaked through the seam of my panties. All from a few kisses and praises.

But who the hell am I kidding? With that fiery glint in his eyes, kisses and compliments coming from Diego are more than enough to have any woman, let alone me, screaming for him to take her.

My best friend.

My subconscious continues to tell me that this shouldn't be happening. That it could ruin everything we've built between us. Yet, the way he's slowly rolling my stockings down, letting his fingers trail over my bare skin, makes me forget all of my doubts.

Common sense flies out of the window when he's so damn good at touching me.

"Let's put these back on," he says, holding up the black, red bottom heels that he'd removed to strip me of my stockings.

The shoes were another gift from him, three years ago when I got a job promotion.

"Oh god," I moan when he begins kissing the insides of my thighs.

"Monique?"

I open my eyes, which had fallen shut. "Yes?"

"Do you know how long I've wanted to know what your pussy tastes like?"

I don't dare to respond that I've also wondered what parts of his … um, anatomy taste like.

"Tonight, I plan on spending the rest of the night finding out." That's his last warning before his mouth makes contact with my pussy lips.

A groan crawls its way up my throat and out of my mouth and I flop back onto the bed. My entire body erupts in a heated passion I've never felt before. It's right at this moment that I remember I'm still in my dress from the wedding.

It's too confining.

But I wouldn't dream of asking Diego to stop pleasuring me the way he is so I can remove the damn thing.

His hands move down my thighs and over my buttocks, rolling the fabric of the dress over my hips. He tightens them almost to the point of pain on my hips, and I groan, wanting him to tighten his hold even more. At this point, his tongue is making me feel like I just might fly away.

I squeeze my eyes tightly and start to dig my heels into his back. But I stop when I remember that I'm still wearing my heels.

"Fuck!" I yell out when his tongue does some sort of magical shit against my clit. I might not survive the night if he keeps this up.

"Diego! Oh, god."

It's as if me calling his name puts a battery in his back. His tongue seeks out my clit over and over again. The sensations start at the top of my head, and before I know it, they rush through me. I let out one hell of a groan as my orgasm rips through my core.

"Shit," I pant out.

A satisfied smile plays at his lips. The moisture on them makes me sit up and yank him to me. I kiss the hell out of him, tasting myself on him. An uncontrollable craving for more overcomes me.

It must overwhelm us both, because before I know it, we're ripping and tearing at one another's clothing to get naked as quickly as possible.

"Condom," I say when we're both nude.

"Just let me look at you," he replies, sounding breathless and in awe, which causes my clit to pulse. "Fuck, you're so beautiful."

His eyes roam over my body, darkening from their normal light brown color. I'm not self-conscious about my body, never have been. But if I were, the way he's looking at me would erase any doubt I ever had.

As it stands, it's doing nothing short of making me want to straddle him and ride him until we're both spent and exhausted.

"I plan on letting you do that soon, baby," he says, making me realize I've said my thoughts out loud.

We're kissing again, his hands touching every inch of me as if he's committing the contours of my body to memory. Though this is the first time we've been together like this, there isn't the usual awkwardness of getting to know a lover for the first time.

There's an ease that part of me feels shouldn't be here. Not yet, so early into this relationship.

"Shh, shh, shh," he shushes me out of nowhere. "You're thinking too much. Let me fix that." He moves in between my legs, forcing me to wrap them around his waist. His thumb finds my clit and starts making slow, torturous circles.

"Do you like that?" he asks as if he can't feel my body's response to what he's doing.

I nod.

"No. Tell me, Monique. Do you like that?"

"Yesss," I hiss.

"Look me in the eyes when you answer me."

I meet his gaze. "Yes."

A mischievous grin crosses his face. "I want you to moisturize my beard again."

"What?"

His answer is to flip our bodies so that he's laying beneath me while I'm spread eagle, my vagina hovering above his mouth. He yanks me down, and before I can take my next breath, I'm riding his face. The trimmed hairs of his beard tickle the insides of my thighs.

I can feel myself dripping onto him.

"Diego, you feel so good," I murmur while my hips ride his face. Tossing my head back, I let out a shout as my second orgasm tears through me.

The only sounds around the room are the groans and moans coming from the both of us as he adjusts positions again. Hovering above me, he takes my hands into his, entwining our fingers.

"Eyes on me when I enter you for the first time," he says against my mouth.

I meet his stare as he pulls his hips back and carefully enters me. He moves slowly, to the point of agony. It's almost as if he's holding himself back.

But I don't want him to hold back. I need him—all of him—inside of me right now.

I wrap my legs around his waist and say, "Take me, Diego."

He searches my face for something. Reassurance maybe.

"Please," I beg.

He curses, and then surges deep inside of me.

Shit!

This is the moment I realize I asked for more than I could take. Diego isn't small. A fact I tried hard not to think about in the past. But somehow, I always knew.

"Breathe, Monique," he says.

I push out the breath I was holding.

"Look at me," he orders. His eyes search mine. He places a kiss to my forehead, and my entire body melts around him. I've always loved his forehead kisses the most.

He must know.

Our bodies become in sync as we find a rhythm that's meant exclusively for us, just like the rest of our relationship. We kiss until our lips become swollen and then kiss some more.

It's like neither one of us can get enough. A third orgasm rolls over me. My pussy walls clamp down around him. But Diego doesn't come inside of me. I can see the strain from the veins in his neck that it takes a herculean effort to pull himself out of me.

He strokes himself once, then another time before jets of his cum splash onto my stomach. I reach down and use my finger to bring it to my lips.

Diego groans as he watches me lick his cum from my finger.

"I'm a goddamn fool for waiting for so damn long," he mumbles. He kisses me again.

It takes a while for us to catch our breaths. When we do, Diego is the first to move. He gets up from the bed. I unabashedly watch the muscles of his ass flex as he walks to the bathroom.

A beat later, he returns with a warm washcloth to wipe me off. A purr claws its way out of my mouth.

"Stop that." He playfully swats the side of my butt.

"Why?" I tease.

"Because if you keep making those noises, I'm not going to give you time to rest before I'm balls deep inside of you again."

My pussy lips squeeze at the thought of having him inside of me again. As much as I would love that, I do need a short break.

He tosses the cloth onto the nightstand and climbs back into bed. His long body curls around mine, and I sigh into his hold.

I'm exhausted. Too tired to contemplate the repercussions of what we've just done. Given my track record, I feel like I'm bound to mess this up somehow.

As I start to dose off, I can't help but to remember the ways in which my past mistakes almost ruined me and Diego.

CHAPTER 9

hen

Monique

I knew he would be here, but seeing his face as soon as we enter this Christmas party puts me on edge. I'm with my parents and siblings for a holiday party at Townsend Manor. We attend it every year on the evening of Christmas.

But this year is the first year that I'm actively avoiding Diego. It's ironic though, seeing how most of our family expects that we'll be inseparable since we both just got back from our respective college campuses a few days ago.

Though Diego and I attend different universities, they're only a couple hours apart by car. So, this isn't the first time I'll see him since we went away to school.

As soon as his eyes meet mine, I look away.

"I'll help with Avery," I tell my mom, taking my little sister's hand. Avery's practically jumping out of her five-year-old skin as I try to unzip her coat to take it off. She's anxious to play with the new toys she's gotten today.

Even as I have to wrestle with Avery's wriggling body to undo her winter stuff, I scan the room. Just like he has a freaking homing device connected to him, I meet Diego's stare. He tries to keep his face as neutral as possible, but I can see he's angry.

Being home with my family and doing all of our holiday stuff has kept me busy enough that I've been able to avoid him. Unfortunately, that won't last.

I know if he doesn't corner me at some point during tonight's party, we'll meet up somewhere, eventually.

I plan to put that inevitable run-in off for as long as possible. I spend the evening helping the younger kids unwrap gifts, fixing plates of food for them, and anything else I can use to stay occupied just so I'm not free to talk to Diego.

Though I have to admit, it sucks not being able to speak to my best friend. Especially on Christmas, my favorite holiday. But he's being an ass.

As I pour my younger brother the last bit of eggnog from one of the dozens of cartons in the fridge, my phone rings. It's my boyfriend, Derek. I find myself mildly annoyed by his interruption but decide to answer since it's the first time we've gotten a chance to speak all day.

"Hey, hang on," I say by way of answer. Then I make sure no one's around as I dip outside to the backyard from the kitchen.

A chill runs through me from the frigid air, and I curse myself for not grabbing my coat first.

"Merry Christmas," I tell Derek.

"Merry Christmas. Did you get my gift?" His speech is slightly slurred, a sure indication he's been drinking.

"It arrived last night. I sent you a text when I couldn't get a hold of you on the phone," I tell him.

"Yeah, I was out late last night."

"With who?"

"What do you mean with who? I went out with friends." His voice starts to rise. "It's the first time I've been back home since the start of the semester. I can't go out with my friends?" he barks into the phone. "Don't be a total bitch, Monique."

"Excuse you?" I squeak, hardly understanding how this conversation went from zero to ten so damn fast.

"You're bitching like I did something wrong—"

That's the last word I hear from him before my phone is snatched out of my hand.

"Who the fuck are you talking to like that?" Diego growls into the phone.

"Diego," I yell and try to grab my phone from him.

He pivots his body away.

"Don't worry about who the fuck this is. If you ever talk to her like that again, you'll find out, up close, who the fuck I am!" He ends the call.

"Why did you do that?" I attempt again to grab for my phone, but he pulls his arm out of reach.

"Does he talk to you like that all of the time? Is that the son of a bitch who you're not speaking to *me* over?"

I flinch at the hurt I hear in his voice.

"Slater is not the reason we're not talking. You are," I say, defending my boyfriend.

"Why? Because I told you about his loser ass friend group?"

Slater is friends with a few guys who go to the same university as Diego. He hates them with a passion I don't understand. Sure, they can be pompous and pricks sometimes, but it's not like we didn't go to high school with the same type of guys.

Besides, Derek's not that bad.

I tell Diego as much which is why his face turns a particular shade of red. The same color as it always gets when he's furious.

"Did you not hear what I told you a month ago? The guy and his bastard ass friends are trouble."

"And I told you that I can take care of myself."

"Then why don't you act like it?" he hisses.

My eyes bulge in shock and anger. "Where the hell do you get off—"

"I get off because I'm your best fucking friend. And you're mine. I told you I would never let anything happen to you, and I meant every word of it."

"How do you know those rumors about Slater and his friends are even true? Is this jealousy or something? Are you angry because his friend, Jake, is dating that girl you liked?"

His eyebrows dip into a V and he looks at me like I have two heads.

"Fuck Jake and that chick. I barely know her."

"But you liked her. I saw it when you came to visit me on campus."

He visited me the first month we were away at college. There's a girl, Jesse, that a lot of guys on campus are enthralled with. She's very pretty and it's not hard to see why the guys want her. I noticed Diego watching her when he came to visit.

I even introduced them since Jesse was in the same biology class as me and we were working on a project together.

They went out once or twice, but nothing came of it apparently because she quickly started dating one of Derek's friends.

"This isn't about her or even his fucking crew, which I've warned you about. This is about the way that asshole was just speaking to you."

"He's a little drunk. It's Christmas … of course, he's going to be a little tipsy. He's not normally like that."

"It's never an excuse to be like that. He called you a bitch."

"Which, if you'd given me the chance, I would've yelled at him about. I'm sure he's sorry, but because you hung up on him, you didn't give him a chance to apologize."

"It shouldn't have ever come out of his mouth in the first place. Could you imagine your dad ever calling your mom a bitch? Or my dad saying something like that to my mom?"

"We're not them!" I scream. Because no, I can't imagine either one of those scenarios happening. But we're different from our parents.

At least, I am.

I'm not getting my happily ever after. I don't deserve it.

"God, what happened to you?" he asks as if he doesn't know me anymore.

That hurts more than anything.

"Why are you even entertaining a loser like him? It's like ever since …" He trails off.

"Since what?" I dare him to say it. The elephant in the room that we've been avoiding ever since the day he found me crying in our spot, over a year ago.

"Since that day, you've changed. All you date now are losers."

"Don't call him that," I yell. "And nothing's changed." I turn away from him so he doesn't see that even I know that's a lie.

I wish I could say nothing in me changed when I found out the truth of my biological father. But it did. Something inside of me broke. For most of my life, I learned to live with the fact that the man who conceived me just didn't want to be a part of my life.

Was it painful? Yes, but I accepted it, and when my mom married Damon Richmond, he became the only father I ever wanted.

Then, I went and discovered the truth. The reality that I was created in something horrific and ugly. I am the by-product of that. How can that not change someone?

Diego comes around to face me. I pull away when he tries to place his hands on my shoulders. I might crack wide open if he touches me. He's the only one who knows everything about me, all of my secrets.

And that's not something I want to look in the face right now.

Yet, he doesn't let up.

"We both know that's not true," he says. "Something's changed, and you won't talk to me about it. Maybe you should talk to your mom—"

"No!" I say louder than I intend to. I look toward the glass door that leads into the kitchen. A few of Diego's aunts and uncles are standing around the kitchen island talking and laughing.

I tug him by the arm, pulling him out of sight of everyone.

"I will not bring this up to her and you know why. Like I said, there's nothing going on with me. I'm just dating a guy you don't like for whatever reason. He's not perfect but nobody is.

"I'm sorry things didn't work out between you and Jesse. You need to get over it. This is the last time I'm going to have this conversation with you."

This is the third time we've argued over my relationship with Derek. Hence, why I've tried to avoid him all night. I didn't want to argue with him on Christmas.

"Monique—"

"No," I cut him off. "Just drop it. I don't want to talk about it anymore. My life is none of your business."

I take a step away from him with the intention of going back inside. Suddenly, a wave of dizziness hits me.

"Monique," Diego calls. "What's wrong?" He doesn't wait for an answer as he instantly checks my glucose monitor. "You're low."

He says what I've pretty much figured out, at the same time he scoops me up into his arms.

"I'm fine," I try to tell him, even though I'm starting to feel the effects of ignoring my numbers for too long.

He ignores me as he bursts through the kitchen door, causing everyone to look our way.

"She's low," he says by way of explanation. "She needs orange juice."

Out of nowhere, my mom appears with a cup of juice and that worried look in her eyes. Even when I do my best to reassure her, my dad, and Diego that I'm fine, they all hover over me as I drink.

The next fifteen minutes are a series of constant checks on my numbers. My mom strokes my forehead and cheek. I hate the concern that lingers in her eyes.

"I'm sorry," I say, peering up from the couch at my mom. "I didn't mean to ruin everyone's Christmas. I'm sorry."

"Baby girl," my dad kneels down beside me while my mom sits at my side, "you haven't ruined anything. We just want to make sure you're alright."

"You need something to eat now," my mom replies. "You have your insulin, right?"

I nod, knowing the drill. Slowly, I rise to my feet to head to the bathroom to inject myself with the necessary insulin before eating. In the meantime, my mom prepares a plate of stuffing, vegetables, and roasted turkey.

I slowly eat my meal while my family continues to linger nearby. When I show them my phone screen, it shows that I'm back in a safe range. "I'm feeling better," I tell them.

My dad kisses the top of my head and stands to move away. His position is immediately filled by my aunt, Kayla, my mom's best friend who's also a naturopathic doctor. I've been a patient at the doctor's office she works at for years.

"Hey, are you feeling okay?" Her tone is so soothing and comforting it almost brings tears to my eyes.

I'm sandwiched between the two women I love the most in this world, and at this moment, I want nothing more than to lay my head on their shoulders and cry my eyes out. For what, I don't even fully understand. I can't do that, though.

If I start to cry, they'll hold me and let me cry and then they'll want to know why. The truth might come out. And I can't burden my mother that way. Not today or any day.

So, I remind myself to suck it up and answer my aunt.

"I'm great. All of the holiday excitement made me forget to check in on my numbers, that's all. Sorry to worry everyone." I look between my aunt and my mom but then immediately look away.

I hate the concern I see in both of their eyes. I know it's out of love for me which makes me feel even worse. When I look straight ahead, I make eye contact with Diego, who I suspect has been watching me the entire time.

Without a word exchanged between us, he comes over to the three of us and squats directly in front of me.

"She's good now," he says with a reassuring smile on his face, looking between Aunt Kayla and my mom. "I probably overreacted. Sorry about that. You two can go rejoin the festivities, and I'll hang out with her. We need to catch up on college stuff."

My mom and Aunt Kayla exchange a look over my head. I can't quite decipher what the look is about but soon my mom gives me a smile and stands. I sigh out the tension I've been holding as she moves away.

"Alright, baby girl. You let us know if you need anything."

"Is Monique okay?" five-year-old Avery and seven-year-old Damian come running up the hall to ask.

My stomach sinks to know even my young siblings are on high alert when it comes to my diabetes.

"She's great," Diego says. "Did you two finish opening all of your gifts?" he asks, sounding cheerful.

"Yeah, but I still can't open the Transformer toy I got. Can you help me?" Damian asks.

"Go get it," Diego answers without hesitation.

He takes the seat on the couch that my mother just vacated. He's as good with them as he is with his own younger brother and sister. Damian and Avery love Diego, probably as much as I do.

I find my head sinking lower and lower until it lands on his shoulder. He looks away from the toy package he's unraveling for my brother to peer down at me.

'I'm sorry,' I mouth to him.

Though this issue is far from over and I have no intention of breaking up with Derek, I don't want to lose my best friend over it.

If only my stupidity had ended there.

CHAPTER 10

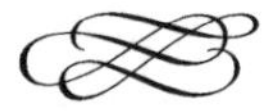

Diego

"We can do more," I tell the room full of stern looking men. It doesn't matter that two of them are my uncles, Uncle Aaron, the CEO of Townsend Industries, and Uncle Joshua, who oversees the real estate division of the company.

At the far end of the boardroom table, mounted on the wall is the big screen with Kyle, my cousin and COO of the company, also present. The two other men in the room are directors of finance and operations.

Uncle Aaron gives me a deep, penetrating look. Most men would flinch at that glare, but I meet his eyes head-on. He steeples his fingers in front of his face.

"Making an assumption like that suggests that we haven't been doing enough." His voice is cold. The hidden insult in his comment isn't lost on me either. I've basically said the company is slacking.

But I won't back down.

The men in this room and my dad all taught me to stand on my word.

"You haven't," I reply.

His only response is to raise one dark eyebrow. Uncle Joshua tilts his head to the side. From the screen, Kyle huffs.

"Do tell?" he says with a challenge in his voice.

I stand and gesture to the printouts I've brought to this meeting.

"This is a side by side of the current projects we have underway contrasted with projects I believe we can take on in the next five years."

"You want us to make a bigger move into commercial real estate," Uncle Joshua says while looking down at the printouts.

"Yes. We've got the manpower, skill, and financial resources to make larger strides in that arena." I look around the room to ensure I have all of their attention. "My expertise is in commercial design."

At my last company, I worked as the lead design architect for large, commercial real estate projects.

They all are well aware of my credentials.

"If you had brought your ass over sooner, we could've started this years ago," Kyle gripes from the screen.

"Shouldn't you be enjoying your honeymoon?" He's only in the first week of his three-week trip to Europe with his new wife and is already on a work call.

"I'm only giving him thirty more minutes, gentleman," Riley says from somewhere offscreen.

Kyle's lips twitch as he tries to withhold his smile.

"He's right, though," Uncle Aaron states, bringing my attention back to the head of the table. "If you had been with us years ago, we could've made much more headway in this arena."

I blink and meet all my family members' eyes in this meeting. Townsend Industries is a powerhouse of a company. They can hire the best and brightest. It never even occurred to me that my family was waiting for me to join the company to enter this subsect of the market.

My stomach twists from the guilt that I could've let them down. I can't tell anyone I needed to wait until what felt like a black cloud lingering over my head was gone.

The death of Gabriel Garcia. My birth father.

"He's right," Uncle Joshua adds. "But you're here now. That's what matters. And this is a great proposal. The project you're overseeing is a step in the right direction," he continues.

I swallow the lump of guilt in my throat and, not for the first time, vow to do and be everything I was meant to be for my family and this job. My life finally feels like it's starting to come together as it should.

The only last piece is the best piece of this puzzle.

Monique.

The night of Kyle's wedding was just the beginning.

We spend the next twenty minutes strategizing. After that, I head to my office with the intention of replying to some emails and then looking over the designs I've been working on.

Unfortunately, my plans get interrupted.

"Diego, there's an attorney from Wolcott & Sons on the line for you."

I've heard of the law firm. They handle everything from estate planning to real estate and family law. But I don't have any contacts with them, nor do any of my business dealings.

A second later, I tell my secretary to put the call through.

"I'm the estate attorney for your father," Donovan Chalmers says, introducing himself.

My head juts back. "No, you're not." I know the attorney my father and all of my family members work with.

"Yes, Gabriel Garcia."

"Fuck," I curse. "That man is *not* my father. Was not," I correct.

"I-I apologize," he stutters out.

"What the hell do you want?"

He quickly jumps into something about Gabriel Garcia's will.

"I don't want any part of it." I start to hang up the phone, but he begs me to hang on.

"Please, I'm not too far from Townsend Industries. Could you please meet with me for ten minutes?"

I know hanging up the phone won't put an end to this shit as quickly as I would like. He or someone else will call again or stop by my office or home.

"Five minutes at the coffee shop across the street."

I hang up before he can respond.

* * *

"DIEGO, thank you for meeting with me," Donovan immediately starts as soon as I reach the table where he's seated.

I don't bother to shake the hand he holds out. I sit. "The timer is on." I tap my watch.

He gives me a contrite look and nods. "I won't take up much of your time."

"You've already taken up too much of it."

With that, he dives right in. "The reading of your fa– Gabriel's will was last week. We were able to hold it in spite of the fact that you weren't present as per his wishes."

I grunt and fold my arms across my chest. Donovan looks at me with hesitation. I don't bother telling him I know the only reason Gabriel Garcia tried to insist that I be present at the reading of his will is to try to maintain some sick sort of power over me.

The bastard was like that. He loved lording control over people—my mother, me, his other family. But fuck him. My not attending was my final middle finger to him. Not that he deserved even that amount of acknowledgment.

"He left you an inheritance."

"I don't want it," my reply is instant. "Give it to his actual children." I stand to leave.

Donovan rises from his seat as well. "It's not that simple, Diego. This inheritance comes with stipulations."

A chuckle passes my lips, but it's tinged with malice. "Of course there is. The son of a bitch was all about stipulations and contingencies and shit." After all, he was a lawyer himself. "I don't give a shit about him or his inheritance. He can rot in hell."

Donovan flinches.

"Your five minutes are up." I head for the door, but he follows.

"Please, Diego, hear me out?"

Irritated, I stop short just outside of the door of the coffee shop. "What?"

"Gabriel knew you wouldn't want anything to do with him or this inheritance."

"Yet, he still made sure to include me." Sick bastard obviously didn't know how to leave well enough alone.

"Yes, well," Donovan continues, "either way the money is yours. Don't you want to know how much it is?"

"No."

"I'm sure you're already well off, given your adopted family's considerable wealth."

"Do not bring up my family," I tell him through gritted teeth.

His eyes bulge, and he takes a reasonable step back. "Still, the money is yours and I cannot allow you to give it away as per the instructions of the will. Especially not to your broth—" He cuts off when I glare at him.

"To Gabriel's other two sons. He insisted that they not receive a penny more than he granted them in his will. Which, admittedly, is less than your inheritance."

I don't have time to figure out Garcia's mind games. He's dead. That's all that matters in my book.

"Then burn it," I say and start to stride off.

"Diego, please," Donovan pleads. "There is a stipulation that after one year you can give the money away if you decide to. But you must hold onto it for one year. Still, under no circumstance is the money to go to Gabriel's other children, however."

"I'm going to say this one more fucking time. Because obviously, I spoke too fast for you to hear me the first time. I don't give a flying fuck about Gabriel Garcia, his money, or his other family. The bastard never did anything out of the kindness of his heart for me when he was alive. I don't expect anything from him now.

"Get the hell out of my way," I seethe.

I brush past Donovan, almost knocking him over. All I can see is red. I hate that even from the grave, that son of a bitch still has some ability to make me this angry. He hasn't been a significant part of my life for two decades, and yet, the mention of his name still brings back the ways in which his words used to taunt me.

"You won't ever be good enough."

"I shouldn't expect more from you."

"You're such a disappointment."

The words he used to tell a child when no one else was around. That doesn't even include the things I overheard him say to my mother when he thought I was out of the room or sleeping.

My hands tighten into fists. I had every intention of going straight to Monique's gallery to check in with her after work. But I don't want her to see me in this state.

Another round at the underground fight club before I go to see her. It's either that or the other method I use to alleviate that dark, angry feeling that comes over me. But I can't bring Monique into that world.

I won't.

CHAPTER 11

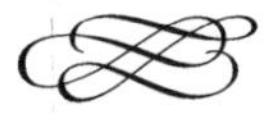

Monique

As I look around the now empty space, I can't believe it. "This is going to be my gallery," I whisper, which is silly since there's no one around. The construction crew have gone home for the day.

The progress that's started in only a few short days since I signed the contract makes my heart soar with pride.

"Mrs. Richmond?" someone calls from behind me.

It's John, the building owner. His smile is sincere. "I'm closing up for the day."

I nod. "I just wanted to look around before leaving."

"Envisioning what it will be like once your gallery opens, huh?"

"Yes," I admit.

"It's a great thing you were able to come up with the money for it. In the past three days, I've had to turn down three offers to businesses who didn't know that I'd already contracted with you."

An image of Diego comes to mind. It's because of him that I even found this space and was able to afford it without having to take out a massive loan or wait for my grant applications to go through.

My heart squeezes and warmth rolls over me as the memories

from the night of Kyle's wedding flood my mind. It's been a little over a week and we haven't been able to see much of each other.

Everything inside of me yearns to see him.

"I'm going in this direction," John says, pulling me out of my thoughts.

"I'm headed that way." I point behind me. "See you later," I tell him and start off for the women's clinic I found a week ago to volunteer at. There are many in Williamsport, including a women's shelter where my Aunt Kayla and her family run.

My mom volunteers there as well.

The place I found is called "Victoria's Home" and is specifically for women and victims of assault.

"Hello, my name is Monique Richmond," I introduce myself to the receptionist. "I have a six o'clock appointment with Joseline Burke."

She smiles and checks the planner in front of her, confirming my appointment, before telling me to take a seat. As I do, I notice the pamphlets on the coffee table in front of me.

So many pamphlets on how to get involved with rape prevention, how to advocate for yourself or someone you love, numbers to call, fundraising events, and more. I briefly squeeze my eyes shut to push out the negative memories and thoughts that want to invade my consciousness.

Not only the imaginings of what my mother went through all of those years ago. And how she had to deal with it all alone. But what almost happened to me because I was selfish and dumb.

"Monique?"

My eyes pop open to find a tall Latina woman, not much older than me, smiling before me.

"I'm Joseline." She holds out her hand.

I stand and shake it. "Pleasure to meet you."

"Thank you for coming in to meet with me as a potential volunteer. Please, come to my office."

Minutes later, Joseline and I are in her office, discussing the various volunteer opportunities. I'm almost overwhelmed with the different needs. I shouldn't be given my experience.

"I see you have some phone experience as well," Joseline says, looking over the resumé I sent in.

"Yes. Three years volunteering for the twenty-four-hour hotline in one of our districts in New York City. After that, I spent the past three years being a companion to women in the ED or in the middle of a crisis."

She looks at me across the desk. "That couldn't have been easy."

I give her a tight smile. "No one does this kind of work because it's easy."

"You're right about that."

The empathy that fills her voice comforts me. I'm also grateful that she doesn't continue to look at me with some sort of expectation that I'll divulge my entire life story to her.

It's as if she knows the women and few men who volunteer or work here come with their own reasons. But no one is obligated to or forced to relay what it is that brought them here.

"Five to ten hours a week is what many volunteers do," Joseline says as she stands from the table. "Naturally, if you can only do that many hours a month, we understand. Most of our volunteers have full-time jobs and lives outside of this service.

Not to mention the toll this type of work can take on someone. We encourage everyone to pace themselves."

I nod as we head out of her office for a tour of the facilities.

"I probably can do a minimum of ten hours. Though, I am in the process of opening my own gallery, which will take up a huge amount of my time."

"Art gallery?" she inquires with interest.

"Yes. It's walking distance from here, which is part of the reason I chose to volunteer here."

She nods. "That's so interesting. What type of artwork will you feature?"

I explain to Joseline my vision for the gallery.

"Most of the art will be contemporary, I'm assuming?" she asks.

"Yes, I have a number of artists that I'm reaching out to from New

York and there are some art fairs I'll be attending over the next couple of months to spread the word."

The next few months will be busy but at the same time, exciting.

"Maybe ..." She trails off. "Never mind." She turns down the hallway, directing us toward the call center. Victoria's House has a twenty-four-hour call line.

However, the look in her eyes before she cut herself off won't let me drop it.

"What is it?" Perhaps she's an art fan.

"It's nothing."

"It's something if you thought to bring it up," I counter.

She stops just before we enter the room. "A couple of months ago, my grandmother, mi abuela, moved to Florida to be closer to my mother and uncle. She left her home to me."

I listen intently, wondering where this story is going.

"While I was cleaning some things out, I found a series of paintings in her attic. They weren't even framed, but they're gorgeous. On the back I discovered that mi abuela signed and dated them.

"Some of the paintings are from the 1950s when she was still a teenager. The last one is dated 1993."

I nod with interest.

"I keep wondering what to do with them. I think she must've forgotten they're even there. My grandmother married when she was just seventeen years old because she got pregnant. She had ten kids with mi abuelo. She even raised two of my cousins. A part of me wonders if ..." Again, her voice peters out.

"If she had been allowed to explore her passion some more, what would've come of it?" I finish for Joseline.

She nods with a smile.

"I've never spoken to her about it though. She's never told any of us that she likes painting. She spent her whole life putting her wants on the backburner to care for others."

"It sounds like her work would be perfect for my gallery."

I haven't even seen the paintings, but I just have a gut feeling they'll fit right in. This is the type of story I desire to have behind all of the work featured in my gallery.

"One day, I can bring the paintings to the gallery for you to look at them? And don't be afraid to let me know if they're not good enough to go into a gallery. I just ..."

"I'm sure they're beautiful. Let's meet at Cup of Joy café over the weekend. Do you know where it is?"

"Of course. I love that place," she gushes.

I nod. "My aunt owns it. It's near my gallery. With renovations going on, it might be too loud to meet there."

We talk for another twenty minutes or so about my gallery and then about Victoria's House. I leave feeling excited.

I pull out my phone to dial Diego's number but stop short.

The dynamic in our relationship has changed. Although, it shouldn't give me pause, it does. Is he my boyfriend? Are we just in the dating stage? If he were my boyfriend, is it too early to call him and gush about the day I've had?

These questions send me into a tailspin, and right as the doubts start to drown out my common sense my phone rings.

It's him.

How does he always know when to call?

My thumb hovers over the answer button. I can't shake the doubts that still rattle through my mind. I want to talk to him but what we did after Kyle's wedding feels like it's clouding my judgment.

I put my phone away and head home, deciding that I'll give him a call later.

CHAPTER 12

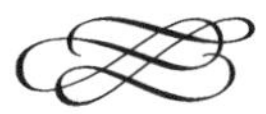

Monique

Two hours pass before later comes. Too many what-ifs have clouded my mind since I received Diego's call.

What if things between us don't work out?

What if I lose my best friend?

What if he expects more from me than I can give?

What if, what if, what if. Even after a shower and some emails sent out to prospective artists, the questions in my head don't stop.

Instead of contending with them, however, I sit down to respond to a web designer who I have creating the website for my gallery. Right as I finish responding to the web designer email and scheduling a conference call with her, there's a knock on my door.

I don't even have to check the monitor next to my door to know who it is. If I was thinking clearly, I would've known that after missing his previous call, he'd show up.

"Hey," Diego says as I open the door.

I can't deny the way my heart rate speeds up at the sight of his gorgeous face. His body takes up the entire space of my doorway.

"Are you going to let me in?"

A smile stretches my lips as I take a step back. I don't make it too far before Diego swoops in and wraps an arm around my waist, pulling my body to him. He dips his head, granting me a whiff of his cologne.

Hints of cedar wood, lavender, and his natural masculine scent mix. I inhale deeply.

My nipples pebble even before his lips reach mine. Once they do, however, my entire body ignites in a wave of passion. I stretch my arms up and around his neck. His hands move over my hips to my butt, squeezing it. I don't miss the bulge that presses against my stomach.

I gasp in surprise when he bites my bottom lip.

"That's for ignoring my calls," he says against my lips.

The deep reprimand in his voice is obvious.

It makes my nipples harden even more, almost to the point of pain.

I shake my head and cover my face, not understanding all of the emotions coursing through me.

"Are you hiding your face from me?" he asks as he closes the door behind him.

He tugs at my wrists.

"No," I say, backing away from him.

"What's up, baby?"

God, does his voice have to be so smooth and deep? It's like ever since we slept together, I can no longer deny how damn sexy my best friend is. Has always been if I'm being honest. But then, I didn't *know* for sure what it was like to be with him.

Now I do and it was better than I could've imagined.

"Talk to me," he says, moving in my direction.

"I can't," I admit.

The frown that appears on his face tightens a vice around my heart.

"You can always talk to me."

"I know but ..." I don't know how to explain what's going on in my mind. "I mean, I could always talk to you. Now I don't know what our boundaries are. There's so much going on in my head and I've had the urge at least ten times today to call my best friend and gush about it but that's you and now we're ... we're ... something else."

He approaches me, taking my wrists in his hand. "We're still us."

"Not really. I mean, I want to call my bestie and tell him all about this new guy I'm seeing but you're him. How can I make that call?"

He twists his lips to the side. "You've never called me to brag about some guy you're dating."

"I know," I admit. "I've never wanted to until now." It sounds ridiculous but that's my reality. I want to gush to my best friend about this new-ish relationship. "How can I do that? I can't say all of that to your face."

"Why can't you?" he asks.

I give him a deadpan expression.

"Don't believe me?"

"How in the world can I call you and—" He holds up his finger, stopping me.

He takes his cell phone out of the pocket of his black sweatpants. Before I can ask what he's doing, my cell phone starts to ring from my kitchen.

I look between my phone and him. "Is that?"

"Answer it."

I go over to the counter and sure enough it's him. "Hello?" I answer.

"Hey, I was just hanging out at home and got the feeling you wanted to talk to me. What's up?"

I pull the phone from my ear. "Are you serious?"

He covers the phone with his free hand. "I'm on the phone right now. Hang on."

I roll my eyes. "You're so damn ..."

He dips his head toward the phone in my hand.

"Did you want to talk about something?" he asks into the phone like this is a real conversation.

"I can't ..." I pause and look around. Then I go to the far side of my kitchen island and put my back to him before I take a seat on the floor.

"What are you doing?" He leans over the island.

"I can't do this while looking at you." I shoo him away and put the phone back to my ear. "Hello?"

"I'm here."

Butterflies rise in my belly at the reassurance in his voice.

"I did want to talk," I start. "I did something this weekend."

"Something or someone?"

I burst out laughing. "You're not supposed to ask me that."

"Why not? We're friends."

He's right.

I roll my eyes. "Someone."

"Was he good?"

I gasp and peer out over the kitchen island but he isn't there. I glance around my living area. He's not on the couch.

"Where'd you go?"

"I told you I'm at home, relaxing. I believe I asked you a question. Was he any good?"

I know he hasn't left my apartment. I would've heard the door close. More than that, I can feel his presence here. There's some rustling noise in the background.

"No, he wasn't good," I say.

"The fuck?"

I crack up but quickly sober up to admit the truth. "He was everything I've ever wanted." *And been too afraid to ever reach for.*

I make myself keep that last admission to myself. The truth is I might still be too frightened to reach for it.

"That's more like it," he says. "But what's with the hesitation in your voice?"

I run my hand across my forehead. He knows me so well.

"He wasn't just anyone," I tell him. "He's the one person that's been a constant in my life and I'm terrified of fucking it all up."

Diego was right, it's a lot easier admitting this to him over the phone than face to face. Though, I know I can't keep doing this. At some point, I'll have to look him in the eye.

"But that's what made that night so special, right?" he asks. "Because he's the one who knows you best."

"Mhmm," I admit.

"That's what it was for me. Can I tell you something?"

"Anything."

"For a long time, it felt like something was missing. I couldn't figure out what it was. Then, something awful happened."

I sit up, my eyes going wide. He never told me about anything terrible happening to him. I rack my brain, trying to remember, but I'd know it if he'd told me already.

"What happened?" Tension fills me as the possibilities run through my mind.

"You told me you were getting married. To someone else."

I cover my mouth for some reason. That is not at all what I was expecting him to say.

"That day in New York when you showed me your engagement ring, I wanted to rip it off of your finger. But you looked happy. Content, at least. So, I knew I couldn't do that. But it was then that I couldn't ignore all of the feelings I buried so long ago.

"I wanted to be happy for you, Mo, but it hurt like hell."

My vision blurs from tears at hearing the pain in his voice.

I did that to him.

"Is that why our calls and visits fell off?" I ask, starting to realize the truth.

He wasn't busy with work. He was trying to let me go.

"I'm sorry," I whisper.

"Don't. You have nothing to apologize for. If I hadn't—" He stops.

"Hadn't what?"

"Nothing. The past is the past. We're here now. You and me. The way it should've always been."

"Diego," I whisper. Tears fill my eyes. Why didn't I see it before now?

The first tear rolls down my cheek. His admission fills my heart, but at the same time it rips the Band-Aid off of the wound of guilt that I've carried around for years. The shame that I've held onto because in so many ways I feel like my relationship with Diego has been so one sided.

He's always looked out for me. He is even going so far as sacrificing his future when my dumb mistakes got me into trouble.

"Are you sure?" I ask.

"I've never been more sure about anything in my life."

I swallow the guilt down and do my best to push it away. I can try to not let my dumb past or my doubts get in the way of the here and now. I can make a genuine effort to build on the rock-solid foundation we already have.

"Okay," I say finally.

"Okay?"

"Yeah."

"Then come down the hall to your bedroom. I want to give you something." His voice is so smooth, it washes over me like the perfect tidal wave, taking me under.

Without much thought, I rise to my feet and let his words lead me down to my bedroom. Unsurprisingly, he's stretched out on my king size bed, stripped down to his white boxer briefs.

I allow my eyes to trail over his beautifully bronzed skin, the tattoo on the underside of his left arm, his washboard abs, and the considerable bulge in his boxers.

"Come here, Monique," he beckons.

* * *

Diego

For the first time today, I take a deep breath as Monique approaches the bed. I can still see the lingering doubt in those honey eyes of hers. I don't break eye contact with her or let her do so with me.

I sit up from the bed and take her chin into my hand. "Do you trust me?"

She nods, but that's not enough.

"Say it out loud, baby. Do you trust me?"

"Of course."

I kiss the corner of her mouth.

"Do you trust *us*?"

Her bottom lip tucks in between her teeth. The hesitation is like a knife slice to my heart. I hate the war happening in her eyes. I want her to trust us as much as I do.

But I have enough faith for both of us.

"Let me convince you," I say against her lips. I capture her perfect lips and kiss her the way I've hungered to do all fucking day.

Just like a flower in springtime, she opens up for me. I can feel the doubt and fear leaving her body as her hands make their way to my hair. Her nails lightly brush against my scalp.

The move sends tingles of sensation coursing through my body. She probably has no idea how much of an aphrodisiac it is for me to have her hands in my hair. In truth, it always has been.

She's the only woman I've allowed to play in my hair so casually.

My dick starts to stretch the front of my briefs, and I become even more impatient. I strip her out of the plaid pajama bottoms she's wearing, and a hiss escapes my mouth when I see she's not wearing any panties.

I grin up at her. "You knew I was coming over, didn't you?"

"No. Oh!" she yelps when I swat her ass for lying.

There's no way in hell she didn't know I would let another day go by without ending up in her bed or her in mine.

I squeeze her ass, and a moan breaks free of her mouth. Monique lets out a tiny gasp when I wrap my arm around her and drag her onto the bed, straddling my body. I kiss her like I won't ever let her get away because I won't.

I may not be able to wash away all of her doubts and fears with one kiss, but dammit, I'm sure as hell going to try. We're both breathless by the time I let up on the kiss. My cock is straining to the point of being painful. But I make it wait.

I need to taste her.

"My beard needs moisturizing," I say against the skin of her neck.

A laugh breaks free.

"Good girl," comes out on a growl when she crawls up the length of my body to straddle my face. "Perfect," I whisper right before she brings her pussy against my face.

Her taste is indescribable. It's a mix of honeysuckle, strawberries, and nothing else I can put into words. It's all her, though.

And I can't get enough of it. I eat like a man stranded on an abandoned island for too long. In many ways, that's exactly how I've felt for years. Since the day she told me she wasn't coming back home.

"Diego," she calls my name at the same time a full-time body shudder runs through her.

She's coming. It's the best feeling in the world to know I'm the one making her come. I lap up the liquid that gushes from her pussy like a cat lapping up whipped cream.

"Take this off," I demand while tugging at her T-shirt. Impatiently, I pull it over her head, exposing her beautiful, round globes. My hands cover her breasts, squeezing and plucking at her nipples.

A tiny scream comes out, and her eyes fall closed. I discovered on our first night together that her boobs are extremely sensitive. That discovery will never go unrecognized. I adjust her body to rim one of her nipples with my tongue while pinching the other.

Another shudder, a scream, and then more liquid soaks the front of my briefs. *Fuck.* She just came again from my playing with her nipples.

"You were fucking made for me," I tell her because, dammit it if it isn't the truth.

She pulls back, slightly panting. I could come from the glossy look in her eyes.

"I want you in my mouth."

Her words scramble my brain. I've honestly tried not to think of this moment. It would've done me in to picture her soft lips wrapped around my cock.

"You're trying to kill me."

Her response is a smile that brings out the dimple on the left side of her face. I've always known this, but right now, I'm certain she could ask me for anything, and I would kill, steal, beg, and cut off my left arm to get it for her.

I move to the edge of the bed, and she starts to fall to her knees.

"Wait." I stop her.

I reach behind me and grab a pillow. Placing it before her, I say, "Okay," releasing her wrist so she comes to her knees on the pillow.

"Thank you," she whispers as her hands find their way into my briefs.

"Fuuuck," I hiss when her soft hand wraps around my rock-hard dick. "Monique, you don't have to do this." I'm barely able to get the words out.

"I know," she says right before blowing air across the tip of my cock.

My eyes roll to the back of my head.

"Which is why I *want* to," she finishes.

Those are the last words I can reasonably comprehend, because a beat later, her hot mouth wraps around my dick. There are no words that humans have invented to describe the surge of feeling that courses through my body. Any thinking or logic flees my brain, and all I'm left with is feeling.

Pleasure bordering on pain is as close as I can describe being inside of her mouth for the first time. Almost too much to bear.

When I look down at her, our eyes lock. She's staring right at me with my dick in her mouth.

My hips jerk upward. Her eyes water. I start to pull out, thinking she's taking me too deep. I know I'm not little. But she dips her fingers into my hips, holding me in place.

I flinch because my hips are slightly sore from the workout I put in at the underground gym earlier today.

Yet, I'll be damned if I move even an inch. Any pain I might feel is outweighed by the immense and thrilling bliss of her taking me to the back of her throat.

I want to call her a good girl again, but words are stuck in my throat.

Our gazes remain glued to one another's.

My hand finds its way into her hair. I undo the high bun she's piled her thick, natural hair into. She might get pissed at me for messing up her hair, but it's worth it.

The next time she takes me all the way to the back of her throat, I know I'm going to come. There's not a damn thing I can do about it.

"Mo ..." I have to stop and inhale before I can complete the sentence. "Baby, I'm going to come." My voice is hoarse as shit.

I almost think this is a dream when her lips stretch into a smile around my dick. Her tongue strokes the vein at the underside of my cock, and that's it.

I'm coming into her mouth.

And my sweet girl takes every drop of it. Watching her throat work to swallow my come almost causes me to go blind. I can feel the energy leaving my body. She's sucking the life out of me, and I'll let her take every ounce of it.

She releases me before I feel like I'm about to pass out. I'm able to get my bearings somehow. I pick her up from the floor to straddle me. A yelp of surprise passes through her when I slam her hips down on my cock. Yes, I'm still hard and want to watch her come as she rides me.

"Take all of me, baby," I insist.

She throws her head back and palms my chest before ... heaven.

That's the only word to describe watching her bounce up and down on my dick. I move my hands to her hips, slowing her pace down. I don't want to rush anything about being inside of her like this.

We watch one another, our bodies speaking the words that won't come out. I've seen just about every expression of emotion one can think of on her face over the years. I've even fantasized about what she would look like taking my dick.

But nothing beats seeing it in person. I want to drink up every second of it. Commit it to memory for the minutes, days, and hours I can't be inside of her to sustain me.

Right when I've gotten my fill, we're both coming. In unison, as if our bodies both waited for only this moment. Our orgasms rush over us in waves. They cause my hips to jerk upward. I do my best not to completely lose myself, however.

I pull out of her. Cum splashes on her thighs and abdomen. I want nothing more than to come inside of her, but this will have to do for now.

"Fuck," she murmurs as she lays her head against my chest.

I caress her back, trailing my fingers through the beads of sweat that accumulated from our vigorous workout.

"I-I didn't think ..." She tries to make out words in between pants but can't.

I don't need her to, though.

Nothing could've prepared me for what this feels like. I assume it's the same for her. I know it is.

I cup her face, making her look up at me. "What the hell took me so long to get to you?"

She presses her lips together before lowering her head to kiss the center of my chest.

"Probably me," she whispers before laying back down against my chest.

We lay like this for a long time. This time, I stroke my hand through her hair and hold her body against mine with my free arm.

Not for the first time, I silently promise to always keep her safe. Maybe we would've gotten together sooner if I hadn't failed at doing it before.

I can't help but think about the time I failed to protect her, and it almost ended in a disaster for the both of us.

CHAPTER 13

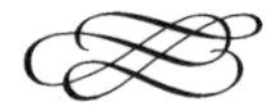

Then

Diego

"The voicemail is full..."

I grunt and disconnect the call. This is the third time my call to Monique has gone directly to her voicemail. All of the different scenarios of where she could be or what could be wrong start to go off in my head.

It's been a few days since I've spoken with Monique. We got into another argument about a different jerk she's been seeing. This one, though, is the douchebag of all douchebags.

Slater Cullen.

His family owns and operates one of the biggest architecture firms on the East Coast. I interned with the company during the summers after my sophomore and junior years of college. I have a standing offer to work for the company full-time once I graduate next fall semester.

I'm in the five-year architect program but plan to double up on classes this summer to graduate a semester early.

While I've worked for his family, I've met Slater on more than one occasion. He's a fucking prick. He's arrogant, swears he's god's gift to women, and is lazy as shit. And those are his best qualities.

Naturally, he's a big shot on Monique's campus, and somehow she ended up dating him. They met when she came to visit me at the NYC office. I kick myself daily for ever making that fucking introduction.

Since our freshman year fight over her loser boyfriend, I've kept my opinions to myself about who she dates. But I couldn't hold back when it came to Slater. They've been dating for nearly two months, and I want to crack the fucker's skull every time I see him.

I know he's no good for her, though he hasn't done anything yet. I have a gut feeling about him. Not to mention, I've heard stories of how he likes to get a little rough with the girls he dates.

"Where the hell are you?" I say to no one since I'm alone in my dorm room.

I pace my room, wondering if I should grab my keys to make the drive to her campus. It's almost midnight on a Saturday. My roommate went home for the weekend, and the rest of my suitemates, including my cousin, Kyle, are out for the night. I came back early because the feeling in the pit of my stomach wouldn't let up.

Something's not right.

Unable to take the feeling anymore, I grab the keys to my Jeep and make a beeline for the door. I stop short as soon as I open the suite's main door.

Standing before me is Monique. Her large eyes are filled with unshed tears, and her arms are wrapped around her body.

"What happened?"

"I-I took an Uber to get here," she says.

I sniff. "Have you been drinking?" I can smell the alcohol on her. She knows drinking too much could be dangerous to her health. Before she can answer, I take her by the wrist to check her watch's numbers.

They're slightly lower than usual but don't look too bad. Still, I don't like it.

"Come in."

"I had one sip of beer," she says when I try to tug her inside. "I know I shouldn't have. I thought it was harmless." She hasn't moved from the entrance. Her eyes cast downward. She's avoiding my eye contact for some reason.

"I believe you."

"The guard downstairs knows me. He said it was okay if I came up. You won't get in trouble for me being here without you signing me in, right?"

There's a nervous tension in her voice that's setting my teeth on edge. Something's the matter, and she's doing her best to avoid talking about it. That only makes me more nervous.

"I wouldn't give a shit if I got in trouble or not." If she took an Uber all of this way in the middle of the night, I know it's because something's wrong.

Very wrong.

"I can go if it's not okay," she says like she didn't hear me.

"Monique." I tug her arm to get her to focus on what I'm saying.

She gasps in fear and pulls away. The flash of terror I see in her eyes makes me see red. I have to fight hard to control my temper. Yet, I want to demand to know who it was that put that fear in her eyes.

Who was it that made her so rattled? Without having to ask that question out loud, I already know it has something to do with Slater fucking Cullen.

I just know.

"Come in." I step back so she has space to enter the suite. "You're safe here. You know that." I have a feeling she needs to hear those words.

She visibly swallows and nods. When she does, I almost become blind with rage. Peeking above the large scarf around her neck is a red mark. I start to reach for the scarf, but I don't want to terrify her even more.

"Ev's gone for the weekend," I say, referring to my roommate.

She visibly relaxes. I lead her into my bedroom and wait for her to sit on my bed before I turn on the lamp on my desk.

Monique doesn't say anything as she remains on the side of the bed. I kneel in front of her, looking over how she clasps her hands in her lap. A couple of her nails are broken, with chipped polish.

She never lets the polish on her nails chip before she changes the color.

Without asking, I reach for the scarf around her neck. I know she's hiding something. It's springtime. Not cold enough for the scarf and heavy hoodie she's wearing.

I pause when she flinches away from me.

"I need to see it," I tell her. I don't move my hands away, but I wait for her to give me the okay.

When her head dips slightly on a nod, I slowly unravel the scarf. She blanches a little as if she's in physical pain.

I drop the scarf on the bed next to her and sit there and stare at the red marks that stretch around her throat.

"Did? When?" The words come out strangled. White hot fury clogs my throat.

My father and uncles have taught me multiple ways to take a man's life. It's a fact among the men in my family. Right now, I'm envisioning using the most dangerous and painful ways to end Slater Cullen's life.

"He did this?" I finally manage to squeeze out through the anger.

She turns her head away.

"Tell me what happened." I need to know to decide just how painful his death is going to be.

"It's my fault."

Those three words are like a punch to my stomach. All of the air races out of me. I don't know what happened. Truthfully, I don't need to know to know that whatever that motherfucker did is not her fault.

"Don't, Mo." I can't help the ice-cold tone that comes out of me. "What did he do to you?"

She grabs the scarf and begins twisting it around and around in her hands. I don't say anything partly because the anger still has a hold on my entire body, making it too difficult to speak. The other reason is because she needs me to be patient.

She came to me because she knows she's safe with me. I don't want to scare her off.

Instead of speaking, I run my hands up and down her legs in an effort to comfort her. Eventually, her breathing slows, and she looks me in the eyes.

"We went to a party at one of the frat houses."

My stomach twists into knots. Nothing good ever started off with a sentence like that.

"It was all good for a while. He started drinking too much, and I got annoyed so I went to talk with some other people." Pausing, she looks off toward the corner of the room.

"I guess he didn't like me ignoring him. He started to say I was flirting with a friend of his. I tried to ignore him and went upstairs where some of my friends were hanging out."

Her fingers tighten around the scarf.

"It was fine for almost an hour. Then he came upstairs and told me he wanted to apologize. I could smell the alcohol on him, but I thought he sobered up a little. We went into one of the other bedrooms.

"Instead of an apology, though, he started to kiss me. I pushed him away. He started to talk crap about how lucky I am to be dating him. How his family wouldn't even approve of him dating a Black girl and ... Diego!" she yells after me.

Before I can let her finish, I'm on my feet, keys in my hand and halfway to the door.

"Where are you going?" She runs in front of me to ask like she doesn't know.

"Stay here," I grit out.

"No!" She plasters herself against the door.

"Move, Monique," I say it as calmly as I possibly can. I won't hurt her any more than she's already been hurt tonight. But I will find that fucker and kill him.

Fuck that, I will take joy in feeling the life leave his body with my hands wrapped around his throat. Let's find out how much he likes being strangled.

"No. I can't," she says. "You can't leave me. Please."

Her words wrap around my heart, softening it. Only she could soften me up in my current state of mind. But still ...

"I'll be back. You're safe here. No one is going to bother you here."

"Diego, no. Don't go." She pushes me away from the door.

I barely budge.

I reach for the door handle around her body and pull the door open. "I'll be right back," I lie. The kind of torture I have planned for that bastard will take at least all night.

"Please, don't leave me," she pleads at the same time she throws her arms around my waist, holding me tight. Her head fits against my chest perfectly.

My instinct tells me to push her away and go find that sorry son of a bitch and make him pay. But the way she's clinging to me, I can't rip myself away from her.

"You can't leave," she starts to say. "You'll kill him if you leave this room. I know it. And then you'll get into trouble."

"Nothing will happen to me."

"Yes it will. Bad things always happen to the people I love because of me." She starts to cry into my chest. "Please don't go. You'll get in trouble and then everyone will find out. My dad will be pissed and will hurt him, too. Then he'll be sent to jail, too. Please just stay with me."

Her arms tighten around my waist.

I stand there, stiff as a board for what feels like forever. I want nothing more than to rip that cocksucker's head off and spit down his throat. But I can't leave her like this. I can hear the terror in her voice.

Slowly, my grip loosens on the doorknob, and I close the door. I lead her over to the bed to sit. And still, she doesn't let go of me.

"You'll stay?"

"Yes." I wrap my arms around her and kick off my shoes. I bring us to lay on the bed, her closet to the wall, me on the outside. "I'll stay."

Her shoulders relax. The hold she has on my arm loosens, but she doesn't let go.

"It's my fault," she whispers.

My head instantly pops up from the pillow. "Monique, I just agreed to stay, but if you say that one more time, I can't keep my promise. I already want to kill him because he put his hands on you. If that bastard has made you believe it's your fault, I can't let him continue to breathe another night."

She goes quiet.

I relax against the pillow again, but tension still flows through me. I'm only remaining here because I know it would hurt her if I left. That's the last thing I want to do. Even as I lay here, I'm envisioning my hands wrapped around his throat.

But I won't strangle the fucker at first. No. That would be too easy a death. He'll have to feel pain first. Lots of pain.

"He didn't, um ..." Her voice trembles. "I fought him off," she finally says. "Barely, but I did." She hiccups right before burying her face into the crook of her arm. The sobs that wrack her body rip my heart right out of my chest.

I pull her into my body and kiss her temple, whispering in her ear that she's safe. That nothing will happen to her here. Most important, nothing she could've done warranted what he did.

"I should've listened to you," she says after a while. "You were right about him. About the others, too ..."

Cullen and her ex, Derek, weren't the only guys she's dated that I warned her about. They were the worst, though. But even that fucker Slater never put his hands on her. She never ended up in my dorm room with tears in her eyes and red marks around her fucking neck because of what he did.

"It's not your fault," I say to her because even though she's not saying it, I can hear in her voice that she believes it is. "Everyone dates people they end up regretting. Making a mistake in a boyfriend doesn't mean you deserve whatever he does to you. You know that, right?"

I wait for her response.

And wait.

"Monique."

"I know," she says after a long pause. "I just should've known better. My parents would be so disappointed if they knew about—"

"They would never be disappointed in you," I insist. I know it for a fact.

"They raised me better than to date losers. My dad taught me how to defend myself." She turns over onto her back to look up at me.

Tears stream down the sides of her face.

I want to beg her to stop crying. Every tear reminds me that I wasn't there to protect her.

"I'm sorry." She curls into my chest. "I'm so sorry for not listening to you."

No words I say will ease the hurt in her voice. Instead of talking, I hold onto her and let her cry.

We must lay there for a long time, maybe an hour or more, before I realize she cried herself to sleep.

Her even breathing is confirmation that she's fallen asleep. The light from the lamp on my desk allows me to examine her. My eyes fall to the red marks on her neck. They've started to turn purple. I again examine over her fingers.

The chipped polish is probably from having to fend that sick fucker off. The more I think about it, the more I know I'll have to break her heart tonight.

There's no way in hell I can remain in this room while he's out there. Not while the bruises around her neck darken and the tears on her cheeks dry but don't fade away.

That son of a bitch has to die tonight.

With my decision made, I softly move her arm from around my waist. She stirs but doesn't awaken. Even as I rise from the bed.

I check and recheck to make sure she's still sleeping. I glance at the bed one last time to verify that her eyes are closed. I exit my dorm room with nothing but my keys and the intention to destroy Slater Cullen before this night is over.

CHAPTER 14

Monique

"These are gorgeous," I tell Joseline as we sit in her office, looking over some more of the paintings made by her grandmother.

"I thought so, too. They're stunning, but I didn't know if I found them beautiful because mi abuela painted them."

I shake my head adamantly. "These are even more eye catching than the ones you showed me last week." The two paintings on Joseline's table are the second set of paintings she's showed me by her grandmother. After our first meeting, I asked her to show me the rest.

Her grandmother has a natural talent.

"The brushwork on these is almost invisible. And the imagery jumps off of the canvas." The paintings are contemporary style, of famous landscapes in her grandmother's native Puerto Rico.

Yet the way she's painted the people in the scenes draw the eye to them. Looking at the painting brings you into it, almost like you were in the middle of this beach scene. Or inside one of the fiestas her grandmother brought to life through her artistry.

"You said she never had any formal training?" I ask.

"No," Joseline admits. "Not that I know of. I asked my father, and he never knew anything about the paintings in the attic or ever saw her with so much as a paintbrush."

"The preservation of the work is amazing, considering these have been left in an attic for over thirty years. It speaks to the quality of the materials used," I gush.

The materials—everything from the types of brushes to paint and canvas—are all important when it comes to the quality of a piece. It also tells a lot about the level of seriousness a person takes in their work.

"She never featured her work anywhere?" I look up at Joseline.

She shakes her head. "Mi abuela spent her life cleaning houses part-time before moving up to become a receptionist and then an assistant at M&S Financial," she explains. "Most important, though, she spent most of her adult life raising her kids, being a wife, and then taking in two of my cousins."

Joseline shrugs.

"I have no idea when she would've even found the time to paint, let alone attend classes for it."

The story Joseline is telling me compared to the story my eyes tell me when I look at these paintings are worlds apart. Yet, they are about the same woman. Given what Joseline has shared with me, I get the impression her grandmother had to shut off the creative side of herself.

She had to let go of her dreams of becoming a full-time artist—if that's what she wanted—in exchange for hard work so that she could raise and support her family. It's not an uncommon story.

But the paintings reveal that the passion to create never entirely went away.

"And you're sure you have legal ownership of these paintings?" I ask.

"Yes, she gave me the house and told me everything was mine to keep. She wanted to move to Florida with as few things as possible."

"I will have to run this past my business attorney just to verify we have the right to feature this once the gallery opens," I warn her. "I know you want to surprise her."

Joseline's face lights up around a smile. "It might be a long shot, but I would love to see her facial expression once she sees her creations hanging up in a real gallery. She's given so much to our family, I want to do this for her."

My eyes water, and I have to blink several times to keep my emotions locked down.

"So many women put themselves on hold for their families." An image of my mom comes to mind. My heart beats against my ribcage.

The guilt of not making more of an effort to see her since I've moved home almost steals my breath. Suddenly, I miss her more than anything.

"Again, I'll talk with my lawyer just to verify. But I would be honored to feature your grandmother's work in my gallery."

"Thank you." Her voice is clogged with an emotion I don't need her to explain.

"I need to get going. I'll be in the call center this weekend to do a couple of hours," I tell her.

Volunteering at the crisis center isn't easy, considering the type of work we do, but I can't imagine not doing it.

Though it's close to five o'clock, I head over to the Williamsport University campus to see the one woman I've unintentionally been avoiding since I returned home.

* * *

"IT'S OPEN," my mother's voice passes through the closed door of her office after I knock.

As soon as I open it, I'm met with the sounds of classical music and the scent of lavender in the air. They immediately take me back to childhood memories of us preparing meals together.

"Monique." My mom smiles as she stands.

I'm across the room in a couple of steps, embracing her. An unconscious need has me tucking my head into the crook of her neck and inhaling. I let the hug linger for a few seconds longer than usual.

"Hey, Mom," I say, pulling back.

"This is such a nice surprise."

I push down the guilt that tugs at my heart. In the month since I returned home, I managed to move into my new place, start renovations on my new business, acquire two artists to feature in said gallery, and start an entirely new relationship with my best friend.

Yet, this is the first time I'm visiting my mom's office. Diego's reminder that my mom misses me and my talk with Joseline about her grandmother brought me here.

"Are you busy? I know it's a weird time, but if you're free, I wanted to take you out to eat."

I should've called her ahead of time and made actual plans, not caught her off-guard like this.

"I just finished up my final class for the day and was grading some papers before heading out. Those can wait. Where do you want to go?"

We decide on a Mexican restaurant close to campus. Though the distance is walkable, we both drive.

"Your father brought me here when this place first opened a couple of years ago," she says as we sit in one of the booths by the window. "I've been a regular ever since."

As if to prove her point, our waitress greets her by name.

"What can I get you started with, Mrs. Richmond? Your regular?"

Smiling, my mom shakes her head. "I'm driving today, so no margaritas this time around." She laughs, and not for the first time, I notice how beautiful my mom is. She's aging like a fine wine, indeed.

More than once, she's been mistaken for my sister. I take it as a compliment.

"I'll just have a lemonade, and please bring extra guacamole," she says.

I order a seltzer water as my drink.

"Do you have your food scale with you? I keep a spare one in my car if you need it."

I wave her off. "I have mine. Why do you still keep a food scale in your car?"

She shrugs. "Habit. I never took it out, just in case."

I've lived away from home for nearly a decade, and she was still thinking of me.

My eyes drop to the pinewood table. I run a finger along one of the fine cracks in the wood. Our waitress arrives with our drinks, which allows me time to swallow down the emotion that's welled up in my throat.

"How's work going?" I ask.

She finishes chewing one of the tortilla chips with guac before answering, "So well. The semester is about halfway through, and I'm loving this new group of freshmen. They're so inquisitive."

She waves her hands in the air, excitedly.

"But this new research collaboration I'm doing will examine the impact of family structures on the development of children's social consciousness. Exciting stuff."

She talks a little more about the nitty gritty details of her sociology research.

"It's early, so I'm still tweaking the specific topic it'll address, but I'm looking forward to seeing where this will go. I have a few grad students who're going to be working with me."

"I'm so proud of you," I blurt out.

She blinks as our eyes meet. "That's supposed to be what I say to you." She laughs.

"A daughter can't tell her mom she's proud of her?"

"Of course she can." She squeezes my hand and starts to say something, but our waitress is back to take our order.

We decided to order the platter of fish tacos to split.

"Speaking of work, how is the gallery coming along? I can't wait to see it."

"Renovations started a couple of weeks ago," I tell her along with the news that I have at least two artists who will be featured.

"There's another artist I found through social media over a year ago but I'm having trouble getting in contact with her. Her page has been deleted. But her work was stunning. In a haunting way," I explain to my mom. "Look."

I pull up the images I've screenshotted. The paintings are all of women of various ages, races, and sizes, but all of their faces are obscured by something. Either their head is down, turned away from the front, or there's a shadow passing over, blocking their face.

"I couldn't take my eyes off of these paintings when I first came across them," I explain.

"Gorgeous," my mother says in awe.

"I think she lives close to Williamsport, but I'm having trouble finding much information on her." I frown because aside from her name, Melinda Blake, I can't find anything else about her.

"Her artistry is perfect for my gallery," I say with confidence although I don't even know her full story yet.

"And the social worker where I volunteer at has these paintings from her grandmother ..." I peter off. I hadn't meant to bring up my volunteering in this conversation.

"Where are you volunteering?" my mom inquires. The question is innocent enough, but I can't give her an honest answer.

"Um, just a local place I found."

A wrinkle appears in her forehead. "You could come work with your Aunt Kay and me," she offers. My mom does a lot of volunteering with the community center my aunt, Kayla, started with her sisters-in-law.

Most of my volunteer work, however, is specific to women who've been sexually assaulted. I can't tell my mom that.

"I'll think about it," I say, again looking down at the table.

I can't help but recall back to the day I found out the truth about my birth father. My grandmother was the one who told me. She was in her final weeks of life and thought I should know.

The work I do as a volunteer is my attempt to restore what was broken inside of me. At least, in part.

It's also my payback. Ever since I've found out the truth, I've felt like I owed a debt for merely existing. Though I know the reality is, I'll never be able to pay back what was stolen from her or make up for the sacrifices she made to have me.

Some small part of me likes to think the work I'm doing now is making an effort.

"Avery was so happy you two came to see her show," my mother tells me, referring to Avery's show the previous weekend.

As I promised her that night, over the phone, I was front and center for my little sister's show.

"She sang so beautifully."

"I know," my mom agrees. "Damon had tears in his eyes," she confesses. "Don't tell him I said this, but he also has tears in his eyes when he watches Damian's games."

"Really?" I let out a small laugh.

Nodding, she waves her hand. "Your dad likes to pretend he's tough, but he has a soft spot for all three of you." She shakes her head.

"Four," I correct.

Our eyes meet, and a sweet smile covers her face.

"Yeah," she admits.

"No one was going to invite me for tacos?" a deep voice interrupts us.

"Speak of the devil," my mom says, grinning up at my dad.

"Speak my name and I shall appear," he says proudly. "I stopped by your office to surprise you for an early dinner, but you weren't there. I checked my phone to see you were here. Hey, baby girl." He leans over to hug me after he does the same to my mom.

"You really do not have a tracker on your phone, do you?" I ask.

Him and my mom exchange a look. Then he looks to me like I'm the crazy one. "Of course I do. I need to make sure she's safe."

My mom rolls her eyes.

"If this is a girls' night out, I can meet you at home, babe."

"No, stay," I insist.

"Are you sure?"

I nod vigorously. My mom scoots over, making room for my dad to fold himself into the bench across from me.

I love seeing them together. It doesn't even gross me out that my closer-to-fifty-than-not-year-old mother feeds my father a fish taco.

"You two," I groan and roll my eyes for show, however.

"Sorry, Short Stuff. I've missed your mom. I've had to put in some long hours over the past few days."

"I'm just teasing." My mom deserves all of the love and tenderness he gives her.

Even as I watch them together, though, I can't help the sadness that starts to sprout in my chest. Women like Sharia McClure will never get their happy ending. Too many to count have never gotten the opportunity they deserve to shine or live a happy life.

A call I took at the center today comes back to mind. The girl's voice on the other end was barely a whisper and full of so much pain.

Another voice shattered and stolen.

"Does Saturday sound good, baby?" My mother's voice catches my attention.

"I'm sorry, what?" I blink, trying to cover the moisture in my eyes.

My mother cocks her head to the side and looks at me with concern.

I smile. "I just got caught up thinking about the gallery. I'm sorry. What did you ask?"

"Dinner this Saturday at home," she repeats.

"I'll buy those lemon bars I used to buy you when you were a little girl," my dad adds. "You know that bakery spot is still open."

I give him the brightest smile I can manage.

"I don't think I can this weekend." My mom's shoulders instantly deflate. "There are a few potential artists I'm meeting at an art fair. And there are a ton of design issues for the gallery I have to work on," I rush to tell her.

"My Short Stuff is so ambitious," my father says. "We're so proud of you," he finishes, mimicking the words I told my mother only minutes ago.

"Well, if it's for work," mom says, reluctance in her voice. "How about next weekend?"

"Um, I should be available. I'll call you and let you know."

"Monique," she says, her voice growing a little stronger. "I know you're busy starting a new business, but we all would like to see more of you."

She holds up her hand when I got to speak.

"I don't want to be that pestering mom who's always nagging their kids about not calling or dropping by enough. But you are a lot closer now and sometimes it feels like you're still as far away as you were in New York."

My stomach ties in knots. How can I tell her that sometimes it feels like I'm that far away, too? Unfortunately, that would open a can of worms that I can't confront her with.

"Your mother's right, baby girl," my father adds, piling on the guilt.

I know they're not doing it on purpose. The two people sitting across from me love me more than anyone else in the world. I shouldn't be hurting them the way I am.

"I'm sorry. I'll be there next weekend. And I'll make more of an effort to spend time with you … all of you," I say.

They both reach across the table and take one of my hands.

"We love you," my mom says.

"I love you, too." I manage to get the words out, but how can I explain to her that her love also makes me feel guilty. Almost ashamed of even existing?

Thankfully, my father lightens the mood by telling a funny story about Damian.

"That boy is a trip," he says with pride in his voice. "Can't believe he beat me at go-kart racing."

"I can't believe he'll be in college next year," I say. Damian was born when I was ten years old. But for much of his childhood I haven't been around. He was only eight when I went away to college. Then I moved to New York instead of back home.

"Yeah, but he's decided to stay close. He's going to Williamsport U," my mom says happily.

"No doubt so he can continue to eat us out of house and home," my dad adds.

My mom snickers. "Please don't pretend like you wouldn't cry buckets if he was going to school far away."

My dad doesn't hesitate in answering, "I would. I'd miss him like crazy. I almost lost it when you went away," he tells me. "I was ready to buy out the entire dorm on your campus and have us all move in. But your mom told me that was a little unreasonable."

My mom laughs.

I do, too. My dad has never been shy about his feelings for all of us. A trait, according to my Aunt Charlotte, his younger sister, that he picked up only after meeting and marrying my mom.

We finish our dinner, and after I promise to make it to dinner the following weekend, we leave. Though I should head home, I can't.

I want to see Diego. He's the only person I ever want to see when I'm in a strange or sentimental mood, but he has a work dinner scheduled for this evening. I won't bother with him.

Instead, I head to a place that gives me hope.

CHAPTER 15

Diego

She's not home, I recognize as I knock on her door. I came to Monique's home before even calling because I wanted to see her as soon as I got out of my meeting.

My phone rings and I answer without even looking, hoping it's her.

"Mo, where are you?"

There's a brief pause. "Diego?" a familiar male voice responds.

A snarl curls my top lip from hearing his voice.

"How the fuck did you get my cell phone number?" I ask Gabriel Garcia Jr. The bastard.

"A friend of a friend," he answers. We don't have any friends in common.

"Why the hell are you using it?"

"We need to talk, little brother."

"If you value your life, you won't ever use those words to address me again," I tell him with a tone so cold I'm sure the bastard feels a breeze through the phone. "Second, if you ever use this phone number to contact me again, I will track you down and dismantle you piece by piece."

He huffs. "And your family tried to make it seem like my father was the savage one. All he did was try to take care of you and your mother after she seduced him into having an affair."

"Where the fuck are you?" I growl. I will find this cocksucker and crack his damn skull for even mentioning my mother.

"We need to talk about the inheritance money."

Of course that's what he wants. I haven't spoken to that lawyer since he came to see me. Haven't even given that money a second thought. He could set it on fire for all I care.

"Here's what's going to happen to that money," I tell him. "I'll receive the payout, and then I'll wipe my ass with every single dollar of it before flushing it down the toilet. It'll be a cold day in hell before you see any of it."

I don't give a shit about the money. But his tracking me down for a second time lets me know that he has a vested interest in it. He needs it a hell of a lot more than I do.

Which gives me the perfect leverage to give him the proverbial middle finger.

"Don't call me again unless it's to give me your location so I can beat your ass." I end the call and then block the number.

That better be the last time I hear from anyone on that side of the family. There will be hell to pay if it's not.

Anger boils the blood in my veins, but I force myself to walk it off. I exit Monique's building and send her a quick text.

Me: **Where are you?**

Mo: **The gallery.**

I head straight to her gallery.

The unlocked door causes me to frown once I reach the storefront. A few of the back lights are on as Monique stands in the middle of the huge space, her back to me.

"Why is the door unlocked?" I ask as soon as I walk in. She should know better. It's after dark, and while this is a safe and busy neighborhood, she can't be too careful. I lock the door behind me.

"Mo," I call when she doesn't respond. I move to stand in front of her. She continues to stare at something over my shoulder. Though the lights are low, I can see the water in her eyes.

"Babe—" I don't even get the question out before she wraps her arms around my waist.

"This has to work, Diego," she says into my chest. She's not crying quite yet but she's on the verge.

"There're so many of them," she says.

"Who?" I cup her face.

She pulls back and glances around the room.

"Them." She gestures toward the blank wall. "The women who'll be featured here. The ones who no longer have voices or took years to find their voice. Even if I could stuff this place full of those artists, there will still be so many women whose stories will never be told."

She turns to face me.

"So many who'll never be able to share for whatever reason. What do I do about all of them? What if this gallery doesn't work out?"

There's a clawing desperation in her voice that calls to me.

"Baby, did something happen?" I ask, knowing I'll take on anything or anyone she needs me to.

She blows out a breath. "I had dinner with my mom, and it reminded me of a call I had at the crisis center today. It was …" She doesn't finish. "I can't say."

I ball my hands into fists. A part of me hates that she does that kind of work. Yes, I know it's valuable and very much needed, but it seems to often take a negative toll on her. I know she's volunteered at these places for years.

However, I think she realized that it bothered me that she did it because over time she stopped sharing about her volunteering with me.

Not that she would tell me much anyway, with the need for confidentiality and all.

"I want this place to mean something, Diego." She meets my gaze. There's a deep pleading in her eyes. "It needs to mean something. I owe it to …" She trails off.

"You don't owe anyone," I say just as passionately. I take her face between my hands. "Your gallery will be everything you envision it to be. Not because you owe it to anyone but because it's yours. Your passion for the artistry of the women who'll be featured here will come across to anyone who passes by this place."

I don't just say that to make her feel better. I tell her this because it's the truth. I know no one will go as hard for the artists in this gallery as Monique will.

"Do you really believe that?"

"We don't lie to one another, do we?"

She shakes her head.

"Then believe it."

Her answer is to lift up on her tiptoes and brush her lips across mine. Before I realize it, her hand moves around the back of my head and starts to play in my hair.

My cock instantly comes alive.

"I need you," she whispers against my lips.

A wild growl escapes my mouth before I kiss her with a fierce abandon. Her body is as responsive to my kiss as mine is to her touch.

Within seconds we're ripping clothes off of one another without a care. Thank god the huge window of her gallery is boarded up due to the ongoing renovations. The only way to see inside is via the top glass panes on the door.

While it's unlikely that anyone can see us from the angle we're at, I move us farther into the space away from the door. I pivot our bodies so that Monique's back is pressed against the far corner wall.

No one can see us from this angle. With that assurance, I drop to my knees to strip her out of her pants. When that's done, I bring one of her legs over my shoulders so I can worship her pussy the way she deserves.

She tosses her head back and thrusts her hips against my mouth. I lap her up like a starving man. Even after doing this a number of times already, I still can't get enough of her taste. It's like she was made for me.

I run my tongue over and over her clit, making her entire body shudder. She calls my name the way I've always wanted to hear her say it, but never fully allowed myself to acknowledge.

"Diego, please," she purrs.

"I know, baby," I say against her pussy lips before outlining the seam of her opening with my tongue. The mewls coming from her are my undoing.

I give her what she needs and let her ride my face as she orgasms.

There's nothing like this feeling.

My hands itch to reach up and grab her. To yank her to me and squeeze her tight enough to see red marks along her skin.

But I absolutely will not unleash that part of me on her.

Monique reaches down and takes one of my hands. The hand that is already moist from her wetness. I stand, and she brings two of my fingers into her mouth, licking them clean.

Seeing that reminds me of having my dick in her mouth. My cock pushes against my pants, desperate to get inside of her.

But my breath hitches in my throat when she moves my hand from her mouth, down her chin, and holds it to her throat. Her gaze meets mine. There's a question in those honey pools of hers.

I drop my attention to where she's still holding my hand, against her soft neck. I allow my thumb to stroke the tender skin there. Everything in me wants to wrap my hand around her throat, tighter. To squeeze it while I'm taking her. I want to hear her tiny gasps for air as I rut into her, building both of our climaxes until neither one of us can take it anymore.

But just as this scene plays out in my head, I see those bruises around her neck. The ones put there by that bastard, that night in college.

I snatch my hand away from her throat.

There's no way in hell I can do that to her. I hate myself for even contemplating it.

To push those thoughts away, I unbuckle my belt and pants before lifting her legs to wrap around my waist.

I kiss her but not as hard or as forceful as I want to. I have to make myself hold back with her. She can't see that side of me. It would ruin everything we're building between us. She's been through too much.

So I kiss her but hold back slightly. She's so slick and ready for me, that it doesn't take a lot of effort to work my cock inside of her. I want to pound into her, but I force myself to go slow.

I push all the way in and then drag myself out inch by inch. I want her to feel every ridge of my cock as it moves inside of her. Monique locks her legs around my waist.

Dragging my hands up and down the length of her waist, I bury my head into the crook of her neck. The skin there is so damn soft, I want to bite it. To mark her so that anyone who sees her for the next few days will know she's mine. But I hold back, only kissing and licking her velvet soft skin.

"I've wanted you for so long," I confess. "Probably longer than I even fucking knew." The words spill out of me without any remorse. It's the whole truth.

For years, I told myself and anyone who would listen that we were only friends—best friends but still friends. For a long time, I thought that would be enough.

I was fucking wrong.

There's no way in hell I can go back to just being her friend after being balls deep inside of her. And there's no fucking way in hell that I'm going to ever let another man know what it's like to be with her like this.

Not while there's any breath in my body.

"Come with me, Monique," I demand. I need to feel her walls milking me.

"Yesss," she moans.

As if we both willed it, we come together. As one.

Just like it should be.

Like it will always be.

This can be enough for me. She is enough for me. I won't ruin this by demanding more. I won't be like that son of a bitch who hurt her.

"Hey," she says, taking my face in her hands. Her eyes search mine. "What's wrong?"

I drop my face to her shoulder, kissing it. I don't want to lie to her, so I settle for a half-truth.

"Just thinking about the past. And what took us so long to get here."

CHAPTER 16

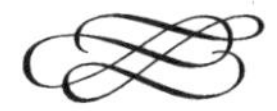

hen

Monique

I awaken to a completely darkened room. Fear seizes me, and my entire body goes cold. Memories of me trying to fight off my drunk and belligerent boyfriend come flooding back. Suddenly, it becomes difficult to breathe.

His fingers tighten like vices around my throat. I can feel him trying to squeeze the life out of me. When I look up into his hazel eyes to beg him to stop, I truly know I'm in trouble. It's as if he isn't there.

The look behind those eyes is blank. There's nothing there, behind that mask besides coldness.

I don't even think he sees me. I scratch at his fingers and try to kick out to get him off of me. For one second something happens, and his fingers loosen just enough that allows me time to suck in a deep breath. He doesn't let go, though.

But that small window gives me enough time to remember what my father taught me. How to defend myself, even against a man twice my size. I crouch low, and with all of my might, I shove my palm into Slater's crotch.

He howls and his hands fly from my neck to his dick.

I crumple to the floor, heaving to catch my breath. But then, I remember my dad's self-defense lessons again. *Don't give them time to recover.*

While he's still holding himself, I push him as hard as I can. He topples to the floor, cursing. I use my remaining strength to pull myself up and escape the locked bedroom.

I don't tell anyone what happened. Most of the partygoers barely notice me as they're either too drunk, dancing, or busy making out. I run all the way back to my dorm room. Even though I lock myself in my room, the feeling of safety eludes me. All I want is to go to the one person with whom I feel the safest.

That's when I sit up from the bed and remember that I'm not alone in my dorm room. I came to Diego. My safe place. He let me cry in his arms.

"Diego?" I call into the darkness.

No answer.

I pat the pillow next to mine to find it's empty. In fact, his side of the bed is empty and the sheets are cool. It has to mean he's been gone for a while.

I get up to turn on the lamp on his desk, and as I already knew, he isn't here.

"Where ..." I don't need to finish the thought. I know where he's gone.

I saw the expression on his face as I recounted what happened between me and Slater. I thought begging him to stay and falling asleep together would put an end to him trying to leave tonight.

I should've known better.

If I had been thinking more clearly, I would've known better.

I can't let my best friend end up in trouble because of me.

That's the last thought I have before I hurriedly put my sneakers back on and race out of the door, to catch a car back to my campus. If Diego's gone after Slater—and I know he has—that's where he would go first.

While I hate Slater, I pray he still isn't on campus. Maybe my open palm fist to his groin was hard enough that he had to go to the hospital.

I think of anything to give me hope that he's nowhere to be found when Diego arrives at my school.

The ride over feels like the longest drive of my life. Even after I promise my driver a large tip if he gets us there faster. We make the hour drive in just under forty-five minutes. I barely spare him a 'thank you' before I'm off and running out of the door, in the direction of where the party was.

By now, it's close to four in the morning but there are still party-goers hanging around the frat house and music is still blaring.

"Monique, oh my god!" a girl shrieks.

I turn to find Gabriella, a girl from one of my art history classes, running toward me. As she takes me by the arm, her eyes are wide with fright.

"Did you go to the hospital? Is he okay?"

My heart sinks.

"Wh-Who went to the hospital?" I hate the way my voice quivers.

She looks at me with wide eyes. "Slater. Some guy attacked him. Wait." She pauses. "He looked kind of familiar. Some other guys said that he knows you." She blinks and then looks at me with suspicion. "Were you cheating on Slater?"

I pull away from her and look around for someone else that I might know. Diego hasn't answered his cell phone the half a dozen times I called him. Now it's going straight to voicemail.

"Robin?" I call another girl, who was at the party earlier. She's also the girlfriend of one of Slater's friends.

She gasps. "Monique! We've been looking for you. What happened?"

I swallow as the events of tonight replay in my head. "Um, I just got back to campus. Where's Slater?" I ask because I hope what Gabriella just said is wrong. If Slater is at the hospital, something terrible happened and I need to find my best friend. Fast.

"Diego attacked him," Robin says, bringing my fears to light. "We were all just hanging out on the back porch. All of a sudden, we hear this screaming from upstairs. Then wham!" She throws her arms around wildly, indicating the chaos that ensued.

"It was totally crazy! Three guys were trying to pull him off of Slater at once, and he was still hitting him. Luckily, the police showed up. He got arrested."

As soon as that sentence leaves her mouth, I take off running. I don't even have a specific intent in mind, but I know I need to find Diego. He can't go to jail because of me.

"The hospital's the other way," Robin yells behind me.

I ignore her.

The only thing that matters is getting to my best friend. He can't get into trouble because of me. He just can't.

* * *

Diego

I push down the guilt I feel for leaving Monique sleeping in my bed. Alone. I know she'll be pissed over what I'm about to do but I can focus on that. All I can see is red.

During the entire hour-long drive to her campus, all I can think about are the ways in which I'm going to torture the life out of this motherfucker. There's nothing else that matters more to me in this moment than ensuring he knows that he fucked up the moment he even thought about putting his hands on her.

I've been to her campus enough over the past three years that I know my way around it well enough. The first place I stop is the off-campus frat house where Slater and a few of his bitch ass friends stay.

"Where is he?" I demand to know as I pound on the door.

Someone yanks it open. It's not him.

"Move." I shove the guy out of the way.

He stumbles back, almost falling. "Whoa, bro. What the fuck?"

"Slater!" I call out at the same time I steamroll my way through the entire house. Aside from a few drunk bastards laying on the couches in the living room, the house is empty.

"He's not here." The guy who answered the door comes up behind me once I've pushed through the last bedroom door on the second floor.

I pivot and grab him by his T-shirt, hauling him to me. "Where the fuck is he?" I demand to know through gritted teeth.

His glossy eyes bulge slightly. He's too fucking drunk to realize the danger he's in. But something inside of that half-full skull of his must click because he soon answers, "He's still at that party. Hooking up with some chick from his chem– Hey," he shouts when I shove him away from me.

Although I only shove him with about half of the force in my body, I hear a loud crash behind me. I'm halfway down the stairs and out of the door before I hear him curse at me for shoving him.

I don't even bother with getting in my Jeep to drive over to the frat house where the party is. With the adrenaline pumping through my veins, there's no way I can sit for even another minute.

My legs propel me forward, my speed picking up as my fingers itch to get my hands around that fucker's throat.

Let's see how he likes being choked. My brain registers the sight of the frat house even before my conscious thinking can put it all together.

Though, it's probably not what it seems, it feels like things move in slow motion from here on out. I can hear hip hop music blaring from the house. Girls and guys alike have spilled out onto the front lawn of the frat house. Red Solo cups litter the lawn.

It's a typical college party scene. Campus police won't be around anytime soon to break it up. The fuckers who own the house come from families who also have names on half of the buildings on this campus. They own campus police as well as the local police in this college town.

"Diego?" some guy says as I push through the open door.

I look over to find Michael, a younger cousin of Slater's, who I've worked with during my internships. I treat him the same as I did that guy back at the house.

"Where the fuck is your cousin?"

His eyes go wild with terror. I always knew he was a pussy. I've barely touched him, and I can feel him shaking underneath the weight of my glare. But this is nothing compared to what his cousin is about to feel.

"Where is he?" I demand again, shaking him.

"Upstairs, I think."

Of course he gives him up right away. He probably knows his cousin's reputation. I briefly wonder if he knows what his cousin did to Monique. If he does and didn't do anything to stop him, I'll beat his ass, too.

"Slater!" I yell as I run up the stairs.

People leap out of my way, pressing themselves flat against the hallway walls as I barrel down it, going door to door. He isn't in the first three rooms I barge into. The fourth one is locked.

My first fist against it leaves a crack in the wood. I don't feel any pain in my hand. All I feel is rage.

"What the fuck?" I hear a voice on the other side of the door. I immediately recognize it as Slater's.

"Who is that?" a woman on the other side asks.

"Open the goddamn door," I growl, punching it again. The second punch creates a dent in the door. A third fist to the door will create a hole right through it.

I never get that chance, though, because the door soon flies open. Now I'm face to face with this cocksucker. But within two seconds of me laying eyes on him, he's flat on his back.

I barely register the blood dripping out of his nose from my first fist to his face. On the way over, I had planned how I would make this motherfucker pay. I wanted to draw it out, slowly and painfully.

As soon as I see his face, though, all I can think about are the bruises around Monique's neck. The way she cried and nearly began hyperventilating as she told me what he did to her. The way she blamed herself.

She actually believes she holds some responsibility for what this son of a bitch did to her. I can't hold my anger in long enough not to attack him on sight.

I hear the yells and screams around me. I think the girl he was in here with even starts crying. I feel someone clawing at my back, trying to pull me off of him. Yet, all I see is Slater and red.

I don't even know how I end up straddling him, but I have him pinned to the ground. He's saying something, but blood is coming out of his mouth, garbling his words. That and the fact that he's now using both of his forearms to shield his head and face from my punches.

"Move your fucking hands!" I scream. "You weren't cowering like a bitch when you had your hands around her throat, were you?"

I completely lose my shit on him. I don't know what's happening around me, who's touching me, who's calling the police or what. All I know is that it's this motherfucker's turn to die. I barely notice the fact that he's passed out.

The continuing rise and fall of his chest lets me know there's still work to be done.

The fact that he's breathing is unacceptable to me.

Unfortunately, I'm not given time to finish the job.

"Put your hands up!" I hear shouted around me.

I don't bother to look. Somewhere in the recesses of my mind I conclude that the police have arrived.

Even that doesn't stop me, though. *They'll have to pry me off of this bastard.*

That's exactly what they do.

It takes somewhere around three police officers to pull me off of an unconscious Slater. Even still, I'm kicking, yanking and fighting to get back to him. He's still alive.

"I'm not finished with him!" I yell at anyone standing in between me and him.

I don't know how, but somehow the police wrangle me away from Slater and out of the room. I don't notice the bite of pain that clinches my wrists as the handcuffs are slapped onto me.

Paramedics rush past us in the opposite direction to get to him. I do my best to trip them to stop them from giving that fucker any type of medical care. He doesn't deserve it.

"Son, you need to calm down," one of the officers says in my ears.

"I'm not your fucking son!" I seethe.

My father would know why I'm doing this. But he isn't around. Not yet. I know there's no way my parents aren't going to be here soon. If I don't get the chance to call them, someone else will.

Even that realization doesn't pull me back from the brink of my rage. I still want that motherfucker's head on a stick. All I keep seeing are the bruises around Monique's neck and it ignites my ire all over again.

"Fuck him," I shout over and over.

As I claw and fight the officers to get back to finish the job, a sharp, slicing pain pushes throughout my entire body. My muscles seize up. I can no longer fight the officers. My body isn't my own.

"Oh my god. They tased him!" someone yells in the distance.

I can't respond to anything or anyone. Everything goes black.

CHAPTER 17

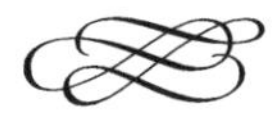

Monique

"Attempted murder?" I hear Diego's mother say as soon as I enter the police station.

It took me a while to find out which police station he was brought to. The campus police transferred Diego over to the local police.

I only found all of this out because Diego's mother called me frantic, asking if I was okay. Apparently, Diego had called his parents with his one phone call. They arrived within a couple of hours.

"Oh, Monique," Diego's exhausted looking mother says as I fully enter the station. I glance around, hoping my parents are nowhere to be found. They likely would've called me if they knew about this.

I know my mom and dad would be right here alongside Diego's parents. But they can't know about any of this. I can't let them find out why Diego went berserk on Slater.

"Aunt Michelle," I say, using the term I've called Diego's mother since I was a teen.

She squeezes me tight. It's comforting and I'm so close to tears that I have to fight hard not to let them spill over.

All around us police officers are coming and going. The scene looks like it's from a movie or one of those primetime cop shows. The officers have one guy, who's obviously belligerently drunk, handcuffed to a chair. He's yelling something about knowing his rights.

Another officer is escorting a woman with smeared makeup down another hall.

An older woman demands to see her son who was arrested three days ago. She's not listening to the officer tell her that he's been sent to central booking. Whatever that is.

"Diego doesn't belong here," I murmur.

"No," his mother agrees, reminding me that she's still here. "He's in with our lawyer and Carter now. I had to step out for a few minutes."

That's the first time I give his mother a real look over. Her eyes are red-rimmed and glossy. The tip of her nose is red also. An obvious sign that she's been crying.

"He won't tell us what happened," she tells me. Her worried look meets mine. "And he got really angry when I told him that we called you."

My stomach squeezes to the point of pain.

"But I didn't know who else to call. He was on your campus, so I just assumed he was with you. Were you with him when the incident happened?"

I rub my lips together and wonder what I should and shouldn't tell her. I tug at the scarf around my neck, trying to think of words to say. Nothing comes to mind. I can't tell her the truth.

"No—"

"Michelle," Uncle Carter's voice reaches us. "Monique," he greets me with a sad smile. His demeanor is as forlorn and dour as his wife's. That makes me feel even worse. Uncle Carter is one of the most upbeat people I know.

I give him a half nod and a small wave.

"He's not alone, is he?" Diego's mother asks worriedly.

"Of course not. Tom is in there with him. Because he's over eighteen there are certain conversations they have to have alone." Uncle Carter scowls, and then his usually sparkling blue eyes, now looking so lifeless, drop to the floor.

"They're not letting up on the charges," he tells Diego's mom. "Because there were so many witnesses ..." He trails off.

She gasps and covers her mouth with her hand. She doesn't say anything as tears flow down her face.

"Why would he do—" She barely manages to choke out before collapsing in her husband's arms.

I feel so sick that I have to clasp my stomach.

"Monique, do you know anything?" Uncle Carter asks. "We know Diego has a temper sometimes, but he's never just flown off the handle for no reason. And he's not talking to us," he tells me.

"He can't go to jail," I say.

Without thinking, I brush past them and head toward the hallway behind the main front desk. I suspect this is where all of the interrogation rooms or whatever they're called are located.

"Diego," I yell, searching for him.

"Mo," he calls out from the first room with the door open.

"Diego, just tell them the truth," I burst into the room and say. I don't pay attention to the older man who stands and demands to know who I am. Or the officers who start to converge on us from either ends of the hallway.

"Miss, you can't be in here."

"Monique, go home," Diego orders.

"Just tell them why you did it. It's fine," I try to reassure.

The headshake he gives me is adamant. "I'm fine," he says.

It's a lie. How can he be fine? He's sitting in an interrogation room with bruised knuckles, his mother crying, and charges of attempted murder hanging over his head. Nothing about this situation is fine.

"He did it because—"

"Shut up!" he yells so forcefully that everyone in the room stops to look at him. "I did whatever I did all on my own. I don't like the son of a bitch. That's all."

With that, he retakes his seat and stares at the glass pane opposite him as if to say 'I'm not saying anything else about this.'

He reminds me of a brick wall. I know there won't be any getting into him. Not even his parents will be able to break that stone-cold demeanor that he's wrapped himself up in.

But I know another way to fix this. There's no way in hell I'm letting Diego pay for my mistakes.

I can't.

With that, I shove past the officers and Diego's parents, and run out of the police station.

* * *

"I WANT HIM ARRESTED!" a woman shrills from the other end of the hallway.

Though I've never met her in person, I know by the sound it's Slater's mother.

"Do you know what that thug did to my son?" She sounds irate.

I would care but I know what type of person her son is. I push away the guilt. The knowledge that this entire mess is all my fault. Diego warned me to stay away from him. He told me Slater wasn't a good guy, and deep down I knew it. But he was the type of guy I thought I deserved.

"I want him to spend the rest of his no-good life in jail," a man's voice declares. Slater's father.

"Diego doesn't deserve to spend one minute in jail!" I say to the lobby full of people.

They all turn to stare at me with wide, indignant eyes.

"Who are you?" his mother asks.

This is the first time we're ever meeting in person. Even though Slater and I had been dating for months. I knew the real reason he never brought me home to meet his parents, though I denied it to myself.

God, how did I think so low of myself to be reduced to accepting that sort of behavior? My parents would be so ashamed of me if they knew the truth.

"I'm Monique," I say with my head held high as I look around the patient waiting room. It's not any hospital waiting room. We're in the private wing of the largest hospital in this city. I knew this is exactly where he would be sent.

"Slater's ex-girlfriend," I declare.

A room full of gasps sound off. My gaze sweeps the room. Even though it's nearly six in the morning, his mother is done up in a full-face of makeup. Her blonde hair is pulled back in a tight chignon, matching pearls adorning her ears and neck.

She looks like she's on the way to host a brunch for the local Stepford wives.

His father glares down at me with dark, beady eyes, his slick dark hair pushed back, dressed in an Italian suit. There are three other men in suits in the room, one doctor and a nurse. I notice a badge on one of the men. He must be a detective.

"That's impossible," Slater's mother scoffs. "How did she get in here?" she asks the others as if they would know.

"Diego isn't going to jail because of your son," I tell them, ignoring her. "He did nothing wrong."

"That vagrant brutalized my son!" his father yells. "He is in surgery right now for a broken eye socket. That ... that ... boy will spend the rest of his life in prison."

"Your son deserved exactly what he got."

More gasps. But I'm not done.

"In fact, he deserved worse. I'm just ashamed that it wasn't me that put him in that hospital bed."

"How dare?" his mother says. "I want her arrested."

The detective actually takes a step in my direction.

"Don't come near me." I meet the detective's gaze, and then look back at Slater's parents. "You both know what type of son you raised. He's a selfish bastard, and this isn't the first ass whooping he's deserved. I'm sure of that."

Both of their faces turn red. My stomach plummets because from their expressions, I can see their guilt. They must know their son isn't the innocent victim they're trying to make him out to be.

For the first time, I wonder if there are any other exes of Slater's that he's done this to. Were they able to fend him off the way I was?

The thought causes nausea to rise in my stomach. I suppress the feeling in order to get my next declaration out.

"You two are the worst type of parents. You've allowed him to become the scum he is. I promise you, if you push ahead with pressing charges against my friend, I will go to the police myself."

I reach up and unravel the scarf from around my neck.

His mother's hand flies to her face and she takes in the bruises. His father's expression turns ghastly as all color drains from his face.

"I know for damn sure the last thing either one of you want to do is have this in the news. But I swear to God if you don't drop those fucking charges, I will scream from every rooftop what your son did to me. Trust me when I say, whatever Diego did or didn't do to Slater, will be a cakewalk if my father finds out what your piece of shit son did to me."

I let my comments sink in. His mother's eyes continue to linger on my neck. The haughty, holier-than-thou expression she had on when I first walked in is nowhere to be found.

Slater's father looks like he's a few seconds away from passing out. This must be what it looks like when you're forced to confront your own sins.

Slater's parents weren't in that room with us, but at this moment, I have no doubt that their coddling behavior of him over the years led to where we are right now.

"And once I start talking, I wonder how many other girls will come forward with similar stories?" I finally say.

Unfortunately, I know from reading about my own sick biological father that these types of bastards never just do this type of thing to one person. The term repeat offender comes to mind.

I take one last look at everyone in the room. They're all silent. I don't say anything more before I leave.

With each step I take, my legs become more and more shaky. I'm able to make it to the far stairwell before I break down into sobs.

CHAPTER 18

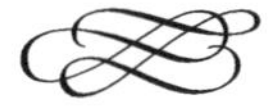

Diego

"Mo?" I call as she stares off, looking at nothing.

She blinks and turns to me as if seeing me anew. "Sorry, what did you say?"

We're spending this Saturday afternoon at the open air art market. Monique scouted a few artists via their social media pages and wanted to check some of them out in person. But she's been a little adrift since we arrived thirty minutes ago.

"Where'd you go?" I ask, wanting to know what has her so distracted.

She gives me a half-smile that doesn't reach those eyes that I love looking into. "I'm right here."

I take her hand and squeeze. "You know the problem with dating your best friend?" I ask. "I know all of your facial expressions. I can tell when you're lying. So let's not do that."

She rolls her eyes, and her smile turns genuine. "Of course you do."

I tug her hand to get her gaze to meet mine again. "What happened?"

She shakes her head. "Nothing." She pushes out a breath. "I was just thinking about ..." Her voice trails off.

I come to a stop directly in front of her. We're surrounded by art enthusiasts, people who are looking to buy, and tables with eager artists standing behind them, ready to sell their work. But I cup her face like there's no one else around.

Because when it's just the two of us, there isn't.

"What's up?"

She pokes out her lips, making my eyes drop to them. My mouth waters because I want nothing more than to kiss her. To kiss away any and all doubts, insecurities, fears, or whatever else is putting that worried expression on her face.

"Are you still worried about the gallery?"

Less than eight weeks before the scheduled opening. She has five artists locked in to debut on opening night. But she's constantly on the look for more artists to feature. More women who've gone overlooked and undervalued.

Between seeking out artists, the time she spends at the gallery overseeing renovations, and the general needs of starting a new business, plus volunteering at the women's clinic, I'm scared she might be overworking herself.

"No," she says with a small shake of her head. "Just thinking about the past, to be honest."

She looks me right in the eyes, searching mine. It's as if she's waiting for me to figure out what she's talking about.

"What past?" We have a lot of history together.

"Junior year of college."

I know immediately what she's referring to. That son of a bitch.

"We never really talked about—"

"We don't need to," I say, cutting her off. "It's in the past and he's … no more."

Slater Cullen met his fate a few years after we graduated college. An ugly car accident.

She opens her mouth as if she wants to protest, but I pull her in for a kiss. As always, I pour everything into the kiss. Almost everything.

The truth is, kissing her makes me want to rip away every shred of clothing, bend her over the nearest table, and not let her up until her voice is hoarse from screaming my name.

The tips of my fingers tingle to squeeze the flesh around her hips until the imprints of my hands are left on her body. I want to drive into her with the force of all of this pent-up emotion.

But I can't do that.

Not to her.

My one and only aim is to protect her. Not to go all caveman on her. No matter how badly I want that. I can keep that part of me in check.

Still, I can kiss her. Which is exactly what I continue to do. Damn the people around us.

"Is he kissing my baby?" That deep, booming voice is like a douse of cold water to my senses.

Monique is the first one to pull back though. She immediately spins around like she just got caught with her hand in the cookie jar.

"Dad, Mom," she says, sounding breathless.

Without hesitation, I wrap my arm around her waist and pull her into my side. I've been waiting for this moment. It's about time her parents and the rest of our family found out the truth. That I'm not about to let her go so they all might as well get used to it.

Not that most of them didn't see it coming.

"Why the hell are you kissing my daughter like that in public?" Uncle Damon demands.

"Daddy, calm down," Monique says. She moves to take a step forward, but I tighten my arm around her waist. I don't want her far from me.

Her father doesn't miss it either. He glares at me.

"I've treated you like a son," he says with narrowed eyes.

I can't help the way my lips curl into a half smile.

"I told you for years this boy was trouble, didn't I?" he says to Monique's mom.

Aunt Sandra laughs and looks at me with the same sweet smile she always has.

Monique's father's reaction doesn't bother me. I know he's just being protective. Hell, I know once we have a daughter, I'll behave the same way.

"Calm down, Damon. This was bound to happen eventually," Aunt Sandra says, surprising me.

Uncle Damon grunts. "Knew I should've kept him away all of these years."

"You've known Diego as long as you've known me," Monique defends. "You were rarely this crazy over my ex."

He waves a dismissive hand in the air. "That's different."

"Well," I finally say, again tightening my hold around Monique's waist. Thankfully, she hasn't tried to pull away. Even if she does give me a somewhat uncertain look.

"It is different because unlike her piece of sh—" I stop myself from saying what I truly want to say. When I look down at Monique, there isn't a doubt in my mind, even though I can see them swimming in her eyes.

"Instead of him, I'm the one she's going to marry."

Everyone around me gasps, including Monique. Her eyes bulge in surprise. I should have expected this reaction. We agreed to three months, but I'll be damned if I can let her go after that. We've spent too much time apart.

I know where my heart is and who it belongs to. It looks like I still need to work to convince her of that.

I look toward her parents. "It's not like you didn't see this coming, right?"

Her mother's smile is proud and wide. It feels good. I know Aunt Sandra has always loved me. To be honest, she's been almost like a mother to me, like my own. I know my mother feels the same way about Monique.

"You haven't even asked me for permission yet," Uncle Damon declares. "I don't see a ring on her finger? Where is it? It better not be a cheap ass—"

"Damon, cut it out," Aunt Sandra snaps.

He closes his mouth but continues to glare at me.

"Well," Monique starts. "Um, we're together," she says hesitantly.

Irritation trickles down my spine but I don't let it show.

"How about you both come over for dinner tonight?" her mother suggests. "Damian and Avery would love to have you both over. It's been a while."

Monique looks to her dad. "Dinner? Where there will be knives and sharp objects?"

I let out a chuckle, knowing that while Uncle Damon isn't a pushover, especially about his family, I don't have much to fear. I'm as protective over the woman at my side as he is.

"We'd love to," I say.

Her father gestures to me and then looks at her mother. "Look, he's talking over her and everything."

"Dad, stop it," Monique says a little more forcefully. "You know Diego would never. He's not being any more possessive than you are over Mom."

"She's right," her mom agrees. "We'll see you both tonight around seven," she finishes. "Come on, babe."

Her father continues to stare at me even as his wife pulls him in the opposite direction.

I turn to Monique. "Looks like we have dinner plans."

CHAPTER 19

Monique

"Why am I nervous?" I ask the empty room as if some mysterious voice will answer back.

After finishing up at the art fair with Diego, he dropped me off at my place so that I could get ready for our dinner with my parents. He should be here to pick me up any minute.

For the life of me, I can't understand why I'm feeling nervous. This is Diego. We're having dinner with my parents. An occasion we've literally done hundreds if not thousands of times throughout our friendship. As kids and teens there was hardly a night that I wasn't over his place for dinner or him over mine.

This is different, the voice in my mind reminds me. All of those times were when we were just friends. This time we're more than friends. A lot more.

We're a little more than a month into our *arrangement,* and every day I can feel myself falling for him more and more. Feelings I didn't know were possible have started to emerge. That, more than anything, is terrifying.

The knock on the door startles me out of my contemplations.

"Coming."

Even though I know it's him, I check the camera on the wall before opening the door. A smile spreads across my lips when I see him in a pair of dark jeans, button-down shirt, and suit jacket. He looks the perfect dressy casual and so damn ridiculously sexy.

"Hey," I say as I open the door.

His lips twist into a frown, and I can't help the urge to run my hand over his beard.

"Did you check the camera before you opened the door?" he asks in lieu of saying hi.

I give him a deadpan expression. "I knew it was you," I tell him even though that's exactly what I did.

"Safety, baby."

"How many times do I have to remind you that I lived in New York City for six years, alone for most of that time?"

His frown deepens. "First of all, I don't like to think about you living in that big ass city all by yourself. And second ..." He stops to pull me into his body. We're now front to front.

I inhale his masculine scent. An unintentional purr escapes my lips.

"I especially don't like to be reminded that you lived with another man." He doesn't give me time to answer by pulling me into a kiss that's certain to smear my lipstick.

I wrap my hands around his neck and pull myself into his body. I don't want any space between us. A sexual hunger that I've never known before has begun to overtake me. It's not like I was a prude before, but being with him has uncorked something inside of me that I didn't know was there laying in wait.

"We definitely should stop there if we're going to make it to dinner with your parents," he says against my lips.

I poke out my lips in a pout.

The deep chuckle that spills out of his lips sends a thrill through my body.

"We'll pick up where we left off after dinner."

"You promise?"

His smile makes my nipples harden. "Have I ever broken a promise to you?"

No.

Not ever.

He kisses the tip of my nose and then pulls away. My body temperature notably drops from the loss of his body heat so close.

"You probably should redo that lipstick." Diego runs his thumb along my bottom lip. He lets out a groan of pain when I stick my tongue out, licking the tip of his thumb.

"You're fucking killing me." He actually sounds like he's in pain.

That's what he gets for kissing me like that with no intention of finishing what he started right away.

I do a quick fix of my lipstick in the mirror next to my door before we head out.

My parents live only a few blocks away from Diego's parents' home. We grew up on the outskirts of Williamsport. Returning here with him feels familiar and new at the same time.

"Don't look so nervous, baby," he tells me, taking my hand in his and kissing my knuckles. "We've done this hundreds of times."

"Not like this," I remind him.

"We're still the same people," he replies, looking over at me.

I stare into his eyes for a long while, letting his sturdy gaze reassure me.

I love you.

We've said those three words to one another many times over the years. I've meant it every single time, but this one is different. I can't say it out loud. Not yet. Even to him. There's still so much uncertainty.

Not to mention the declaration he made earlier today to my parents.

"They're probably waiting for us."

As soon as he says that, my parents' front door opens. My father's standing there, arms folded across his broad chest. I remember that pose every time I brought a boy home while in high school.

I stopped bringing any boys home after I went away to college.

Though I defended the losers I dated to Diego, deep down I knew they weren't worth my time. Nor were they worth being introduced to my parents.

The last guy I introduced to them was my ex-fiancé.

"Hey, you two," my mother says, brushing past my father before he can even greet us.

I suspect she does it to stop him from being all overprotective.

"Hey, Mom," I murmur as she pulls me in for a hug like she hasn't seen me in weeks instead of hours. I somehow get the sense that she hugs me like this because she's afraid she won't see me again for a long time.

"Come in," my mother says, pulling my father, who's eyeing Diego up and down, inside of the house.

"Diego!" my brother Damian shouts as he barrels down the steps.

"You don't see me standing here."

My kid brother gives me a half-smile. He reminds me so much of my dad when he smiles like that. He's practically our father's carbon copy.

"Sorry, sis." He wraps his long arms around me.

I sniff him. "Are you wearing cologne?"

"He put too much of it on," Avery says as she rounds the corner, her face wrinkled in disgust. "He smelled up the whole upstairs bathroom."

"Shut up," Damian barks at her.

"What did I tell you about talking to your sister like that?" my father asks, silencing the entire argument with one question.

Damian mumbles an apology to Avery before taking Diego by the arm.

"It's been a minute since we played a game together. Let's go a few rounds before dinner," he tells Diego, pulling him toward the TV room which is down the hallway.

"Yeah, why don't we have some guy time?" my dad says, slapping a palm to Diego's shoulder.

I don't miss the way he tightly grips it either.

"Da—"

"That sounds perfect," my mother answers. "I wanted to have some time with my girls, too." She loops her arms around mine and Avery's.

Smiling, Diego winks at me like it's no big deal.

The look he gives me speaks to his confidence. Not for the first time, I wish I had as much confidence in this situation as he did. Not that I don't trust him. It's myself I can't fully bring myself to trust.

As I'm guided by my mother to the living room with my sister on her other arm, I'm reminded even more of where I came from. The truth hits me like a ton of bricks. This is why I keep my distance from my parents, especially from my mom. Even though I yearn to be closer to her, I can only be around her for a certain amount of time before the questions start coming to mind.

There's so much I want to ask her and know about her perspective on how my life began. Doing that would only bring up too much pain for her. It would likely unravel the carefully crafted bandages she's placed over those wounds.

Therefore, I keep my distance so that I don't accidentally blurt out the truth.

"Look what I came across this past week," my mother says, holding up a gold photo album book.

"What's that?" Avery asks, sounding only half-interested. Her phone is already out in her hand.

My mother quickly snatches her phone and shushes Avery's whining.

"This is what us old folks call a photo album," she replies.

"Mom, you're not old," I tell her.

"Thank you, baby."

"Besides, you're like a fine wine," Avery says, grinning.

I narrow my eyes on her. "What do you know about wine?"

"Nothing." She shrugs, but I side-eye her.

"You better not," my mom adds.

Avery lets out a frustrated groan. "I meant it as a compliment. Sheesh. I heard Daddy say it to you a couple of weeks ago. He said you're like a fine wine. You're just getting better with time."

My mom and I look at one another and burst into laughter. That's exactly something my father would say to my mom. Given the reddening of her cheeks, I know that Avery overheard him correctly.

"Thanks, hun." My mom kisses Avery on the cheek. "Just make sure you're not going around repeating everything you overhear your father say."

I stifle a laugh with my hand.

"Anyway, I got lost looking over these photos. Some of them I hadn't looked at in years. So many great memories came flooding back. I wanted to see if you girls remembered any of these. Hush!" my mom scolds Avery when she moans again.

Though she's playing the role of the grumpy teen who'd rather mope in her room than spend time with her parents, Avery curls up close to our mom and places her chin on her shoulder.

The picture they make reminds me of the times I used to do that when I was a kid. Back when it was just me and my mom. The first nine years of my life it was just the two of us. When my dad came along, I pretty much loved him from the beginning.

He never once made me feel like I was in the way of his and my mom's relationship.

He treated me like his own. I've been his "Short Stuff" from the very beginning.

"What's that smile about?" my mom asks, looking over at me.

"Just remembering when you and Daddy met."

Her face softens that way it does whenever my dad is brought up.

"He was so good with you. I would've never tolerated anyone who wasn't," she tells me, looking me directly in the eye.

I know that for certain. One thing I've never doubted is how much my mother has always loved me. Which, for some reason, has made me feel even guiltier over the years.

"I can't believe you have this," Avery interjects, bringing our attention back to the photos. It's a picture of when she was around four years old. She was in a play at her pre-school, singing on stage.

"Of course I still have this. It was your first public performance." My mom laughs. "Your dad just about climbed on stage to get these pictures. He has a video, too. For years, anyone who came over to our house was made to watch that video, the one of Damian in his football practice, or of Monique's drawings on the refrigerator."

Avery and I groan in unison.

"I was a terrible artist." It didn't take me long to realize that I didn't have the talent to be an actual artist. That never stopped my dad from showing off my painting.

"You weren't. You just never found your niche," my mom contradicts.

I shake my head and reply, "I found my niche. It's just not on the actual canvas. I have a better eye for spotting talent than creating the work myself."

"Which is why your gallery is going to be phenomenal," she tells me.

We continue looking through the photo album. Every page she flips, my mom stops and recounts the story behind the photo. I love listening to the pride in her voice. In most of the pictures, my brother and sister are laughing and smiling toothless grins.

It makes me happy that they had such a beautiful childhood with two parents who loved them so much. With an entire village that loved them. Our extended family, my dad's mother, his sister, the Townsends are all throughout the photos, too.

"Ah, this is the day you were born," my mom says to Avery.

In the photo, my mom is smiling at the camera, holding a pink bundled up Avery in her arms.

Something tightens around my heart. I can't help but to think about how different my birth day must have been from Avery's. And Damian's for that matter. I was ten and twelve years old when they each were born. Old enough to remember how happy my dad and mom were to welcome them into the world.

It has to have been such a contrast to how my mom felt when she gave birth to me. I get lost in my thoughts.

"Look at Mom in the hospital." Avery points at a photo.

In it, my mother is smiling holding Avery again, bundled up in a pink blanket. I blink and focus on her smile in the picture.

"You were so happy when she was born," I say as I run a finger along her face in the photo. That smile says it all.

"That's true. I was," my mom agrees, looking over at my sister. Then she turns to me. "But that isn't Avery I'm holding."

She looks me in the eye. "That's you."

I look back at the photo, blinking. It takes a few beats for it to register, but I can see the differences. The hospital room is different, my mom is younger in the photo. Almost like a kid herself. But the smile ...

The smile is the same.

"You were happy?" I didn't mean for it to come out as a question but a part of me can't conceive of it.

"Of course I was," my mother states as if that's a silly question. She doesn't say anything more as she flips the page.

I wonder if the smile on her face was just for the camera. Some hospital staff asked her to pose and smile with her new baby and she did it for them. But the expression on her face was so similar to the pictures of her posing with Damian and Avery.

I can't fathom it.

For years, I've told myself my mom had to grow into the love she has for me. She never let me know it or showed it, but ever since I discovered the truth, I've known it. How could anyone love something that began the way I did?

"Oh, this is Monique in the hospital," Avery says.

I look down and sure enough it's a picture of me waving at the camera from my hospital bed. I had to be around thirteen or fourteen. Throughout my childhood, I was lucky for the most part, not having to make too many trips to the hospital on account of my diabetes.

But there were still times when things went wrong. That day was one of them.

"I'm sorry," I apologize out of nowhere.

"For what?" My mother asks.

I manage to give her a tight smile because where would I even begin with an apology?

"There's Diego," my mom says, pointing to him sitting by my hospital bedside. "He wouldn't leave your side."

I remember that, too.

He's always been by my side.

"Let's go make sure your father hasn't done anything to him, huh? It's time for dinner anyway."

She closes the photo album and rises from the couch. The weight of all of the emotions moving through me makes it difficult for me to stand. However, I manage to push past them.

"I need to check my numbers before I eat," I tell my mom as a way to dismiss myself to the bathroom. My statement is true, but I also need a minute alone. Everything feels suddenly overwhelming, and I'm not sure how I'm going to make it through this dinner for some reason.

CHAPTER 20

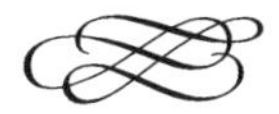

Diego

I knew this day would eventually come. Ever since I made the decision about my intentions to make Monique completely mine, I knew I would have to have this talk with her father.

"Diego, did you see that?" Damian shouts in laughter. He just killed off my last remaining power source on the video game. "I thought you said you were good at this," he quips.

"Guess my thumbs are out of shape," I joke.

He rolls his eyes.

Damian's a good kid so I don't bother telling him that I'm letting him beat me. It's his father whose eyes I can feel like lasers on my back. Watching us intently.

My aim is to get the game that I promised over as quickly as possible to have this so-called confrontation with Uncle Damon.

"Damian, why don't you upstairs for a few minutes while Diego and I talk?" Monique's father finally says.

"Yeah, I bet I can find better competition online," Damian declares. "When's dinner? I'm hungry."

"Give us ten minutes," his father answers.

"Cool. I've got plans tonight."

Uncle Damon tells him something about making sure all of his schoolwork is done before he even thinks about going out for the night. Within a few minutes it's just the two of us.

I rise from the chair and meet his eye contact.

"You wanted to speak with me?"

He looks me up and down.

"You know I own two guns, right?" he finally says.

I lower my head to hide my grin.

"Is that all?"

His eyebrows raise. "Don't think because I love you like one of my nephews that I won't hesitate to use them if you hurt her."

"I would never," I tell him in complete seriousness.

A small grin appears on his lips but quickly disappears.

"It's about time you went over to Townsend," he says, surprising me.

If I'm not mistaken, there's admiration in his voice.

"What took you so long to go over there?" he asks.

My mind flashes back to the aftermath of losing the job waiting for me after what happened junior year. I never gave my parents the full story of why I went after Slater. They supported me wholeheartedly, though, sparing no expense when it came to legal representation.

Even more in the aftermath I needed to prove myself to them. To let them know I wasn't just a trust fund kid who got into trouble, fucked up with his shitty temper, and ran to his family when things got too hot to handle.

I decided to forge a way on my own. I worked at bullshit, small architect firms until a major firm in the city hired me five years ago. There I cut my teeth on real design work, worked long hours, and took extra classes to improve. All so I could be worthy of the weight of my last name.

"Life," I say.

He raises a dark eyebrow. "And that five-year probation you were on?" he inquires.

"Four years," I correct without an ounce of shame.

He grunts and folds his arms across his chest. "It's been seven years and I still don't know the entire story of what happened in that situation."

And he won't ever know.

Monique wanted it that way. I'm her secret keeper.

"I never liked him," I say.

"Because you didn't like him, you beat him to within an inch of his life."

I slide my hands into my pockets because just thinking about that fucker makes my fingers itch. I want to dig him up from his grave and wrap my hands around his throat once again. The first time wasn't enough.

But he eventually got what he deserved.

No one questioned how since he reportedly had a blood alcohol level two times the legal limit.

"Something like that," I tell Mr. Richmond.

He takes a step closer. "Can I trust my daughter with you?"

There's a hard edge in his voice. My defenses kick up. Not because of the question. But because any man—her father or not—asking if Monique is safe with me brings on that reaction. As far as I'm concerned, I'm the *only* man she's ever been truly safe with.

"Uncle Damon, you know the answer to that question," I reply.

He lets out a chuckle and then sighs. "I've always known it would be you two in the end."

It's my turn to raise my eyebrows.

"I'm no dummy."

"Never thought you were."

"When you were kids, you two had that secret language thing going on. I thought your friendship would grow apart as you got older." He shrugs. "It happens. Kids grow up and make new friends. Not you two. Eventually, the way you started to look at her changed."

He points at me.

I cock my head to the side because I'm interested in his take on things.

"I don't remember exactly when, but late teens, twenties, something changed. I also felt the change in her. She started pulling away from all of us more.

"No matter how much I asked what was up, she insisted that nothing was the matter. That she was just growing up."

There's a sad look in his eyes.

"She's my oldest. I never raised a child before her, so I thought it was growing pains. Needing to assert her independence. When she told us she was moving to New York after college, I was happy for her. But I hated it. I always assumed she'd come back home after college."

You and me both.

He shakes his head. "But Sandra told me that our girl needed to go off and find herself. She said that when she was ready, she would come back home. I know it's selfish of me, but I want to have all of my kids close by. When she told us she was getting married to that artist in New York, I almost lost faith."

My body tenses. I don't like to be reminded that she was engaged to someone else. That was a low point in my life. Probably even worse than after my arrest and subsequent punishment. Deep down, I knew her marrying someone else would result in a change in our relationship. Even more so than her living so far away.

"But, the truth is, I never saw her ending up with him. He was ..." Uncle Damon rolls his eyes. "Maybe he was what she needed at the time. I've got strong instincts though. They've kept me alive this long.

"I knew it wouldn't last with him. Not for very long."

He meets my eyes. "I asked you if my daughter is safe with you, but I already know the answer to that. I would've never allowed you to be around her this long if I believed otherwise."

"All due respect, Uncle Damon, even you couldn't have kept me away from her." I say the words without thinking. I know for damn sure there isn't hell or highwater that could've kept me from her. No one and nothing.

He chuckles again. "You know what they say about that *all due respect* shit, right?"

I return his laugh. "Just telling you my truth."

"I expect nothing less," he quickly replies. "Anyway, I'm not the one that needs convincing."

He pauses, allowing me to figure out the meaning behind his words. He's right.

"I saw that look on her face when you mentioned marriage," her father says. "You're sure, but my baby girl will need some convincing."

"I'm certain enough for the both of us," I reply.

Monique still has doubts, I can see it in her eyes, but there's nothing I'm more sure of in my life.

"You've got your work cut out for you," he finishes, and then wraps his arms around my shoulders. "If I know you—and I have since you were a little boy—I know you'll figure it out."

I nod. "I don't have a choice," I reply. "She's my entire world."

That's the truth.

"If you ever forget to treat her like it, just remember I keep my two guns nearby. And that's not the only way I know how to kill a man. I haven't been down to the gym in quite some time, but my hands are still lethal."

He looks me directly in the eye. Uncle Damon hasn't been a part of it for years, but he was also once a part of the underground gym.

"I'll remember that."

"See that you do."

"Damon, babe," Monique's mother knocks and enters the room. "Good, you haven't hurt him."

He tightens his arm around my neck. "Not yet."

I grunt and step out of his fake headlock. "Monique?" I ask her mother.

"She's in the bathroom monitoring her numbers before dinner. How about we head to the dining room?"

I follow them out of the room but not before checking Monique's numbers on my phone. I'm relieved to see they're in a safe range.

The relief is short-lived, when I think about her father's words. She still isn't convinced, which means I have more work to do.

CHAPTER 21

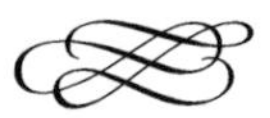

Monique

As we enter Diego's place, my feelings from earlier continue to weigh on me. I was able to make it through dinner with smiles that I didn't feel but I know Diego noticed.

He has a way of noticing everything about me.

"Come here," he says as soon as the door closes behind him. He doesn't give me time to completely enter his five thousand square feet luxury condo before he pulls me into his arms. I've been to his place plenty of times, but I always love viewing the pieces of art on his walls.

There's something so comforting about being in his home. Everywhere reminds me of him.

Diego traces my jawline with his finger. My body's response is instant. At this point, it doesn't surprise me how I react even to his simple touches.

"You were quiet during dinner. Are you feeling okay?" He scans my face with worried eyes.

I attempt to hide my true feelings with a nod. "Hey, there's an art fair next weekend in Blairwood. An artist I've been trying to track down for some time might be there. Are you up for coming with me?"

He looks over my face before agreeing. "You don't even have to ask. You know that."

I do know that. A sigh slips from my lips as the picture in the photo album of me in the hospital comes back to my mind.

"Being with someone with a long-term chronic illness isn't easy."

A wrinkle appears in his forehead as he pulls back, looking down at me in confusion. "Are you talking about your diabetes?"

I pull out of his embrace and move to the far end of his expansive living room. I bypass the low sitting leather couch and chairs to stand in front of the painting of smoke emitting from a volcanic landscape. The piece beautifully highlights the fuchsia colors of the volcanic mountainside against the gray smoke in the background.

Diego and I were together when he purchased it at an Art Basel show in Miami five years ago. However, at this moment, I can't help but to recognize how deeply I relate to the image.

My life feels like a mix of the beautiful fuchsia—a wonderful family, finally getting my gallery off of the ground, a man who would move mountains for me. Yet, the billowing overhang of the dark smoke in the background—the way my life began that I can't talk about with the one person I want to talk to about it with, my disastrous past that almost resulted in my best friend in jail, and my illness.

Diego takes me by the waist from behind. My back presses against his strong chest.

"Do you remember when I gave Johnathan Baker a bloody nose for teasing you about wearing a glucose monitor?" he asks.

I turn to face him because that was the last thing I expected him to say.

"We were in fourth grade."

He nods. "You had come to Excelor Academy a few months earlier," he says of the exclusive private school I started going to when my mom married my dad.

Johnathan, from what I remember, was a loud mouth boy who liked teasing girls he thought were an easy target. The day he first saw the glucose monitor attached to my arm I became one of his victims.

When he started teasing me, I didn't say anything because I was frightened that he would recruit other kids to join him. That was my experience at my previous school. It got so bad that one day I decided to leave my extra insulin at home. I ended up in the emergency department and scared the hell out of my mother. Soon after, I got the continuous monitor.

"I hated bullies and I couldn't stand that little prick," Diego declares while tucking a few strands of my loose curls behind my ear.

I smirk.

"But what really pissed me off was the look on your face when I overheard him talking shit to you. I saw red." He lifts and lowers one shoulder. "The two-week punishment I received from my parents was worth it. Because no one else dared to say anything about your diabetes after that."

"You shouldn't have gotten in trouble for me," I mumble. I hate being reminded of the times he's put himself on the line for me.

"I was pissed that anyone would dare to make fun of something so serious." He takes my hand and leads me to the couch. After sitting, he pulls me to his lap.

My hands immediately go to his hair.

"What I never told you was that the week before that I overheard my dad telling my mom about the scene of a car accident he and his team worked. They had to pull the driver and her two-year-old daughter out of the car."

I pull back and look down at him. Diego's father is a firefighter. Back then, he was still working at Rescue Four, one of the most elite stations in the city. Today, his father is a deputy chief in the emergency operations sector of the department.

"He told my mom that they later found out the woman had type one diabetes and her insulin dropped while she was driving. She lost consciousness. She survived, and so did her daughter, but that was when I first realized that diabetes could be dangerous," he continues.

"That night I asked my dad what diabetes was because you told me you had it but never talked about it. I hadn't thought much about it. But hearing that someone could've died because of it scared the hell out of me. Because my best friend could get sick. I wanted to know how to help you if I needed to."

I cock my head to the side. "You've never told me this."

He moves my hand from his hair and presses a kiss to my knuckles.

"I had my dad stay up with me all night long while he explained to me what low blood sugar meant, and insulin levels. We watched videos of how to do insulin injections, even though you had a continuous pump at the time. I even had him teach me CPR just in case I ever needed to know how to do that."

"Diego."

"I wanted to be there for you if you ever needed me. I didn't tell you because somehow, I knew you would tell me in your own time. I was okay with that," he says casually.

How the hell could he have been so young and yet so attuned to my needs?

"Your illness was and never will be a burden to me. It's a part of you, and I'm in love with every piece of you. I want all of you, Monique. Not just the convenient parts."

My vision blurs.

He wipes away the first tear that falls with his thumb. "That wasn't supposed to make you cry."

I laugh. "What did you expect to happen when you say something like that to me?"

"There's a few things I can think of." He cups my face and kisses the tip of my nose. Then he presses his lips to the corners of my mouth. Finally, he kisses me where I want him to. It's unhurried and tender.

Too tender.

I turn in his lap to straddle him. I pour everything into the kiss. A noticeable bulge rises in his pants.

He pulls back, hands still cupping my face. For a while he doesn't say anything. Just continues to stare at me, searching my eyes. I search his as well. As much as I can see he wants me, there's a hesitance that I don't quite understand.

This is the same man who just declared his love for me. Hours earlier he told my parents that he was going to marry me. Now, there's a look in his eyes of uncertainty or hesitancy or something that I can't quite read.

He blinks and the expression disappears. I wonder if it wasn't all in my head.

Before I can figure it out, we're rising from the couch. I wrap my legs around his waist, and let him carry me to the bedroom.

* * *

I WAKE UP HOURS LATER, wearing one of Diego's T-shirts. When I turn over to run my hand across his chest, I find his side of the bed empty. The room is mostly dark save for some light streaming in from the slightly opened door.

A part of me wants to lay back down and wait for him to return to bed. But then I check the number on my watch. My blood sugar is low. I have to get up and find something to eat.

As soon as I exit the bedroom, I see light coming from the room down the hall. It's Diego's home office. After I go to the bathroom, I head for the kitchen. The first cabinet I check has my favorite granola bars. Boxes of them, in fact.

A smile creases my lips at seeing them all line up.

"Monique?" Diego's worried voice calls behind me. "Are you okay? I heard you up and then I just checked my phone. Your numbers are low."

I hold up the half-eaten granola bar. "I'm on it," I reassure.

He pushes out a breath of relief. "I should've checked on you."

I wave him off. "It'll be okay in a few minutes. What were you doing in your office?"

"I had a phone call and didn't want to disturb you."

"A phone call? One of your exes looking to get back with you?" I tease.

His face turns serious. The next thing I know I'm in his arms, tightly pressed against his hard chest.

"There is no one else," he says adamantly. "No one else has mattered." He leans down and kisses my lips with a firmness that cements his words.

In truth, I never doubted his feelings or if there was anyone else. It was a joke, but I would be a liar if I said I didn't enjoy the way he gets all possessive. I want him to deepen the kiss, to bend me over the counter and make me yell out his name fiercely until we both come, to make me pay for even bringing up the idea that he could think about someone else.

But he pulls back from the kiss. The fire burning in his eyes, however, tells me he's just barely hanging onto his control.

"I'm sorry," he mumbles.

"For what?" I'm confused.

"Your numbers. I shouldn't have kissed you before we know you're okay." He captures my wrist in his hand and looks over the numbers on my watch. Even before I can get a look at them myself, I can tell they're moving in the right direction.

The way the tension eases from the lines in his forehead is an indication. Sure enough, once I check, they're back in a safe range.

"Still a little low."

"Give it some time," I tell him. "I'll finish this granola bar." I take another bite of the bar still in my hands.

"I should've let you finish before kissing you." He rolls his lips together in a way that speaks to his guilt.

I hate the way my illness can sometimes take the spontaneity out of my life. More than one ex of mine made comments on how they wish they didn't have to plan things out ahead of time so often on account of my potential to fall ill or need extra insulin or food.

Even the "nice guys" I dated would get slightly annoyed at times, including my ex-fiancé.

"I think the kiss is helping my blood sugar." I show him my numbers again. They've risen a little and are now in a comfortable range. "Who was the call from?" I ask just to change the subject.

"No one important," he says dismissively. The hard set of his jaw indicates otherwise. "I started working on something in my office."

"Can I see it?" I love seeing his designs. "I've talked to you ad nauseam about the gallery and the artists I want to feature. You haven't shared any of your recent designs with me. Not since your new job at Townsend."

I don't wait for him to respond. I pull him by the hand down the hall to his office. Diego isn't the type to brag on himself. Though he's an excellent architect and has a masterful eye for design, he'll rarely make a big deal out of his own work.

We enter his spacious office. This room was intended to be the second largest bedroom in his three-bedroom condo, but he turned it into a private office. Three of the four walls are lined with desks, covered in large building mockups. I recognize them immediately because they're designs that he's worked on in the past.

Across the room is his beautiful wooden drafting table. On the table's work surface sits a large piece of grid paper with pencil sketches on it. The design itself takes up most of the table's workspace. It must've taken hours to complete the design with this kind of detail.

"This is the project you're working on for Townsend?" I ask, looking down at what will become a ten-story building, octagonal in shape.

When I feel him come up behind me, I lean back to lean into his chest. His arm wraps around my waist, securing me to him.

"Our client wants an eco-friendly building. The design shape allows for different parts of the building to receive a considerable amount of sunlight throughout the day."

He points to the area where the building's roof will be.

"We'll place solar panels all along here." He drags his finger across the roof portion. "And it'll capture and store the energy in electric battery banks. The client wanted to be able to run the building on fifty percent solar power. With the design we're utilizing and the panels, I believe we can get to seventy percent. Maybe even eighty."

"That's amazing, Diego."

"In the center, here," he points to the middle area, "will be a park. Since the building will be composed of residential and commercial spaces, I insisted we create room for sufficient greenspace. The walking trail within the center of the building will be about a half a mile around."

"That's a lot."

He nods when I look up at him. "Too much?" He peers down at me as if genuinely seeking my opinion.

"No." I shake my head. "I love greenspace, especially in something like this. Coming from living the past few years in New York, I always appreciated it when building designers considered greenspace as part of their design. It allows for a place for people to forget they're in the middle of a city with millions of people. I think it's good for stress relief."

He nods and kisses my forehead. "I thought so, too. It kind of reminded me of that park you took me to in New York when I came to visit the first few times."

I snap and turn to him. "Yeah, the one that was right next to my first apartment up there. I loved that area."

I turn back to look at the design. "With this area, you can have landscapers create some beautiful gardens."

"That's the plan."

"You're so talented," I tell him while continuing to look over his design. I know a little about design considering my father is a real estate mogul himself and my best friend is a top-notch architect.

"This is your art," I say just above a whisper.

"Hm?"

I run my hand over the design, again smiling at what he's created. "You're an artist, Diego. Instead of paint and canvas, the city is your background. Phenomenal," I whisper as I study the design plans. "I knew your talent would be limitless. I can't wait to see this design in person."

"I'm not the only one who worked on this plan," he reminds me.

I shake my head. "Doesn't matter." I turn and run my hand through his hair. "You came up with it. I know you did."

He dips his head in the incredibly cute way he does whenever the compliments become too much.

"Why did it take you so long to go over to Townsend?" I ask because I need to know. Something held him back for years.

He meets my gaze. "My past."

I lift an eyebrow.

His eyes drift upward to look at something over my shoulder. "I needed to make it on my own before I went to work with my family," he responds.

"Now was the right time?"

He nods.

"Why?"

The truth is, he made something of himself long before now, but I choose to listen instead of countering his belief.

"Gabriel Garcia died."

It takes me a minute to place the name. When I do, my eyes go wide. "That Gabriel Garcia?"

He nods slowly.

I obviously don't call that man Diego's father, even though, biologically, he is.

"When?"

"Four or five months ago."

"Right before I decided to move back."

"It was then it felt like the past that'd been hovering over me for so damn long was gone. For the most part," he adds.

My heart sinks at his last comment. "I'm sorry," I mumble. "You shouldn't have ever felt like you had to wait to live your life because of my actions."

He wrinkles his forehead.

"Gabriel Garcia might've been part of the reason you felt like you weren't Townsend enough to work there but that's not all of it. I know it," I tell him. "It's because of the record you carried because of me."

I can't hold back the guilt that has lingered all of these years over that situation.

"Monique—"

"No, let me say this. I'm sorry I wasn't strong enough back then. I should've been the one to call the police on Slater that night. If I had, you wouldn't have gotten in trouble."

"Stop talking," he demands, taking my face in between his hands. "Listen to me when I say this." His eyes drill into mine.

"There's not a damn thing you could've done to stop me from beating the living shit out of that bastard. I don't care if he had been locked up. I would've gotten arrested just to be thrown into a cell with him to fuck him up. The moment I found out he put his hands on you, there wasn't a soul on this Earth who would've stopped me."

He's so certain and sure but I still feel like I could've done something differently. Diego lost more than an internship and job opportunity after that. He was practically a leper in his industry for years.

Most people would've gone and worked directly for their family business. Especially when that family business is supported by the weight of the Townsend name. But he felt like he had something to prove.

"You know it isn't true, right?" I ask him.

"It's true. I would've—"

I press a finger to his lips. "Not that. I don't doubt you would've found a way to get to Slater come hell or high water. I mean, it's not true the lies your father put into your head."

I know about the bullshit his father used to tell him. I was the only person he confided in about the way Gabriel Garcia used to talk to him.

"The Townsends always accepted you as one of their own. You're just as much Carter Townsend's son as Samuel, or Taylor is his daughter," I say of Diego's younger siblings.

He nods. "I know."

"Do you?"

Instead of answering, he runs the tip of his tongue across my finger that's still on his lips. My nipples instantly pebble.

His hands move to my ass, gripping it and pulling me into the obvious bulge in his pants.

"I said yes the first time," he pulls back to say. Right before he buries his head into the crook of my neck.

My vision blurs when he runs his tongue along the beating vein there. I'm so close to surrendering, but there's something I need to give him.

"Wait," I say.

He audibly growls when I step out of his hold.

"I have a present for you."

Before he can protest, sprint out of the door and to the bedroom. As I knew he would, I hear his heavy footsteps following me.

"Your ass better be naked in the next—"

"This one first." With one hand behind my back, I hold out the ring box which is one of two gifts I brought with me. "I made sure to bring this since I knew I'd be spending the night at your place."

"What's this?" he asks, taking the box from me but not opening it.

I roll my eyes skyward. "Why do you always do this?"

He chuckles because he knows how it gets under my skin. Instead of just opening the damn present he has to ask what it is.

"Open it, please."

He looks at me over the box before proceeding to open it slowly. His face ignites into a bright smile.

I peek over the edge of the box as if I don't know what's inside.

"I thought these would look great with your suits at your new job," I say, taking one of the sterling silver cufflinks out of the box. I turn the square cufflink so that his engraved initials are clearly visible.

'DT' are engraved into the cufflinks.

"I know it's a little late, but it took a few weeks to get these especially made for you," I tell him.

"These are beautiful, but you shouldn't have. Whatever you spent on them could be put into your gallery."

I wave him off. "I used some of my savings, and don't you dare think about guilting me over buying these for you. If you would've told me about the new job at Townsend sooner, I could've gotten you something a lot nicer."

"These are great," he says, looking me in the eye. "They match my navy blue suit perfectly."

"That's the suit I was thinking of when I bought them." Navy blue is his color. He looks phenomenal in it.

"Okay, that was the first one." I pluck the cufflinks' box from his hands and place it on the nightstand. "This is gift number two." I hold out the second box.

He scrunches his face as he looks from me to the box.

"Don't ask. Just open."

He chuckles that deep way that makes my nipples harden as he takes the box from my hand. He opens it, and I watch as his eyes widen.

"What's this?" He holds up one of the black mixed martial arts gloves.

I take the glove from him and undo the Velcro to slip it onto his hand. "These are the best quality gloves I could find," I answer at the same time I secure the glove firmly around his hand, making sure it fits.

The look of confusion on his face remains.

"This way when you get into one of your underground fights, you won't come back to me with bruised knuckles." I meet his eyes. "Your hands are too pretty for all of that bruising."

His shoulders slump, and he exhales slowly. "You know."

I lift on my tiptoes and press a kiss to his lips. "You aren't the only one in this relationship who can read the other so easily."

He clears his throat. "I'm so—"

I press a finger to his lips. "If you're about to apologize, save it. There's nothing to be sorry about." I know all about the underground fighting group or club or whatever they call it. My dad was a part of it for years.

"You know ..." I draw out as I slowly start to unbutton his shirt that I'm wearing.

A smile spreads on my lips when his eyes light up. His gaze moves slowly over every inch of skin that I reveal with each release of a button.

"You don't always have to turn to fighting to work out any intense feelings you might have." I finish unbuttoning the shirt and let it fall to the floor.

Diego's nostrils flare. He steps closer, his bare chest grazing mine. "What are you saying?"

"I'm saying ..." I take one of his hands in mine and bring it to cup my neck.

He instantly squeezes but quickly backs off. As if he's once again working to control himself.

"You don't have to handle me with kid gloves," I say just above a whisper.

"I don't." His voice is low, as if even he knows he's not being fully truthful.

"No?"

He shakes his head.

"Then show me." I hold his hand to my neck, waiting for him to do something.

His body remains completely still; his breathing quickens, though.

"What are you saying?"

"I'm not as sensitive as you think I am," I answer without thinking. "You don't have to be afraid to be rough with me."

He shakes his head slightly. "Stop." He pulls his hand away.

Before I can answer, he cups my face and kisses the life out of me. The kiss is intense but not rough. While my body lights up from the kiss, I can tell he's still holding back.

But when his hands go to my waist and he lifts me to him, I lose track of my thoughts. We spend the rest of the night tangled in one another's arms. In the back of my mind, however, the knowledge that he's still holding back remains.

CHAPTER 22

Diego

"I'm going to break that cocksucker's face," I mumble as I stare at the missed call number on my phone. Though I didn't answer the call, I suspect it's from Gabriel Jr.

I haven't talked to him or that fucking attorney in weeks. Nor do I plan to.

"I hope that wasn't meant for me," Uncle Josh says from my office doorway.

"Never for you."

His brows draw down in concern. "Someone giving you trouble?"

I should've known that would be his next question. "No," I tell him. That's the truth. Gabriel Garcia's family aren't trouble. His son is just pissed that, for whatever reason, his father left me a sum of money. I know it was nothing more than some sort of manipulation technique on his part.

That's what he was good at. Manipulating people. I refuse to let him or his fucking sons reel me into their mess, even from his grave.

"You know if someone is, you come to us first," Uncle Josh tells me.

"I know. I swear."

He eyes me. "I had lunch with your dad the other day. He said you've been busy. I told him about the work you're doing here. You should've seen his face."

He smiles wide. My chest warms because I know my dad's face when it fills with pride for me.

"Pretty soon, he's going to tell anyone who will listen that you designed half of the buildings in this city."

We both laugh.

"I'll tell him to cool it with the bragging. We're meeting for lunch today."

"Nah." Uncle Josh waves a hand in the air. "Don't bother. He's right. As far as I'm concerned, every building worth looking at is going to have the Townsend name on it. And yours will be front and center."

He squeezes my shoulder. "That's a hell of a job you did on the Johnson Project. They're thrilled with how it's shaping up. Given we get the permits and licenses on time, we should break ground in about two months."

"That's a hell of a turnaround," I reply. For a building and project of this size and scale, it can take years before ground is broken.

"Things move fast when you know what you're doing. Next week, we're meeting with Aaron and Kyle to talk more about our venture into commercial real estate. Are you up for it?"

"Hell yeah." Like he even needed to ask.

"That's my boy." He pats me on the back of the head and starts for the door. "Tell my big bro he has a hell of a kid."

"I already know it," my dad's voice booms from just outside of my office door. He's dressed in his department's button-down white top and black trousers. He looks every bit the part of the head of the fire department. He's not quite the head but he is pretty high up.

"Dad."

He barrels right past Uncle Josh and envelops me in a bear hug.

"I thought we were meeting at the restaurant," I tell him.

"We were, but I had to have a meeting this afternoon that brought me closer to this side of town. Why?" He pulls back and looks at me. "Your old man can't stop by your job?" He looks over this shoulder at

Uncle Josh. “You think your boss is going to have an issue with it? I used to beat his ass for fun when we were kids.”

Uncle Josh snorts. “It’s been a long time and your knees aren’t what they used to be, old man,” he scoffs.

“Still in good enough shape to best you.”

“Yeah right.”

“You two.” I laugh at their bickering. They’ve always been like this. My dad is the oldest out of the four of them and his brothers and he never lets any of them forget it.

“You and Samuel will be bickering like this for years to come, too,” my dad says of my kid brother. Sam’s only seventeen but I do give him shit every time I see him.

“True,” I agree. “Are you ready? I’m just finishing up a few emails.”

“Yeah, but first I want a tour.” He plops down on the chair in front of my desk.

“You grew up here. Why would you need a tour?” My father never came to work at the family business. He went directly from high school into the military, despite what my grandfather wanted. Then he went from the military into the fire department and has been there ever since.

Though he’s never worked at Townsend, he knows the company like the back of his hand. As the oldest, he was expected to take over the company when he came of age. As a result, he spent a lot of time here when he was growing up.

“Because I’ve never been here with my son giving me a tour. Don’t question your father. Do as you're told.” He gestures toward my computer. “Finish those emails.”

I shake my head, laughing. “You can’t boss me around in my own office.”

“Can and will.”

Rolling my eyes, I take my seat to finish my emails. Within minutes, I’m done and start showing my dad around the office like he’s never been here before. The pride I see in his eyes is uncanny.

Not for the first time, I realize how lucky I got when Carter Townsend became my father.

Lunch runs a longer than I expected, and ends with me promising my dad to bring Monique over to the family home for dinner soon. He wasn't the least bit surprised when I told him we're together. Not that I thought he would be.

Apparently, me and Monique are the last ones to get onboard with our romantic relationship. Once I finished lunch with my father, I had a few afternoon meetings that I took out of the office.

By the time I finish with work, it's close to six o'clock. Which is the perfect time to head over to Monique's gallery to check in on her. I know she's there. Even still, I call her to let her know I'm on my way.

I leave a message when it goes to voicemail.

A trickle of concern moves down my spine. I do my best to shake it off as I head over to her gallery. Just because she didn't answer her cell phone doesn't mean anything's wrong.

Yet, I can't shake the feeling.

And as soon as I enter her gallery, I know my senses were right.

The bell that sounds overhead alerts Monique as well as the other man standing in the middle of the gallery with her that they're not alone. My gaze lands on Gabriel Garcia Jr.

I'm barely able to suppress the anger that rolls through my body.

I'm gonna kill this motherfucker.

For his part, Gabriel Garcia is standing there with a fucking sinister smile on his ugly face. I plot exactly how I'm going to rearrange it as I stride over in his direction.

"Diego, hey," Monique says, cheerily. "This is Santos and his friend. He said he was passing by and got excited to see a new art gallery opening up in the neighborhood."

She gestures to the bastard on the other side of the room.

I blink as I stare at her. It takes me a second to realize she has no idea who this fucker is. She would've never met Gabriel Garcia or his other children. I never spoke of them because once I was adopted into the Townsend family, none of them were relevant to me.

She wouldn't know what he looks like.

"Is that right?" I ask, coming to stand in between him and Monique.

She steps beside me and gives me a funny look. "Yes, he's an art admirer himself."

"How could I not be in this neighborhood?" the bastard says, speaking for the first time since I entered the gallery. "I'm thrilled to see another woman-owned gallery entering the market. Ms. Richmond was just telling me about the artists she plans to feature here in the gallery. I think it's very brave of her—"

"I'm sure you do. But as you can see, the gallery isn't open yet. You should leave. Both of you," I say the words as calmly as possible but the fists at my sides are a dead giveaway of how much I want to punch this motherfucker in his face.

"Diego," Monique scolds.

I ignore her.

"Matter of fact, why don't we speak more outside?" I grab Garcia by his arm.

He grunts in pain from the bruising hold I have on his arm. I glance over my shoulder to see the bastard he brought with him following us outside as well.

Behind us, Monique asks me what the heck I'm doing.

"I'll be right back, babe."

My entire concern is to get this bastard and the asshole he brought with him out of her gallery and away from her.

I pull him out of the door and toward the alleyway that's a few buildings down from Monique's gallery.

"Get the hell off of me," Garcia yells, snatching his arm away. At the same time the bastard who was in there with him comes up behind me.

"I will fuck you up," I tell him as he gets too fucking close.

"Leave him be for now," Garcia says like he's a fucking don with his own personal bodyguard.

"I told you the next time I saw your face I would break it, didn't I? Did you think I was playing? And you have the audacity to show up at my woman's business?"

I move on him, but he leaps back and holds his hands up.

"Now you know I mean business," he dares to say. "I've been calling you for weeks and you've been ignoring me."

"Why the hell are you still calling? How many ways do I have to tell you to fuck off before you to get it? I'm done talking."

I lunge for him; all I see is red. The fact that he would dare to come to Monique's gallery as a way to get to me, tells me he doesn't value his life.

"Get the fuck off of me," I yell at the burly motherfucker behind me.

He lets out a grunt from the swift elbow I give to his midsection. But he recovers and starts to advance on me. I'll beat the living shit out of both of these fuckers, if need be.

"Look, I'm not looking for a fight," Garcia says, coming in between me and the fucker.

"The minute you showed up to my woman's gallery that's exactly what you got."

He jumps back when I start for him.

"It doesn't need to be this way," he claims. "I came just to let you know how serious I am. All we want is for you to show up at this meeting we're having in a few days. We'll go over how you can forward us the money."

"Who the fuck is we?" I bark at him.

"Your brothers. Me and Rodrigo."

"Call yourself my brother again and I beat your head into the fucking concrete."

His eyes balloon in fear. He takes a step back, nearly knocking over the big bastard still standing behind him. Some type of bodyguard he is.

Everything in me wants to rip both of their heads off. The memory of Monique standing next to this bastard with a smile on her face, thinking he had some sort of genuine interest in her business, pisses me off to no end.

I will myself to think strategically instead of acting on my emotion.

"Where?" I finally grit out through clenched teeth.

"A small accounting firm we have on the outside of Williamsport. I own it. We'll meet there, and I can tell you how you can serve us by forwarding us the money my father left. After that, I'll be out of your hair for good."

"Fine. Text me the address." I brush past him, nearly knocking him over when I shoulder check him.

I have no intention of giving him a dime. At this point it's based on principle. He has no idea the world of hurt he just unleashed.

"I'll see you there," he says behind me.

I don't stop or acknowledge him. If I do, I know it will end with me slamming my fist into his face. That'll happen eventually, but right now I need to go make sure Monique is alright.

"What was that about?" she blurts out as soon as I enter the gallery.

I lock the door behind me as soon as I close it. "Why did you let him in here?" I demand to know.

She looks up at me in confusion. "What are you talking about? He's a potential customer. Why did you treat him like that?"

"He's not a customer. He's a lying son of a bitch."

Her eyes balloon. "What happened?"

I grind my teeth together, wondering how much I want to tell her. I don't want any part of my biological father or his fucking kids touching her.

"Nothing happened. He's not a customer."

"Who is he then?" She folds her arms over her chest.

I know she won't let it go. "He's Gabriel Garcia Jr."

"You mean ..."

"Yeah." She doesn't need to finish the sentence. I can see from the expression on her face she now gets it.

"Apparently, that cocksucking sperm donor of mine left some money to me in his will. He didn't leave it to his other kids, and now they want it."

"Why would he show up to my gallery?"

My anger sparks all over again, just thinking she was here alone with him.

"He's been trying to get a hold of me, and I've been ignoring him. This was his way of getting to me."

"Diego—"

"I'm taking care of it." I move to stand in front of her, cupping her face. "He didn't do anything to you, right?" I look her over, making sure there isn't a hair out of place.

"Of course not. He was only here with that guy for a few minutes before you showed up."

"Good," I say against her lips before kissing her with everything inside of me. I don't even give her time to take her next inhale before I'm walking us backwards toward whichever wall we reach first.

I don't stop when I hear tools clatter to the ground. We'll take care of it later.

"Diego," Monique pants as I frantically search to undo the button on her jeans. As soon as it's free, I'm yanking her pants down her hips. Her panties are the next to go.

She's stripped and naked from the waist down in a matter of minutes. I place her legs over my shoulders and begin feeding on her like a starving man. Every time I taste her pussy, I crave more. I don't think I'll ever get enough.

An entire lifetime could pass with my head between her thighs and it still wouldn't be enough.

"Baby," she pants over and over again.

When she moves her hands to the back of my head, I halfway go blind with need. Her hand in my hair is my weakness. And I take it out on her pussy, lapping her up and still demanding more.

The first orgasm she gives me isn't enough. My hunger for her is nowhere near satiated. I try to remind myself to not go completely insane on her. Not the way I want to.

Visions of me turning her over onto all fours and smacking her ass until it's good and red before I take her from behind assault my mind. I want that so fucking bad.

But I can't do that to her.

I won't allow myself to do that to her. She's been through too much. I can be the nice guy that she needs me to be. For her I'll control my base instincts.

Instead, I undo the button of my suit pants and take her nice and slow. I deep stroke her, making sure she feels every ridge of my cock inside of her. The most beautiful sight in the world is Monique with her head thrown back, eyes half-closed and my name pouring out of her mouth.

The way her pussy grips my cock, I can't help but to think about what would happen if she weren't on the pill. An image of her belly swelling with my baby has me gripping her thighs even tighter.

When she screams my name again, I know she's coming. The squeezing of her walls around me, pulls my orgasm from me.

"I love you," I tell her over and over.

Three words that I've held on for too long. It feels better than my orgasm to say them out loud. Monique wraps her arms around my shoulders and pulls me into a searing kiss.

It's not the words I want to hear but I take the kiss because I know that's the best I'm going to get for now.

CHAPTER 23

Monique

"Are you sure you're up for tonight?" Diego asks as he comes up behind me, wrapping his long arms around me.

On instinct, I push my hips against his groin.

A smile creeps across my lips at the growl he makes at the back of his voice.

"For that, I should keep your ass inside all night." He emphasizes his meaning with a squeeze of my ass.

I spin away from the floor-length mirror in his bedroom and hold up my arms. "Absolutely not. This dress deserves to be seen." I wiggle my hips.

He looks me up and down in the form fitting, black and gold, sleeveless dress. It stops inches above my knees. I know it's a scene stealer by the way his eyes darken as he checks me out in it.

"Even more reason to keep you home."

He reaches for me again, but I dodge his hold and sidestep him. "What's the matter? Afraid you can't keep up?" I tease.

He snorts. "You're all the incentive I need to keep up."

My nipples tighten from the deepness of his voice. But I don't let his sexiness suck me in. We haven't been out to a club in forever, and I feel like dancing. I'm in a good mood.

"I haven't seen Kyle or Riley since the wedding. Didn't you say Kennedy's going to be there?" I ask of his younger cousin.

He nods but lifts an eyebrow. "Are you sure you haven't overexerted yourself this week? You've put in back-to-back twelve-hour days working at the gallery."

Though there is so much caring in his voice, I can't help the way my shoulders slump slightly. I love that he cares for me. The way his gaze darts to my wrist, tells me he's thinking about my numbers.

"Where's your watch?" he asks.

I jingle my wrist with my gold bracelets instead of the smartwatch I usually wear. With my other hand, I point at my clutch on his bed. "I'm not wearing it tonight. I have a read out on my phone just like you do. You've worked just as many hours this week as I have."

His ongoing work project keeps him in the office well past dinner time most nights. I've even taken him dinner a few evenings this week.

"Yeah, but—"

"Not buts," I cut him off. I wrap my arms around his neck and give him a quick kiss. "I'm fine and we're going out."

To end any further discussion, I take his hand in mine, grab my clutch, and pull him out of the bedroom.

About thirty minutes later, we arrive at the exclusive Black Opal nightclub and lounge.

"Mr. Townsend." The security guard nods at Diego as he undoes the velvet rope to allow us in the private entrance.

Diego extends his arm for me. I wrap my hand around his and follow his lead as we enter the nightclub. After a few hellos to some business associates, we take the glass elevator up to the second floor VIP area.

"It's about time," a deep voice booms from across the room. "We've been waiting for hours," Kyle Townsend says, glaring at Diego.

"Don't listen to him," the beautiful woman to his right says. "We just got here ten minutes ago," Riley, Kyle's wife, tells us.

Kyle frowns. "How am I supposed to guilt him if you keep telling on me?"

She rolls her eyes. "Don't guilt family. Besides, does it look like he's even paying any attention to you?" she argues.

Both Kyle and I turn our attention to Diego, whose gaze is firmly planted on me. Has he been staring at me like this since we got off the elevator?

Without a word, he leans in close to my ear. "Did I tell you how beautiful you look tonight?"

"Only twice."

Though I can't see his face, I know he smiles because his lips brush against my ear, making me shudder.

"You look good enough to moisturize my beard," he growls in my ear.

It takes me a beat, but when I realize his meaning, I cover my mouth and gasp. "You—"

"Oh my god!" a voice screeches behind us.

I turn to find Kyle's twin sister and Diego's cousin, Kennedy, staring between us wide-eyes, mouth ajar.

"Is this *finally* happening?"

I turn to Diego, who's looking at his cousin with a raised eyebrow.

"Don't everyone speak at once," Kennedy says. "First of all ..." she throws her arms around my neck, "welcome home."

I laugh as I hug her tight. Kennedy is a few years younger than me, but we practically grew up together. She's like family. As we hug for the first time since Kyle's wedding almost two months ago, I realize how much I've missed her.

"I'm not the only one who deserves a welcome back," I say as we pull apart. "You've been quite busy, I hear."

She shrugs. "Traveling for work." Ken's an up-and-coming investigative reporter. "I'm home now." Then she gasps. "I can't wait to hear all about your gallery."

She takes my free arm and starts toward the main area of the VIP section. I come to a stop when Diego's hold doesn't let up. I turn back to him.

The look in his eyes is so pitiful that I can't help but laugh.

"Of course, he's all clingy now," Kennedy gripes. "Can you please let her arm go so we can gossip about you in private?"

He makes a face at his cousin and then lowers his gaze to me. I see the kiss coming only a split second before his lips touch mine.

My body burns from the kiss.

He cups my chin at the same time he pulls back. "Don't go far."

"Where are we going to go?" Kennedy answers for me. "All the men in this family are so possessive." She rolls her eyes. "That's exactly why I'm not getting married. With my luck, I'd end up with someone like one of them."

"You don't need to get married," Kyle says as he approaches.

His twin sister sucks her teeth. "Don't start with me. Come on, Monique. You too, Riley." She loops one arm in mine and the other in her sister-in-law's, and we start toward the other side of the lounge.

Our group is the only one in this quartered off section. Kennedy grabs two flutes of champagne, handing them to us before taking one for herself.

"Are we celebrating?" I ask.

She nods. "Your art gallery is opening soon."

Butterflies flutter in my stomach. The excitement that's been mounting for weeks is almost palpable. My dream is coming true.

"Tell us all about it," Riley insists, taking my hand so we can take a seat on one of the black leather couches.

"I have four confirmed female artists so far," I tell them of the details of the gallery. "Next weekend, Diego and I are going to an art festival to find this one artist who I think would be perfect for my gallery. Her art just speaks to me. There's one painting when a girl is hiding behind this wall of hair and—"

"Yeah, we can't wait to see it," Kennedy interjects. "Before we get into that, though ..." She pauses and glances across the room in the direction of Diego and Kyle.

I'm surprised to see Diego looking my way. I smile and take a sip of my champagne. His expression instantly turns from sexy to a frown. His attention lingers on the glass in my hand.

It's not hard to decipher what he's thinking. Without thinking, I reach inside of my clutch and pull out my phone, waving it in his direction.

A silent communication between us that my numbers read perfectly safe. I'm okay with one glass of champagne.

Even as his shoulders relax, though, I can't help but think about how much extra work he puts into taking care of me. He knows my eating schedule better than I do. I wonder if he ever considers it a burden.

"I need to use the restroom," Kennedy says, pulling me out of my thoughts. "Come with me."

* * *

"HE'S SO DAMN CLINGY," Kennedy says in disgust of her brother.

Kyle grabbed Riley by the waist before we could leave the VIP area.

"She can't even go to the bathroom in peace."

"Doesn't look like she minds," I say as I glance back at Riley laughing at something Kyle says in her ear with his arms wrapped around her body.

"You would agree," she replies. "I barely got you away from my cousin."

I smirk because she's right. I barely made it out of the lounge area without Diego insisting on following along like a puppy. I love how attentive he is, but it also makes me wonder if he pays such close attention out of fear.

"Now spill," Kennedy says as we exit the elevator on the first floor.

"Spill what?"

"Don't play," she shoots back. "There are private restrooms and staff falling all over themselves to serve us drinks upstairs. I didn't bring you down here for the bathroom or to go to the damn bar."

She moves in front of me and places her hands on her slim hips. "I brought you down here for some privacy. How long has it been since you and Diego finally got together? Is that why you moved back from New York? Oh my god, are you two engaged yet?"

"Whoa!" I hold my hands up in front of me. "Who said anything about marriage?"

She frowns, and it scarily reminds me of her father, Aaron Townsend. "You two have been joined at the hip since what? Like, third grade or something crazy like that."

"Fourth," I correct.

"See? Anyway, we all saw it coming. But then you got engaged to that artist in the city. Diego got really dark after that. I remember barely seeing him smile."

I glance up toward the VIP section. "Really?"

Kennedy nods. "I had a feeling it had to do with your engagement. Anyway, is that why you broke up with your ex?" Gasping, she takes my hand. "Oh my god, did he do, like, some big dramatic move and declare that he couldn't live without you forever? Is that why you and your fiancé broke up?"

"No." I laugh and try to ignore the way my chest tightens up. It's not the mentioning of my ex-fiancé that causes the feeling of rejection to rise up inside of me. The reasoning for his dumping me is, though.

"What's happening between me and Diego has an expiration date," I admit to Kennedy.

"What?" comes her immediate reply. Her light brown eyes widen. "There's no way. How—"

"I actually need to use the restroom," I cut her off. "How about I meet you at the bar?"

She looks me up and down, obviously not content with my non-answer, but she doesn't push. Thankful, I give her a nod and head to the bathroom.

Luckily, I don't have to wait as I enter the beautifully marble-floored and wall mirrored bathroom. The trim along the ceilings is the same blood red color as walls of the VIP section.

I marvel at the grandeur of this club as I do my business. Whoever owns this place obviously spared no expense to create the luxurious, exclusive environment.

As I move to wash my hands, a woman enters the bathroom. We make eye contact, and I give her a quick smile out of politeness. She's beautiful, I can't help but notice. Long, dark hair, smokey brown eyes, and a rich caramel complexion.

She moves to the sink next to me and turns to look me over. "You're really pretty," she says, surprising me.

"Thank you. So are you," I return.

When I think that's the end of our conversation, she surprises me again. "What's that on your arm?"

I don't need to look to know that she's pointing at my continuous glucose monitor. Annoyance prickles through my body. Haven't most people learned not to ask questions about other people's bodies, yet? Especially not of a complete stranger.

"It's nothing." I turn to grab one of the folded linen clothes to dry my hands.

"It has to be something if you're wearing it out here, right?" She swings her hair over her shoulder. "Is it because you have diabetes? My boyfriend's ex had that. He told me."

My frown deepens. "Your boyfriend shouldn't be telling you about his ex's health information."

She waves a hand. For the first time I see the glassy look in her eyes. She's at least a few drinks in. Not an excuse to be messy but whatever. This girl isn't my problem.

"Yeah, well, he broke up with her." She shrugs, not paying attention to the fact that I'm not interested in this conversation. "He said she was too needy. Always wanting to be taken care of because she was sick. Are you always sick? How are you able to wear that and come out to a nightclub?"

"Excuse me."

I brush past her, knocking her out of my way with my shoulder. I typically have patience with drunk people, but she just pushed my damn buttons. I yank the door open with all of the force I can muster and start for the bar to meet Kennedy.

"Hey," Ken says as soon as I come up next to her. "Did you want something? I don't know your drink of choice."

I start to say yes but hesitate. I glance down at my wrist and realize that I'm not wearing my sports watch with my numbers on it. And I left my phone upstairs in the VIP section.

Once again, even in a minor way, my illness plays a role in the choice I have to make. I shake my head.

"I'll hold off until I can check my numbers," I tell Kennedy. "I can order something once we—"

"Hey, were you upset by what I said?" that annoying voice from the restroom asks behind me.

I slow blink and wait for a beat before slowly turning around. Yup, she's still there.

"Who is this?" Kennedy asks.

"No one." I glare at the woman.

She has the nerve to blink like I'm the one who said something wrong. She looks over at Kennedy.

"I was just asking—"

"Leaving," I interject. "You were just leaving because you obviously can't take a fucking hint." At this point, she's starting to piss me off.

"I'm not going anywhere." Her voice grows louder.

"Babe, what's the matter?"

A familiar male voice shocks me. For a beat, I can't move. *Did I hear that voice correctly?*

"I heard your voice a few tables away," his voice continues. "What happened?" Finally, he turns my way and our eyes lock.

Nope, it wasn't a figment of my imagination. Staring me in the face with his arm wrapped around the irritating woman from the bathroom is my ex-fiancé, Lawrence Jordan.

"Monique." His eyes widen, looking as surprised as I am.

"Do you know her?" the woman at his side asks.

He looks down at her but pinches his lips together.

As I stare at the two people in front of me, it dawns on me. I'm the ex she was talking about. The one her boyfriend dumped because she was … what was it? Oh, right. Too *needy*.

"Monique, h-how are you?" he dares to ask.

Sudden anger infuses all of my senses. Without thinking, I take

Kennedy's drink from her hand and throw it in his face. The woman at his side screeches.

"Real mature, Monique," Lawrence says through gritted teeth. "I figured you wouldn't be over my dumping you, but this is beyond unreasonable ... especially after you cost me all of the shows that I had planned over the next year."

I blink in confusion. "What the hell are you talking about?" I hold up my hand before he can answer. "I don't care. Just don't speak to me ever again."

I turn to Kennedy. "Sorry about your drink. I'll buy you another."

There's a smirk on her face. "Losing the drink was worth it."

"You're going to pay for this dress," the woman at Lawrence's side insists. "It's vintage! Getting this dry cleaned will cost a fortune," she whines.

I smile at the dark maroon stains that pepper her cream dress. My grin widens as I look over at Kennedy.

"Red wine. Nice."

She laughs at the thumbs-up I give her. I hadn't even paid attention to the type of drink she had in her hand.

"I like to keep it classy," she jokes.

"Grow up, Monique," Lawrence's voice interrupts our mini celebration. "This is insane behavior on your part. If—"

"I suggest you calm your fucking tone when speaking to her," a deep, thundering voice interjects from behind Lamond.

The chill that runs down my spine tells me who the voice belongs to seconds before I look over behind Lawrence to find Diego glowering down at him.

"Unless you want your ass beat in front of your new girlfriend a second time."

Glancing down and noticing Diego's fists are clenched tightly, I move to him without thinking. I practically push my ex to the side to step into Diego's warm embrace. As soon as I lay my hand against his chest, some of the tension ebbs out of his body.

He peers down into my eyes, and I can't help but to feel so comforted. Safe and protected.

"He's not worth it," I say just above a whisper.

He leans down and brushes his lips across mine. My entire body heats up and suddenly I forget where we are.

Until …

"What's this?"

Diego's top lip curls as he looks over at Lawrence who just asked that question. His hold around my waist tightens, but he moves me to his side.

"You don't like having your teeth, do you?"

"Diego." I squeeze his hand.

Lawrence looks over at me, suspicion in his eyes. "It isn't bad enough that you got me fired from my upcoming shows? Huh? Are you telling me you were lying to me the entire time in our relationship when I asked you about him?"

My forehead wrinkles as I try to work out what the first part of his question even means.

"I never did anything to your or your shows," I tell him.

"That was me," Diego says, stepping into Lawrence's face. "You lost your shows and ongoing projects because I put in a few calls. Trust me when I say I wanted to do a lot worse. I still can if you have specific feelings about it," he threatens.

Everyone in our vicinity understands it's a threat as well. The woman with Lawrence has gone completely silent, though she peers my way scowling from time to time.

Lawrence takes an obvious step back. He points at me. "She told me there was nothing more than friendship going on between you two." He looks at me with narrowed eyes.

"Don't fucking look at her," Diego says through gritted teeth. "She told you the truth. You made a choice. Deal with it." He takes a step forward.

I grab his arm. "Diego, no."

"What's going on here?" another deep, slightly raspy voice asks.

I turn to see a tall Asian man dressed in all black. He's a bit hypnotizing with his perfectly square jaw, perfect, clear skin, and eyes the same color as his clothing. The hard set of his square jaw speaks to his irritation.

I can't help but to notice that he would be absolutely gorgeous if it weren't for the wicked scary scowl on his face.

"This son of a bitch needs to leave," Diego says without looking the guy's way. As if he knows who he is. "Now," he barks out.

"This is my club, remember?" the new man says. "I don't take orders."

"Yeah," the woman with Lawrence suddenly finds her courage, "you can't kick us out."

"But I can," the owner says. His voice isn't raised at all. But it's as if with those three words all other noise dies down.

"Wh-What?" she demands.

"I don't repeat myself." He dismisses her with a look. Then gives a barely noticeable nod of his head.

Before I can blink, there are two huge guards standing beside Lawrence and his girlfriend.

"Come with us," they say in not too friendly tones.

They must not be too stupid because neither of them puts up much of a fuss. My ex does start to look my way, but Diego moves in between him and me, blocking his view.

He mouths something to Lawrence that I can't hear. Whatever it is, it causes Lawrence's face to drop, fear invading his features.

I make a mental note to ask Diego what he told him later when we're alone. When I look over at Kennedy to make sure she's alright, I'm surprised by the expression on her face.

She's paled, her mouth ajar, and it looks like she's seen a ghost. I glance back to find her staring at the owner of The Black Opal.

He turns her way. His eyes scan the length of her body, and I swear I see his jaw go even more rigid. How that's possible, I don't know. Then he turns and disappears into the darkness of the nightclub.

The exchange happens so quickly I have to ask myself if I made it up.

"Are you alright?" I ask Kennedy.

She opens and closes her mouth a couple of times before looking over at me. She blinks and then pulling herself together.

"Fine. Great. Let's go back upstairs." The words are barely out of her mouth before she's dashing off in the direction of the stairs to the VIP section.

"What was that about?" I mumble.

"Did he touch you?" Diego suddenly asks, sounding irate.

"No." I press my hand to his chest. I can feel his heartbeat through his clothing. I rise to my tiptoes and run my finger along his bottom lip and then through the hairs of his beard.

My ex isn't even a thought in my mind as I look up into Diego's eyes.

"How about we head home?"

His eyes darken in that way that makes my nipples tighten. Never in my life did I imagine I could want someone this badly.

"Let's go," he says before wrapping me up in one of his long arms and practically carrying me toward the exit.

CHAPTER 24

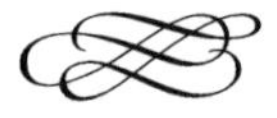

Diego

"Are you sure you're okay?" I ask as we enter my condo.

I grab Monique from behind and spin her so that she's facing me. I search her pretty face for any hint of dissatisfaction or injury.

If that shithead ex of hers laid one finger on her, I'll track his ass down tonight. There won't be anything left of him for his family to find.

The smile at her lips leads to her dimples exposing themselves. It's like a balm to my soul. I run my hand down the left side of her face, palming it. She's so damn beautiful that it steals my breath away.

"I want to beat my own ass," I tell her just above a murmur.

Her forehead wrinkles in confusion. "Don't worry about Lawrence. He's nothing," she says.

The words should calm the annoyance bubbling inside of me but they don't. I shake my head.

"Not him." I pause. "Well, yeah, fuck him. But I want to kick my ass for taking so goddamn long to make you mine."

Her eyes widen in surprise. I lean in and capture her lips. Fire ignites inside of my veins from the contact. A small groan escapes her mouth as she wraps her arms around my neck.

Everything inside of me is urging me to pick her up, strap her to my bed, and make her scream my name for hours until she begs to let her up for air.

When I pull back, the pout on her lips is almost too much to bear.

"How are you feeling?" I ask instead of picking her up so I can bury my face between her legs the way I want to.

"Um." She glances around as if uncertain.

I remove my cell from my pocket and pull up the app that has the readout of her blood glucose numbers. My frown is instant.

"You're low." I curse under my breath before taking her hand to lead her to the kitchen. "I have some orange juice in my fridge," I tell her, knowing the drill.

She doesn't bother trying to hide the sigh that falls from her lips.

"I'm fine," she insists but follows me to the kitchen.

"You're low." I grab one of the cartons of orange juice I keep in the fridge and hand it to her. I watch as she drinks it, our eyes locked on one another's.

She's so damn beautiful that it's almost painful.

"I have some of those lentils you like. I can whip up a quick salad to eat." I check my watch, noting the time. We'll have to wait for fifteen minutes or so to make sure her blood sugar reaches a safe range.

"Now we wait." The smile she gives me doesn't reach her eyes.

"What's wrong?" Not liking the way she's holding her head down, I step in front of her. I move my fingers underneath her chin, giving her nowhere else to look except at me.

"Did that son of a bitch say something to you?" The growl in my voice can't be helped. I will shatter every bone in her ex's body before making him go to sleep forever if he did.

"Who?" Her eyebrows furrow. "No," she quickly replies.

"Don't lie to me to defend him."

I watch as she visibly swallows. Her eyes dart away from mine. "*He* didn't say much," she finally offers.

"Then it was the woman he was with?"

Heat starts at the back of my neck. I can see it in her eyes. Whatever that woman said to her, is making her feel something I don't like. A bevy of options start to run through my mind as to how I can handle both of them.

I would never put my hands on a woman, but I have no problem breaking both of Lawrence's kneecaps for whatever it is he said to that woman that she felt comfortable repeating to Monique.

"Stop it," Monique says, pulling me out of my thoughts.

"What?"

"I see the way your eyes are darkening. You're already thinking of ways to get back at him … at both of them."

Damn.

I sometimes forget how well she knows me. My aim is to always keep the angry beast inside of me locked away from her. She doesn't need to see that part of me. Not ever.

My lips part. On the tip of my tongue is my refusal but I stop myself. I won't lie to her.

Instead, I lift her free hand to my lips and kiss her palm.

"I'll help you with the insulin," I say, gesturing toward the insulin she's retrieved from the refrigerator.

Fifteen minutes are almost up, and thankfully, her numbers are on the rise. The next step is an injection and then food.

"I can do it. I've been doing this for years."

"And I'm going to help tonight. Alright?"

She pauses before her lips split into a genuine smile.

After following her into the bathroom, I take the insulin pen from her hand. I look at the numbers on my phone before checking with her the amount of carbs she'll have with the salad and putting the adequate amount of insulin in the pen.

Having memorized this part, I lift her dress and swipe the right side of her stomach, close to her hip, with an alcohol wipe. A few seconds after the alcohol dries, I pinch her skin and quickly do the injection. She doesn't even flinch.

My brave girl, I think as I lean in and place a kiss to the site I just injected. A sigh escapes her lips as I lower her dress.

"You're the only man who's ever done this." Her voice is barely above a whisper.

For some reason, that knowledge lights up my insides. "Good," I say before pressing a quick kiss to her lips. "Time to eat."

I take her hand in mine as we exit the bathroom and head to the kitchen. Then, I prepare a salad with enough lentils to give her the right amount of carbs for the injection she just received.

"I'm sorry," she murmurs, after taking her first bite.

It might be sick, but I love watching her eat, especially when it's food that I've prepared.

I lean across the kitchen isle.

"I'm a hundred percent certain that your answer to my next question is going to piss me off but I'm going to ask anyway."

I pause, watching as she takes another bite of the salad.

"What are you apologizing for?"

She rubs her lips together as she chews.

"Stop that," I tell her. "I'm the only one who gets to use my mouth to smear your lipstick tonight."

Laughter spills out of her, making me inhale a little deeper. Our eyes lock.

"I know you had other plans for when we got in tonight."

"Oh, you mean like stripping you down, laying you in my bed, and making you scream my name until your voice is hoarse?"

She bites her lower lip, and I see the vein in her neck pulse a little quicker. I love seeing the physical evidence of the impact of my words on her body. It's as if she wants me as badly as I want her.

"Yes." Her voice is breathless. "But instead of going right at it, we have to do all of this ..." She gestures to the salad in front of her.

"Stop."

I close my eyes and can't help the way my nostrils flare as I do my best to rein in my irritation.

Slowly, I open my eyes once I've calmed myself to a reasonable level. "Who was it?" I ask, looking her directly in the eye. "Which one of your fucked up exes made you believe taking care of yourself before he could fuck is some sort of inconvenience?"

I try to temper the tone in my voice but it's useless. Because I know once she tells me who, I'm going to look the fucker up and make him wish he'd never come across her let alone said some bullshit like that to her.

Dropping her head, she pushes the remaining salad around her plate, not answering.

"Who was it?"

She shakes her head. "No one."

"Monique." Her name comes out as a warning. It takes everything inside of me not to tell her that if she lies to me again, I'll have no choice but to bend her over my kitchen island and turn her ass red as I make her take every inch of me as punishment.

I can't do that with her.

I have to clamp down on those urges.

"I'm not lying," she says with emphasis. "No one ever said it out loud. But I saw it. In the roll of their eyes or the deep exhale whenever I had to pause things to check my numbers or do an injection and then eat. Having a chronic illness can take the spontaneity out of a relationship."

She says it like she's trying to warn me against something.

"And?"

"And, it doesn't ever go away," she replies.

"You know what else can take the spontaneity out of a relationship? Being tired, a long day at work, kids, bills. Should I go on?" I don't wait for her reply. "Life can take the spontaneity out of a relationship. Diabetes is a part of your life. I know it's not going anywhere. It's as much a part of you as the honey color of your eyes. Or the way your dimples appear when you smile at something you really love. You don't ever have to apologize to me for wanting all of you."

She bites her lower lip, looking as if she's trying to hold back her smile.

A groan pushes through my lips at the way I want to fill that mouth of hers with the rod pulsing between my legs.

I rise to my feet and cup her face. I bring our lips to touch but I don't deepen the kiss the way every cell in my body wants me to. I can't.

"Finish eating," I order.

"This is really good by the way," she says around another bite of the lentil salad. "You still won't tell me what's in that dressing of yours." She side-eyes me.

"I made sure to include the carbs from the dressing in the calculation of your insulin."

She rolls her eyes. "I know. You always take care of me. But what if I want to make it on my own?"

I shrug. "Why would you when you have me?" I wiggle my eyebrows, making her laugh.

"What if I asked really nicely?"

Around a smirk I reply, "It's a secret."

"Is it?" She raises a perfectly arched eyebrow. Her expression turns saucy.

My heart rate kicks up a notch.

She leans across the kitchen isle. "What if I gave you something in return?" She runs her tongue across her bottom lip.

A shudder runs through me. I swear she wouldn't tease me like this if she knew how thin my restraint is.

Noting the empty salad bowl, I move it to the side.

"What do you have in mind?"

CHAPTER 25

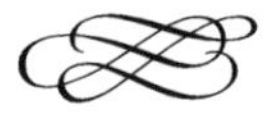

Monique

My nipples harden from the way Diego's eyes darken. A moan rises up my throat and out of my mouth from the way he bites his bottom lip. With his smoldering gaze on me like this, I feel like I'm the center of his entire world.

To be honest, it's not an entirely new feeling. He's always had a way of making me feel like I am the only person in a crowded room. The only person worth looking at.

My stomach muscles tighten as the many memories of him watching me with such an intense focus stream through my mind.

How long has he looked at me this way?

It's a question I don't dare try to answer right now. Or ask out loud. The response might be more than I'm ready to hear.

Instead of saying anything, I wrap my arms around his broad shoulders and hover my mouth just above his.

"My numbers are fine. Let me convince you to give me that recipe."

A gasp escapes me when Diego rises to his feet, lightning fast. His large hands move to my thighs as he lifts me to wrap my legs around his waist.

Diego takes long strides toward his bedroom, not once breaking eye contact with me.

The automatic lights illuminate the room as we enter. The way he lays me down on the bed isn't soft. My back hits the mattress harder than usual. Before I can blink, Diego hovers above me. His expression is unreadable as he stares down at me.

But his eyes give his emotions away. He's fighting hard to restrain himself. I know this look. But I don't want him to hold back. I want more of him.

I lift up to run my tongue along that throbbing vein in his neck. A wild growl pierces the air. It almost takes me a few beats to realize it came from the man holding me. My brain kicks into gear when I feel the hard length in between his legs press against my stomach.

But he remains still. He just looks at me as if trying to figure out what to do with me.

I know he knows. Yet, I get the feeling he's restraining himself from taking me the way he wants … again.

Fuck it.

I take it upon myself to begin ripping and tugging at his belt buckle. His eyes grow wide. The expression only lasts a nanosecond before he wraps both of my wrists in one of his hands. He lifts my arms above my head.

"Stop," he says, but it comes out at a grunt.

"Stop what?" I ask in my most innocent voice.

"I'm trying to control myself, baby." There's a plea in his voice that I don't like.

I wiggle my body, trying to break free. His grip on my wrists tightens. Ironically that causes the wetness in my panties to increase.

"Kiss me, Diego," I say and tilt my chin up, giving him better access to my mouth.

His mouth is on mine in less than a second. He devours my mouth. His hands feel like a vice around my wrists. I don't try to break free from his hold. Instead, I raise my legs to plant my feet on the bed before lifting my hips.

Diego breaks off the kiss and hisses loudly. "Fuck," he groans.

His voice is so damn sexy when he's turned on. Hell, when he isn't turned on his voice is the only sound I could listen to day and night.

"Take me, Diego. Please," I beg, needing him more than ever for some reason. I can't explore my deeper feelings now. I just want this with him, right now.

I don't know if it's the tone of my voice that spurs him on or what, but before I know what's happening, Diego flips me over onto all fours.

My dress is unzipped and stripped from me before I can figure out what's happening.

"Ohh," I cry out when he buries his face in between my cheeks. I arch my back on instinct while Diego's hands move to my hips, gripping tightly. The liquid from my pussy begins to slide down the inside of my thighs.

I can't keep still. It feels too good. But when I try to move my hips, his hold on my waist tightens almost to the point of pain. I want him to hold tighter, to make it hurt, but he doesn't.

To encourage him, I push back against his face.

"More," I groan out. My throat is tight but I'm able to get the one word free.

His fingers dig into the skin of my hips. He pulls back but doesn't go far. I feel his warmth right behind me.

Smack!

The first slap against my ass stuns me. My body reacts before my mind as a shiver courses through me. The stickiness between my thighs increases.

Smack!

The second slap on the other side of my ass doesn't surprise me as much but it turns me on even more. I arch my back and peer over my shoulder at him.

"Face forward," he orders.

The command in his voice almost makes me come right there on the spot.

I raise an eyebrow and continue to stare at him, daring him.

He narrows his eyes, and I see a muscle in his jaw tick.

"What if I do—" I can't even get the last word of my question out before another swat lands on my clit this time.

My arms tremble, threatening to give out from the weight of all of the feelings coursing through my body.

Diego pushes himself in between my legs, spreading them wider to make room for him.

"You like me spanking you?" he asks as he covers my pussy with his palm. He can feel how wet I've become.

"Answer me!" he demands before smacking me again.

I can't answer because his next hit steals my breath.

"More," is all I can get out.

I grip the sheets tightly, almost pulling them from the bed. Every smack of his causes a wave of energy to crash through me, heightening my body's drive to come.

"Please," I call out.

"Please, what?"

"I need you inside of me," I tell him in between pants.

All kinds of relief fill me when I hear ruffling sounds behind me. I hope that means he's removing his clothes, but I don't dare turn around. The idea of him stopping for even a moment will cause me to pass out from pure agony.

"Is this what you wanted?" he asks before slamming himself inside of me.

I throw my head back while my mouth falls open. A silent scream emanates from me. I'm already half breathless. But when Diego's hand presses against the back of my head, forcing the top half of my body down against the bed, the rest of my air is stolen.

He's absolutely relentless as he plunges in and out of my sopping wetness. His hand moves to the back of my neck, holding me down as if I could move even if I wanted to.

I groan and bite the sheets. His free hand curls around my hip so tight that I know that I'll have his mark on me tomorrow morning. That knowledge alone causes me to grow wetter.

Or it could be the result of the way Diego's pounding my pussy relentlessly.

Either way, my toes curl on their own, and before I know it, a blinding orgasm rips through me. For a short while it feels as if my body is levitating from the bed. I don't feel anything beneath me. I'm wrapped up in the wave of this orgasm and Diego's all-encompassing want for me.

This has to be what pure bliss feels like.

When I can't take much more, the emotion begins to ebb. I'm slowly released from the web of bliss back onto the softness of the plush bed beneath my body.

I can't see anything. It takes almost a minute for me to realize that my eyes are closed. Slowly, I open them and meet Diego's dark glare staring down at me. His lips are twisted in worry.

"Are you okay?" he asks, his voice hoarse.

I'm on my back, the lower half of his body next to me while his top half hovers over me.

"I was rougher than I planned. I'm so—"

I raise up and cup the back of his head, bringing our lips to touch. I kiss the apology back down his throat. I can't bear to hear it. Not in this state.

I tell him with the kiss that there's nothing for him to apologize for.

"I need you again." I know he's up for it. I can feel his cock poking into the side of my thigh. I wonder if he even reached his climax.

"You're going to be sore in the morning," he says like that's a bad thing.

"So?" I run my fingers through the soft hairs of his beard.

A low growl starts in his throat. He doesn't move, though.

I move my hand to his hair and start twining one of his curls around my finger. The growl becomes louder. In seconds, he's climbing on top of me again.

My one hope is that he doesn't regret what we've done in the morning.

CHAPTER 26

Diego

"This is better than even I expected," our client, Ronald Johnson, says from his position at the far end of the boardroom table.

My team and I have just presented the plan we created for his commercial property. The building features all of the renewable energy features he wanted and more.

He glances at the presentation on the large screen behind me before asking, "And you're saying this can be up and running within the next twenty-four months?"

I nod. "That's the worst case scenario. We need your approval for a few more features. Once that's cleared, I will send these plans up to our guys in construction. We've already received the necessary permits."

"Wow." He claps his hands and grins as he looks around at his team. "These guys told me Townsend was the way to go. I shouldn't have waited this long to work with you. My family worked with the Cullen family for so long that I was too damned stubborn to break out from underneath them."

I thrust my fisted hand into my pocket to keep it hidden. The mention of the Cullen family reminds me of their piece of shit son, Monique's ex, and the way he hurt her.

The fact that he's dead doesn't dampen my desire to dig him up and crack his eye socket all over again. Even after all of these years my ire for that son of a bitch hasn't calmed.

A memory of my weekend with Monique flashes across my mind. Guilt weighs like a metal balloon in the pit of my stomach.

I was too rough with her.

The morning after our night out at the club I woke up to find bruises of my handprint along her hips. I wish I could say seeing that disgusted me, but the opposite is true. My cock grew rock hard at the sight.

I wanted to take her right then and there. Brutally.

But I held back. I forced myself to get up and take a cold shower.

I jerked off twice while in there to calm my dark urges.

"Get it done," Wilson says, clapping his hands together, which brings me back to the present.

"We need your signature on a few documents." I hand him some papers so we can get this shit over with. As much as I wanted this project to go through and to receive his approval, once we have it, my mind is already onto the next hurdle I need to tackle.

My piece of shit half-brother called me two days ago to have me meet him at his accounting office just outside of the city to discuss his father's money.

The jackass honestly thinks he has me by the balls. He's too fucking stupid to realize that showing up to Monique's gallery was him signing his own death certificate.

"You're in a rush," Uncle Joshua says as soon as I step out of my office.

I double check my watch. It's ten of six.

"The papers should be on your desk," I tell him.

His smile grows. "They are. Johnson had a huge grin on his face when he left."

Ronald Johnson and his team exited our office almost two hours ago.

"You did a hell of a job on that project. I knew making you the director was the right way to go."

I won't lie. It feels good to hear my uncle compliment my work. And more, to know he's not just blowing smoke up my ass. I did a hell of a job on this project. I can't wait until the construction of this design is completed. It's going to be a sight to fucking see.

"The Williamsport Sky will be painted with your designs." Monique's words from weeks ago come back to my mind.

I dip my head as a smile crests my lips.

"No wonder you're in such a rush to get out of here." Uncle Josh chuckles.

I give him a look.

"What's that look about? I know what that smile means. You think you're the only one who's in love?" He slaps my arm. "Some of us have been doing this for a while." He snaps at the same time he says, "Oh, that reminds me. Your Aunt Kay wanted to barbecue this weekend since the weather's going to be nice.

"She wanted to make sure I told you about it in person and she insisted that you bring Monique."

"I already said we'd be there in the family group chat," I remind him.

He rolls his eyes. "You know she doesn't keep up with that chat. She'll post a question and then won't check for weeks."

I chuckle, knowing it's true. Aunt Kayla's notorious for doing that.

"We'll be there, except we'll probably be late since we're going away this weekend."

This is the weekend that Monique is going to scout one of the last artists for her gallery at an art fair a few hours outside of Williamsport.

"I remember," he says. It doesn't surprise me. Uncle Josh has a mind like a steel trap. No wonder he's been able to run Townsend Real Estate for so long. "Enjoy your weekend away."

He looks me in the eye as he squeezes my shoulder.

"Great work." He holds up a hand. "Don't give me any shit about it being a group project. I know who works for me. And I know who stayed late nights and demanded more from their team when they weren't satisfied with the bare minimum."

He gives me a nod before sauntering off.

I watch him over my shoulder before striding to the door.

I have one more piece of business to take care of for the day before going home to see the love of my life.

* * *

"DIEGO, you made the right decision in coming," Gabriel Jr. says with a wide grin on his face as I enter the backroom of this accounting office.

I glance around and scowl at the big bastard standing in the corner. He's the same son of a bitch who was with Gabriel before. I have something for his ass, too.

Gabriel must've wizened up after our last meeting, though, because he's brought more reinforcements. There are two other security-guard looking jackasses in the room. One of them are seated directly next to Gabriel at the small, wooden table at the center of the room.

The other stands in the opposite corner behind me.

I glance back, meeting his eyes and scowling his way, too.

"It's a little crowded in here, isn't it?" I ask. "Your office isn't big enough for this many people," I mock as I glance around at our underwhelming surroundings.

Gabriel's office barely fits two people and the table where he's seated. The ceiling stained with old water marks and the flickering overhead lights tells how bad business is going.

"No wonder you're so hard up for the money."

He grunts and pounds on the table with his fist, but quickly calms himself when I glare down at him.

"The fact that *my* father left you even a dime of his money is bullshit. All you have to do to turn it over to me and Rodrigo—his real heirs—is sign on the dotted line."

He slides a folder with the documents inside.

From my standing position, I glance at the folder before my eyes go back to him.

"I thought your father's will was rock solid," I say. "How is this … whatever the fuck it is, supposed to override his will?"

I don't actually give a shit about the answer.

"What's the hesitation about?" he asks. "I thought you didn't want the money."

"I still don't," I reply. "What the hell is in those documents that overrides a dead man's will?"

Gabriel clicks his teeth, and I flex my hands to keep from ramming my fists down his throat. It's too early for that.

He pushes out a harsh breath. "If you must know," he says with a roll of his eyes, "I had my attorney do a work around. Instead of going through the courts to contest the will, which could take months or even years, I had a few friends of mine …"

He pauses and looks at the three other men in the room like they're his personal goon squad.

"Help that lawyer realize the error of his ways." He smiles triumphantly. "Thus, contesting the will isn't as much of a hassle and that document there states that you willingly give up the money and forfeit it to myself and Rodrigo. My father's *real* heirs."

He says that last part like it's supposed to sting or something. His father is not mine. I got the better end of the deal when my mother married Carter Townsend.

I look between him and the folder in front of me. Slowly, I lift the folder and open it to the documents inside.

"Do you have a pen? I forgot mine at the office," I lie.

Gabriel sits up straight in his chair. "I brought a special pen for this occasion." He holds up a red rollerball pen.

I instantly recognize the style and design.

"It's Montblanc. This was my father's," he says proudly. "This'll be the only time you'll ever use one of his pens. I thought it would be fitting to have you sign using this one, anyway," he continues to speak as he hands me the damn thing.

"How fitting," I respond, taking the pen from him.

I look from him to the papers in my left hand. "You remind me a lot of your father," I tell him.

His eyes squint as if deciphering what that's supposed to mean. I don't bother hiding the malice in my voice.

"He was a controlling, manipulative, and abusive son of a bitch. I see where you get it from."

Gabriel's eyes bulge, and I sense the shifting of the other three men in the room. All of my instincts tighten in response.

"I told you before that I planned to wipe my ass with this money." I meet Gabriel's hard stare. "Fuck you and him." I spit on the documents in my hand before tossing them aside.

Before Gabriel can even react, though, I flip the top off of the pen and grab one of his hands, yanking him across the table.

His scream of pain when I ram the tip of the pen into the fleshy part of his right palm, isn't enough to quell the rage that has been simmering inside of me ever since I saw him standing in Monique's art gallery.

Gabriel's screaming turns to a grunt of agony when my first punch cracks his jaw. The sound of the bones in his face breaking help to soothe the jagged edges of my ire. Sometime between the second and third punch I feel hands on me, but they don't stop me.

I'm somewhat aware of a breeze behind me. I know someone has come through the door that I recently entered. Yet, that knowledge doesn't stop me from beating the hell out of Gabriel Garcia Jr.

With every hit I remind him of why he should've kept his fucking distance. Money is one thing. Threatening the woman I've loved since before I knew what the hell love was is an entirely different situation.

"I will fucking kill you!" I yell, again hitting Gabriel.

"Son!"

I vaguely hear the word in my ear but it doesn't register.

"If you ever in your fucking life ..." I trail off because Gabriel's life won't last much longer. Hell, the way he's flopping around after each blow I send to his face, coupled with the blood covering it, I'm not entirely sure he's alive right now.

Does that stop me?

No.

The dark, uncontrollable rage that I've learned to suppress over the years has found its outlet.

"Son! Diego!" a deep, familiar voice calls.

I recognize the voice. The sound of comfort and love and everything a father is supposed to be.

"Son, you're going to kill him," it says. This time the statement is accompanied with a steel vice wrapping itself around my upper body.

The fire burning inside of me starts to diminish.

"It's okay," he says just like he did when I was a little boy and would get upset over something.

That's when I finally turn away from an unconscious Gabriel to meet the cerulean eyes of my father.

"Not here," is all he says.

Still breathing hard, I take a step back and stumble due to the way my body continues to tremble from the adrenaline rushing through it.

My father holds me upright.

"It's over. He won't hurt her," he assures.

I look over at Gabriel who's labored breathing lets me know he's still alive. But he's in no condition to hurt anything at this point.

"Our guys will take care of this mess," my father says. "Come on."

I barely register the guys from our family's security coming in and out of the room. I assume they've already taken care of the goon squad Gabriel had with him.

"I still don't know where Rodrigo is," I tell my father as we exit out of the back of the tiny office building.

He stops us in the middle of the parking lot behind the building. "We'll find him wherever he is," he replies, placing a hand on my shoulder. "Are you alright?" He looks down at my bruised knuckles.

I glance around, only seeing our security coming in and out of the shop. "Should we be out here?"

"There's no security cameras. Everything's been managed. No one will ever know you or I were here," he says with confidence.

My shoulders slump from the release of tension his response provides. I trust my father implicitly.

"Are you okay?" he asks again, this time clapping my face with his palm.

I ball and flex my hands. "I'm fine." I meet his eyes. "Sorry about that. I moved before I could ask him about Rodrigo. I know you told me to keep my hands off of him, but—"

He holds up his hands. A chuckle rushes out of his mouth.

After that day when Gabriel Jr. had the balls to pop up at Monique's gallery, I knew he was going to be an issue. Or should I say, I knew that I would need help getting rid of his body.

So, I went to the man I trust with my life.

My father.

We had a plan for how I was to get information out of Gabriel because we knew that he wasn't working alone. Rodrigo is a part of Gabriel Jr's bullshit somehow. Even if he hasn't shown his face yet.

"Did you honestly think I believed you when you said you'd keep your hands off of him until we arrived?" my father asks, still laughing. He shakes his head. "I knew as soon as you mentioned Monique's name he was as good as dead. You're lucky I gave you that five minutes alone with him."

His grin shrinks a smidge.

"You did enough damage in that amount of time." He looks back at the exit we just left.

"Not enough," I reply. "He's still breathing."

My father's hand on my shoulder tightens. "Not now. You have places to be. Don't you?"

I'm meeting Monique at her gallery so I can take her out to dinner. That thought reminds me to pull out my phone and check on her numbers. I exhale in relief at seeing she's in a safe range.

I send her a quick text to let her know I'm on my way. Then I follow it up with a reminder to make sure all of the doors of the gallery are locked and to not come out until I'm there to meet her.

I laugh when she immediately replies with an eye roll emoji followed by an emoji with its tongue sticking out.

I meet my father's smiling eyes.

"Thank you."

He grips both of my shoulders and looks me in the eyes. His expression changes to one of total seriousness.

"I want you to know something." His voice is thick in a way that tells me he's getting emotional. "You never needed to prove anything to me."

I dip my head, but his eyes chase mine, demanding without words that I continue to meet his stare.

"You've been my son since the day I met you. There's nothing you ever had to prove or accomplish to earn your last name."

Warm comfort starts in my chest and spreads throughout the rest of my body. Even though deep down, I always knew this, I never realized how much I needed to hear him say it.

"You're my son. Just as much as Sam and Taylor," he says of my younger brother and sister. He cups the back of my neck. "Don't ever forget that. You have a problem like this and you don't come to me immediately, I'm going to break my foot off in your ass."

I grin. "I don't need to involve you in every problem," I stubbornly reply.

He lightly punches my shoulder. "No, you have a whole fucking family who will go to war for and with you if we need." His voice loses its playfulness, letting me know he's serious. "The next time you wait to come to me, we're going to have a problem."

"Yes, sir."

He pats my neck a few times before stepping away. "Go home to your woman. Because I'm damn sure going home to mine. Oh, she told me to tell you to have your ass at your uncle and aunt's barbecue—"

"This weekend," I finish for him. "I know. I told Uncle Josh I'd be there. I remember."

He smiles and claps the side of my face before heading to his car. A beat later, I'm climbing into mine and heading to see the only person I want to see every night when I get home.

CHAPTER 27

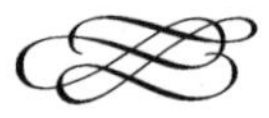

*M**onique***

I lay my head against the headrest and take in Diego's profile. His perfectly trimmed beard outlines his strong jaw to perfection. The muscles in my stomach tighten as I picture his beard wet from the moisture in between my legs.

My knees pull together from the sensations that start in my core. The movement catches his attention. From the driver's seat he glances over at me. A smirk tugs at his gorgeous lips.

He knows exactly what I'm thinking.

"It should be illegal," I say.

"What?"

"To be as fine as you are." I let out a sigh. I never missed how gorgeous my best friend is. It was just that before we crossed this line, I never felt comfortable saying it out loud. Not directly to him, at least.

"You think I'm fine?" he asks.

I swat his comment away. "Shut up."

He chuckles.

I allow my hungry gaze to drink him in without shame. My eyes trail down his face, over his broad shoulders, and down the length of his arm until I reach his hands on the steering wheel.

My lips fall into a frown at the sight of the bruises on his knuckles.

"What happened to the gloves I bought you?" I ask him.

He flexes his hand as he looks at it and then back at the road. A muscle in his jaw ticks.

We're on our way to the art fair in Blairwood, a small city about five hours from Williamsport.

"Tell me what really happened," I say with a gesture toward his hand.

"It's nothing." He adjusts himself in his seat. A dead giveaway.

"We don't keep secrets from one another, remember?" We've had that saying for years but I know the reality is there's a boatload of shit we haven't shared with one another.

"Secret keepers," I reiterate.

"Gabriel Garcia Jr.," he says.

I nod.

"You got into a fight with him?"

He snorts. "More like he walked into my fist a couple of times."

My stomach tightens from nervousness. A flash back to our junior years of college comes back to mind. I remind myself that this is not the same situation.

I won't push him on the details. Not this time.

"Is he taken care of?" I ask, needing to know at least that.

He glances my way and gives me a short nod.

I don't say anything else on the matter. Instead, I reach over and start playing with one of his curls. My mind drifts off to someplace else.

I start to think about our upcoming weekend. My priority for this weekend is making contact with a fabulous artist I found online. She only posted a handful of paintings on her social media page before suddenly deleting it.

However, a post from a few months ago mentioned that her work would be displayed at Blairwood's Art Fair. I'm banking on that to find her and convince her to let me showcase her paintings at my gallery.

I can't quite put it into words yet. I just know that her story will fit right in with the theme of my gallery.

"Baby, as much as I love it when you play with my hair ..." Diego says, yanking me out of my thoughts. He takes my hand from his hair and presses a kiss to my knuckles before settling my hand on his thigh. "I can't have you doing that while I'm trying to concentrate on driving safely."

A grin splits my lips. "And my hand on your thigh is safer?" I start to slide my hand toward his dick.

He grunts and wraps my hand in a vice grip, trapping it before I can reach the promised land.

"We have two more hours in this damn car. I have no problem pulling into the first hotel we find and tying you down to the bed until you beg me to let you up for air."

I slowly close my eyes and have to clench my teeth together to keep from asking him to do just that.

Then I recall his exact words. My eyes pop open as I ask, "Did you say tie me to the bed?"

His lips purse. "A figure of speech." His voice is thick.

I think it was more than a figure of speech on his part.

As much as I would love for him to do exactly what he said, I need to get to this art fair.

With reluctance, I pull my hand away. "Work then fun." I nod more to myself than to him.

"Good girl."

Why do those two words cause my nipples to harden? Again, I have to fight my own instincts not to go in the direction my body is leading me. I can't recall ever wanting a man as much as I want Diego. At all times.

It's probably because he's always been my safe space. My best friend. My protector even when I didn't ask him to be.

I love you.

Three short words that we've said to one another hundreds of times before. But this time would be different.

I'm *in love* with my best friend. That adds a whole other layer to those three beautiful words. Even though he's said them to me, I can't say those words to him.

This relationship was only supposed to be a short-term thing. I should've known better.

You're a burden. The thought flashes through my mind.

That reminder causes me to look at the bruises on his hand again. It occurs to me that whatever happened between Gabriel Jr. and Diego, he did it to protect me. Because Gabriel Jr. showing up at my gallery was an unveiled threat.

A lump forms in my throat at the reminder that I could, yet again, be the cause of strife in Diego's life.

I sit up straight in my seat and turn to look out of the passenger window.

"Are you hungry? It might be time for you to eat something," Diego says, concern in his voice.

Yet another reminder that he thinks he has to manage me. To take care of me because I'm too damn fragile.

"I have a granola bar," I answer.

Before I can dig in my bag, Diego pops his glove compartment open and pulls out two different kinds of granola bars.

"The peanut butter one is the best," he says with a smile.

Butterflies flutter in my belly at that look. But the wave of passion is stamped out by the guilt of feeling like he has to take care of me.

I hate the way memories of my ex-fiancé come to mind. The things that woman he was with that night at the Black Opal said.

What if Diego gets tired of taking care of me?

"I'll have what I brought with me." I pull a packet of gummy bears out of my bag before checking the numbers on my watch.

I don't look Diego's way as I tear the bag open and start eating. I know he must be wondering what that was about, but I can't explain it. I don't want him to think he has to constantly take care of me. That's not what this relationship is supposed to be about.

Though conversation about the art fair takes up the rest of our car ride, in the back of my mind, the fear of me being a burden and what that means for me and Diego continues to crowd my thoughts.

CHAPTER 28

Monique

"There are some amazing artists here," I tell Diego as we stroll the rows of artists showcasing their work.

He nods in agreement while eyeing a black and white portrait of a bird's eye view of Williamsport. The artist is a semi-famous photographer from our home city.

"Do you like that one?" I ask, coming up beside him.

With his gaze still on the photo, he wraps a long arm around me, pulling me into his side. The unease I felt in the car gets pushed aside by the feeling, though it doesn't entirely go away.

Maybe it never will.

"It's decent," he says.

I observe the photo and then give a quick shake of my head. "Not yet."

He peers down at me with a wrinkle in between his brows.

"That picture lacks your designs. Once your building designs are developed, I'll hire a photographer to take pictures of the new and improved Williamsport skyline. So you can hang it up in your home."

His eyes light up in a way that makes the butterflies in my belly start flapping. He leans down and presses a kiss to my lips. The feeling of his lips on mine linger even after he pulls away.

"Let's go find your artist."

I blink and shake my head, suddenly remembering what we're actually in town for.

"Melinda Blake," I say, naming the artist I'm looking for. "But her name's not on the listed artists."

Pursing his lips, Diego scans the list of artists on the fair's program that we grabbed on our way in.

"What about this one?" He points to a name that's just initials. "M.E.B. could stand for Melinda Blake."

"Contemporary," I read the short bio provided underneath the artist's name. "Let's give it a try."

We head toward the other side of the fair to find the row and table where M.E.B.'s work is displayed. My heart sinks as soon as I see a young man standing behind the table.

I start to tell Diego that this isn't her, but one of the paintings on display catches my eye. Picking up speed, I head straight for the table.

"Amazing Grace." I point at the beautiful image of a woman cloaked in a hoodie, half hiding her face as a bright spotlight shines down on her. "Who painted this?"

I know the painting.

The blond-haired guy behind the table blinks at me. He's young, probably early twenties. A quick scan of his hands tells me he's not the painter. Most of the painters here have paint-stained hands.

"I'm sorry?" he asks, taken off guard.

"Amazing Grace. That's the name of this painting, right?" I know it because it was one of the paintings I came across on Instagram by Melinda Blake.

"Yeah, that's right." He smiles but quickly stifles it. "How did you know?"

I observe the other paintings. Most show a young woman hiding her face in one way or another. They're hauntingly beautiful. However, none of them have names or titles displayed the way most other artists name their work.

Also, there's no signature on these paintings.

I turn to Diego, who's quietly observing me. "She painted these."

I look at the man behind the table. "Do you know Melinda Blake?"

His hazel eyes widen in surprise, I suspect. "How do you, um ..." His gaze drifts off to the side before he finally replies, "These are the works of M.E.B."

"Do those initials stand for Melinda Blake?"

He grows nervous as he glances between me and Diego.

"Did you steal this work from her?" I blurt out the question. Anger starts to rise inside of me at the idea of someone ripping such a talented artist off. How the hell did he get these paintings?

"What? No," he insists while waving his hands in front of him. "I would never steal from my sister—" He stops short.

"Your sister?" I pounce, moving closer to the table, almost getting in his face. "Is she Melinda Blake?"

Pressing his lips together, he looks over my shoulder.

"Your sister is extremely talented," Diego says. It's a simple statement but it seems to relax the guy ever so slightly.

His shoulders drop a little. His gaze turns to the paintings on the table.

"She's so freaking good," he says, sadness lacing his tone. "But she doesn't like coming to these types of things." Slowly, he looks back up at me. "She doesn't go out in public much. Something like this ..." he scans the open-air space with all its hundred if not thousands of people strolling around, "it's too much for her. But it's one of the biggest art fairs in our area. I told her she couldn't miss it."

He shrugs.

Relaxing a bit, I move back a little from the table, to give him room. There's a deep, resounding emotion in his tone that speaks to how much he cares for his sister. That instinct of mine, that is so keen when it comes to scouting out great art, piques. I believe even more now that Melinda Blake is perfect for my gallery.

"Melinda painted these, right?" I have to verify.

He nods. "How did you know that? Her full name, I mean?"

"Months ago, I came across her Instagram page. I probably spent a few hours looking at and analyzing the paintings there. I even bookmarked the page to reach out to her, but when I went back a few days later, the page was gone."

His eyes light up in surprise. "I created that page for her. It was only up for a few weeks. It got some good attention, but after a few art galleries reached out and wanted to meet Mel, she made me delete it," he explains.

"I've been searching for her work ever since then," I confess. "Her work is haunting in a way that you can't take your eyes off of it." As I say this, my gaze falls back to the painting of the young woman in the light.

I'm so tempted to buy it for myself. In fact, I'm surprised that no one has purchased it yet. When I say as much to the guy behind the table, he tells me that he's just arrived. Unlike many of the other artists, he hadn't posted images of the paintings on the fair's website beforehand.

"Lucky me," I say. "I want to feature your sister's work in my new art gallery." I get right to the point. "What's your name by the way?"

There's more hesitance on his part, but he finally tells us, "Ben Blake."

"Melinda's brother," I comment, taking in this new information.

He nods.

I glance over at Diego, who's watched the entire exchange mostly in silence. The pensive expression on his face tells me that though he's been quiet he's taking everything in.

"I'm opening a new art gallery in Williamsport." At the mention of my home city, Ben's eyes expand. "I would love to feature Melinda's work in my gallery. The opening is only a few weeks away."

I pause before making my next request.

"I know you said Melinda doesn't like meeting people or public events," before I can finish my request, Ben is shaking his head, yet I persist, "but I'd really love to at least meet her. Are you from around here?"

"No, she can't," he blurts out.

"Is she ill?" At this point, I know I'm being rude to press like this, but I feel it in my gut that this is too right to let slip through my fingers. "I'm sorry," I say. "It's not that I want to violate her privacy. As the owner, I need to verify each piece that I want to feature in my gallery. I like to meet the artists or at least make an effort to do so before I can approve of their work.

"Maybe I can at least talk to her. Could you give her a call?" I prod.

He looks uneasy, his eyes moving between me, Diego, and the paintings on the table. Yet, he doesn't want to turn me down. I can feel it. The fact that he set up an Instagram account to feature his sister's work, and came to this fair, shows how much he believes in her work.

"Just a phone call," I reiterate.

With a nod, he pulls out his cell phone. I watch as he dials his sister's number.

"Mel?" he says after a beat. "Um, there's someone who wants to talk to you." He thrusts the phone my way.

"Hello? Melinda Blake?"

There's a long pause on the other end.

But I hear her breathing.

"Yes?" Her voice is so low I barely hear it.

"My name is Monique Richmond. I'm an art curator and owner of a brand-new art gallery opening up in Williamsport. I love your paintings and would love the opportunity to discuss the possibility of featuring your work."

I can almost hear the 'no' before it comes out. Instead of letting her finish, I push on.

"Before you turn me down, please know that I can be persistent. I've seen your work. You have an amazing brother who obviously believes in your talent." I pause to look over at Ben.

He's grinning but dips his head in shyness.

"It's because of the Instagram page he created that I discovered you. I was mesmerized by your talent. I've spent months trying to find your work after the page was deleted. I remembered one of the captions mentioning that you would have a table at this year's fair."

"That was Ben's doing," she suddenly says.

I let out a small laugh. "I figured. Your work deserves an audience. They're truly amazing. I know this is a long shot, but would you mind meeting with me? I can come wherever you are."

I look over at Diego who has both eyebrows raised. He moves closer, his hand going to the small of my back. I want to lean into him and rest my head on his strong chest. But I don't.

"I promise I won't take up much of your time," I tell Melinda when there's no immediate answer. "While I'm sorry to make you uncomfortable, I can feel in my gut that your work would fit right in with my gallery. You're the type of artist I'm looking for."

She pushes out a breath, and I hold mine.

"There's a diner over on Riverdale Avenue. Do you know it?"

I pull the phone away from my ear. "A diner on Riverdale Avenue?" I say to Ben.

"Scotties," he replies.

When I peer at Diego, he's already got his phone in his hand, using his GPS app to search for the address.

"Got it. It's only ten minutes from here."

"I can meet you there in fifteen minutes," I tell Melinda.

"Um, I'll need twenty," she says with some hesitance.

"I'll be waiting."

As I hang up the phone, I feel like one of the final pieces of my dream becoming a reality is falling into place.

CHAPTER 29

Monique

"Um, Mel, doesn't really like to meet too many people at once," Ben says right before we enter the diner. He says it to me but his gaze skirts over to Diego before looking back at me.

"We'll meet you inside," I tell Ben.

When he leaves us to enter, I squeeze Diego's arm. "Thank you for coming with me."

He cups my cheek. "There's nothing to thank me for." His lips meet mine in a quick kiss, but I can feel every tender emotion in it. He moves to kiss my forehead.

"I'll take a seat in one of the back booths."

God, those three words are on the tip of my tongue. I want to say I can hardly believe I've fallen in love with my best friend but that's a lie. The truth is this type of love may have always been there in one form or another.

A few more weeks.

That's when my gallery opens. Also, the ending date of our *trial period* or whatever this is between us. I was so certain I could let him go after this. But Diego proves to be as amazing a lover as he is a friend.

With a sigh, I push those thoughts away and walk through the door he holds open for me.

I take a seat in the third booth next to the window. From where I sit, I can see Diego sitting at the far end of the diner at a small, round table with Ben.

"What can I get started for you?" the waitress asks.

"Just a coffee. Black," I tell her. "I'm waiting for someone."

She nods and disappears quickly. A few beats later, the bell over the door rings. I turn to find a medium height figure walking through the door. I say figure because at first, it's hard to tell if the person is a man or a woman.

They're wearing an oversized hoodie with the hood covering not only their head, but a large portion of their face as well.

"Mel?" Ben calls from the opposite end of the diner. He hurries toward the door.

My stomach rolls with anticipation. I watch the brother and sister whisper between one another. Melinda has her back to me, her hoodie still up.

A couple of minutes of watching them pass before Ben points toward me. Melinda turns my way, but her face is still obscured.

Ben nods my way before he slowly walks past. He's not only a proponent of his sister's talent but he's protective of her. I don't know their story, but I bet the two of them are lucky to have one another.

It makes me think of my younger siblings. I make a silent vow to show up more for both of them.

"Melinda?" I ask as she approaches my table.

The closer she gets, the more I see brown tendrils hanging over one side of her face. The hoodie falls back slightly but she doesn't push it all of the way down. Now, I can also see that she's wearing a pair of oversized sunglasses.

"Yeah," she answers in a paper-thin voice.

"Please, take a seat."

She pauses for a breath but eventually slides into the seat across from me. Her eyes are pinned to the glossed wooden table between us.

She doesn't say anything as she lets her pointer finger start tracing the lines of one of the cracks in the table.

I quickly spot the telltale paint stains on her fingers. Oddly, this brings me a little more comfort.

"Thank you for meeting with me."

The waitress interrupts whatever, if anything, Melinda is about to say. "One coffee, black." She slides my piping hot cup in front of me.

"Melinda, is that you?" the waitress asks, sounding slightly surprised.

"Yeah, Kathy. It's me." Melinda doesn't look up from the table or remove her sunglasses as she answers.

"I'm glad you got out today. It's not even Tuesday," she continues. "How about a cup on the house?" The waitress doesn't even wait for Melinda to respond. She heads behind the counter and pours a fresh cup for Melinda. A few beats later, she's sliding the cup in front of her.

Melinda barely responds but she does mumble a, "Thank you."

Once the waitress leaves us, I slide my coffee to the side and look across at her. I won't ask her to lower her hoodie or even look at me. I get the feeling she's doing the best she can.

"Melinda, I promised not to take up much of your time, so I'll jump right in," I explain. "You're a rare talent. I was hooked from the moment I saw your first painting. The painting Ben had at the art fair, Amazing Grace, man ..." I push out a breath as I try to find the words to describe my feelings when I first saw the painting.

"It was majestic, mysterious, haunting, and alluring," I say. "And that only describes the tip of the iceberg as far as the depths of feelings your work elicits."

"You're good with words," she mumbles. She plays with her fingers, picking at her already short nails.

"No," I counter. "You're good with a paintbrush and canvas."

At that her hands still.

"You think so?" she asks. Like she's never been complimented on her work before.

That can't be the case.

"Melinda, you have to know how talented you are. Don't you?"

Her hand goes to the hair hanging over the left side of her face. She tousles it a little but doesn't tuck it behind her ear.

"I don't know anything." She goes back to picking at her fingernails.

"I don't think that's true."

For the first time, she lifts her head. She must realize what she does because she quickly dips her attention back to the table.

"Maybe you don't believe what you've heard so far," I continue. "I know Ben believes in your talent."

She glances over her shoulder at Ben before dropping her head again.

"The comments on your Instagram posts before it was deleted also prove how talented you are. Also, the fact that I'm sitting here across from you."

I pull out my phone and open its gallery. I slide it across the table so she can see the pictures. One by one I flip through pictures of me at my former job in New York.

"I worked with some of the best curators around. Not to toot my own horn, but I was damned good at my job as well. I've seen talent. I know the difference between someone just running a brush across a canvas and someone who's working from an internal passion that can't be seen but can damn sure be felt.

"I feel that when I look at your work, Melinda."

I hedge, knowing what I say next could make her stand up and run right out of this diner.

"I also know when someone's hiding. Running from their own destiny."

She completely stills across the table.

"You don't know me," she says, her voice sounding a little stronger but still low.

"No." I shake my head. "But I don't need to know you to know that you were born to be an artist. Whatever's stopping you from reaching your full potential, is something you have to push through."

I stop as I tuck my bottom lip between my teeth. Those words felt like they came from a deeper place inside of me. As if they aren't only meant for Melinda.

Shaking the thought loose, I focus on the woman across from me.

"Why are you opening your gallery in Williamsport? If you're so successful and so good at this? Artists must come a dime a dozen in New York. Why are you doing this here?"

I open my mouth to tell her the truth. That the start-up costs in New York were too high and that I couldn't get a loan or a grant and I didn't want to burden my family with asking them for money.

But what I say instead is, "Williamsport is my home. It's where I was born and raised." Without thinking about it, I look over Melinda's shoulder. My eyes lock with Diego's.

He gives me a reassuring smile, and my whole heart melts.

"It's where my heart is," I tell Melinda without taking my gaze off of Diego.

That is the actual truth. I always wanted to start my gallery in Williamsport. Somewhere along the line I lost sight of that vision. I spent so many years running that I convinced myself, I wanted a different dream.

"Home," Melinda repeats.

I hear yearning in that one word.

"Where's your home, Melinda?"

Without hesitation, she answers, "The canvas."

Her answer draws a smile out of me.

"Let me bring your home to my gallery."

Slowly, she lifts her head. The oversized sunglasses and hair hanging over the left side of her face obscure me from seeing her completely.

I can't see but I think she's looking me directly in the eyes. Assessing me.

With a slowness that reveals she's questioning her own movements, Melinda reaches her hands towards her sunglasses. She pauses for a beat.

Then, with deliberate action, she removes the sunglasses from her face. When she pushes her hair behind her left ear, I see it.

The entire left side of her face is scarred over. Rough, red skin covers the entire half of her face. If I had to guess, I would say they're a result of third- or fourth-degree burns. My stomach tightens from the unimaginable pain Melinda must've endured from whatever happened to cause this.

"Is this the face you want to represent your gallery?" she asks, cynicism peppering every word.

"Yes."

I supposed she wasn't expecting such a fervent yes.

Melinda's eyes narrow, assessing me.

I glance down at my left arm, and without thinking, I remove my arm from the blazer I'm wearing and roll up my short sleeve to show her the monitor on my arm.

"I've been wearing this thing in one form or another since I was ten years old," I confess. "I got it after a trip to the ER because I neglected to take my insulin with me to school because some of my classmates made fun of me," I tell her.

She looks from my arm to my eyes. The skepticism is still evident in her eyes, but it's dimmed slightly.

"I'm not comparing what it is you've been through to my living with type 1 diabetes. All I'm explaining is that I know what it's like—even a little bit—to be othered. To feel different from everyone around you. And to not have a meaningful outlet to share that with anyone."

Melinda slowly nods as she slides her sunglasses back over her eyes. I don't take it as her pulling away from me. It's more like she's not used to being in public for too long without her disguise.

I get it.

We all wear masks in one form or another.

"I won't ask you to do anything you aren't comfortable with. My gallery will feature women who have something to say through their art. But for one reason or another the world has shut them down. At my gallery, your voice will speak loud and clear. Through the canvas."

I can't see them, but I feel Melinda's eyes reaching out to mine. "What's the name of your gallery?"

A smile crests on my lips. This is the first time I'm revealing the name of my gallery to anyone.

"Stolen Voices," I reply, satisfaction filling my heart.

CHAPTER 30

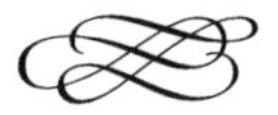

Monique

"Are you sure you're feeling alright?" Diego asks with a crease in between his brows. I know why he's asking. My blood sugar numbers have been wonky this morning. Even after I've eaten my numbers are lower than normal.

However, I feel fine, and for now, I'm not going to stress too heavily about it.

"I'm great," I say with excitement. "Melinda has agreed to let Stolen Voices feature her work. We're going to visit some more wonderful artists at the fair today. And I get to spend the rest of the weekend with you."

I press a finger into his chest and run it up to his chin. A small chill runs through me from seeing how Diego's eyes darken.

He drops his head and presses a kiss to my lips. "You'll tell me if you weren't feeling well, right?"

I press my lips together. That slight disdain for my own ailment and the way it invades even my most peaceful moments prickles at the edges of my mind. I do my best to ignore it.

"You will be the first person I tell if I start feeling off," I tell him. "Let's go," I say with urgency, in part just to change the conversation.

We're meeting Melinda and Ben at the diner again so I can see a few more of her paintings.

After that, the plan is to spend the day at the art fair. There will be more artists today since it's Saturday and I can't wait to see them all. With Melinda, all of my slots for opening night featured artists are filled, but I can always find artists for the future.

"Art awaits!" I say with a little twirl as I head to the door of our hotel suite. Diego went above and beyond the room, of course. When I told him as much, all he did was kiss me breathless and tell me that he wanted an even better room but this was the best suite available within a ten-mile radius of the art fair.

He chuckles as he follows me out of the room. We spend the first hour of the day with Ben and Melinda at a local park since Melinda didn't want to go to the fair. Melinda warms up to me, but she keeps her face hidden whenever Diego is near. Only once he and Ben go off on a separate trail does she lower her hoodie.

Little by little, I find out that a fire, when Melinda was ten years old and she was home alone with Ben, caused her scars. Right before we leave, Ben pulls me aside and reveals that Melinda got the scars after she ran back into their home when she realized he hadn't made it out.

He was only five years old at the time. She was able to get him out right before a piece of the roof collapsed on top of her.

"I wouldn't be here if it weren't for her," he tells me with emotion welling up in his eyes. "Our parents …" He trails off and shakes his head. "Drugs and their fucked-up relationship meant more to them than we ever did. She's all I have."

I return the squeeze on his arm. "I'll take care of her," I say just above a whisper. "I promise."

He nods before heading in the direction of the car they share.

I watch as they pull out of the parking lot and drive away. Diego's right by my side, his hand moving to the small of my back.

"She's trusting me with the one thing in her life she has," I tell him, not knowing what else to say.

I feel his lips on my temple. "She couldn't trust a better person." He says the words with such confidence that I have no choice but to believe I'm going to pull this off.

"You need to eat," he says, that telltale concern in his eyes. As if to prove his point, he holds up his phone, showing me the readout of my numbers.

They're even more off than when we left the hotel about ninety minutes ago. Worry starts to build in my chest because I've been down this road countless times. So many times I don't want to think about it.

"I may need to do an adjustment," I tell Diego, trying to infuse my voice with nonchalance. "I'll eat something from the food I brought and then we can wait fifteen minutes or so. I'm sure it'll be fine after that."

The look he gives me isn't one of reassurance that I wanted. Concern is etched in his forehead. "Why don't you eat something from the diner? It's close by. I can call ahead and order you some of their oatmeal or a side of eggs and multigrain bread with some orange juice."

"That's way too much," I insist as he starts to lead me to his car.

"You'll have your pick of what to eat. What you don't finish, I will," he says like it's not a big deal.

He picks up his phone and puts a rush order on the meal at the diner. We're only about a ten-minute drive from it. We make it there in just over five. Our food arrives at our table as soon as we take a seat in the booth.

I weigh out the appropriate amount of carbs on my traveling food scale and proceed to eat my toasted bread with some butter and drink the fresh squeezed orange juice.

We make small talk as we wait fifteen minutes or so before checking my numbers again. A part of me wants to scream about how much I hate things like this. When I make plans for my day, or my life in general, and this uncontrollable part of my life rears its ugly head, it can put the brakes on all of my plans.

But I'm determined not to let my illness stand in my way today. I want to get to see more artists at the fair.

"We're good to go," I tell Diego. I thrust my wrist with my watch on it in his face so he can see that my numbers have gone back up to the safe zone.

He nods, eyeing the numbers. Minutes later we're on our way. Unfortunately, I notice my glucose numbers start to drop again. Not quickly but they shouldn't be moving so much when I've just eaten.

"What's wrong?" Diego asks, glancing over at me.

I hadn't even said anything. "How do you do that?" I ask. "I haven't spoken a word."

"The corners of your lips curled downward a little and you're biting the inside of your cheek. You do that when you're worried. That or you play in my hair," he finishes.

I look down at my hands because I have them clasped to keep from reaching over to play in his hair. I thought that was my only giveaway. But he knows me too damn well.

"I'm fine," I say, but he gives me a look. "My glucose dropped a couple of points but I'm still in the safe zone." I rush to say that last part.

His hands tighten on the steering wheel. "How are you feeling?"

Instead of my immediate reaction to tell him that I'm fine, I take a beat to assess how I'm feeling. Am I feeling woozy, sluggish, or otherwise out of it?

No. On all fronts.

I do feel a little low on energy, but after a somewhat long travel day yesterday, accompanied by the excitement of the fair and meeting with Melinda to finally acquire my final artist for my gallery, that's to be expected.

"I feel okay," I answer with honesty.

He glances over me and looks me over, taking his own inventory.

"I'm fine for now. Let's go to the fair. We don't have to stay that long, and I've brought plenty of things with me to eat and extra insulin." I pat the bag sitting on my lap for emphasis.

"We'll be doing a lot of walking around at the fair. Are you sure—"

"I'm fine," I say a little more forcefully than intended. "Sorry. I promise to tell you if I feel off. Please, let's go to the fair."

When he finally nods, I release a breath in relief. While I am a little concerned as well, I don't want to put this off.

"It'll be okay," I tell him. But I'm certain we both know it's to assure me more than him.

* * *

Diego

I keep a close eye on Monique as she talks with one of the artists at today's fair. The woman's paintings are appealing enough, but I've barely been able to keep my attention on anything except for Monique.

Her and my phone. Her numbers keep dipping.

In the two hours we've been at the fair, she's had to drink one of the cartons of orange juice, and then have a half of one of the granola bars she brought with her. Even though she's not hungry at all. When she eats her numbers rise again, but within a short amount of time they take another dip.

This isn't usual. I know it and so does she. Though I can see her trying to downplay it and keep a straight face. I don't know if it's for me or for her. I want to tell her she doesn't need to be strong for me.

It's my job to be strong for her.

But I don't want to take away from the happiness she's having meeting the artists and looking over their works. Under different circumstances, I'd be right there with her.

However, her well-being takes precedence over everything.

My instinct tells me to take another look at my phone. Her numbers have dropped even more. I don't know what's happening but I don't like it.

"Hey," I say, placing my hand on the small of her back. "I think you need to sit down for a bit. You might need to do an adjustment," I say low so she's the only one who hears me. "Are you sure you're feeling okay?"

She nods. "Yeah, but my numbers ..." She doesn't finish the sentence, but I already know what she's thinking.

The device that helps to keep her alive tells her that something inside of her body is off. The machine is reliable ninety-nine percent of the time. This could be that one percent where it's off.

Yet, I'm not willing to take that chance, not with her.

"Listen, I know you're going to hate me for saying this, but may we need to leave early. Tomorrow's the last day of the fair. We can come back in the morning before we head home."

She scans the area surrounding us. There are rows and rows of artists. Many of whom she hasn't gotten a chance to see yet.

"Not all of them will be here tomorrow," she tells me.

I manage to control my voice as much as possible when I reply, "Anyone worth visiting you will come across tomorrow or some other time. Right now, we have to take care of you."

I don't wait for her to reply. Taking her hand in mine, I start to lead us toward the parking lot and back to the car. It's a twenty-minute drive from the fair to our hotel.

Before we leave, I hand her one of the cartons of orange juice. She drinks it with an almost tortured look on her face.

I take her hand in mine and kiss her palm. We wait for fifteen minutes, and then do an injection instead of opting for one of the granola bars I keep on hand in my glove compartment.

I've made sure to bring enough food to keep on hand for her to eat a proper meal in case we need it. She eats some multigrain crackers and cheese with a side of sliced vegetables as her meal.

"Okay," she says after she swallows the last bite.

By the time we get back to the hotel, her numbers look strange. Though she's recently done an injection, her insulin levels are dropping.

"Sit down," I insist when Monique starts pacing our suite.

She keeps telling me that she feels fine. Slightly off, but nothing serious. Nothing that would warrant the readout of her insulin numbers.

"Maybe I did the injection wrong," she says, a note of worry lacing her voice.

When the monitor's alarm starts to go off on both Monique's watch and my phone, my heart begins to beat out of my damn chest.

It's the signal that her insulin numbers are dangerously low. Even after another injection of insulin, her numbers continue to drop.

"It's time to go to the hospital," I finally say.

Monique's shoulders slump. The tears in her eyes tear at my soul. She parts her lips, and instinctively, I know it's going to be to tell me that she doesn't feel that sick. I'm aware that she knows her body better than I do but those numbers scare the hell out of me.

Even if I have to carry her kicking and screaming, she's going to the hospital.

"It's been hours," I say, cutting off whatever she's about to say. "You've done all that you can, and it's not working," I tell her this at the same time I call for an ambulance. It will be quicker than driving. Plus, if something happens, the paramedics are better equipped to handle it than I would be.

I also call the front desk of the hotel to alert them of the situation. Within a minute, there's a hotel employee in our suite assisting us. While Monique continues to tell me she doesn't feel that ill, I know it's more for me than it is for her.

I can see the fear in her eyes.

"It's going to be fine," I tell her as the medics load her onto the gurney.

I hate how fucking helpless I feel in this moment. My sole purpose is to protect her, but I can't. Not when I don't even know what the problem is. And not when the threat is from her own body.

The only thing I can do is hold her hand. Even as the paramedics insist that I need to back away from her so they can do their job, I stay close.

"I'm going with you," I tell one of the medics when he tries to close the ambulance's doors in my face. Like hell is she going anywhere by herself.

All I can think about is how she's putting on a brave face for me. I know she is. The smile on her face doesn't reach those beautiful brown eyes that I love staring into. The dimple that pops out when she smiles for me is nowhere to be found.

"I can't believe this is happening again," she says, looking at me as we ride to the hospital. "I've done everything right. I eat when I'm supposed to and don't when I'm not. I keep a close eye on my numbers and still ..." She presses her head back against the gurney.

"This isn't your fault," I tell her. "You know that. We're going to find out what's wrong and get it fixed. We'll be back at the hotel before morning," I assure.

I don't know if what I'm telling her is true. Yet when she looks at me with that uncertainty and doubt in her eyes, my entire being wants nothing more than to reassure that everything will be okay.

It takes only a handful of minutes for us to arrive at the hospital.

"Sir, you're going to have to remain out here," the ER doctor says, extending his arm as if he intends to stop me from following the love of my life.

"Like hell," I respond between clenched teeth.

"You can't—"

"Can he come?" Monique asks, lifting her head to see me. "Please?" she begs the doctor.

The sound of her begging causes me to clench my hands into fists.

I look over at the doctor. "My name is Diego Townsend," I place emphasis on my last name. "My grandfather, Robert Townsend, is friends with Scott Wolfe who's on the board of directors of this hospital. I don't mind giving Scott a call to ask him if it's okay if I can accompany my wife throughout her stay."

I stare him in the eye and wait for his response. The entire time I have to remind myself that he's the doctor whose job it is to take care of Monique. He won't be able to do that if I break his fucking nose.

I'll keep my hands off of him but I'm not above throwing the weight of my last name around. Not when it comes to her.

"O-Okay, Mr. Townsend," he says, his tone sounding vastly different than it did a minute ago.

"Diego is fine," I tell him. "Just take care of my wife." I don't even think twice about calling Monique my wife. Sometime along the last few months I silently made the decision that she's mine forever.

Hell, I probably knew this all along. This was my intention with the deal we made. I never had any plans to give her up after three months.

"Let's run some tests," the doctor says. He runs down a litany of tests to the nurse to start running on Monique after checking the stats that the paramedics give him.

Monique is rolled into a separate room in the emergency department. We're secluded from the main area and there's no waiting involved, as they start running tests on her immediately.

"Can you tell me when your symptoms started?" the doctor asks Monique.

"Her numbers were slightly low when we woke up around seven this morning," I answer.

They both look over at me.

The doctor looks like he wants to tell me that he wasn't talking to me, but when I narrow my eyes at him, he closes his mouth. He writes something on Monique's chart.

"He's right," Monique starts to say.

We go through the usual rigamarole of checking all of her stats. A slight sense of relief courses through me when I see that her stats are stable for now. The doctor tells Monique the tests that he's going to run for her.

She starts to name them before he's even finished.

"Been through this before?" he asks.

My top lip curls in anger. What the hell does he think? She's only lived with this illness for most of her life.

"Once or twice," Monique replies gracefully.

I glare at his back as he exits the room. Then I pull out my cell phone.

"Who are you calling?" She asks.

"Scott Wolfe, he can get a better doctor out here within the hour. Then we—"

"Hang up the phone," she says.

I don't.

"I'm serious," she insists.

The phone continues to ring in my ear.

"We don't need Mr. Wolfe or anyone else from the board of directors to get involved. I'm sure Dr. Grieves is a perfectly competent physician."

I narrow my eyes. "We can always get a second opinion." That's when Scott Wolfe's voicemail kicks in.

Monique narrows her eyes at me.

I turn away from her as I leave a voicemail for Wolfe, letting him know to call me back ASAP.

"It's Saturday. He's probably enjoying the day with his family or something," Monique declares.

I shrug. "And? It's just a few phone calls he needs to make."

She snorts. "Yeah, now it's a phone call. But in a few minutes, I bet you'll be on the phone with your grandfather and have your entire family raising hell to get the best endocrinologist in the state on their way over here."

"That's not a bad idea—"

"Don't you dare."

She stretches out her hand as if she's reaching for my phone. I'm not close enough for her to reach, but I don't want her to strain herself, so I step closer. I let her take my cell from my hand. She puts it in the hand farther from me and slips it under her left hip as if hiding it.

"Sit." She points to the chair beside the bed. "I've been through this before. Now, it's a waiting game," she says, staring up at the ceiling.

I'm left with nothing to do but to take the seat by her bedside.

She's right. Now we wait to find the answers.

CHAPTER 31

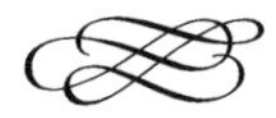

Monique

I put on a brave face for Diego but inside I'm a trembling mess. I hate hospitals. I know they're supposed to be a place of healing. Where sick people come to get better.

That's what my mom would tell me when I was a kid. However, I'm old enough now to know that there are quite a few people who enter those doors and don't make it out alive.

"Stop thinking like that." Diego's stern voice pulls me out of those dark thoughts.

I stare at him. "You're not a mind reader. You don't know what I'm thinking."

He gives me a smirk. One that sends butterflies in my belly fluttering. "This little crease in your forehead ..." he says at the same time his thumb lightly traces the very crease he's talking about.

I smile from his soft touch as I turn my head his way.

"Says it all," he finishes. "You get it whenever you're concentrating on a difficult problem. Or when you have bad news and you're trying to figure out how to say it."

"When have I ever given you bad news?" The question spills out of me without thinking.

"The day you told me you were moving to New York. At our spot." His voice is low, but I hear him loud and clear. He moves his hand to my hair, stroking the top of my head in a way that lulls the fear raging inside of me.

"We were standing in my favorite place in the world, and all I could think about was how my life was turning upside down," he confesses.

A lump in my throat forms. It's painful to look him in the eye. It's as if he's reliving that moment all over again.

"I planned to tell you how much I loved you that day."

At that, I sit up, but he presses a hand against my shoulder, pushing me back against the bed.

"You what?" I ask.

He nods slowly. "I've loved you for as long as I can remember. For years, I thought it was only the type of love a friend feels for his best friend. Even when my family and almost everyone around us were trying to tell us it was more than friendship, I ignored them."

He takes my hand in his. "It wasn't until after that situation in college with your ex that I realized the truth. What I feel for you is much deeper than friendship. I was going to tell you then. But ..."

But I told him I wasn't coming back to Williamsport. He doesn't need to finish his sentence.

"I knew it was my fault."

That's the comment that makes me stop in my tracks. "What?"

His gaze meets mine. "I was the reason you weren't coming back. I made everything worse for you when I attacked that fucker." He shakes his head, dropping his eyes to the bed. "My rage, I couldn't control it. Not after seeing those bruises he left on you. My temper put you in a terrible position."

"No," I say, adamantly.

When his eyes balloon, I realize my tone must've been sharper than I intended. But I don't care. I can't let him continue to believe that lie.

"Is that what you think? That it was your fault why I chose to not move back home after college?"

He tucks his lower lip in between his teeth, his jaw going rigid. "Not what I believe. It's what I know for certain."

"You're wrong." I push his hand away when he tries to stop me from sitting up. "Listen to me right now," I say with urgency. "You were never responsible for my decision to stay away." I swallow the emotion welling up in my throat. "I told you the reason I decided to move away."

"But—"

"But nothing." I cup his beautiful face between my hands, forcing him to look at me. "Listen to me. If anything, you were the main reason making the decision to move to New York broke my heart into a million pieces."

I've never confessed to anyone what I'm about to say, but it feels right to say all of this to him. The main person who matters the most in all of this.

"I knew what happened back in college was my fault. Don't," I warn when he tries to protest. "I brought that scumbag into my life, and I knew he was a jerk yet I defended him over and over. No, what he did to me wasn't my fault, but ..." I can't quite find the words to make him understand that I know I made decisions in my life that weren't the best for me.

"He was what I believed I deserved at the time. Learning the truth about my biological father ... it changed something inside of me. Something that's taken a long time to fix."

Despite growing up with a loving mother and the best stepfather a person could ask for—who, for all intents and purposes, *is* my father —knowing that I am the product of something horrific, isn't easy to live with.

"Then you lost the job position you had been looking forward to because of what happened. On top of that, you got into legal troubles and then no other architecture firm that you were interested in would hire you. I knew it was all because of me," I explain.

"I never blamed you for any of that. I never would."

I laugh, though there are tears in my eyes. "I know. That's what made it worse." I laugh again, not even understanding what's so funny.

Maybe it's the expression on his face. There's absolutely no anger or heat.

Just pure, unfiltered love that he's no longer hiding.

Looking at him in his face like this, the way he refuses to look away or hide his emotion, makes me realize just how much and for how long he's been holding back.

It's overwhelming.

"Maybe if you had gotten angry with me it would've been easier to handle," I tell him. "But you didn't. I knew you never would. You'd never say *I told you so* or anything like that. Yet, your world was turned upside down because of me. Then you refused to go to work for Townsend Industries like everyone expected."

"I wanted to make it on my own, first," he says.

I nod. "I know. And I felt like it was me who stood in the way of you being able to do that. I can't explain it, exactly." I release his face and lay back against the bed.

I stare up at the ceiling because it's easier than looking him in the face. Not when he's staring at me with such love and adoration. It's hard to believe I'm deserving of that much love, although I want to reach for it so damn bad.

"Diego, please," I start. "If there's one thing you believe in this world, please make it the knowledge that it's not your fault that I moved away. Your temper never, not once, frightened me. I know without a doubt in my mind that you would never hurt me."

I turn my head to face him.

"You never had to convince me to love you," I say, referring to the words he said the night of Kyle's wedding. "There isn't a day since we met at nine years old that I haven't loved you." I turn and look him in the eye.

"There isn't anywhere else in this world that I feel the safest than in your arms."

I reach my hand up to cup his cheek and run my fingers through his beard.

"I love you," he says.

"I love you, too," I whisper because even though I mean it with my entire heart and soul, there's still fear.

But the smile that spreads over his face dulls the ache of fear in my chest. It leads me to start to believe that all of our years of separation were worth it. Just to see that expression.

"I—" My next sentence is cut off when the doctor reenters, reminding me of where we are.

For a few minutes I forgot that I was in a hospital bed, waiting to find out what's wrong with me this time. What a wonderful few minutes it was. That I could pretend to be just a woman finally confessing to her best friend how deeply in love with him she is.

Except reality comes spiraling back down. It's more than that. I'm more than that.

I'm me, the human form of a black cat, confessing her love to the man who would do anything to protect her.

It seems like any girl's dream.

The truth is, though, I don't want to become a burden to my best friend. The man I love. I don't want him to have to always be the one to look over me and after me. What if he gets tired of it? What if I become too much of a strain on him?

I know Diego, he wouldn't say anything. He would keep it to himself because he believes it's his duty. But I don't want to become a duty to him. Like I am right now.

Right as I have that thought, the door of my hospital room swings open and in walks a nurse to assist the doctor. The files in her hand are a reminder of exactly where we are. The hospital because of my illness that, at times, likes to rage out of control. No matter what I do.

Diego is immediately on his feet. The way he's staring the doctor down makes him lean away. There he is again, fully in protective mode.

"What's wrong?" he instantly asks.

The doctor looks between me and Diego until deciding to focus his eyes on me. There's a plea in them.

"Diego," I call, reaching my hand out for his.

He doesn't hesitate to take it. I give it a squeeze, urging him to relax a little. He exhales and rolls his shoulders, doing his best to answer my plea. My heart almost explodes in my chest with how much I love him.

How I could've ever thought of marrying someone else is beyond me. A trick my mind played on me when I truly believed I couldn't have Diego.

But can you have him now? the small voice in the back of my mind asks.

"All of the tests we've run so far have come back and there isn't anything that's concerning in them," the doctor continues, bringing my attention back to him.

What he's saying is a relief but not completely. The last time I was in the hospital I was there with my fiancé, but by the time I left our relationship was over. He couldn't handle the ups and downs of life with me.

I know Diego would never leave me like that. But can I subject him to this life with me? Will I have to push him away to keep from bringing him down?

Like I already did once in his life?

CHAPTER 32

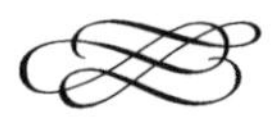

Diego

"Are you sure you slept enough? I could've extended our stay at the hotel," I tell Monique as I glance over at the passenger seat.

We're on our way back to Williamsport from the art fair. Monique and I were at the hospital until a little after midnight. Though the first round of tests came back positive, I wasn't satisfied. I asked—maybe demanded—the doctor run the tests again just to make sure everything was stable.

We still aren't sure what it was that made her numbers drop so rapidly yesterday. Monique suspects it was a recent update in the monitor she uses. She's already ordered a new one that should arrive today.

Though everything's been stable since we left the hospital, I've felt an unease from her that I'm not sure is a result of yesterday's medical emergency or something else. She's been quiet since we started driving a couple of hours ago.

"I know you don't like to sleep in cars," I say, "but maybe you should try. We have a few more hours before we arrive back home.

And we're expected at Aunt Kayla and Uncle Josh's place for their barbecue. But I can cancel that if you want," I quickly add.

"No way." Monique shakes her head adamantly. "Our families will be there. They'll ask questions if we don't show up. Aunt Kayla texted me twice this weekend to make sure we were still going."

I grind my teeth together. Monique hasn't told her parents or family about our trip to the ER. She begged me not to call them or tell my family. Because our families are so close, if mine found out there's no way her mother and father wouldn't know about it.

I let out a sigh that I can't hold in.

"Babe, it's not a big deal to tell our families what happened. They'd want to know."

"I know," she turns to me. "We can later. I just don't want them to worry. You know how my parents can be. Since all of the tests came back positive and my numbers have been stable for hours now, I just don't want to add to anyone's stress."

"What stress?" I ask. "Caring about you? You know your family, and mine," I add, "would be more stressed over the fact of finding out that you were in the hospital and they didn't know about it."

"It was only a few hours. I can tell them later when I see them. Let's just get home, go to the barbecue, and have a good time. Plus, I get to share that I finally have all of my artists chosen for opening night."

She smiles over at me, and for the first time today, it's genuine. I reach over and take her hand into mine, kissing the back of her palm.

"It's going to be amazing."

"Thank you. I explode with anticipation just to see all of their beautiful paintings hanging on the walls of my gallery."

"Stolen Voices," I say, repeating the name of her art gallery.

She squeezes my hand. "What do you think of the name?"

"It's perfect."

Her smile grows as if my answer was exactly what she needed to hear.

"I have something to show you," I say, glancing over at her with one hand on the steering wheel and the other firmly wrapped around her hand.

"What is it?"

"A surprise," I say.

"I like surprises." She squirms in her seat, her smile growing. The uneasy silence that was present a few minutes ago evaporates as Monique attempts to guess what the surprise is.

I laugh at every guess. She's terribly impatient even though, unlike most people, she likes surprises.

"Where are we going?" she asks with a lifted eyebrow, an hour later when I take the exit before the usual one that will take us directly to Williamsport.

"A shortcut."

She narrows her eyes suspiciously, her lips twisting to the side in that cute way of hers. I tighten my hold on the steering wheel to keep from pulling over and taking her right here and now.

It's been days since I was inside of her. While I didn't even think of it while we were so concerned about her health, knowing she's okay and having her this close reignites that need.

"It's not that far out of the way," I tell her but it's more for myself.

A few minutes later, I take a right, and Monique gasps. I know she's realized where we're headed.

"Is it still here?" she asks.

"We're going to see."

Minutes later, we come to a gravel road that leads to a field. In the distance, I start to make out a beat-up, old barn.

Our spot.

"It's still there," she says happily.

As we get closer, though, our joy is slightly tamped out from the fence that surrounds the property. There are multiple "keep out" signs on the fence.

"Let's stop here," she suggests when we reach right outside of the gate.

I park the car and tell her to stay inside while I make sure we're the only ones out here. This place, the spot we found so many years ago, has been abandoned for years, but the fence is new. Which could mean new property owners who have some sort of security system involved.

When it looks like we're all clear, I open the door for her.

"I can't believe the building's still standing," Monique says as I help her out of the car. Leaning back against the door, she stares at the building.

"I haven't been back here since that day," I confess.

She looks up at me, sadness invading her eyes. "I visited a few years after I moved to New York. I couldn't go inside." She shrugs. "It didn't feel right being here without you."

I watch her as she closes her eyes and squeezes my hand. My gaze drops to the serene smile that covers her lips and I can't help but stare.

"Do you hear it?" she asks with eyes still closed.

I don't have to ask what because I already know. She's referring to the river that runs behind the barn.

"I've always loved the sound of running water," she says like I don't know. "Reminds me of peace."

I intertwine my fingers with hers, making her eyes pop open.

I crush our lips together, not meaning to kiss her so aggressively but the emotions running through me won't let me go easy.

Monique moans into the kiss.

It takes all of the strength in my body but I pull away, placing my forehead against hers.

"This wasn't the surprise," I admit. "Not entirely."

I wave my head toward the back of my car at the same time I open the back of the SUV. Pulling down the back hatch, I display the picnic basket I hid there. I managed to fill it with sandwiches, fruit, an array of cheeses and crackers, and a bottle of champagne.

"When did you do all of this?" she asks as I lay out the red and white checkered picnic blanket over the back area of my car for us to sit.

"I brought some of the stuff with us. Then this morning when I went to pick up breakfast, I bought the rest."

I lift her to sit before I take my place next to her.

"Champagne?" She holds up the bottle.

"I wanted the chance to celebrate with you before anyone else."

"I haven't done anything yet."

"Like hell you haven't," I retort. "You have eight artists with at least twenty paintings between all of them to display. Your gallery is less than two weeks away from opening and it's going to be huge."

"Oh, that reminds me," she says with a smirk. "I still need a date for the opening." She lifts an eyebrow.

I pull her hand between my hands. "I know you didn't think there was any way in hell I would let anyone else be on your arm for your big night, did you?"

I lean in and steal another kiss.

"Oh." I pull away from the kiss before I lose myself.

Monique groans. "You can't keep kissing me and then stopping," she complains.

"One more surprise, baby."

Out of the bottom of the picnic basket, I pull out a box. "I hope you don't mind too much, but I took the liberty of having some business cards made for you."

"Really?" Her eyebrows lift in anticipation.

I nod. "You were having trouble coming up with a design, so I just drew something I thought you would like. Then when you revealed the name of the gallery this weekend, I called a nearby printshop to have them do a rush order. It's just a mockup but I ordered a few hundred in case you liked them. If not, you can toss them. No worries."

"I'm going to love them," she says at the same time she claps her hands in anticipation. "You're so good at this stuff. I didn't want to ask but let me see," she squeals.

Monique doesn't even wait for me to hand her the box. She rips it from my hands and opens it to pull out one of the cards.

It's a sleek black card with gold trim in the shape of falling leaves. At the center in block letters is the name "Stolen Voices Gallery." Underneath the gallery's name is the website, telephone number, and email address.

"I went with the leaf trim since fall is your favorite season." She loves that time of year.

"It's perfect," she says in an almost whisper.

"You're perfect." It's cheesy as fuck but it's the only thing I can think of to say.

Yet, when she looks up at me there are tears in her eyes. In part because of gratitude. I can see that plainly. But there's something else. That lingering doubt that I remember from last night while we were in the hospital. I hate that it's returned to her eyes, threatening to overshadow this moment.

I don't want it to come between us. Not when this moment is meant as a celebration. I quickly pull out my phone and do a quick check of her numbers to make sure she doesn't need to eat.

When I see they're fine, I toss my phone aside and take her face in between my hands. I kiss her senselessly. I kiss to push away any and all lingering doubt that I saw in her eyes.

I've known for years that this chemistry, this love between us, was enough to last a lifetime and beyond. Anything else is just bullshit.

Monique moans into the kiss, and my dick responds by pressing against the zipper of my jeans. We're going to be late to my aunt's barbecue. Hell, that's if we make it at all.

"I want you," Monique says against my lips.

Yup. That's the moment I know we're definitely not going to make it.

I make quick work of putting the food back in the basket to move it out of our way.

Next to go is Monique's shirt followed by her bra. I bring her to straddle my lap, placing her breasts in the perfect position for me to suck. Her hands move to the back of my head.

My cock becomes even more demanding. Monique's hands in my hair have always been an aphrodisiac. Long before I even knew what the fuck that word meant.

I circle her nipple with my tongue until it becomes nice and rigid. Then I move to the next one, alternating between her two globes.

"Diego." When she starts to pant my name, I can't wait much

longer. It's either that or coming in my jeans like a fucking sixteen-year-old boy.

I work to strip us both of our clothing before laying her on her back. With a firm hold on her ass, I push inside of her with all of the impatience rushing through me. The gasp she lets out calls to that deep darkness inside of me.

Images of me with my hands around her neck, squeezing and letting go while I fuck her into her orgasm, stream through my mind.

I tighten my hands on her thighs, doing my best not to be too rough with her. I force myself to remember she was just in the hospital less than twenty-four hours ago. Even though it turned out to be nothing, she was still there.

I can't let the monster that rages inside of me out. Not in front of her.

I keep chanting that to myself until Monique surprises me. She reaches for one of my hands and brings it to her neck.

"This is what you want to do, right?" she asks, breathlessly.

"Mon—"

"Do it," she says with an eagerness I think I might be dreaming up.

"You're …" I trail off because I don't know what to say. She's not sick. Not exactly. She's not fragile. She's the strongest person I know.

But I don't want to hurt her.

"Do it," she urges again.

My fingers move on their own accord. When I clamp down around her neck, she presses her head against the bed of my SUV, giving me more of her neck to hold onto. She arches her back into me.

"Take me, Diego."

Fuck!

How the hell am I supposed to turn that down? I'm strong, but dammit if she doesn't make me weak as fuck.

So, I do what she asks. What we both want, apparently. I tighten my hand around her throat. It's tentative at first. But Monique looks me directly in the eye, silently imploring me to take her in the savage way my body desperately craves.

I try to hold on to the control I've worked to carefully control over the years. I do my best to remind myself that my main objective is to take care of her, to be her protector. Not the boogeyman she fears or tries to get away from.

But when I look into her eyes, I can see the love and trust shining back at me. I see how much she craves this side of me as well. Something inside of me snaps. Before I know what I'm doing, I have my hand on my belt buckle, undoing it.

In a handful of seconds, I've removed my belt and my hand from her neck so that I can tie it around both of her wrists. After trapping her arms above her head, I pull my fully erect cock out and use my knee to spread her legs wide for me. As I move in between her parted legs, I return my hand to her neck.

"Take me, Diego," she pants.

I don't need more urging. Any control I thought I had is obliterated by those three words.

Crushing my mouth to hers, I savagely kiss the life out of her while squeezing her neck in a rhythm that feels natural. I impale myself inside of her, causing her to let out a silent scream.

"You feel so fucking good," I growl into her ear.

She tries to raise her hands to my face but I hold them down.

"Don't move," I order. "You only get to move when I say so."

Her lips part but I tighten my hold around her neck. The next sound to come out of that beautiful mouth of hers is a purring cry. I already feel her legs tremble around me.

"Don't come until I tell you to."

"I-I-I can't," she cries out when I loosen my hold on her neck.

"You can't?" I ask at the same time I pull completely out of her.

A whining moan escapes her lips.

"Die—"

I don't give her time to finish my name before I flip her onto all fours. Her hands still above her head, I push her face down against the blanket and make her back arch for me.

She's so fucking wet, that I easily slide inside of her from behind. Her entire body shivers. I want to hold out for as long as possible. For the both of us to hold out for as long as we can.

I don't ever want this feeling of being bare inside of her to go away. To know that right now, she's mine. Only mine. The way it was always supposed to be.

"Mine!" I ground out with each stroke of my cock. "Say it, Monique. Tell me you're mine," I demand.

When she doesn't respond fast enough, I pull her up, bringing her back against my front. I move my hand around to the front of her neck before biting her earlobe.

"Say it."

"Y-Yours," she pants out. "I'm yours."

The words are the soft balm my soul needed.

"Then come on my dick like a good girl."

I use my free hand to massage her clit. It doesn't take much before she's exploding around me. I feel every contraction of her pussy muscles as her orgasm tears through her. Monique lets her head fall against my shoulder while she continues to call out my name.

It's music to my fucking ears.

How I went so many years without claiming her is a fucking wonder to me. That shit is over now, though.

"I love you, too," she says, breathlessly. More than feeling her orgasm around me, those three words set off the explosion of my own orgasm.

She's mine. And I'm never giving her up.

CHAPTER 33

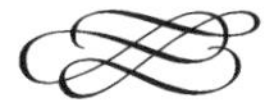

Monique

"I can't believe this is happening," I say to Kennedy Townsend with the biggest grin on my face. We're standing in the middle of my gallery.

The opening is in less than a week. Aside from some minor touches, it's complete. I'm waiting until the last moment to hang all of the paintings on the walls. However, I know where every single painting is going. My only question is which piece to make the centerpiece. The main painting that visitors will see first as they enter the gallery on opening night.

I'm having trouble deciding between one of Melinda Blake's works and one of Jocelyn Burke's grandmother's paintings.

"What you've created in a few short months is amazing," Kennedy says as she looks around. "You're going to have a full house on opening night. Theo Bilkens, the head of the Arts & Culture department of my paper, has already name dropped your gallery in a few writeups," she tells me.

Kennedy is an investigative reporter for a major imprint based here in Williamsport. The fact that the name of my gallery has even made it into the rooms of her paper's headquarters is music to my ears.

I grin. "I'm sure your cousin had something to do with that," I tell her. I don't know how, but I'm sure Diego went and name dropped my gallery to someone to get the array of bloggers and social commentators that have already RSVP'd for opening night.

"What? Is that a bad thing?" Ken asks.

With a shake of my head, I answer, "Not at all." I shrug. "A few months ago, I might have said that it was too much and that I didn't want to ask anyone for help, but ..." I trail off.

"Times have changed," Kennedy finishes for me with a lifted eyebrow.

"Something like that."

"Good." She claps her hands together. "Because it's taken you two long enough to get your shit together."

"Excuse—"

My question is interrupted by a knock on the door. Assuming it's one of the renovation workers coming to finish up a few minor details, I yell for them to come in.

Yet, my eyebrows lift in surprise when I see who it is.

"Ms. McClure," I say, recognizing the woman immediately. Even though it's been months since we last spoke, I still think about Ms. McClure and her grandson, Mikey, often. And, of course, Sharia.

I make my way over to hold the door open for her to pass through.

"Hi!" a little voice says, catching my attention.

Standing next to Ms. McClure is two-year-old Mikey, Sharia's son.

"Mikey," I say with a smile.

He lights up in that way toddlers do when you know their name without having to ask them.

"I hope this isn't a bad time," Ms. McClure says.

"No, I was just waiting on some workers to stop by to finish up on some minor details. You caught me at a great time."

I turn to look over my shoulder. Stretching out my arm, I say, "This is Kennedy Townsend. A good family friend."

"Hello," Kennedy waves.

"If you're busy, we can come back," Ms. McClure says.

"No, please. I actually have a meeting that I need to get to," Kennedy tells her. "Mo, I'll stop by a little later on for dinner," she tells me, reminding me of our plans to get dinner.

When she leaves, I place my full attention on Ms. McClure and Mikey. "Are you visiting Williamsport for vacation?"

The older woman shakes her head. "Not exactly." She does a three-hundred-and-sixty-degree inspection of my gallery. I watch her as she takes in every detail, her eyes stopping on the name tags of the artists posted along the walls.

"You have quite a few artists lined up," she says as she moves farther into the gallery.

Mikey follows her, looking up at the walls, too.

"Yes," I reply. "So far, I have nine artists lined up for our grand opening. There are a few others that I am lining up to feature in the coming months."

It feels good to say that out loud. I'm reminded of how despondent I felt the last time I spoke with her, months ago. So much has changed since then, in such a short amount of time.

I open my mouth to ask her how things are going with the gallery she chose in New York for Sharia's paintings, but I'm cut off.

"Would you like one more?" Ms. McClure asks.

"Excuse me?"

"Grandma, I'm hungry," Mikey whines, interrupting us.

Ms. McClure frowns. "I was in such a rush from the hotel, I forgot his cereal."

"I have some granola bars and fruit snacks. Does he like chocolate chips?" I ask.

When she nods, I move to my bag behind the counter and pull out two granola bars, one chocolate chip and the other peanut butter.

"Which one, buddy?" I ask, squatting in front of Mikey.

He chooses the peanut butter one, and I open it before handing it to him.

"Sit down and eat so you don't get crumbs all over Ms. Richmond's gallery," his grandmother tells him.

I smile as I watch him do as he's told. Ms. McClure hands him a small tablet that he takes with one hand. Without question, he places the granola bar down in the seat next to him so that he can turn on his favorite game before he goes back to eating.

"I don't like to give him too much screen time, but that thing comes in handy sometimes," Ms. McClure says with a laugh. "Anyway, like I said, I don't want to take up too much of your time. It's just that I received a call a couple of months ago from Diego Townsend."

My eyes go wide. I already know what she's going to say before she tells me the rest of the story, but I let her keep talking.

"He said he heard about how wonderful my daughter's art is from you."

I nod, not knowing what to say just yet.

"He explained how hard you were working here in Williamsport to open the art gallery. Then he went on to tell me how he felt like he knew Sharia just because of the way you talked about her and her art."

She pauses and smiles at me.

"Listening to him talk about my baby ..." Tears fill her eyes as she shakes her head.

I squeeze her arm consolingly.

"I miss her." She lets out a humorless laugh. "So many of my days now are filled with caring for Mikey, making sure the bills get paid, and work. Most of the time, I don't have time to feel just how much I miss her."

"Ms. McClure—"

She waves a hand in the air. "I'm sorry, I didn't come here for you to see me cry." She meets my eyes. "I came here because of the way that young man talked about my daughter. Because of you. He believed Sharia's art can and will still touch many others. Her story will live on. He believes it because of the way you talked about it. And then he asked me if I could believe it too."

She wipes a tear away.

"I came here today to ask you if you would do the honor of featuring my baby's art in your gallery?"

Her question steals my breath.

It's not just that I'm gaining an artist that I've wanted to have in my gallery for months. It's the fact that Ms. McClure, this mother, trusts me with the legacy of her deceased daughter.

"The honor, Ms. McClure, would be all mine," I reply.

I don't know who moves first. Maybe we both moved at the same time. All I know is that somehow, we ended up in one another's arms. Tears streamed down our faces. Mixed in with the mourning and sadness, though, was hope. And love and adoration.

As if he didn't want to be left out of the moment, a tiny arm makes its way around my leg. I glance down to see Mikey hugging both his grandmother and me. There's an ear-to-ear grin on his face.

I don't know if he truly understands what's happening, but it feels like his mother is in this room with us. Something falls into place and the doubts that have been running through my mind for months regarding my gallery are erased.

My mind goes to one person. The one person who knows me inside and out. Who holds all of my secrets and who has proven time and time again that he is my soulmate.

After we dry our tears and go over the logistics of featuring Sharia's work in my gallery, I give Ms. McClure and Mikey a hug before they leave for the day.

I immediately call Diego. It goes to voicemail since he's still at work.

"I love you. Thank you," I say before hanging up. I follow up the message with a picture I take of one of Sharia's paintings that Ms. McClure brought with her.

All of the pieces of my gallery are finally in place. Now all that is left is for my personal life to follow suit.

CHAPTER 34

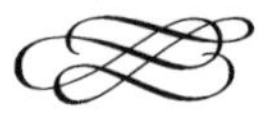

Monique

"He called her to convince her to feature her daughter's work at your gallery?" Kennedy asks after I tell her the story about Ms. McClure and what happened earlier.

We're heading out of the Mexican restaurant where we just had dinner. It's only a few blocks from my gallery, so we decided to leave our cars parked there.

"Yes," I say with a smile. I haven't stopped walking on cloud nine since Ms. McClure and Mikey left my gallery hours ago. The only thing that would make this moment more perfect is if Diego didn't have a work dinner. I wouldn't mind spending all night showing him how thankful I am.

He's meeting me at my gallery after his dinner though.

Kennedy sighs. "I'm not one for love, but what you two have is special."

I stop short directly in front of the doors of my gallery. "What do you mean you're not one for love?"

Though unconventional, Kennedy's parents have been married for years and she grew up in a family full of love. I should know, our families are deeply intertwined. One in the same, practically.

If anyone is to believe in love, I would think it would be her.

She shrugs like it's no big deal. "I mean it sounds cute and all, but with my luck I'd probably come across a guy like my dad or my brother or something. Someone who's all controlling and possessive." She rolls her eyes. "No thank you."

That reminds me of that night at the Black Opal. When she looked as if she'd seen a ghost.

"Hey, do you know the owner of The Black Opal?"

Her eyes squint as if she's trying to place what I'm referring to. She quickly shakes her head vigorously. But the movement looks too exaggerated. "No."

It's as if she's trying to convince herself more than me.

"Anyway, I assume once your gallery is open and operating smoothly, I should expect a wedding invitation in the mail soon, huh?"

She changes the subject back to me, but I let it slide.

"Why would you think that?"

I unlock the door and let us both inside of my gallery before flicking on the lights.

"Uh, because if you haven't noticed my cousin is head over heels in love with you. And, you know, part of my job as an investigative reporter is to be observant of my surroundings. He's not the only one who's in love."

My stomach tingles from the butterflies that just thinking about Diego produces. She's right.

But marriage?

"No, he's not," I admit. "Marriage is a huge commitment, though, and I don't know if either one of us are ready for that."

"Why not?" a deep voice asks behind me.

I spin around to see Diego filling up the entrance of my gallery.

"Hey, cousin," Kennedy says into the thickness of the tension his question and my ensuing silence brought on.

He nods at Kennedy.

"Yup, that's my cue to go." Kennedy pulls me into a quick hug and mumbles, "Good luck," in my ear.

I don't have time to ask what she means before she's headed for the door.

"Text me when you get in so I know you—"

"Got home safe," Kennedy says, finishing the rest of Diego's comment to her. "Yeah, sure."

As soon as the door closes behind her, Diego spins back to face me, pinning me with his gaze.

"How was your meeting? Did everything get signed?" I ask.

"Fine. What is it that you're unsure of?" he asks, getting straight to the point.

"Diego, don't you think this is a discussion for another time?"

"No." His answer is firm. "Let's have it now."

"Seriously? It's the end of the day and neither one of us is in a position to talk about this right now."

"My position is solid. Because I know exactly what I want and who I want it with," he retorts. His voice is so unyielding and solid that I don't doubt he knows precisely what he wants.

"What is it you want?" I ask.

"A life with you. I want you to be my wife. Mother of my children if we choose to have them. To grow old together. To—"

"Take care of me when I get sick? Or to constantly hold back your deepest urges because you're terrified of hurting me?" I throw back at him.

His head juts backward and he narrows his eyes on me.

"That's what a life with me would be," I tell him, finally verbalizing my fears. "You know that, right? Taking care of me if and when I get sick. Or you holding back because I'm too damn fragile."

"Fragile?" he interjects.

"Yes. Soft, weak. Whatever. That's really what you think, isn't it? That I need rescuing."

"How could you even believe that's what I think?" he replies back with something filling his eyes. Something I can't identify.

"Isn't it? That's why you hold back when we make love," I finally say what I've been thinking for months. "You're scared of hurting me somehow, but ..." I blow out a deep breath, feeling the tightness in my chest that starts to take hold of me.

"But what?" he questions when I don't say anything more.

"You're hurting yourself," I confess. "You can't be your full self with me because you're too frightened that I can't handle it. Whatever it is. You think you have to constantly look out for and take care of me. That's how I become a burden to you. Just like I was to my ex. I—"

"Don't compare me to that son of a bitch," he says through gritted teeth.

The anger in his eyes doesn't frighten me. There's never been a moment that I've ever had fear of Diego. Even when I've seen his eyes darken with rage and anonymity for someone else, it never repelled me.

But it did reveal how far he would go to protect me, which is what has the potential to get him into trouble.

"You'll cut off parts of yourself to protect me. While I love you for it, I don't want to be your burden," I tell him. "Not like I was to my ex and not like I was to my mother."

"You've never been a burden"

"I have!" I yell back because I can't help the emotions that spill out of me at revealing my deepest, darkest fear. "My entire life is a burden to everyone I love. My own mother ... she shouldn't have had me. My very life started out of something horrible. How can I be anything more than a burden?"

A single tear falls from my eye as I state my biggest fear out loud.

"Baby," Diego starts for me, but we both stop when a gasp followed by the sound of shattering glass sounds behind me.

I jump and spin to face the door. Standing there with mouth ajar and tears filling her eyes is my mother.

A second ago, I didn't think I could feel any worse. Yet, seeing the profound sadness in her eyes makes my legs go weak. I might have fallen if it weren't for Diego's hand at the small of my back. He's at my side in the blink of an eye.

"Monique," my mother says just above a whisper. Her voice is thin, as if the emotion in it weighs too heavily for it to fully come out.

"I—" I don't finish because I don't even know what it is I want to say. My gaze drops to the ground, and I see the shattered pieces of a glass vase that held a beautiful bouquet of rainbow roses.

I continue to stare at the broken glass, puddle of water, and flowers on the floor because I can't meet my mother's eyes. The shame welling up inside of me is too much.

"No," Diego says when my mother starts to bend down to pick up the pieces of the vase. "Let me," he says in a voice that breaks my heart.

It reminds me of how utterly and deeply in love with him I am. As I watch him grab a broom and go about the work of cleaning up the flowers, I avoid my mother's eyes. Neither one of us speak. I don't know what to say, but I can tell by the glances I sneak over at her, she wants to say something.

"I'll take the broken glass out to the garbage," Diego breaks the silence, the dustpan in his hand, holding the broken vase.

"Diego," my mother stops him with an arm, "can you give me and Monique some time to ourselves?"

I swallow the lump that's formed in my throat. He looks back at me. I can see by the look in his eyes he doesn't want to leave. But he turns and gives my mother a small smile.

"Of course." His voice sounds so strained. "I think you two need to talk." He says the words to my mother but stares at me as he says them.

He moves to me, placing a kiss on my cheek. When he pulls back, our eyes meet. The look in his eyes silently conveys me that our talk isn't over either.

I watch him exit the door, as does my mother, before she turns back to face me. The tears still in her eyes make it difficult to breathe.

The quiet that fills the space between us goes on for an indeterminate amount of time.

My mother is the first one to break the silence.

"You know the truth," she says.

CHAPTER 35

Monique

Those four words cause the band around my heart to tighten. I don't have to ask what truth she's referring to. It's the same truth that's been a wedge in our relationship since I was seventeen years old and found out how I was conceived.

I nod because words refuse to form in my mouth.

"How long?"

I pinch my lips together. I know the answer is going to hurt her, but lying at this point is futile.

"Nana told me right before she passed," I tell her.

My mother's hand covers her mouth but not before I see the quivering of her bottom lip.

"Monique," she moves closer, taking my arms in her hands, "that was ..."

"Eleven years ago," I finish for her.

"You've known the truth this long and never said anything."

I dip my head because the tear that rushes down her cheek feels like a knife slicing its way into my heart. "How could I?"

The question comes out as a whisper.

Her hands tighten around my arms as if she's trying to make sure that I don't get away.

"I can't believe ..." She pushes out a harsh breath. "You had to deal with that all alone."

"I had to deal with it?" My voice is borderline incredulous. "You were the one who was ..." I can't say the words. Not to her. "And then you got kicked out of your home because of me and then I got sick."

A full body tremble runs through me. I tried to bury these thoughts and feelings for so many years. It seems like my entire body is reacting to having them resurface and shown to the light.

"It's my fault your life was so hard for so long," I say. "If you hadn't had me, everything would've been easier for y—"

"Don't you dare," she says with a sharpness that stuns me.

I blink before meeting her gaze. Though the tears remain, her stare is focused as she meets my eyes.

"Do not finish that sentence."

I swallow the words that remain on my tongue.

"Nothing that happened to me is your fault. Do you hear me?" For emphasis, she shakes me by the arms.

"You did nothing, *nothing* wrong." Her voice is so fierce. I'm not sure I've ever heard this tone from her.

Still, the wall and insecurity that's built up in my heart over the years is thick. Hard to penetrate.

"I know I didn't purposefully cause those things to happen to you," I start. "But the truth of the matter is most of it wouldn't have happened if I weren't a part of your life. You wouldn't have gotten kicked out of your home so young. You wouldn't have had to work those terrible jobs to support me, or put off your dream of going to college. Or worked a career that you didn't love just to be able to afford insurance to take care of me."

"And yet, I wouldn't have had you," she says with so much sincerity I can feel the crack in that wall around my heart growing deeper.

She steps closer. "What happened to me ..." She pauses, and I watch as she visibly swallows. "The way you were conceived is an experience no one should have to go through."

More tears stream down my cheeks.

"I wouldn't wish it on my worst enemy. But," she stops and places her hand underneath my chin, making me pick my head up to meet her eyes, "that night, aside from being the beginning of your life, has *nothing* to do with you."

I can barely see her through the haze of tears in my eyes. "But ... how could you not hate me? After that and everything else that happened because of me, how could you not hate me just a little?"

It's a question I've wondered about for years. My mother is the most loving person I've ever known. She deserves the entire world. The idea of someone hurting her and me having that person's blood running through my veins sickens me.

"Hate you?" she asks as if it's a totally foreign concept. "I could never."

I believe her but I still don't understand.

"How could you not, though?"

She moves her hands to my cheeks and wipes my tears away with her thumbs. "This is why you've been so distant for years." I hear the realization in her voice. "Is this why you moved to New York?"

I look past her shoulder. "Part of it. I didn't want you to have to worry about me anymore."

To my surprise, she smiles and shakes her head. "That's not possible. You're my daughter. My first born. It was me and you for almost the first ten years of your life. Since the day you were born, a piece of me has been living out in the world. I'll always worry about you. Not because of some obligation or ... what did you just call yourself? A burden," she answers.

"You were never a burden. Not once did I think of you as a chore. You are my baby girl."

Though it's wobbly because we're both crying at this point, her smile reminds me of the one in the picture from the photo album. The one of her in the hospital bed after just having me. She was looking down at me like I was the most precious thing in the world.

I close my eyes, and all of the occasions throughout my life in which I've seen that same expression on my mother's face come back to mind.

The day of my kindergarten graduation.

When I got my driver's license.

My first job.

Every time I brought home an A on a paper or straight A's on my report card.

My high school and college graduations.

And my favorite times …

Whenever I walked in the house or a room and she saw me. As if she was just happy to see me, not because I did something special. Just because I existed. She loved me.

I still remember the moments I overheard her crying over unpaid bills or worrying about the cost of medical expenses. Those moments are overshadowed, however, by the love I've always experienced.

"You know," my mother continues, causing me to open my eyes to look at her again.

I wipe the tears away to see her clearly.

"You're the reason I ever met your dad." Her smile grows at the mention of my stepdad. "Without you, your brother and sister wouldn't exist. And I wouldn't have met your Aunt Kayla."

I wrinkle my forehead in confusion.

"You're the reason I sought out a doctor's office that had a naturopath. I read somewhere that some patients with diabetes were helped by working with a naturopath as well as their regular medical doctors. I wanted to get you the best care. That's how I found the office where Kayla used to work."

My aunt is a naturopath, who, for many years, worked alongside MDs to treat patients together. Now, she works full-time for the community center she started with her sisters and mother-in-law.

"Kayla and I became friends, and through your uncle, Joshua, is how I met your dad. So, if you want to blame yourself for anything in my life, you can take responsibility for quadrupling the amount of love I have in my life today."

I don't know why, but that's the moment that I break out into a full body sob. The truth of how deep and profound my pain around all of this ran never occurred to me. I had just been masking and doing my best to bury this guilt and shame I felt for so many years. I thought I'd managed to become numb to it.

Yet, the tears I shed as my mom holds me, rocking me back and forth just like she did when I was a little girl, tells the story.

"It's okay," she murmurs in my ear. "Let it out."

"I can't believe you knew all this time," my mother says as we slowly pull apart.

The lump that was in my throat seems to have dissolved with the numerous tears I shed.

"I'm sorry," I whisper as I wipe away the remaining tears.

"You have nothing to be sorry about. I just wish you would've come and talked to me."

I shrug at the same time her hands slide down my arms, coming to rest around my hands.

"I didn't know how," I admit. Honestly, how was I supposed to go to my mother with that information? "I believed what you told me as a kid. Then Nana let it slip what that group you used to go to was for. I asked her about it, and she admitted what my ..." I pause because I refuse to call that man my father.

"What *he* did, and that I ..." My lip quivers and I find it too difficult to let those words fall from my lips. Not to her.

"I can't believe she told you," my mother says, the first hint of irritation rising in her tone.

I know her dismay isn't directed at me. She and my great-grandmother had a complicated relationship. I didn't know the woman who raised my mother for the first decade of my life.

"Please don't be mad at Nana," I say. "It was in the last few months of her life. I don't even think she meant to tell me the truth, but she was on so many meds and you know how she used to say things she didn't mean or realize."

My mom squeezes my hands and nods, understanding.

"Damon was right." She pushes out a breath. "He told me a long time ago that secrets have a way of coming out."

"He knows?" I don't know why that surprises me. For some reason, I assumed that my mother kept the truth from me, she must've kept it away from him as well.

She nods. "There isn't anything that your father doesn't know about me. And vice versa. On this I wish I had followed his advice. Maybe you wouldn't have stayed away from us for so long. And you wouldn't feel like you're a burden to anyone. Especially the man you love."

She gives me an expectant look.

My heart muscles tighten because I know she's referring to Diego.

"Do you want to talk about what I walked in on tonight?"

I squeeze my eyes closed because I've kept so many of my feelings to myself for so long it's almost painful to tell my truth out loud. But if there's anyone who I can talk to about this, it's probably my mom.

"I love him," I say.

She lets out a laugh. "Baby, I might be oblivious to a lot of things, but you being in love with Diego Townsend has never been one of them."

She intertwines her arm in mine and leads us over to the receptionist area where there are chairs for us to sit. She picks up one of the roses that Diego placed on the counter.

"I brought these because I wanted to congratulate you on your opening before the big day. Just you and me."

She hands me the rose. I bring it to my nose and sniff. I've always loved the smell of flowers.

"He's serious about wanting to marry me," I say as I lower the rose to my lap. I decide to skip over the fact that our relationship was supposed to have a three-month expiration date.

"That was inevitable." She says it so casually that it surprises me a little. Another laugh spills from her. The sound of it warms my heart. I've always loved hearing my mom's laugh.

Despite the whirlwind of emotions swirling around inside of me, I feel lighter somehow. Like the fact that she knows I know the truth, coupled with the cry I just had, lifted something from my soul.

"Baby, he's a Townsend. If there's one thing I know about the men in his family, is that they don't hesitate when they've made the decision to go after the woman they love. Your father may not be a Townsend, but he has that in common with them."

The corners of my lips tip upward because I know what she says is true. One of the things I love most about Diego is how dogged and determined he can be in the pursuit of something he wants.

"I know, but that's the problem," I say after a while. "What happens when I become too much for him?"

My mother wrinkles her forehead in confusion. "Too much? What do you mean by that?"

Pushing out a breath, I tilt my head toward the ceiling. "My sickness." I gesture toward the monitor on my arm. Looking at my mom, I tell her, "I had to go to the emergency room two weekends ago."

Her eyes balloon.

"I'm sorry for not telling you," I immediately say. "It turned out to be nothing, and I didn't want to worry you."

Despite my explanation, there's concern and a little bit of hurt in her eyes. Even as I explain the entire situation and that, for the most part, it turned out to be nothing.

"It was most likely an issue with my glucose monitor. But that doesn't mean the next time won't be something serious." I hate saying these words out loud, especially because of the fear I see in my mother's eyes.

It's the same fear I remember seeing when I was a child. Anytime I didn't feel well or had to go to the hospital, that same haunted look would appear. Seeing it now is a reminder of what I don't want to bring to Diego's life. A constant state of worry, of what-ifs.

"My ex broke up with me because it became too much for him," I tell her.

Her eyebrows lift. "Lawrence?"

I nod. To my surprise, she rolls her eyes and waves a hand in the air.

"We all knew that wouldn't last."

"What?" I sit up straight, looking her in the eye.

She nods, shamelessly. "Your father and Joshua even had a bet going." She shrugs. "Of course, I had to convince Damon *not* to fly to New York to break his legs."

She laughs at the shock on my face.

"We all never saw the chemistry between you two. He came across nice but selfish at times. Plus, there was always Diego.

"But when your father heard you two broke up, he was convinced that boy did something to you. He had a plane ticket to New York booked. I had to make him cancel it." She shakes her head laughing.

"He didn't do anything to me," I tell her. "Not really. He was just honest about what he could and couldn't handle. My illness was too much for him."

"Then he wasn't right for you." My mother takes my face into her hands. "A lifetime commitment is filled with ups and downs. You think you're the only one who has the potential to become sick? What if one day on the way home from work Diego gets into a car accident and becomes seriously injured? Are you going to leave him?"

"Of course not," I answer without needing to think about it.

"Or if all of a sudden he received a scary medical diagnosis. Are you going to treat him like a burden then?"

"Mom." My voice comes out as almost a whine because she knows the answer.

"No, you won't," she answers. "Because love goes beyond illness. When you love someone with your entire heart the way that boy loves you, it's not a burden to care for you in the ways you need to be cared for."

She pulls back, lowering her hands from my face to my lap.

"You were never a burden for me. Not because of the way you came to be. Or because of your illness. You filled my life with a love I never knew before you existed."

With glossy eyes, she looks around my art gallery.

"And I'm so damn proud of you. Let Diego love you with his whole heart, too. Don't hold back. You both deserve the kind of love your father and I know."

She brings my hands to her lips and kisses them.

Fresh tears stream down my cheeks. A catharsis I didn't know I needed.

A beat later, I find myself wrapped up in my mother's arms. I cling to her tightly. Once again, crying more tears than I thought I had inside of me. I cry for the young woman she was when she became pregnant with me, who fought to keep me and then set her dreams on hold to provide everything I needed.

I also cry for myself. For the seventeen-year-old girl who found out the truth about her conception and developed the sense that she was inherently bad because of it. And the young woman who dated losers because she didn't believe she was worth more.

More tears are shed for all of the women in my life who I've encountered who believed the same thing. For the women whose voices were shouted into a void. The women whose art I may never get a chance to feature in my gallery but who I'll do my best to ensure they'll be heard wherever and whenever they can.

When my mother and I finally pull apart, I feel even lighter. Heavy in other ways, though.

"I need to talk to Diego," I say.

A knowing smile covers her face. "He probably hasn't gone far."

"He lives close," I respond as if she doesn't know.

She nods. "And if I had to guess—" The ringing of her phone interrupts her. She laughs. "Right on time." She turns her phone screen to me.

I smile, seeing it's my dad.

"He'll want to say hi." She hands me the phone.

"Hi, Daddy," I answer.

"Baby girl?" His surprised, deep voice comes through the line.

"Yeah."

"Your mother's with you?"

"She's right here. She stopped by the gallery to drop off some flowers." I look at the beautiful flowers on the desk.

After a few more pleasantries, I pass the phone to my mother. For a few seconds, I watch the interaction between my mother and dad on the phone. The only father who ever mattered in my life.

Another urge to speak with Diego pushes through me. My mother must realize it as she tells my dad she's on her way home now.

A hug and promises to talk more, and an invitation to come over for dinner with Diego before my opening night, and the both of us are heading out of the gallery.

We split, going in opposite directions to our cars. I've parked in the parking lot about a half of a block away from my art gallery. I typically walk but I needed to carry a few heavy items today.

As I start for my car, I notice a few other cars parked near mine. It doesn't worry me since it is a public parking lot. However, the hairs on the back of my neck start to stand on end. A quick sweep of the parking lot doesn't bring any answers as to the sudden wave of anxiety that pushes through me.

I only have about ten more steps until I make it to my car.

I pick up my pace, but a sound behind me has me spinning around. I come face to face with a man with a dark, grave expression on his face.

"Are you Monique Richmond?" he asks, the pinch in between his eyebrows giving him a devilish appearance.

"Who wants to know?" I ask, knowing better than to tell a stranger my name.

"Rodrigo Garcia," he answers.

Before I can register the name, everything goes black.

CHAPTER 36

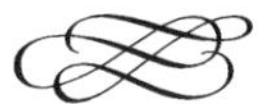

Diego

I didn't want to leave Monique's gallery. Everything inside of me wanted to stay. To make her understand that there is no way in this world that she would or could ever become a burden in my life.

The burden would be to live a life without her. Up until a few months ago, I had conceded that the only way I could have her in my life was as friends. I made myself believe that that would be enough.

It was a lie.

What started as a friendship between us, grew into something deeper, more profound over the years. The past three months have shown me just how deep what we both feel for one another runs. I can't go back to just having her as a friend, even as my best friend.

I want her for a lifetime—in my home, in my bed, as my wife.

Pacing my living room, I wonder if coming back home was the right thing to do. As much as I wanted to stay with Monique, I knew she needed to speak with her mother. It's a conversation that has been years in the making. Ever since Monique found out the ugly truth about her biological father.

I know all too well the scars she carried as a result of a past she honestly had no part of but somehow believed lived on through her anyway. More than that, the belief that she's somehow a burden is what almost did me in.

I crack my knuckles at the thought of finding her ex-fiancé wherever he is and cracking his skull for being yet another person to make her believe such bullshit.

When I check my watch, I see that close to forty-five minutes have passed since I left the gallery. I don't know if her conversation with her mother is over yet, but the idea of her possibly leaving the gallery alone, as it's getting dark, doesn't sit well with me.

She's capable of handling herself but something in the pit of my stomach has me on high alert. I don't know if it's because of the way we left things at her gallery, or if it's a general sense of unease that has me grabbing my phone. Either way, I call her.

I'll apologize if she's still with her mother, but just the sound of her voice right now would put me at ease.

Her phone goes straight to voicemail. I pull my phone from my ear and stare at it. Before I can process it, I'm dialing Monique's mother's number.

"Hey, Diego," her mother answers.

"Hi, are you still at the gallery with Mo'?"

"No, I'm on my way home. She was on her way home, too."

That pit in my stomach starts to grow. Before she's even finished with her sentence, I'm on my way out of the door. Monique's gallery is walking distance from my condo. I want to make sure she didn't decide to walk here on her own.

I tell Monique's mom that I'm going to head back to the gallery to meet her. I do my best to keep the concern out of my voice, but I have a feeling she hears it anyway.

Though the area is safe with plenty of pedestrians around most of the time, anything can happen.

I decide to hop in my car since it'll be faster than if I were to walk. I scan the street she would've taken to walk back to place but don't see her. The idea that she could've gone back to her place passes through my mind.

If she did, though, that doesn't explain why her phone went straight to voicemail. When I pull up in front of the gallery to see all of the lights turned off and door locked, my mind starts racing.

I start out taking long strides in the direction of the parking lot where I know she likes to park when she drives to the gallery. My strides turn into a full out run when I hear yells coming from the parking lot.

As I round the entrance of the parking lot, one of the overhead lanterns provides enough light for me to see some sort of altercation happening in the far end of the parking lot.

My heart starts racing as I pick up my pace. I hear a scream that I quickly identify as coming from Monique.

"Don't … you … ever …" she's saying.

"Mo!" I yell.

As I get closer, it takes me a moment to realize what's happening. Monique isn't being attacked.

My woman is standing over whoever is on the ground, sending—from what it looks like—another kick to his groin. I reach them at the same time that she actually stomps on his nuts.

The move both sends a wave of pride through me and makes me cringe in pain.

"Baby," I call to Monique.

She spins in my direction wide-eyed, hands on guard as if she's just waiting for the next son of a bitch to take down. Another sense of pride courses through me.

I hold my hands up in the universal *I'm not a threat* sign.

"D-Diego?" she asks as if coming out of a trance.

"What happened?" I look between her and the man crouching on the ground, holding himself in pain. I still can't make out his face in the position he's in.

"Your brother attacked me," she answers, breathless.

It takes seconds for her words to fully sink in. "My what?"

"Rodrigo."

I finally take a good look at the bastard on the ground. It's Rodrigo

Garcia, the son of a bitch my family and I have been trying to track down for weeks. All I see is red.

That familiar haze of anger blankets me at the knowledge that this prick attacked Monique. At least, he tried to. He's about to get worse than a few stomps to his groin. Though, from the way he's still writhing on the ground, I know he's in a serious amount of pain.

It's not enough, though.

"You're about to meet your brother in hell," I tell him through gritted teeth.

"Hey, are you alright?" someone calls from behind us.

I don't pay them any mind as I start for the coward on the ground. Monique jumps in front of me.

"Diego, don't." She pushes against my chest. "We have an audience." With her head she gestures over my shoulder.

I don't immediately turn around, still intent on getting to the cocksucker who thought he could put his hands on her.

"Diego, please," she begs.

"Oh my god," a woman's voice says, sounding as if she's getting closer. "I saw the whole thing. That guy attacked her. I've called the police."

I look over at the woman and then back at Monique. She's silently begging me not to lose my control.

I wrap my hands around her arms, needing to hold onto her to verify that she isn't hurt. I pull her into me. The feeling of the rising and lowering of her chest against my stomach is the only thing that relieves the anger raging inside of me. It continues to remain, but I can manage it.

I won't take care of this piece of shit right now. Not in front of witnesses and not in front of her. In the distance, I hear the wailing of police sirens. Though it's not the way I would prefer to handle this, knowing that this bastard won't be able to put his hands on Monique ever again, gives me a little bit of solace.

As the police arrive and rush toward the dirtbag on the ground, Monique pulls back and looks up at me.

"How's that for weak?"

I put my forehead against hers. "You've never been weak."

She smiles. "I know. I'm sorry," she says in a whisper.

She doesn't need to explain or tell me what she's sorry about. I don't need an apology. But with those two words comes the realization that she's learning to let go of those bullshit misbeliefs she had about us.

"I'm never letting you go," I tell her with all of the fierceness my body contains.

Her eyes water. "Good, because I'm not letting go of you either."

The sentence my heart has been waiting to hear for years. It washes away years of doubt and fear.

CHAPTER 37

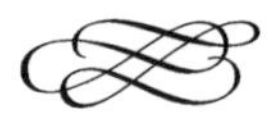

Monique

I inhale as I look around my art gallery. The beautiful paintings on the walls make my heart sing. Right now the gallery is empty, but in less than two hours is my opening.

Everything is set up and prepared since I had the caterers come in early. Bottles of champagne are chilling on ice in the back where the industrial kitchen I had installed to be able to host events is. Hors d'oeuvres are in the refrigerator, waiting to be served or being created. I've come out to survey my space before everyone arrives.

I asked Diego to give me a few minutes alone. He's supervising in the back. I can't believe my dream is staring me in the face. What I've longed for, for so long. In addition to my best friend and the love of my life being here to support me, he's also responsible for this dream of mine coming true.

I thought I would feel like a failure or more of a burden if anyone besides myself was responsible for helping to open this gallery. Yet, as I look around all I can feel is immense gratitude and love.

My heart is bursting open with love.

As this thought rolls through my mind, there's a knock on the front door of the gallery. Thinking it might be one of the caterers who couldn't get into the back door, I move to open it.

"Lawrence?" I say, surprised to find myself face to face with my ex-fiancé. There's a bouquet of flowers in his hand.

Tulips.

"Hi," he says as if he isn't quite sure of where to go from there. "These are for you." He extends the bouquet my way.

"Thank you." I take the flowers. "Would you like to come in?"

He shakes his head. "No, I don't want to mess up your big night.

"I, uh …" He pauses and runs a hand over the back of his head. "I was in town, and I heard tonight was your big opening. I wanted to drop by and say congratulations." He shrugs.

"That's really kind of you."

I scan over my ex-fiancé. The man I once thought I was going to marry. And I don't feel anything. No anger or disappointment.

Well, in all honesty, there's relief. I'm grateful he was the one who ended things because I might have moved ahead with marrying him. That would've been a terrible mistake. My heart has always belonged to Diego Townsend.

"Um, I also wanted to apologize," he finally says.

I wrinkle my forehead. "For what?"

"That night at that club."

I think for a beat and realize that he's referring to the night at The Black Opal. "Don't worry about it."

"It wasn't true, you know," he says. For the first time since I opened the door, his eyes meet mine. "The reason I gave you for breaking up."

That stuns me. "You mean because of my illness."

He shakes his head. "I'm sorry I even said it. It was just …" He sighs. "Do you remember that night you were in the hospital?"

I think back, vaguely recalling that night. I remember being frightened and once again feeling helpless, at the mercy of a disease I couldn't control.

"You wanted him," he says, bringing me out of my memory. "The first person you thought to call was Diego, even though I was right there."

I frown, trying to remember specifically what he's referring to.

"I don't think you even remember," he concludes. "You were somewhat out of it. But you asked me to call him. You said he was the one person who helped make you feel calm when this sort of thing happens."

I watch as Lawrence visibly swallows.

"That was the moment I knew you were in love with him," he confesses.

It steals my breath.

"The whole time we were together, whenever he visited or you mentioned him, I tried to tell myself you two were just friends. But it always felt like I was stepping into something that I had no business getting in the middle of."

He shrugs. "But my pride wouldn't let me admit that to you. Not back then. So I made up a lame excuse about not wanting to take care of you. I'm sorry, Monique. I never meant that shit. It was a terrible thing to tell you."

"It damn sure was," a deep voice that sends chills down my spine says behind me.

I have to keep my lips from curling into a smile as I turn to look at Diego over my shoulder. His face is a storm cloud as he peers down at my ex-fiancé. I fold my arms over my chest to hide the way my nipples harden at seeing him so damn sexy in the tuxedo he's decided to wear for tonight.

One would think the scowl on his face would be off-putting. It's the opposite for me. I have to remind myself that I don't have time to jump his bones.

Diego's glare drops from Lawrence's face to the flowers in my hand. His frown deepens.

"She doesn't even like tulips," he scoffs.

"Really?" My ex sounds surprised.

In the time we were together, he never bought flowers for me. I never got the opportunity to tell him that I didn't like tulips.

Diego rolls his eyes and reaches around to take the flowers from my hands. My ex stands there, a dumbfounded expression on his face, as if he doesn't know where to go from here.

"Well, I just wanted to tell you that and to wish you luck with your gallery. It looks amazing," Lawrence says.

"She doesn't need luck," Diego retorts. "She has talent, savvy, the drive, and everything else she needs." As if to emphasize his point, he wraps his free hand around my waist, pulling me to him.

"Thank you, Lawrence."

"Bye," Diego says for me.

He gives a quick nod of his head before he turns to leave.

I turn to Diego. "That was rude."

"Fuck him." He stares over my shoulder as if he's thinking about going after Lawrence to settle some unnamed score.

"He just wanted to wish me luck and to apologize."

He snorts. "He did that. Good thing that's all he wanted." A devilish smile spreads his lips as he leans down. "Because I wouldn't hesitate to fuck him up for thinking of doing anything else to you."

His lips press against mine, again igniting that usual warmth that starts in the pit of my belly and slowly starts to spread throughout my body.

"Ugh, here he is again, maiming my baby in public."

I pull away from Diego to find my parents and brother and sister approaching. They're all dressed up, looking fantastic. My heart feels overwhelmingly full.

"You look beautiful, baby," my mom says as she pulls me in for a hug. Like most of the hugs we've had lately, it lingers for a little while. I breathe in deeply, allowing my mom to hold onto me and I her.

After years of the emotional distance between us, these hugs feel like making up for lost time.

"Hi, Daddy," I say as he pulls me into a hug.

When we pull apart, there's a frown on his face. He's looking over at Diego. Not at him, so much as the flowers in his hand.

"She doesn't like tulips," my father says. "I thought he was your best friend. The boy should at least know you don't like tulips."

Diego scoffs. "I would never buy her such a small bouquet of flowers. I'm going to throw these out."

I don't have time to tell him that wouldn't be nice before he turns to presumably head for the garbage. My father follows him in, and I escort my mom and siblings inside.

Within the next thirty minutes my gallery starts to fill up with all my closest family and friends. Right before the doors open for the general public, I look around and realize how full my gallery is already.

Not just the gallery.

My heart as well.

My heart is the fullest it's ever been.

When my eyes connect with Diego's, tears fill them. He walks over to me and places a kiss on my cheek before lightly blotting my cheeks to wipe away the tears.

"Ready?" he asks in my ear.

My smile grows impossibly wide as I nod. "More than anything."

A minute later, I officially open the doors of Stolen Voices Art Gallery.

The line waiting to enter is longer than I dreamed of even anticipating. I stand at the entryway to greet each and every visitor.

"Jocelyn," I say to my friend and director of the women's shelter where I volunteer. "You didn't have to wait in the line." I take her hand in both of mine.

"I know, but I have a special guest who I wanted to surprise." She steps to the side to reveal an older woman seated in a wheelchair.

I gasp and cover my mouth as I instantly recognize her grandmother.

"Monique, I would like for you to meet my grandmother. Mi abuela, Arysilys Diaz."

"It's a pleasure to meet you," I tell her grandmother in Spanish.

Her eyes lift in surprise. "¿Tú hablas español?"

I nod. "My best friend taught me." I happen to look up and see the very man I'm talking about standing by my side. "This is him," I say, placing a hand on his shoulder.

He leans down and presses a kiss to Mrs. Diaz's hand. "I've had the honor of seeing your paintings and they are absolutely stunning," he tells her.

Her eyes light up, delighted. He offers to escort her in so she can see for herself the display of her artwork on the wall. I watch as he rolls her wheelchair in. He smiles at me over his shoulder, winking at me before entering the gallery with Mrs. Diaz.

"I have to say, I think he's a keeper," Jocelyn says.

"Don't I know it." I couldn't agree more.

The night flies by. Every time I walk past someone as they admire one of the paintings on the wall, my heart soars a little more.

"The stroke work on this piece is beautiful," a woman who owns a local bookstore says as she stops me. "Melinda Blake is the name of the artist? I can't believe I've never heard of her before. I know most of the well-known artists in this area."

A smile grazes my lips. "She's a new artist," I answer with pride. "It took a little convincing to get her to sell her work here, but she's worth the trouble. Wouldn't you agree?" I ask and turn to the painting for emphasis.

"Wholeheartedly. Is she here? I would love to meet her."

I shake my head. "Melinda isn't quite ready to make a live appearance. She'd rather have her artwork speak for her at this time."

I secretly hope that one day Melinda will be here to talk about her art in person. Until that day, however, I am proud to be her voice. To tell the world about what a wonderful talent she is.

Which is exactly what I do for the next fifteen minutes with the shop owner. Whatever I say must convince her because she decides to purchase the painting on display as well as come back the following week when I tell her I'm expecting two new pieces from Melinda.

A little before nine o'clock, I decide it's time to make my speech before the night gets too far from me.

As if he's a mind reader, Diego brings over a flute of champagne. I watch as the caterers hand out flutes to the guests in attendance. My eyes land on my mother. Her eyes are full of tears. That almost does me in. I feel my knees get a little wobbly, but Diego places his hand at the small of my back.

"I love you," he says in my ear, and then steps away, giving me space to be the focal point.

Though nervous, I tap my glass with the edge of a knife to get everyone's attention. When all eyes turn my way, I search the crowd and seeing all of my family's smiling faces brings a peace to my heart that I didn't know was missing.

On instinct, I turn to the one man in the room who seems to always have his attention on me. My gaze lingers on him for a few moments as I gather my thoughts. I find strength in his eyes.

He gives me a small nod.

"I know you're all enjoying the beautiful art surrounding us. So I will make this quick," I say. "First, thank you all for coming. I can't put into words how much it means to me that you're here.

"For years, it's been my dream to open an art gallery. Not just any gallery." I make it a point to look at as many guests in the eye as possible. There's Jocelyn and her grandmother, Sharia's mother, Ms. McClure, Melinda Blake's brother. Just a few of the artists or their representatives that helped to make tonight such a success.

"I wanted to provide a space for women artists whose voices have been stolen, robbed, or otherwise taken away, a space to showcase who and what they are. A place where shattered voices become whole again through the magic of art."

I wave a hand toward the paintings on the walls.

"As you can see, the magic is all around us. I'm in awe of the women who've placed their trust in me to bring this vision to life. This gallery wouldn't have been possible without them."

I nod toward the artists. "Thank you."

"And thank you to all of you," I say again. "Welcome to Stolen Voices Gallery. I'm certain this will not be your last visit. There is so much more art to come."

I hold up my glass of champagne and wait for everyone else to do the same.

"To restoring those stolen voices one piece of art at a time."

Cheers sound around the room as I take a sip of my glass.

CHAPTER 38

Diego

I can't take my eyes off of her. As much as I want to be alone with her—to be inside of her—I want her to soak up every second of this night. I've kept my distance from the love of my life tonight for two reasons.

First, I don't want to interrupt her time with the artists and the guests on her opening night.

Second, I know as soon as I touch her for too long, I won't be able to keep myself from stealing her away. As I watch her in that long, black and red dress that beautifully accentuates the curves of her body, I imagine all of the ways that I will be taking her after tonight's event.

"Have you bought the ring yet?" Uncle Damon's voice asks behind me.

I turn around to face the man who raised the woman who owns my heart. There's a sparkle in his eyes and a small smile on his face.

"I did," I confirm.

"Do you have it on you?"

I shake my head. When I approached him a few weeks ago to let him know I planned on asking Monique to marry me soon, he asked to see the ring. Since I was having it specially designed, it wasn't ready for anyone to see.

"I have a picture," I tell him. "She'll be the first one to see the real thing."

He nods, his smile growing as if I have his approval. Not that I ever asked, but it feels good to know I have it.

He places a hand on my shoulder. "You never needed it, but you've always had my approval," he tells me for the first time.

He lets out a chortle when I lift an eyebrow. "I knew you would keep her safe. Whatever type of relationship you had with her."

He squeezes my shoulder, his eyes full of emotion.

"It'll be a proud day for me to walk her down the aisle if you're the groom."

I drop my head and swallow the lump in my throat. Hearing him say this is almost as welcomed as it was to hear my father tell me that I never needed to be anything other than exactly who I am to be his son.

"Let me see the ring," Damon says.

I pull out my phone and bring up the picture of the ring I had designed for Monique.

He whistles low. "Look at that." His hand goes back to my shoulder, and he squeezes. "She's going to love it."

"Yeah, just don't expect him to call you dad anytime soon," my dad says as he comes up on my other side.

His blue eyes sparkle in pride. "It's a beauty, isn't it?" he says to Uncle Damon.

I can't say anything as they both pat me on either shoulder. Instead, I stare across the room as my entire heart continues to talk with the artists and the guests in her new gallery. She's arm-in-arm with her mother, proudly introducing her before talking about the pieces on display.

For a brief moment, our eyes lock from across the room. My entire body fills up with all of the love I have for her. She smiles at me, and I know, on instinct, that she's thinking the same.

"You're not proposing tonight, are you?" Damon asks.

I shake my head. "Tonight's her night."

"Good," he answers. "You have other things to take care of before you propose to my daughter." A slight gravity enters his voice.

My father squeezes my shoulder, knowing exactly what Uncle Damon is referring to.

Yeah, there is some business I need to take care of before calling Monique my fiancée. I owe it to her to finish it before I put this ring on her finger.

* * *

"Oh my god," Monique moans as she lays back against the couch cushion. I'm on the floor in front of her, her left foot in my hands, massaging it. "You have magic hands," she groans when I press my thumb into the ball of her foot, releasing the tightness I find there.

"You've been on your feet all day."

I lower her left foot to the carpeted floor before moving to her right foot.

"It was so worth it." She suddenly sits up. "Every single painting on display sold out!" she exclaims. "I knew it was a good decision to keep some paintings in inventory. We're getting more next week. And we're booked out for events for the next three months."

Her eyes are so wide with happiness and joy that I can't help but laugh. I take her head in between my hands.

"I'm so proud of you, baby," I tell her before pulling her in for a kiss. I intend for it to be quick, but she deepens it.

She slides her body onto the floor so that we're both on our knees facing one another. She wraps her arms around my neck.

"Thank you," she says against my lips. "Tonight wouldn't have happened if it weren't for you."

I shake my head and move a few strands of her hair away from her face. "This was all you. I'm just a proud bystander."

She rolls her eyes. "You're so much more than that. Let me show you how much," she says. Her hands slide to the button of my pants, undoing it.

I place my hands over hers. "Wait." I pick up my phone and check the app on my phone that tells me her numbers.

A grin touches my lips when I see her numbers are nice and stable. She's done her injection and eaten her final meal of the day, so we're good to go for what I have in mind.

When my gaze meets her eyes, there's a small pout on her lips.

"Don't even think of pouting. I plan on keeping your ass up all night long. I needed to make sure you're ready for it," I promise.

At that, her grin returns as I lift her to carry her to my bedroom.

"I want you to use your silk tie tonight," she says against my mouth.

Pulling back, I look down at her. There's a plea in her eyes. I can't look at her and refuse her anything, not on my worst day.

I've held this part of myself back from her for so long. Thinking I would hurt her. I now know it hurt us both not to give her all of me. It only served to reinforce the insecurities she harbored over the years.

With a nod, I lay her down on the bed before pulling open the drawer of my nightstand. I've kept an array of silk scarves in here for months. Never used them with anyone else.

Slowly, I pull out the black silk scarf. I don't miss the way Monique's eyes light up with interest. Though she remains quiet.

"Give me your wrists," I order.

A smirk crosses her lips. "You can ask better than that, can't you?"

My cock jumps against the zipper of my tuxedo pants at her act of rebellion.

I press a knee onto the bed, moving closer to her. "You're cute as hell, but don't think I won't make you regret defying me."

Without warning, I cover her body with mine, taking her wrists into my hands, and proceed to tie her arms to the headboard.

"This dress was really pretty," I say, trailing my finger between her breasts. In my other hand, I raise the other item I retrieved from my nightstand.

Monique's eyes widen at the sight of the sharp blade in my hand. For a beat, I wonder if I've scared the hell out of her.

But the surprise quickly turns to interest with a spark of desire.

Her lips spread into a tempting smile as her eyes meet mine. Warmth fills my chest at the silent conveyance of trust she bestows in me.

I slide the blade down the front of her dress, cutting it open, then make quick work of discarding the needless fabric.

"But it looks so much better on my bedroom floor," I say before giving the same treatment to the lacy bra and matching panties she's wearing.

"You know you're buying all new items for me, right?"

A chuckle spills from my lips. "Anything you want, baby."

I make that promise before diving face first in between her legs. I relish the sweet taste of her pussy on my tongue. Monique's thighs clamp tightly around my head. Her moans and the curses spilling from her lips have my dick pressing hard against the front of my pants, begging to get free.

But I won't let myself have my release anytime soon. Not before I make her pay for her little act of defiance earlier. I lick and suck on her clit until I feel her legs start to tremble and her body tighten all around me.

She's close to coming, so I pull away from her.

The yelp of surprise sends an instant thrill through me.

"What happened?" I ask in the most even voice I can muster.

She blinks and moves to sit up but can't because of her bound wrists.

Fuck, I love seeing her in this position. All helpless in my bed. Her body completely exposed to me and the desperate look in her eyes, begging me to give her the release she needs.

"Why did you stop?" she pants.

"Because it's not time for you to come yet." I finally start to unbutton my shirt, taking off of my clothes.

"I can do it myself," she says, her eyes narrowed.

"With your hands tied to my headboard?"

"Untie me," she orders.

Another chuckle is my reply.

"Diego," she growls through gritted teeth.

My dick jumps against my zipper. Her anger is such a fucking turn on. The little flare of anger in her eyes turns to a different kind of fire when her gaze drops to my cock in my hands.

I slowly stroke myself. She watches in obvious hunger as my hand moves up and down my length.

"That's it," I croon as her lips part.

She widens her mouth. I move closer to her and lift one of the pillows from the other side of the bed. I place it underneath her head to give her a better angle to take all of me inside of her mouth.

It's not enough though. I'm not able to go in as deep as I want from this position. I untie her arms from the bed and move her so that her head hangs upside down off of the side of my bed.

From this angle, I slide the entire length of my cock deep into her mouth. I go in so deep that her throat starts to expand. She gags, and I can't help how the sound turns me the fuck on.

"Relax your throat, baby. Be my good girl and take all of me," I encourage.

She visibly does as I tell her, keeping her eyes on me. I pull back a little to let her catch her breath before pressing in again. This time she takes me so well.

In and out, I move, relishing in the feel of her hot mouth on me. My hips start to pick up speed on their own accord.

"Touch yourself," I tell her. "Play with my pussy for me. Keep her nice and wet."

Monique reaches down and begins to do as I say. Muffled moans sound around my cock.

"But don't come," I order. "If you come before I tell you to, you're going to wake up tomorrow morning with a sore ass."

Her eyelids lower slightly, as if she's angry with me but her mouth is too occupied for her to be able to say it.

"Do you know how fucking good you look with my dick in your mouth?"

Another moan.

"You look like you're right where you belong. Mine," is all I can say because it's too difficult to speak in full sentences at this point.

When I notice her back arch off the bed, I know she's getting closer to coming herself. I can't let that happen. Not yet.

I lean over and smack her hand out of the way before pulling my dick out of her mouth. My knees almost buckle when I see the way her head chases after my dick.

"On your knees," I order through clenched teeth. "I want to fuck the hell out of your face."

When she's on her knees in front of me, I take her face in between my hands. "Hands behind your back."

She complies immediately.

"Tonight, I'm spilling my come down that pretty throat of yours before I fill up your pussy. Open."

Her lips fall apart, and I push myself inside of her mouth as deep as I can go. I'm satisfied when she takes me with ease. My body can't hold on much longer. I start to fuck her face in the same way I plan on fucking the rest of her body soon.

Tears stream from her eyes, and drool spills out of her lips. I love the contrast of how put together she was earlier this evening and how she is now. Only for me.

"Keep your hands behind your back," I grunt when she starts to move her hands to my hips. "In the morning, we'll have to talk about safe words," I say in between thrusts.

A second later a blinding light happens behind my eyes. My body comes apart from the orgasm that rips through me. I can't stop my hips from moving even if I wanted to. My dick feels like a fucking water fountain as stream after stream of my come spills out.

My girl takes all of it. She swallows my come like a fucking champ.

Right before I collapse on the bed, I pick her up from the floor and bring her to the mattress with me. I lay like that for a while, with her in my arms. We're both breathing in unison, my arm draped over her body, holding her to me like she's my lifeline.

When I catch my breath, I lift my head to see her eyes are semi-closed.

"Oh hell no," I say. "I told you, I'm keeping you up all night long."

She giggles when I spin her onto her back before slipping in between her legs.

"Then you better keep your promise," she teases.

"Always, baby," I groan before slipping inside of her. "This time I might even let you come for me."

She arches her back off the bed before wrapping her legs around my waist. I pull her up to wrap her arms around my neck.

"Mine," she says against my lips.

I almost come again right then and there. But the next orgasm will be hers. I want nothing more than to feel her pussy walls vibrating around me as she orgasms.

I grip her hips firmly and impale her over and over with my cock. She tosses her head back, gasping for air.

"Come on my dick, Monique," I order.

Like the sweet girl she is, she does.

It's the most beautiful sight I've seen all night. Once she's sated, I let my body's natural response take over. Another orgasm rushes through me, just as powerful and fierce as the first one.

If this is what I have to look forward to for the rest of my life, I'll gladly welcome it.

But first, there's a matter I need to take care of before I can fully claim Monique as my wife.

CHAPTER 39

Diego

"I've seen some crazy shit from all of your uncles and even my crazy ass nephew," my dad says as he gestures in Kyle's direction.

My cousin, along with my uncles, grandfather, my father, and even Monique's dad were all out here in an isolated part of the woods. Way on the outskirts of Williamsport, a parcel of land that our family owns for less legitimate matters.

"But I think this might take the damn cake," he says as he stares at the bow and arrow in my hands.

"You think so?" I ask as I slide one of the arrows into position on the bow.

"Definitely crazy as fuck," Damon says as he comes up on the other side of me. "Kind of wish I had thought of it for … the bastard who hurt my wife." Unmistakable rage crosses his face. I know instantly he's talking about the cocksucker who assaulted Monique's mother.

Hot anger curls through me at the thought of that bastard as well. I decide to take this anger and the rage I feel toward my intended target out right here.

"You can untie him now," I say to Uncle Josh, who has Rodrigo on his knees in front of him.

Before he undoes the rope binding his wrists, I rip the electrical tape from over his mouth.

"You guys are fucking crazy!" he shouts, looking around with wide, frightful eyes.

"You think so?" I line up the arrow, point the bow directly at him, and hold it only a few inches from his face.

He crouches low to the ground.

Frowning, I stand up straight. "What the hell are you doing?"

"Please, please," he begs. "Don't!"

I roll my eyes. "I won't."

He pushes out a heavy breath and looks at me with terrified but hopeful eyes. "You won't?"

I shake my head. "No." I shrug. "Not like this. I just brought you out here to talk."

I crouch low before placing the bow and arrow in my lap.

"You know attacking my woman was fucked up, right?"

He blinks and looks around.

"Don't look at them. Look at me since you did it to hurt me, isn't that correct?"

He nods cautiously. "I-I just needed the money and it's not right that my father left the money to you. When Gabriel went missing, I thought you did something to him."

"So you decided to attack the love of my life," I finish for him.

"Why is he still fucking talking?" Damon demands to know. "Put an arrow in his fucking head and let's be done with this."

Rodrigo looks over my shoulder in confusion.

I look from Damon back to him. "The woman you attacked is also his daughter."

He blinks as if understanding.

"He's the one who taught her how to fight, too." I chuckle, remembering the way Monique had this bastard on the ground crying out for help.

"And shoot a gun," Damon adds. "You're lucky she didn't have her piece on her. This conversation wouldn't be happening."

I frown. "Then I wouldn't have the satisfaction of doing this." I rise to my feet. "Stand up."

When he doesn't move fast enough, I pull him to his feet.

"I told you I wasn't going to shoot you."

I hear Damon suck his teeth behind my back. I glance back to see Uncle Josh place a hand on his shoulder and whisper something in his ear. He visibly relaxes.

"I won't shoot you … without giving you a chance to run."

He stands there, mouth wide as if waiting for me to say more.

I push out a harsh breath and step to the side, out of his way. I spread my free arm toward the open forest around us.

"I'm giving you a head start. A full sixty seconds before I come looking for you. Once I catch you …" I punctuate the sentence by lowering my bow and aiming it.

"Your time starts now," I say when he doesn't move.

He continues to stare at me with wide eyes.

"Fifty-nine, fifty-eight, fifty-seven," my dad starts counting.

"I suggest you start moving. We don't have all fucking day," Kyle says with his usual amount of impatience.

"As much as I would like for this to take all day, my cousin is correct." I move behind Rodrigo and shove him with my foot. "Fucking move."

He stumbles but doesn't fall to the ground. He looks over his shoulder as he takes tentative steps away from us. His pace gradually picks up until he's in an all-out sprint.

"How much time?" I ask, staring after my prey. I watch him until he disappears into the brush of the forest. I'm not too worried about it.

"Twenty-five seconds," my uncle, Tyler, answers. "I swear this younger generation is slightly more crazy than us." He chuckles, as do the rest of my uncles and my father.

The only one not laughing is Damon. "As long as you take care of him before I do," he says.

I nod slowly.

"Five … four …" my father counts down. As soon as the word one passes through his lips, I take off in a run, bow and arrow in hand.

"Stay here," I tell them over my shoulder. I won't need them to take care of this piece of shit. He signed his fate the moment he decided it was a good fucking idea to go after Monique.

Now, he's about to meet his brother in hell. I start off in the direction I watched him go. Eventually, I drop my eyes to the ground, searching out footprints and sights of broken twigs or branches.

His trail isn't difficult to find at all. He obviously hasn't spent much time in the woods at all. No idea how to cover his tracks. Great for me. Not so much for him.

When I pinpoint where he is, I turn away so that my back is to him. I get really quiet as if I'm searching for him. I want the son of a bitch to think he's got the upper hand.

I hear the moment he starts to make his move.

"You son of a bi—"

He doesn't even get the full comment out before I spin and release one of my arrows right into his stomach.

He stops abruptly, the branch in one of his hands halting halfway above his head. It drops to the ground with a thud.

His eyes go wide, and then drop to the arrow protruding out of his stomach.

I lower the bow and arrow before walking over to him. I don't say anything as I yank the arrow out of his stomach. A silent scream wrenches from him and he falls to his knees.

My frown returns. "You could've at least made it a little more difficult." Disappointment laces my tone.

He crumples the rest of the way to the ground. "Please," he wheezes out.

"Please?" I crouch beside him. "Is that what you would've said if you'd succeeded in attacking Monique? If she hadn't been able to defend herself, would you have given her the mercy you're now begging for?"

Rhetorical questions I know the answer to. This bastard has a record of domestic violence. He has no problem attacking women.

"Please," he begs some more. A trickle of blood forms at the corner of his mouth.

"Fuck you." I give him one final look before telling him, "Give your father and brother my pleasantries."

I lift the arrow up high and then send it plunging into his neck, ending him quickly. I'm done with this piece of shit.

"Is it done?" I hear a few beats later.

I glance over my shoulder to see Damon staring at me expectedly. He's surrounded by the rest of the men in my family. I give him a nod.

He releases a breath. "Now you have my permission to marry my daughter."

A smile curls the corners of my lips. "You know I was never asking, right?" Like I needed anyone's permission to marry the woman who's owned me since we were little kids.

My uncle, Josh, laughs and claps his best friend on the back. "Let's go."

The usual clean-up crew for this type of mess starts to do their thing. With this mess out of the way, my mind already starts to think about the best way to ask Monique to marry me.

The perfect way pops into my mind without having to give it too much thought.

EPILOGUE

Monique

One month later

"What are we doing out here?" I ask Diego as he turns onto a long, gravel road. I immediately know where the road leads. My heart sinks a little at the reminder that this place that once was ours is owned by someone else.

We haven't been out here since that day we returned from the Blairwood Art Fair. Though, I've yearned to come out here again. So many of the special moments in my life, along with some of the low points, were followed by a visit to this place.

"The fence will prevent us from going in," I say before he can answer my previous question.

"There's a new owner."

My frown is instant. I hate the idea of this place being owned by someone else.

"The gate is locked," I tell Diego when we come to the same fence that kept us out last time.

"Hang on," he says as he throws the car in park.

I watch as he climbs out and heads directly to the fence. To my surprise, he pulls a key out of his pocket and opens the lock. Next, he undoes the chain and tosses it to the side, opening the fence.

I can't sit in my seat. I climb out of the car. "What is this?"

"I thought I told you to wait in the car." He narrows his eyes on me.

I can't even help the way my nipples tighten from that look. "I'll let you spank me later for not listening."

A spark passes through his eyes, and I know I'm going to be a little sore later on. It'll be worth it.

"Why do you have the key for the fence?" I ask, although I've already put two and two together.

He takes my hand in his and brings it to his lips. "Since you don't listen, let's walk the rest of the way."

It's not an answer to my question but I know he won't give up any information before he's good and ready. *Stubborn man.*

"The barn's still standing but it won't be for much longer." He points about a hundred feet ahead of us where the old barn stands. "It's too dangerous to go inside," he says, turning to me, "so I opted to do this outside."

He spins me around, and I see a beautiful red and white checkered blanket spread over a part of the lawn. An array of food sits on top of the blanket.

"Is that champagne?" I ask.

He nods and leads me to the blanket. "A celebration always needs champagne."

I want to ask what we're celebrating but I bite my tongue. I have an idea and I'm halfway bursting at the seams to yell out an answer.

"Are you hungry?" he asks as he helps me to take a seat in front of the beautiful spread of food. He obviously had to have help to set all of this up.

"Yes," I say. "But we can get to the food later. Answers."

He lowers himself in front of me and presses a quick kiss to my lips. "So impatient. Didn't I warn you about that last night?"

I squirm a little remembering the way he made me wait over and over last night. And when he finally let me orgasm, I almost passed out. The seam of my panties becomes saturated just from the memory.

"Patience does have its benefits," I concede.

His smile widens. "That's my girl."

"But you can still ask me the question."

He tosses his head back and a deep laugh reverberates out. God, he's so damn sexy and fine and all of the things I've ever wanted. And he's been mine all along. I could still kick myself for the amount of time it took me to get over my insecurities.

"Okay," he says before giving me another quick kiss. "First, let me make sure." He pulls out his phone, and I already know what he's doing.

"I'm fine," I say as I thrust my wrist in his face to show him my numbers. "Perfect range."

He nods and places his phone down.

"I want to show you something." He reaches around the picnic basket set in the middle of the blanket and pulls out a roll that I identify as architecture plans. When he unfurls the papers, the drawings on them confirm it for me.

"I thought the main house would take up the space where the barn now sits. We'd build our bedroom back here so we can look out onto the stream from our balcony. But if you want the bedroom to face the front of the property, we can do that as well."

He points to the different rooms in the design.

"Diego," I cover his hand with mine to stop it from moving, "what are you saying?"

His smile lights up his whole face. "The new owners of this property," he does a sweeping gesture with his free arm, "are us, baby."

My eyes water. "You bought this? You're the new owner?"

He nods. "I had to buy it from the guy who bought it a few years ago. He tried to be a hard ass, but I got what I wanted in the end. We'll have to add you to the title and everything of course. I just couldn't let you in on the surprise."

I look around the open field and make out the stream that runs through the property in the back. The barn where he and I spent so many nights talking about our future, confessing our secrets to one another. Where I cried in his arms when I found out the truth about my mother and when I broke his heart when I told him I wouldn't be returning home.

All of those moments happened right here. This place is the story of us.

"We're ... it's ours?" I ask again to make sure.

He nods before wiping away a tear.

"Oh," he says and holds up a finger. "I can't buy you a house and land without making it official, can I?"

He slides a black ring box into the center of the design drawings before opening it.

I gasp at the beautiful pear-shaped diamond ring. It's stunning, and we're in the perfect position for the sun to catch the sunlight glinting off of the pink diamond and the rest of the diamond stones that encircle the band of the ring.

"Monique," Diego's voice captures my full attention, "I've loved you for as long as I've known you. You have been my best friend and my biggest cheerleader and the owner of my heart ever since I can remember.

"Will you do me the honor of being my wife?"

I throw my arms around him and cry into the crook of his neck before he even finishes the question. "Of course I will," I mumble into his neck.

I feel his body rumble with the deep laughter he lets out.

He pulls back and slides the ring onto my finger. "Thank you for loving me."

As if I ever had a choice.

ABOUT THE AUTHOR

Looking for updates on future releases? I can be found around the web at the following locations:

Newsletter: Tiffany Patterson Writes Newsletter
Patreon: https://www.patreon.com/tiffanypattersonwrites
Website: TiffanyPattersonWrites.com
FaceBook Page: Author Tiffany Patterson
Email: TiffanyPattersonWrites@gmail.com

ALSO BY TIFFANY PATTERSON

More books by Tiffany Patterson

The Black Burles Series

Black Pearl

Black Dahlia

Black Butterfly

FOREVER SERIES

SAFE SPACE SERIES

Safe Space (Book 1)
Safe Space (Book 2)

RESCUE FOUR SERIES

Eric's Inferno
Carter's Flame
Emanuel's Heat
Don's Blaze

NON-SERIES TITLES

This is Where I Sleep
My Storm
Miles & Mistletoe (Holiday Novella)
Just Say the Word
Jacob's Song
No Coincidence
Personal Protection

THE TOWNSEND BROTHERS SERIES

Aaron's Patience
Meant to Be
For Keeps
Until My Last Breath
Aaron's Gift

TIFFANY PATTERSON WEBSITE EXCLUSIVES

Locked Doors
Bella
Remember Me
Breaking the Rules
Broken Pieces

THE TOWNSENDS OF TEXAS SERIES

For You
All of Me
My Forever

THE NIGHTWOLF SERIES

Chosen

THE A**HOLE CLUB SERIES (COLLABORATION)

Luke

Made in the USA
Columbia, SC
03 December 2024